OUTPOST

OUTPOST

SCOTT MACKAY

TOR®

A TOM DOHERTY ASSOCIATES BOOK
NEW YORK

OUTPOST

Copyright © 1998 by Scott Mackay

Edited by David G. Hartwell

A Tor Book
Published by Tom Doherty Associates, Inc.
175 Fifth Avenue
New York, NY 10010

Tor Books on the World Wide Web:
http://www.tor.com

Tor® is a registered trademark of Tom Doherty Associates, Inc.

Library of Congress Cataloging-in-Publication Data

Mackay, Scott.
        Outpost / Scott Mackay.—1st ed.
                p.   cm.
        "A Tom Doherty Associates book."
        ISBN 0-312-86467-1
        I. Title.
    PR9199.3.M3239093   1998
    813'.54—dc21   97-36367
                                                        CIP

First Edition: March 1998

Printed in the United States of America

0 9 8 7 6 5 4 3 2 1

To my wife, Joanie,
with devotion, gratitude, and love

ACKNOWLEDGMENTS

I would like to thank the following people for their invaluable contributions to this book: Aldo Pullano, Cathy Pullano, Mary Biagioni, Sal Nappo, Claire Mackay, Settimo (Sam) Ursomarzo, Tony Martella, Fatima Cardoso, Tony Cardoso, and Joe Silvaggio.

I would also like to thank David G. Hartwell and Tad Dembinski for their superlative editorial support.

And a special thanks to my agent, Joshua Bilmes, for his advice, effort, and faith.

I

PRISON

1

Seventeen years old, and she couldn't remember murdering anyone, couldn't remember a trial or sentencing, or who, exactly, she had killed. As Felicitas looked up at the twin suns, her memory felt nearly blank, with only enough of it left to tell her that most of it was missing. But the image persisted, and if most of the details of her life were forgotten, she at least remembered this one thing: the identification tag stapled through her victim's ear.

She sat against the north wall and gazed at her hands. They no longer felt numb, and she knew that something must be different. Enough memory left to tell she had a lived a life here, inside these four gray walls. But she still didn't understand. How could these small delicate hands crush someone's throat? There. Another memory. Surfacing through the mental fog. The hands around the throat. She turned to her friend, Adriana, and held out her hands.

Adriana stared at Felicitas, but her eyes remained glassy.

Felicitas wasn't going to get answers from Adriana.

She couldn't understand where all the questions had come from, couldn't figure out who she was, why she was in prison, or who had put her here. She let her hands drop to her lap. Was it murder? The question gnawed. She couldn't comprehend how she had ever had the motive or opportunity for murder. A *carceriere* walked by, its gray skin corroded with age, its shoulders jerking. Men banged metal over by the east wall. Women stitched old pieces of cloth together. Children played a game of tag around the women.

She got up and followed the *carceriere*. No, it couldn't be murder. She felt incapable of murder. Adriana touched her arm.

"Don't go," said Adriana, her voice toneless.

"I'll be back," said Felicitas.

She followed the *carceriere*, keeping several paces behind. It walked toward the group of men who banged metal, its arms twitching, its eyes flashing. Not only was there the question of murder, there was also the question of the *carcerieri*. Why were they dying one after the other? What was she going to do when they all finally stopped working? Who would feed her? Who would put her to bed at night?

The *carceriere* halted in the middle of the yard, beeped a few times, and drew its *pistola*. Even this was different. Every time a *carceriere* drew its *pistola* the prisoners scattered, fled for their lives, took cover from the jailer's deadly aim. Yes, she had a clear memory of that now. But this time the men continued, unalarmed, hammering at old bits of metal, moving only after another series of beeps.

The *carceriere* fired, like an old man. It couldn't see anything. Its arm was too stiff to follow so many moving targets. Felicitas backed away, frightened by the hiss of the *pistola*. The *carceriere* fired once more. The *pistola*'s charge scattered over the east prison wall in a shower of yellow sparks, and smoke rose to join the mist in the air. The *carceriere*'s arm jerked once more, then the old machine toppled into the foul-smelling muck of the yard.

The men went back to their work as if nothing had happened.

Felicitas circled behind the *carceriere*, hardly able to understand why she took such a risk when most of the time she stayed against the north wall. She was scared, like in the middle of the night, when the sleeping pallet gripped and drugged, and the dreamphones sang. Dreamphones. Another memory. Unlocking yet more details about the murder: a woman's body lying in the rain, her fingers stiffly curled, and, yes, here it was again, the *uominilupi* identification tag stapled through her ear. Now she remembered. *Uomolupo.*

When she was certain the *carceriere* wasn't going to move, she crept behind it and had a close look.

A hum came from somewhere inside, and a purple light flashed on its chest. What did that mean? And what did all the glyphs etched over its metal casing mean? So many things she had never questioned. So many things she had never examined. Like why she had no mother, no father, no brothers or sisters, why she was so hungry all the time, so thirsty, why, for the first time in her life, she looked at the world with more than a surface understanding. She curled her fingers into a fist and tapped the *carceriere*'s chest. Other *carcerieri* lay in similar derelict condition around the yard.

She tapped again. She pressed a few buttons on the *carceriere*'s console, thinking she might get it working, believing if she could bring it back to life she could in some way make up for the death of the woman she had murdered. Nothing happened. The purple light continued to flash. The *carceriere* didn't move. Her eyes clouded with tears. Here was another one, dead, no one knew why. She put her hand on its cheek.

Then someone gripped her chin and lifted her head. She cried out, startled.

A man, somewhere in his fifties, with a ruddy face, blue eyes, and black hair, peered at her. She recognized the man, but couldn't immediately think of his name. He jerked her head one way, then the other, examining each eye. His own eyes narrowed, and several creases came to his dirt-smudged brow. "Felicitas?" he said, his voice hard. She couldn't understand how he knew her name. "Are you there? Do you recognize me?" He brought his face closer. A smile softened his features, and she wasn't so afraid anymore. "I've been watching you." She didn't like that, being watched, especially by this man. "It's me, Piero."

Piero. The name sounded familiar. The smile slipped from the man's face. A huge dark shape flew over the prison, the mist coiling in its slipstream as it banked over the south wall. All heads lifted. The dark shape disappeared behind the wall.

Felicitas broke away from Piero and ran to the north wall.

"Felicitas!" cried Piero.

She didn't turn back. She ran until she reached her spot beside Adriana. She sat down, feeling safe now. Piero stared at her, and again the smile came to his face. He stooped over the dead *carceriere* and pried the *pistola* from its hand.

"Didn't I tell you?" said Adriana.

Felicitas turned to her friend. Adriana stared straight ahead. Felicitas felt sorry for Adriana because she knew Adriana hadn't changed, didn't look at things the way she now did. And it was the same all over the yard. Some now had the spark of life. Others, like Adriana, were still dead, their eyes leaden. Felicitas knew she was somewhere in between, no longer dead, but not yet alive.

She turned back to Piero, now curious.

He checked the *pistola*, aimed it at the dead *carceriere*'s head, and fired. The head exploded into fragments. Felicitas glanced up at the twelve *sentinelle*, big metal guards who roamed the catwalks along the parapets, wondering if the one nearest would aim its *cannone* and blow Piero to bits. But the nearest *sentinella* whispered by, oblivious to Piero's blatant transgression, a menacing silhouette against the twin suns, and disappeared into the northeast guard tower, emerging a few seconds later along the north wall, its eye dim, as if it too were getting old and could no longer see the things that happened in the yard.

In the food dispensary, her stomach growled. Some of her dreamphone haze came back, and she nearly convinced herself that everything had returned to normal. She believed she was finally going to get a food-brick. The army of *carcerieri* would emerge from the rear doors and make sure everybody stood in their rightful place and got their rightful share. But the doors remained shut. No *carcerieri* came.

Piero's men worked the machine manually. The dispensary wasn't the same. It reeked of human feces and urine, and the wood chips on the floor hadn't been changed in a long time. Three *carcerieri* sat by the entrance, like old men on a park bench.

The bell rang, her eyes glazed, and she walked over to her spot by the machine, her mouth watering, and watched the chute at the top of the ramp. The machine whined, her hamper slid open, but her food-brick didn't appear. Tears came to her eyes. She wanted her food-brick, the pasty gray cube that looked after all her nutritional needs, wanted it badly because she was weak and her legs shook.

"I want my food!" she called to Gasparo. "Where's my food?"

But Gasparo, a big man, ignored her and walked to the other end of the machine.

She looked down the row, where Adriana greedily ate her food-brick. Adriana was one of the lucky ones today. Felicitas resented it. She left her place at the feed chute, walked over to Adriana, ripped the food-brick out of her hands, and took a ravenous bite. Adriana, still dazed by the dreamphones, turned to Felicitas with glassy eyes, her arms hanging at her sides, and watched Felicitas eat.

Felicitas stopped, couldn't go on. Adriana had no way to defend herself. As a brain-numb prisoner of the *uominilupi,* she was helpless. Felicitas gave the food-brick back. Adriana was just as skinny, hungry, and weak as Felicitas. Felicitas had no right to take her food.

2

Felicitas waited for a *carceriere* to take her to her cell that night. She was tired. She sat in the north cellblock cross-legged on the floor and watched the confusion. Prisoners tried to find their way to their cells by themselves, but many weren't having much luck.

Felicitas struggled to her feet. The clumsiness had come back. She looked at Adriana. Poor Adriana. Had they both been born in this prison? There must have been something before this prison. A memory fluttered through her mind: sitting around in a circle with other children, an old woman reading a book to them, all the children in a dreamphone haze, but some less so than others, some actually learning from the book. The memory disappeared. She helped Adriana to her feet.

"Why don't they come for us?" asked Adriana.

Felicitas brushed the hair from Adriana's face.

"Follow me," she said.

They walked down the corridor through the prisoners and *carcerieri*. Another recollection passed through her mind: The *carcerieri* hardly ever took her to her cell anymore; she had been finding her way up the stairs in the north cellblock for a long time now.

Why didn't the *uominilupi* come out of the sky anymore? Another memory. And where was Maritano, the boy who had kept her safe all these years, who took her in his arms in the hidden spots of the south tower, and told her everything would be all right?

"Where are we going?" asked Adriana.

"To our cell."

She looked around. Many prisoners shuffled from cell to cell. Mist curled in from the barred windows above and slithered down the walls in a slow-motion cascade, breaking apart as it hit the floor. Some adults had children in tow.

They walked to the end of the corridor. Each cell looked the same, with wood shavings on the floor, two sleeping pallets, and dreamphones above. She stopped at the second cell from the end and had a close look. Lichen grew around the window. There was a chip out of the third tile to the left. The bloodied rag from her recent monthly flow lay on the floor next to the chamber pot. She recognized the cell. But was recognition the same as memory?

"We're here," she said.

"Are you sure?" asked Adriana.

"This is it," said Felicitas.

They entered the cell. She was uneasy. With this new amnesia, she felt uncertain about the nightly lockup, wasn't sure how to proceed. She looked at Adriana. Adriana was bewildered.

"You lie there," said Felicitas, pointing to Adriana's sleeping pallet.

Adriana obeyed.

Felicitas looked up at Adriana's dreamphones, checked the sleeping pallet's leg and arm straps. She inspected the console along the side. She'd seen the *carcerieri* do it all her life. Yes, here was another memory, a dim vision of a nightly routine. She pressed the first button twice, relying on this hazy memory. The dreamphones came down over Adriana's head and two red lasers entered either ear. The routine, it was there, locked away in her mind.

Felicitas threw a few switches and the sleeping pallet straps automatically gripped Adriana's arms and legs. A few faint memories: the dead woman with the *uominilupi* identification tag stapled through her ear, Maritano, and now this nightly routine. But other than that, not much else. She couldn't find a focus on any particular events in her life, but knew, without knowing how she knew, that this was how they bedded down every night. Here was this routine, ingrained in an automatic part of her brain.

She watched Adriana's face, waiting for the telltale vacancy. But Adriana remained awake.

"Anything?" asked Felicitas.

"It's not working," said Adriana. "My arms are still cold."

"I'm sure I did everything right." Felicitas rubbed Adriana's brow affectionately. "Try to relax. Maybe it will start working in a while."

She walked to her own pallet and climbed in. She worked the controls. Her dreamphones came down, and the straps gripped her arms and legs, drew a little blood, and, as usual, the whole apparatus hummed. As usual. The same thing, done every night, all her life. Her body remembered it more than her mind. But she didn't feel the usual warmth spreading through her arms to her chest, nor did the usual visions fill her eyes. More of the murder: the rain, the chunky scarred hands floating before her in the dark, the woman running away from her, auburn hair flying in the wind.

Her background memory seemed intact; she knew the names of things, of places in the prison, all the routines of her life. But again, she had to wonder, was that just recognition? Finding their cell, was that just more animal instinct? All the sharper details of her memory seemed gone. She remembered surfacing through the mental fog this morning, yes, another specific memory, but she couldn't remember much before that, couldn't remember yesterday, or the day before—as if coming awake in the yard this morning had marked a watershed.

She tried to relax, closed her eyes, hoping the dreamphones would send her to sleep, that after they forced her to look at the murder one more time, maybe as punishment, maybe as rehabilitation, they would give her the sweet and oblivious darkness of the long night.

But she lay awake. For minutes. Then hours.

Until the shuffling of the baffled prisoners died down and she heard only the occasional metal clank of a *carceriere* footstep on the cold stone floor.

In her dream, she swam to the center of the south bath, where the water was way over her head. This wasn't her usual dreamphone dream, the one where she murdered the young woman. This dream was different. Her arms tingled. A strange sensation. One she had never had before. A tingling associated with this . . . this dream.

A dream . . . but not really a dream at all. She felt the warm water on her skin, heard the echo of water sloshing against the sides of the bath. Was this real? She felt as if she had become unstuck.

She dove beneath the water and swam with powerful strokes to the bottom.

She felt her way through the darkness and entered a subsurface tunnel, where she found a current. She struggled against the current, the water nearly too hot. Her lungs hurt, clawed by lack of oxygen. Her throat strained but she continued to swim, determined to get through the tunnel before she ran out of breath.

The current about-faced midway, and she allowed herself to be carried along, knowing she was almost there. She floated . . . floated . . . spiraling upward.

When she broke the surface she was under the south wall in a hidden chamber.

A creature, manlike, but also wolflike, wearing a black prison uniform, stared down at her with amber eyes. She gazed at the creature, and she knew, without having to be told, that this was a *uomolupo*, and that his name was Lungo Muso.

Lungo Muso pulled her out of the crack in the floor where the water fissured through. Then he pointed to the far wall.

She looked at the wall and her eyes narrowed with interest.

Scratched on the wall she saw glyphs. And she remembered: these were the glyphs of the *uominilupi*. She also saw English letters.

She had been here before, more amnesia lifting.

She walked to the wall, picked up a stone, and etched *uominilupi* glyphs into the hard gray surface. Dozens of them. As if she were skilled in the writing of *uominilupi* glyphs. How could she do this? She knew nothing of their writing. Or did she? Was this one of the memories she couldn't remember? Lungo Muso watched her.

When she was done, he picked up his own stone and scratched an English translation into the rock.

> *You saw me with your night eyes, saw my daunted soul, and how it burned brightly like a star through the long dark night, and you kissed me, touched me, and gave me back my hope so that I could one day rise like the cliffbird and call to my lonely brothers and sisters. You made me the hunter, and with my brothers and sisters I was everywhere, in the sky, on the earth, and in the water, so that my vanquishers, in their confusion, scattered like leaves in the wind. I walked silently, and my vanquishers could not hide from me.*

He then scratched a picture into the wall. Not a glyph but an actual picture. A building, impressive, even magisterial, a series of oblong slabs, one stacked on top of the other, a temple or shrine, not an ordinary building but a building of significance, a building of power. He took a chunk of lime-rock from his pocket and colored the building white.

She looked at Lungo Muso, hoping for elucidation, but he simply nodded.

She turned back to the picture.

"I don't know what that means," she said.

But even though she didn't know what it meant, she got a bad feeling from it.

The big white building posed a threat.

The big white building was somehow dangerous.

Felicitas opened her eyes. Prodded awake by her dream, by its sense of danger. She had never before been awake like this in the middle of the night. Lungo Muso. She glanced at Adriana; her friend was asleep. Lungo Muso, the glyphs, the white building sketched on the wall. Felicitas stretched her fingers and worked the console. The dreamphones lifted and the straps opened. She sat up, and she didn't feel dizzy or heavy, the way she usually did, but alive and bright.

She got off her sleeping pallet and looked out the open door. The several small ceiling lights did little to dissipate the gloom. Everything was blurred with a fine mist. She had to shake the dream from her mind. She walked to the window and looked out at the yard. Forget it. At least for now. The searchlights crisscrossed in a thorough pattern, filling the mist with dancing shadows. Take a deep breath and relax, she told herself. The *sentinelle* whirred along the catwalk.

A figure emerged from behind the clock tower. Felicitas recognized the black hair and rough square face. Piero.

Piero walked to the middle of the yard, heedless of the searchlights, and stared up at the walls. He pulled his *pistola* from his belt and aimed at the nearest *sentinella*, swung the *pistola* to the left as the *sentinella* moved along its chain-drive. Was he going to destroy it? Didn't he understand that the other *sen-*

tinelle would kill him instantly? But he didn't fire. He was only pretending. She wanted to be out there with him. If Piero could find his way out to the yard, so could she.

She moved from the window and walked into the dark corridor . . .

But got no farther than halfway down when a metallic hand gripped her arm. She spun round. A *carceriere.*

The *carceriere* lifted her arm and scanned the symbols tattooed on her skin as the loose sleeve of her uniform fell back. Making an identification, it then wrenched her toward her cell, as if she were a truant schoolgirl. But something was wrong, and with each step the *carceriere*'s grip tightened. She groaned, frantic with fear, and tried to push the *carceriere* away.

"Let go!" she cried.

But it wouldn't let go.

Just when she thought she would faint from pain, the *carceriere* beeped, came to a halt, and collapsed to the floor beside her.

She staggered backward, holding her arm, and stared at the fallen machine. The purple light flashed on the *carceriere*'s chest, and a high-pitched whine came from its abdomen. Was this what the prisoners had to look forward to, machines so old and decrepit they were now a menace?

She looked up and down the corridor. A few curious prisoners peered out at her. Two of them left their cells, men she recognized, one named Aldo, the other Anteo. They were both dead, but dead in different ways.

"You shouldn't be out here," said Aldo. "You should be in your cell. If you go to your cell right now I'll have a book for you tomorrow."

She rubbed her arm, still breathless from her encounter with the *carceriere.*

"You have books?" she said.

He nodded, but he nodded like a simpleton. "I know people," he said. "I can get a book for you tomorrow. You should stay out of the corridors at night. The *carcerieri* don't like it."

But she only half heeded his warning. Books. She again remembered sitting in the circle with other children. Had she undergone some kind of schooling? Here was a dead man telling her of books, a dead man who could speak properly but who was still obviously dead, with only a dull sense of the things around him. By contrast, Anteo was zombielike, looked as if he weren't capable of stringing even the simplest sentences together. Anteo stared at her, his eyes like burnt-out lightbulbs. Both Aldo and Anteo were dead, but why was there such a big difference between them?

She again looked at Aldo, curious about him. He was concerned about her. She wondered if his memory had been damaged like hers, or if the amnesia came only after the mental fog lifted. His perception did indeed seem blunted. But because he was still dead, were all his specific memories intact? Conversely, her own perception was sharp, but her specific memories were mostly gone. Aldo shifted from foot to foot, waiting for her to say something.

"Where can you find books in this prison?" she asked.

"I know people," he repeated.

She gave Aldo a grin. "Okay," she said. "I'll go to my cell. But I'm counting on that book."

Aldo nodded sluggishly, then peered nervously down the corridor.

"You'd better hurry," he said. "There'll be another *carceriere* along soon."

3

The next day, as she walked across the yard to the south tower, she was wary of the remaining *carcerieri*—her arm was badly bruised from last night's encounter.

She was surprised she could remember the specific events of yesterday so well: the lifting of the mental fog in the morning, taking Adriana's food-brick in the afternoon, performing the nightly lockup in the evening. She remembered the unsettling dream about Lungo Muso.

It was still early, with only *Stella Piccola* glowing over the wall. The air was damp and cool. No sign of Aldo or her book. She remembered Aldo too. Remembered Anteo. She remembered Piero out in the yard last night, aiming at the *sentinelle*. New specifics. Gems to treasure. Maybe they would help her remember old specifics.

She hurried past the dispensary, looking up at the south tower.

She didn't know why the *carcerieri* never went to the south tower, or why it had been allowed to fall into ruin by the *uo-minilupi*, or why so many of its rooms were sealed off while others had been gutted by fire. She didn't know why it was made of steel and plastic when the rest of the prison was made of mortar and stone.

As she reached the tower, she brushed a lock of hair from her face. She walked around to the back of the tower, leaving footprints in the morning dew, and entered the structure through a large gash in the metal.

Inside, tiny perforations were visible, pinpoints of light, enough to see by.

She climbed a spiral ramp up through a central chamber, where walkways led at regular intervals to chambers, platforms, and balconies. She saw gleaming *topi* eyes staring out at her from dark corners. She saw glyphs engraved on the walls, like the glyphs she had seen in her dream of Lungo Muso. She stopped. She was startled. These were the exact same glyphs she had scratched into the wall in that dream. She looked for a picture of Lungo Muso's strange building, but she couldn't see one. She had a closer look at the glyphs.

None of them made any sense to her now, not the way they had in her dream. And it hadn't really been a dream but more of an episode. She lifted her hand and traced one of the glyphs with her finger. She pricked her finger on a metal sliver, and, pulling it away, saw blood beading through the dirt on her fingertip. She lifted her hand and tasted her own blood. She knew so little about herself. Every small discovery might help.

"Felicitas?"

A voice drifted out of the darkness. She turned around. It was Maritano, the boy who had kept her safe for so many years. They always met here, in the south tower.

He walked into the dim light near the glyphs. She now knew why this place had become special, why she sometimes came here without even eating her food-brick in the morning. It was here, in this crumbling metal tower, that she could be with Maritano.

He was a slight but tall man, young, with a fair freckled face, tawny hair, and eyes the color of an overcast sky. His nose was broken, now healed crookedly.

She reached out and stroked his immature beard.

"Maritano," she said. "Where have you been?"

With painful slowness a grin came to his face, and his thin lips parted to show uneven rows of brownish teeth. Felicitas seemed to see Maritano for the first time. She searched her memory, tried to find him—a memory of him from last week, or last year—but she uncovered only a vague outline, nothing concrete at all. Today he looked pale, as if he had been hiding away sick somewhere. She wasn't sure she felt the same way about him anymore.

He put his skinny arms around her and pulled her near. This embrace was what she lived for, yet now it felt strange.

"You look . . . different," he said, without inflection. "You smell funny."

She pulled away and studied his face, trying to discern a flicker of light in his eyes.

"I don't know what's happened," she said. "Maritano, can you hear me, can you understand? Everything has color and depth and texture. Everything's come out of the shadows and into the light. My memory's vanished but I . . . since yesterday . . . I don't know, I feel like someone's opened a door and I . . ."

She stopped. Her words were lost on Maritano. She turned away, not sure what to do.

She heard hammering outside. She moved to the wall and looked out one of the perforations. Maritano lumbered behind, his footsteps echoing through the darkness. He put his hand on her shoulder, but with her curiosity aroused, she shook it away.

"Maritano, please," she said.

She stared out the perforation.

Piero and twelve others smashed apart dead *carcerieri* with improvised hammers. How odd to see prisoners working without the supervision of the *carcerieri*. She stared at Piero, drawn to the man. He pointed at the head of a decapitated *carceriere,* said a few words, and one of the prisoners, a young man about Maritano's age, moved it into a pile of three or four others. She wanted to be down there helping them, not up here with Maritano. Something had been lost with Maritano, an innocence and spontaneity. She turned around and looked at Maritano. He had no vigor, no purpose. And there was certainly no joy in his eyes. That's what she needed right now. Some joy.

"Maritano, you're ill," she said. "You should go rest somewhere."

She turned away. She couldn't look at him anymore. She peered through the perforation again. Her eyes immediately found Piero.

And she knew that Piero had a plan—she could see it in his forthright movements—and she wanted to be part of that plan.

She didn't belong up here with Maritano anymore.

She belonged down there, along the east wall.

Later the same day, twenty-two *carcerieri* gathered in the yard, the tarnished remnant of a once strong army, responding to the landing-pit klaxon. Forty of fifty prisoners stood around, necks craned, watching the sky. Felicitas stood near Piero. Maritano looked on sullenly from a distance.

The inside bars came down over the *carcerieri* and the gate opened. This was her only view of the outside world, this yearly opening of the west gate, when the unmanned ship came out of the sky with fresh supplies. And the view didn't tell much. A barren expanse of charred rock stretched up to the lip of the landing pit. A few sparse patches of grass clung to the dirt. Some of the children pressed their faces against the bars to get a better look.

The *carcerieri* filed out the west gate. The prisoners were kept back by the inside bars. The searchlights crisscrossed the yard with stark beams. Both suns shone in the murky sky. But no ship descended out of the mist. Watching this futile exercise of the *carcerieri*, Felicitas now had the unspecific sense that a ship hadn't come last time, or the time before.

She glanced at Piero. He had a grin on his face. Did he know the *uominilupi* weren't coming, that their unmanned ship wouldn't materialize through the upper atmosphere? Were they all going to starve? Were the *uominilupi* actually going to let them die?

The *carcerieri* marched up the hill three abreast, their movements strained, as if this long-familiar terrain were now strange to them. How old they looked. Piero glanced down at her, gave her a nod.

"You, too, are alive now, Felicitas?" he said.

She looked up at the sky. "I don't see anything," she said. "They're not coming, are they?"

But Piero just looked at her, and Felicitas couldn't tell whether he pitied her or if he were amused by her. Up on the catwalks, the *sentinelle* whirred back and forth on their chain-drives with manic urgency.

"Why are the outside bars so thick and widely spaced?" she asked. "If they forgot to put these inside bars down, I could easily squeeze through those outside ones."

A smile came to Piero's face, showing a squarish flat set of teeth.

"The outside bars aren't meant to keep us from getting out, Felicitas," he said. "And are you really so eager to escape? The prison offers security and food, and a dry warm place in winter."

She stared pensively at the *carcerieri* as they continued their uphill march.

"I want to see what's out there," she said.

The *carcerieri* climbed the rocky slope, manlike, yet with no fluidity of movement. The prison offers security. Yes, now she remembered the fear of the outside world, the things that moved through the mist, that occasionally shook the ground outside the prison, memories, fleeting and mysterious, of strange and unintelligible cries, of ghostlike howling.

The *carcerieri* walked right up to the lip of the landing pit, and, under the impression there might be a ship's ramp, continued onward, toppling into the pit. Several prisoners laughed—such a rare occurrence. The *carcerieri* tried to climb out of the landing pit, heads just visible over the lip of the pit, but kept falling back in, unequipped to angle themselves properly.

That's all she saw for a while. *Carcerieri* coming up over the lip of the crater, then falling back in. And many of the prisoners soon got tired of watching, and their stomachs growled, and they knew that the ugly square ship wasn't going to come, and that they were going to go to bed hungry once again.

4

The north wall still had its pull.
Felicitas sat against the north wall with Adriana, trying to feel the sense of security and belonging the north wall had always given her. *Stella Piccola* and *Stella Grossa* shone down on her from over the south parapet, and the *sentinelle* up on the south catwalk cast moving shadows on the colorless dirt of the yard as they rumbled by. She glanced around at her fellow prisoners along the north wall, wondering if any of them besides herself had grown sensible to the world. But their eyes remained dull. Even the eyes of the north wall children remained torpid.

Across the yard, against the east wall, the men still worked. So did the women. And children played. Children who were alive.

A woman chased a small girl. The small girl laughed as she ran away—she couldn't have been more than six or seven.

The woman called, "Come to me, *figlia*, I have a surprise for you."

"No, *signora*," cried the child. "You're going to have to catch me first."

The child, with the light of life in her eyes, darted around the clock tower. The woman chased after her.

Figlia. Something jogged in Felicitas's memory, she wasn't sure what, a bit of the dreamphone haze lifting again, an idea about the words the woman and child used. *Figlia* and *signora.* Terms of affection between a mother and daughter, yes, but also something about the words themselves. They were different. She looked up at the suns. *Stella Piccola. Stella Grossa.* Different words again. More of the dreamphone haze lifted. The language she and the others used here . . . in this prison . . . a hybrid . . . yes, she remembered puzzling over it before, when she'd been a dead girl, but now she couldn't remember anything about it. *Sentinelle. Carcerieri.* She turned to Adriana, her brow furrowing. *Amica.* Friend. Two different words, each meaning the same thing.

Adriana looked at her shyly. "You don't talk to me anymore," she said.

Felicitas glanced past Adriana's shoulder, where she saw Maritano sitting with two of his own *amici.* More of the amnesia lifted. She recognized his friends, and, after a moment, remembered their names, Marco and Ottavio. Marco was a short squat man of about twenty with an unruly head of coarse brown hair, a flat wide brow, and bushy eyebrows. Ottavio had lighter hair, nearly blond, was taller, and broader across the shoulders. He exercised with a piece of stone as he sat cross-legged with Maritano and Marco, bending his arm at the elbow as he lifted it up and down. She had lived a life with these people, she sensed that now, but she could hardly remember any of it.

"Do you want to play cards?" asked Adriana.

Adriana produced a deck of worn playing cards from under her blanket. Felicitas looked at the cards. And her memory jogged again. Italian playing cards, cards with coins and swords and goblets on them. She looked at Adriana. A stray breeze from the parapet blew one of Adriana's blond curls from her face. *Italian.* Yes, she remembered now. Italian and English. Languages. And the notion of languages unlocked a further memory. Of a room somewhere in the prison, crammed with books. She remembered spending hours there, reading the books, understanding the English ones, fighting to understand the Italian ones, marveling over the differences between the two languages, wondering why the language in the prison seemed to be a mix of both.

"I don't remember how to play," said Felicitas.

Adriana stared at her with her doll-like blue eyes. She looked desperately malnourished.

"But we play all the time," said Adriana. "*Tresette, briscola, scopa,* we've played them all."

Tresette, briscola, scopa. Italian. She looked up at the east wall. It rose starkly out of the mud of the yard, the windows gaping through the stone in the haphazard pattern of a punch-card. Was the room with all the books up there? She glanced over at the men working by the east wall. She saw Gasparo, the man who supervised at the dispensary, a huge man, nearly seven feet tall, with a big square head, shoulders like a ox, and thighs as thick as her waist. Maybe Gasparo would tell her if the books were up there. Or maybe some of the children playing by the east wall might tell her.

She turned to Adriana.

"Adriana, I have no memory of playing card games with you," said Felicitas.

"But how could you forget?" asked Adriana.

She had no answer. She stared at her friend. Obviously Adriana remembered the card games. But in coming out of the dreamphone haze, she herself, though now alive, could remember none of them.

"I'm going up to the east cellblock," she said.

Adriana put the deck of cards away. "To see the books?" she asked.

Felicitas peered at her friend closely. "You know about the books?" she asked.

"We go there all the time," she said.

Felicitas leaned over and put her hand on Adriana's wrist.

"Could you take me there now?"

"I don't know the way," said Adriana.

"But you said we go there all the time."

"You've always brought me there," said Adriana. "I've never paid any attention to how we got there. I've always followed you, Felicitas."

"But the books, they're up in the east cellblock, aren't they?"

Adriana's eyes went even glassier than normal as she tried to remember. "I think so," she said.

Felicitas stared up at the east wall. "I guess we'll just have to find out," she said.

As they left the north wall, she saw Piero stand up from his work at the forge—he was melting down scrap. He stared at her. Watching her again. She cast a nervous glance his way, then climbed the steps up through the archway into the east cellblock.

Like the others, the east cellblock had five levels overlooking a central common area. The place smelled. Shafts of morning light cut through the misty air from the upper windows. Felicitas tried to remember where the books might be but nothing came to mind. She would simply have to search.

They walked from one end of the first level to the other.

"Why don't we go back into the sunshine?" asked Adriana. "It's cold in here. And it's damp. You know I hate the damp, Felicitas."

"I want to find the books," said Felicitas.

They climbed to the next level. They searched cell after cell, well over a hundred on each side, but not a single one had books. The third and fourth levels produced the same lack of results. On the fifth level they found a large holding pen at the south end, and inside, Felicitas saw hundreds of old books stacked on makeshift shelves. A man sat at a table just inside the barred gate. The holding pen was large, easily ten times the size of a normal cell. Instead of stone and mortar walls, it had steel slats all around.

More of the amnesia lifted. She remembered this place. And she remembered the man sitting at the table, though she couldn't readily remember his name. He was a tall willowy man, with a thin face, a bald pate with a rim of fine brown hair worn shoulder length. His fingers were long, spidery. He wore a *pistola* in his belt. His eyes were alive. He had come out of it. He wasn't of the north wall, he was of the east wall.

He got up from his table, approached them, and looked through the steel slats at them.

"Felicitas?" he said.

Her brow knitted, and she stared at the man.

"And you are?" she said at last.

He smiled, revealing a ragged line of teeth. "Francesco," he said. "You know, Francesco. I guard these books for Piero."

"Francesco," she repeated. She turned the name over in her mind. "It sounds familiar, but I . . . I seem to have lost my memory . . . I seem to have—"

"Don't worry," he said, "you'll come out of it." Francesco glanced at Adriana. His face darkened. "Is she . . . you know . . . is she still dead?"

Felicitas glanced at her friend. "I think so."

Francesco nodded. "It's all right," he said. He opened the gate. "She can come in. She's such a slight young girl, I don't think I'll have any trouble with her." He swept his long thin arm toward the books in a gesture of welcome. "Come in," he said. "Get yourself reacquainted. Piero says I'm to encourage you, especially now that you're alive."

"*Grazie, signore,*" she said.

The words came reflexively to her lips. Italian words. Popping suddenly into her English speech.

She entered the holding pen. A big blue ball stood on a gold pedestal in the middle of the holding pen.

"What's this?" she asked.

"That's a globe," he said. "A globe of the earth." Francesco seemed to enjoy explaining this to her. "You look at that all the time."

"I do?" she said.

"Yes," he said.

She studied the globe. This was a model, a representation of a planet. She suddenly understood, as yet more of the amnesia shredded away, that she possessed at least a rudimentary understanding of astronomy. She looked at some of the land masses while Adriana walked toward another table farther down. *Africa. Asia. Europe.* She turned to Francesco, shaking her head.

"I'm afraid I don't . . . it's not coming back . . . I'm not sure exactly what these—"

"No need to rush, *bella*," said Francesco. "It takes time. I've been out of it nearly three years, and I still don't remember everything, not by half." He glanced toward Adriana. "Why don't you join your friend? She's at your table. I've left some of your favorite books out." He gave her an ingratiating nod. "I knew you would come back."

She stared at Francesco, trying to remember something about him, but there was nothing.

Finally she just said, *"Grazie, signore, grazie,"* and walked to the table.

At the table, Adriana pointed to a picture in one of the books.

"Look, Felicitas," she said. "A horse."

The animal in question was a hoofed creature with pointed ears, a mane on its neck, and a long tail. Horse. An earth animal. The memory jogged. She looked at another book. She read the title. *Trees for English Gardens.* She flipped through the book. Yes. Trees. Plant life. She'd taught herself about plant life. Knew what plant life was, but had never actually seen it, at least none except the pond scum that floated in the drainage pools and the few bits of grass around the landing pit. Often wondered if there were any trees around the prison. No windows facing outward. They all faced the yard. Here was a chestnut tree. And here was a plane tree. And these dark tapering ones were cypress trees. How pretty. And this oak, she longed to sit under its spreading branches on a sunny day and enjoy its shade. The words in this book were all in English.

She picked up another book. The words in this one were Italian.

Italian. English. She could tell the difference just by looking at them. And now recalled reading references to other languages. French. German. Russian. But why just English and Italian in the prison? And how had she ever been able to tell one from the other? Who could answer these questions? She glanced at Francesco. He was absorbed in paring his nails with a makeshift shiv. He didn't seem a likely candidate.

Who could she ask, then? Piero?

She decided there was no one else.

She would have to summon her nerve and talk to the man who always watched her.

5

Piero took her to his workshop later that same day, a room near the top of the south tower. He told he'd been alive for five years, longer than anybody, and that he'd been trying to figure out the prison's various mysteries ever since. He told her the whole place was run by machines.

She in turn told Piero about her Lungo Muso dream, her dreamphone dream, and about her visit to Francesco up in the east wall.

"And I've had some memories," she said. "I remember sitting around in a circle with some children listening to a woman read a book." She was talkative now. Piero, exhibiting a novel friendliness, had put her at ease. "I thought I would have a lot more memories. But I don't."

"It's just a matter of time, Felicitas," he said. "Your memories will come back to you."

In his workshop, Piero searched under some junk on a table, pulled out a shiny disk, brought it to his workbench, and gave it a spin. The disk spun faster and faster, and soon hummed like a spinning top.

"Have you ever seen a *uomolupo?*" she asked.

"No," he said, "Though I imagine we call them *uomolupo* for a reason. You say you see the hand of one in your dreamphone dream stapling a tag through the dead woman's ear?"

"Yes."

"What's it look like?"

"Four fingers, two thumbs, claws, and fur."

Piero took a deep breath, pondering her description.

"Rosario says he's seen two of them in his dreamphone dream." He turned to her, peered at her as the disk gained speed on the table. "Lungo Muso . . . he shows you glyphs?"

"Yes."

His eyes narrowed.

"What about this memory I have of sitting around with a group of children listening to a woman read?" asked Felicitas.

"Yes . . . that . . . well . . ." He rubbed his bearded chin with his hand. "The dead have a school of sorts, Felicitas. And you were part of that school."

"That's one of the only things I remember," she said.

Piero's eyes softened with sympathy. "It's this amnesia, you see, this inability to recall things once we come out of the dreamphone haze. A side effect. We know enough to recognize things, to know who we are, but it takes time for us to remember the details. Don't worry. It will come back to you. But it takes time. Rosario's trying to figure out a way to make the amnesia go away faster."

"Who's Rosario?" she asked.

"He's my . . . my *consigliere.* You've seen him in the yard."

"I never murdered anyone," said Felicitas, her voice sullen.

Piero brushed the dust off a viewscreen with the back of his sleeve and hooked it up to a keyboard. "That's always troubled you, Felicitas," he said. "Even when you were dead, you didn't believe you killed that woman."

Piero searched through broken bits of *carcerieri,* his calloused hands moving among the junk until he found a couple of pieces of wire. He inspected the wires and put them on his workbench beside the humming disk.

"The dreamphones lie," she said.

He looked up from his workbench.

"Who can say what the dreamphones do?" he said. "There are so many things we can't be sure about. How can we be sure how we got here? We all have dreams, but are they genuine, or simply made up by the *uominilupi*? You see a claw in your dream, and now Lungo Muso appears, and we say the *uominilupi* look like wolves, that they walk like men, and that this is the reason we call them *uominilupi*." He shook his head. "But who can say for sure?"

"You've been alive longer than any of us," she said. "You must have learned something."

He didn't answer, at least not right away. He walked over to another work-table, moved aside some dust-covered circuit boards, and came back with a corroded gold plaque.

"Look at this," he said, handing it to her.

She took the plaque and stared at the engraved glyphs, small ones in complex configurations. These glyphs were less representational than the ones out on the ramp, more technical. As much as she tried, she couldn't make sense of them.

"What is it?" she asked, handing it back to Piero.

"It's a *carceriere* schematic. We've figured out enough of their language to at least understand some of it. Right here," he said, pointing, "this shows service life. The *carcerieri* have a service life of a hundred and thirty years. All of our *carcerieri* are now dead." He cocked his head to one side, his eyebrows rising. "Does that mean we've been here for a hundred and thirty years?" He shrugged. "Who can say?"

"You think we've been here that long?" asked Felicitas.

"Possibly. Maybe as a population we've been here for centuries. Who knows?" He tossed the *carceriere* schematic onto his workbench. "What bothers me most is that we might not be so much prisoners of the *uominilupi* as we are of a fully auto-mated, antiquated, and now abandoned penal system."

Piero fastened one wire to the viewscreen, one to the key-board, then attached the opposite ends to the baseplate of the power disk, which hummed quietly. He pressed a few buttons, threw a few switches, and the screen lit up.

"Raise your left arm," he said.

She obeyed.

Piero entered her identification code into the keyboard.

The picture of a man appeared on the viewscreen. The man was around forty years old, entirely bald, with a pasty com-plexion, a protruding brow, and predatory eyes. He was ugly. Piero pressed a button, flicking forward to a new screen: blocks of *uominilupi* writing appeared.

"I've studied a thousand examples of this writing," said Piero. He leaned forward and examined the script more closely. Felicitas leaned forward with him. "A lot of these words I've never seen before. But I understand some of them."

Piero pressed another button and flicked to a third screen.

She was surprised. Here was her dream, the scarred white hands floating in front of her, the woman running away through the rain.

"You have to watch that every night?" asked Piero.

She nodded.

"You should count yourself lucky," said Piero. "Mine's a lot worse." He pressed a button and flicked back to the second screen, the one with the writing. "This is a report of some kind. Maybe it tells how the bald man in the first screen killed this woman, the evidence against him. It's the same with all of us. Someone else has committed our crimes, but we're the unlucky ones to be imprisoned."

"I see hands . . ." She felt chilled to see her dream on the screen. "And they're floating in the air before me." Her voice sounded breathless as her fear intensified. "And when I chase that woman . . ." She was losing track of her thoughts. "Large

white hands with terrible scars all over them . . . and I can't . . ."
She felt close to tears.

Piero put a hand on her shoulder. "It's all right, Felicitas,"
he said. "You can be afraid. We're all afraid." He let his hand
slide from her shoulder and flicked back to the picture of the
bald man. "Those hands, they probably belong to this man," he
said. "Of course, there's no way of knowing. Maybe the original prisoners somehow schemed to make us take their places
by tattooing their identification codes onto our arms. The
carcerieri wouldn't know the difference, not when they identify us that way."

Piero leaned back and gazed at the screen with skeptical
eyes. The screen flickered a few times, as if it were losing power.

"You don't sound . . . too convinced," she said.

Piero's grin disappeared, and he now looked irritated.

"When I look at all the evidence," he said, "I believe we
must be the offspring or descendants of the original prisoners.
This man on the screen might be your father or grandfather, or
maybe even your great-grandfather. The identigram on your
arm might have been handed down to you as a kind of family
heirloom, a way to make sure the *carcerieri* looked after you."

His voice now had a restless quality.

"I believe that as a population we've been here for a long
time, longer than any of us can imagine. Maybe centuries. I'm
not sure what happened to the *uominilupi* but I don't think
they've been here for hundreds of years. The machines run the
place now. Maybe the *uominilupi* don't even know we're here
anymore. The machines keep doing what they're supposed to
do. No one's ever turned them off. They keep us here, generation after generation. But now they're breaking down."

The screen flickered again, the face disappeared, the screen
turned red, then went dark as the power disk finally gave up.

"What about the dead?" she asked. "Some of them seem to
be smarter than others."

Piero stared at the screen. "I don't know," he said. "Not even
Rosario really knows."

Felicitas was curious. "Is Rosario . . . is he supposed to know?"

Piero lifted his eyes and looked at her. "Rosario's a . . . a *genio*. He understands everything. He's figured out most of the machinery in here. This business with the dead . . . well . . . he says it's just human nature, that we're all different, even we who have come out of it. Some of us can work all day in the yard without having to stop, while others are exhausted by noon. Some of us have blue eyes, others have brown. Some are right-handed, some are left-handed. Some can bear the cold, some can't. Rosario believes that some dead are more resistant to the dreamphones and sleeping pallets. Others . . . well, you can see for yourself . . . they're buried. So buried they're never coming back. We don't think too many others will come out of it now. With some, the damage seems permanent, with others, it doesn't."

Rosario. He had some good ideas. She would have to meet and talk to this man. Piero seemed to think a great deal of him.

"Adriana can't even seem to find her way around the prison," she said.

He looked away, and his face settled. "Adriana seems to be . . ." He turned to her. "They all have different aptitudes. Some, you show them where their cell is one night, and they forget the next day. Others, they only have to learn something once. As for Adriana . . . she relies on you a great deal. We'll just have to hope she comes out of it."

"What about the Italian?" she asked. "Why do we all have Italian names when we're all so obviously anglophones? Why is the English we speak peppered with so many Italianisms? And why do I recognize one as Italian and the other as English?"

Piero shook his head slowly. "I can't give you any definite answer, Felicitas. We have only English speakers in this prison now. But there must have been Italian speakers at one time, and they obviously had an influence on the way we speak."

"But why should I know about Italian and English?" she asked. "Why can I tell one from the other?"

Outside, the wind whistled around the tower.

"From the books you've read," he said. A smile came to his face. "When you were dead, Felicitas, it was always books with you. It was always language." His smile broadened, as if this were a topic of particular interest. "You were always curious and observant. You could always express yourself when you chose to. Now that you've come out of the dreamphone haze . . ." He gave her shoulder a pat. "Well . . . I'm surprised by how well you speak. You have a talent for language. We always knew this. And it's surfacing through your amnesia. That's why you recognize the English and Italian. This is why Rosario and I have watched you. It's these books, you see. Most of them are with Francesco in the east cellblock, but we have others cached safely here and there. You were always looking into them. You even struggled with the Italian ones. It was always language with you, Felicitas."

"But where do these books come from?" she asked. "I can barely remember them."

Piero raised his eyebrows as he slid onto his stool. "No one knows for sure," he said. "But I remember one incident, when Rosario and I first searched the basement of the east cellblock, about a year or two after we came out of the dreamphone haze. The corner room, where the east wall joins the north wall, had no books, at least not when we first looked through it. But then the north bath sprang a leak and the water emptied into that section of the east basement, and we went to have another look. This time, the corner room was full of books. We had no idea how they got there. Rosario's looked into it, and the only explanation he's come up with is that, as with everything else in this prison, there's been a malfunction. Maybe these books were intended for somewhere else, and they wound up here because of a breakdown of some kind."

*   *   *

She swam to the middle of the south bath, to where it got deep. Was it here, the subsurface passageway, the one that led to the room in the south wall, to Lungo Muso? She concentrated on her arms. No tingling. She had to find that passageway, had to convince herself that her dream—her episode—wasn't a dream at all. She glanced at the central island, ten yards to her left. This seemed right. This was the spot.

She dove under and kicked to the bottom. She searched and searched but she couldn't find the subsurface passageway. What she found instead was a spot that looked as if it had been patched up, exactly where the tunnel should have been. The patch was made of a rough gray compound.

And that was enough for Felicitas. She knew she hadn't been dreaming. Her visit to Lungo Muso under the south wall had been real. . . .

6

Felicitas sat in her usual spot against the north wall looking up at the sky, thinking about everything Piero had told her. *Stella Grossa* and *Stella Piccola* shone weakly above the parapets. Adriana sat beside her, still dead to the world.

What kind of life had she lived? She couldn't sit still, got up and paced in front of the dead, who slouched against the wall. None showed a flicker of interest, not even the smarter ones. If she'd been anything like these prisoners along the north wall, she must have lived a life of squalor and monotony. And that wasn't fair.

She kicked a piece of mortar. She felt robbed. Her memories, the few she had, were so patchy, so indistinct, she couldn't tell whether they were real or imagined. She felt cheated. Except for a few small bits, her childhood had been wiped clean, and she could only hope that the amnesia would lift soon.

She walked over to the east wall, where Piero's men worked on broken *carcerieri*.

She was restless, wanted to help them, but wasn't sure if the men would let her. Most were young, but a few were Piero's age. At least thirty children, all of them alive, were running around here and there, playing games.

The women worked by the clock tower. She remembered the name of only one, an older woman, Concetta. Was this the woman who had read to her? She couldn't recall. The women looked familiar.

She walked past the group of men to see what the women were doing.

They sorted pieces of cloth, stitched them together to make larger sheets. Some made capes. Others made hoods. Concetta came over to her and held out a uniform.

"You see this?" said the old woman. "You see what I've done? I've stitched this orange and yellow bird onto the breast pocket. I'm going to wear this uniform once it's done. Don't you think it's pretty?"

Was there something familiar about the woman's voice? Felicitas thought there might be. Felicitas thought this might be the woman who had read to her.

"Yes, very pretty," said Felicitas.

"This bird is a symbol of freedom," said Concetta. "It's a symbol of light. Why don't you help us?" Concetta waved at all the various pieces of cloth and fabric. "We found most of this material in the old supply room behind the dispensary. We're making tents. It's lots of fun. Why don't you join us?"

Concetta even spoke like a teacher of young children.

Felicitas gave the woman a timid smile. "Thank you," she said. "But I think I'll see what the men are doing."

She walked over to the east wall and joined the men.

They all looked purposeful.

Without saying a word, Piero put his hand on her shoulder and guided her through the knots of men. Most were dismantling *carcerieri* or machinery scavenged from the south tower. A few worked the makeshift forge, while others constructed, with hammers and bolts, a metal lattice, the purpose of which wasn't immediately clear.

"I knew you would come, Felicitas," Piero finally said. "After our talk yesterday, I knew you wouldn't stay away much longer. I couldn't ask you. You had to show me." He surveyed his small outdoor factory, pleased with it. "Maybe you can help Rosario," he said, pointing. "He'll show you what to do."

She stared apprehensively at Rosario, feeling shy and unsure of herself. He was about ten years older, had a stern face with well-defined features. His thick blond hair was combed back from his face and tied in a ponytail. His blue eyes were intent on his work. He was tall, muscular, slim. His movements, as he worked, were competent and proficient. Felicitas had a funny feeling in her stomach; it was as if she had never truly looked at a man until she had looked at Rosario. He glanced up from his work. Their eyes met. And it wasn't at all like looking into Maritano's eyes, eyes as mute as stones, but like gazing at stars. Rosario's eyes were bright with meaning.

Piero gave her shoulder a squeeze.

"Go on," he said. "Rosario will teach you."

Felicitas walked through the workers.

As Rosario gazed at her, she felt self-conscious, wondered if she had dirt on her face, or if her eyes looked dead like stones. Was she pretty? She wasn't sure. There weren't any mirrors in the prison. Would Rosario consider her just a girl, nobody special? Rosario gave her a nod. She felt the color rise in her face.

"Don't be afraid," he said. He picked up a *carceriere* arm and handed it to her. "You can start with this," he said. "Use this metal shiv. Pry the gray plate off by popping the rivets. Save the rivets. When you get the plate off, strip the musculature until you get to the underlying support. It looks like this." He held up a thick metal bar, the length of a *carceriere* arm. "Put it in that pile with the rest of them."

"What about the musculature?" she asked.

"Get rid of it in that pile over there."

She squatted beside him and took the shiv. Yes, this was where she belonged, among these men of the east wall, not with the dead of the north wall. She stuck her shiv under the thin layer of gray metal and pried. She felt fearless, calm, buoyant. Life had truly begun. Nothing could frighten her, not the *mostri* that flew through the sky, not the dead woman running through the rain, not even the *uominilupi*. She was strong. She was courageous. She did not know fear.

But then something crawled out of the *carceriere* arm onto her wrist, and her fear instantly returned. She shrieked like a child, pitched the arm to the ground, and shook her hand wildly until the thing dropped to the dirt.

"Topo!" she cried. *"Topo!"*

The rodent darted away, but it didn't get far. With lightning speed, Rosario chopped off the creature's head with his shiv, grabbed its quivering body by the tail, and tossed it into a basket of several others.

Rosario knelt beside her and put a hand on her knee. His touch reassured.

"It's dead now," he said. "You don't have to worry. I should have told you. There's a certain oil in the *carcerieri* the *topi* love." He lifted the *carceriere* arm, shook it, and peered inside. "I think it's empty now. You don't have to worry."

She felt like a fool, couldn't meet his eyes, kept staring at the *topo*'s head.

"Thank you," she said. "I'm all right now. It startled me, that's all."

She went back to work. No, she wasn't brave after all. But she would have to find courage somewhere. She stuck the shiv under the plating and worked the metal free, taking care to collect all the rivets.

Then Rosario laughed. His laughter was like music, forthright and sure of itself, the laughter of a man who didn't have to prove anything to anybody.

"What's so funny?" she asked.

"You," he said. He didn't mock. He wasn't making fun of her. "You're funny. The way you moved, the way you shook the *topo* off your wrist. That was funny."

He laughed again, congenially. And she wasn't sure whether she should laugh with him or not. After all, the joke was at her expense. But then why not? Why couldn't she laugh at herself, especially when she could laugh with Rosario, who wasn't being at all mean about it? Laughter was a good way to turn fear into something harmless. So she laughed, and it felt good, natural. She liked the sound of her laughter, especially the way it mixed with Rosario's.

But then a stone landed next to Rosario and her laughter stopped, and, looking up, she saw Maritano standing nearby, disheveled and dirty, staring at her with his dead blank eyes. He picked up another stone and threw it in Rosario's direction, narrowly missing him. Rosario stood up and looked at Maritano.

Maritano ignored Rosario.

Maritano gazed at Felicitas, targeting her with his eyes, as if there was no one else in the yard. And she now saw blame in his eyes, as if Maritano thought she had betrayed him by laughing with Rosario. A dim light shone in his eyes. She didn't know what to make of that. She had never seen a light like that in his eyes before. Maybe he was coming out of the dreamphone haze.

Maritano turned around and shuffled away, zombielike, his arms hanging at his sides.

Felicitas turned to Rosario.

"Is he . . . he's never acted like that before," she said. "I've never seen him . . . he's never been angry like that before. And his eyes, he seems to be . . . do you think he's coming out of it?"

Rosario's jaw jutted. The amusement of a moment ago had vanished. He glanced at Piero, who had stopped his work by the forge. The two men stared at each other. She couldn't read their expressions. The two of them seemed to talk without the use of words.

Rosario turned to her, and the hardness eased from his face.

"No," he said. "I don't think he's coming out of it." Rosario smiled, but she could see he was forcing it. "He just . . . he just doesn't like you and me having fun together, that's all."

She finally removed all the gray plating.

As she pried away the electronic musculature, several cracks, buzzes, and pops came from the parapet. She looked up. The searchlights went out, casting the yard into unfamiliar darkness. The *sentinelle* clanked to a stop on their chain-drives, slowly shouldered their *cannoni,* and beeped, two short and one long, over and over again, each flashing a small purple light.

All work stopped and a hush fell over the yard.

Piero stepped away from the forge and gazed at the nearest *sentinella,* his eyes narrowing. He spun round and looked at the *sentinelle* up on the west wall, then at the ones on the north wall.

He strode to the north wall, pushing a few of the dead out of the way, and peered more closely at the *sentinelle* up on the north catwalk, even as their beeping began to fade and their purple lights went out.

"Has it finally happened?" he said, to no one in particular.

A deep silence such as none of them had ever heard before enveloped the prison yard. The *cantus firmus* of their lives had always been the constant whispering of the *sentinelle* up on the catwalks, but now that was gone. The only sounds Felicitas heard were the wind and, curiously, the lapping of water. Was there a lake outside the prison?

Piero turned from the north wall and strode back to the east wall. He ignored everybody. He gripped the lattice with unexpected strength, pulled it upright, and leaned it against the east wall. He climbed it with the agility of an acrobat.

Anybody could see the lattice reached only a quarter of the way up, but Piero was blind to this fact. He climbed to the top, balanced precariously on the last rung, and clawed the wall in a desperate effort to get out. It was pathetic. But also heroic. Heroic because she finally understood Piero's plan. Escape. What other plan could there be?

When she opened her eyes, the north cellblock's overhead lights were out, and she stared into darkness. The lights, another breakdown. It was so dark, she touched her eyes to make sure they were open.

Something was making her nervous, a change in the way her cell felt, the way it smelled, even the way it sounded . . .

She sat up—she no longer used the restraints—and listened, her eyes wide, the tiny auburn hairs on the back of her neck rising. Why did she feel so nervous?

"Adriana?" she called.

But Adriana, still one of the dead, slept soundly, her breath barely audible. Felicitas looked up at the window, where she saw the dim outline of the bars. What was making her so anxious? She slid off her sleeping pallet and walked to the open cell door. Maybe she was anxious because daily the lattice grew longer and she knew that she must soon leave the prison for good. But that wasn't it. There was something else, something more immediate, something more . . .

A hand came up from behind her and clamped over her mouth. The warm narcotic teeth of a pallet restraint latched onto her arm and she felt the drug seep into her nervous system. She turned around, tried to see the intruders—she was certain there was more than one—but it was too dark, and with the old narcotic warmth spreading through her body, numbing her, rushing through her limbs, she quickly lost control. Her legs buckled, her head lolled forward, and she collapsed. Strange arms reached out and broke her fall.

She couldn't understand, didn't even try to understand, simply surrendered because as a dead girl she had always surrendered. She grew faint, dizzy.

They carried her out of the cell and down the corridor. She couldn't figure out why or how this was happening, whether some of the *carcerieri* had come back, whether this was Maritano with some of the dead, or if it were the *uominilupi.*

They carried her to the end of the corridor and out through the main archway into the open air. She closed her eyes, couldn't keep them open, and sank into her old dream, her dream of murder. The white scarred hands floated in front of her. Up ahead she saw the woman running away from her through the rain. *Please, not this again.* She shook herself awake.

She was short of breath as the men took her across the yard to the south tower. The world spun end over end in a mounting wave of vertigo.

She drifted back into blackness, back into her dream. But it wasn't the same dream, because now one of the murdering hands carried a long sharp knife.

They put her on the floor of the south tower.

She opened her eyes. She was in one of the many alcoves. She saw the glimmering of oil lamps rippling over glyphs, saw faces above her. Was that the bald man from her dream, her father or grandfather, now holding not a knife but a stainless steel scalpel? They wore hoods fashioned from old prison uniforms. Were those wolfish eyes gazing out at her from the darkness—were they the eyes of the *uominilupi?*

They rolled her onto her stomach, forced her face into the dirt, and flicked her long hair out of the way. She twisted her head to one side, could see the bald man out of the corner of her eye. He poised the scalpel above her. But now it wasn't the bald man. This wasn't a dream. This was real. Her body stiffened, and she squirmed, trying to get away. These men were going to cut her. These men were going to kill her.

"No, please," she cried. "Please don't hurt me. Please don't hurt—"

But the knife sliced into the tender flesh at the base of her skull, and blood spilled over her skin. She was so heavily drugged, she was numb to the pain.

Then darkness overcame her.

7

She woke up on her sleeping pallet the next morning with no idea how she got there. She was groggy, her muscles were stiff, and the back of her neck ached. She lay on her stomach, her face turned to one side, her cheek pressed against the steel. She didn't want to open her eyes. She was afraid to open her eyes. But she finally opened them anyway.

Adriana sat on the edge of her own pallet staring at Felicitas, her eyes like marbles. Adriana slid off her pallet, and, on unsteady legs, walked over to Felicitas. She looked emaciated. She was starving. She hadn't had a food-brick in three days. Who made the decisions about food-bricks?

Adriana stroked the back of Felicitas's head, then leaned over and kissed her cheek.

"Adriana," said Felicitas, "Adriana, can you see what they've done to me?"

Felicitas tried to push herself up but it was too painful to move. Her friend stared at her as the wheels of understanding turned slowly in her mind. Adriana lifted Felicitas's thick auburn hair and gazed at the back of her neck.

"They've put a bandage on your neck," said Adriana.

"Take it off and see what's there."

Adriana looked into Felicitas's eyes, then at the bandage, and a crease came to her brow.

"I might ruin it," she said. "I wouldn't want to ruin your pretty bandage, Felicitas."

"You won't ruin it," said Felicitas. "Just peel it away."

Adriana swallowed, now apprehensive. She moved Felicitas's hair and leaned closer.

"Is the bandage clean?" asked Felicitas.

"Very clean," she said. "Where did they find such a white one?"

Adriana peeled the corner of the bandage away, the adhesive tugging gently against Felicitas's skin. When it was off, Adriana stared for a long time. Felicitas grew impatient.

"Well?" she said. "What do you see?"

"They've cut you, Felicitas. They've had to stitch you up."

"Yes, but is there anything odd about the cut?" asked Felicitas.

Adriana's eyes glassed over; she didn't understand the question. Felicitas wasn't sure she understood it either. Wouldn't there have to be something odd about this cut? Didn't there have to be a reason behind the whole brutal procedure? If they hadn't been trying to kill her, what had they been trying to do?

"It looks deep," Adriana finally said. She rubbed her hand over Felicitas's brow. "Are you going to be all right, Felicitas? You're not going to die, are you?"

Felicitas took Adriana's hand.

"No," she said. "I'm not going to die. You can put the bandage back on now."

A vacant grin came to Adriana's face; she was glad she didn't have to struggle with any more questions.

"There," she said. "That's better. I wish I had a pretty white bandage like that on my neck too."

Felicitas waited all morning in the south tower for Maritano, passing the time by puzzling over the badly worn glyphs, intermittently fascinated by them, then bored by them, sometimes feeling as if she were on the verge of understanding them, then baffled by them. She compared and matched, counted and grouped. Was this her education coming into play, this methodical approach to problem-solving? She had a memory of a smooth wall with chalk writing on it; and the same old woman—was it Concetta?—writing a sentence, something about a red fox and a brown cow. Concetta went over each word, explaining what each one was, how each one worked in relation to the others. Felicitas believed if she worked long enough with these glyphs she might understand them the way she had understood Concetta's sentence.

A figure walked up the ramp, emerging out of the shadows. It was Maritano. She hoped she would see life in his eyes, but his eyes remained dead. He had lost a lot of weight. His ragged uniform hung around his bony frame like a flag around a flagpole, his jaw jutted, and his arms and legs were as skinny as poles. He carried a bundle of something wrapped in rags. Even from this distance Felicitas smelled the stale reek of his prison uniform.

"Maritano?" she said. "Maritano have you—"

"You don't sit against the north wall anymore," he mumbled.

She stared at him, wondering how she should answer him.

"You look so thin," she said. "I don't see you at the dispensary. Don't they give you your food-brick?"

He looked away, walked past her with a feeble shuffle, put his back to the wall, and slid to a sitting position, clutching the bundle to his chest.

"They don't feed me anymore," he said. "Gasparo doesn't like me."

Her lips stiffened. "It's not that he doesn't like you, it's just that he has to—"

"I don't know why he doesn't like me," said Maritano. "Maybe some day I'll get him to like me. He always gets his food-brick. I never get mine. Maybe if he starts to like me, he'll open my hamper and I'll get my food-brick again."

His voice was flat, his reasoning lateral. He couldn't see the hundreds of questions opening up in ever expanding complexity the way she could. Had he been one of the children sitting around the floor listening to Concetta? Or had he been one of the truants? She now had another memory, how some of the children didn't bother with books, how they preferred their own pursuits.

She sat beside Maritano.

"Maritano," she said, wondering how she could make it clear. "Haven't you noticed a change? Haven't you noticed how the *carcerieri* no longer look after you? And the searchlights? They're not working anymore."

"Maybe I'll have to hurt Gasparo," he said. "Then he'll like me again. Maybe I'll have to throw a stone at him. I can make him like me."

"Maritano, you can't make anybody like you by throwing stones at them. Please, try to . . ." She stopped, wasn't sure if there was any point. "Where do you sleep at night? Are you still in the west cellblock?"

But he didn't answer, scratched his ankle in a distracted movement, then looked down at his bundle. He lifted the bundle and offered it to Felicitas. A gift, she wondered? She took the bundle and pulled away a corner of the cloth.

Inside lay five dead *topi*, cleaned and skinned. She had a vague recollection that she had seen the large rodents prepared this way before, ready to be roasted on an open fire. A gift. Another memory: children sitting around the north archway watching a young man skin a *topo* with a sharp piece of metal.

Her stomach rolled as she remembered the gamey taste of *topo* meat, how she got it caught between her teeth, and how, if she ate too much, her stomach hurt.

She put the bundle down. "No, Maritano," she said. "You eat them. You look as if you need them more than I do."

He took the *topi* back, disappointed.

She leaned over and kissed him on the cheek, trying to find some of the old feeling, some of that special friendship they had shared since childhood. But it wasn't there. She couldn't remember him sitting in the circle with other children learning from the books. All she remembered was Maritano always throwing stones, from sunup to sundown, chalking a target on the prison wall and practicing all the time.

She turned around and lifted her hair from her neck.

"Do you see this?" she said. "Do you see what they did to me the other night? They came for me, and they did this to me. I don't know who they were. Do you know why they did this to me?"

Maritano was silent. He put his hand on her shoulders and pulled her near. He preferred kisses and touches. He never liked to talk.

She knew she wasn't going to get any answers from Maritano.

She knew that things would never be the same between her and Maritano again.

She left him sitting up there with his bundle. She knew his feelings would be hurt, that he was going to sulk for a while, but she left him there anyway.

She exited the south tower and saw Piero foraging through the pile of debris near the south wall.

He stopped his foraging and looked at her.

"You were with Maritano?" he called.

"He's up there right now," she called back.

Piero's face grew slack, and he nodded, but there was something strange about his nod. She stared at him, wondering what was wrong. He went back to his foraging, making a big show of ignoring her. Then she understood. He was suspicious of her. And the thought surprised her. Why would he be suspicious?

Piero came to her in the yard a short while later.

"Are you hungry?" he asked.

His suspicion had evaporated.

"Of course I'm hungry," she said. "I'm always hungry."

He nodded. "You go to the dispensary today," he said. "You'll get a food-brick. Go there every day. Gasparo's going to make sure you're fed. We need you strong. You're one of the *superstiti* now, Felicitas," he said. "You're one of the survivors."

In his brusque way, he quickly retreated, without any further explanation.

Superstiti. She glanced at the north wall, where the dead, Adriana among them, huddled together, half starved.

By implication, there would be some who didn't survive.

8

Felicitas carried scrap metal from the heap behind the south tower. *Stella Piccola* and *Stella Grossa* shone weakly. Scrap metal to melt down and make chain links with. Chain links for the crane. The crane that would hoist the lattice into place, now that it was so heavy.

She walked along the west side of the dispensary, felt perfectly fine, happy with the work she was doing.

But then the tingling came to her arms again, that same tingling she'd felt when she went under the south bath to visit Lungo Muso. That dream, that episode. She stopped, overcome by a sudden breathlessness. This was no dream. She dropped the scrap metal and sat down. She closed her eyes. She didn't know how, didn't know why, but she felt as if she were rising, as if she were once again becoming unstuck. Her arms tingled so badly they hurt. She had the sensation of movement, of wind through her hair. The tingling wouldn't go away. And she couldn't feel the ground beneath her feet. So she braced herself and got ready to open her eyes . . .

And when she finally did, she was no longer in the prison yard . . .

She was sitting on a hill, and it was pouring rain. It was night-time and the prison was nowhere to be seen. Another dream, another episode. And she didn't understand any of it.

She stood up, trying to catch her breath. The rain soaked her instantly. Lightning flashed, and in the momentary brightness she saw a large house in a valley below, with a village nearby, and a church steeple. She saw oak trees, plane trees, a barn, several paddocks, some sheep hiding under a spreading chestnut. Things she remembered from the books. Several people cowered in a cave nearby, people dressed in old-time clothes, the men in frilly shirts and tricorn hats, the women in frocks and bonnets. They were looking down at the house in the valley, as if they were afraid of it.

Where was she? Lightning flashed again and the surrounding hills were lit up, and she tried to see the prison but she couldn't see it anywhere.

She stood there for several minutes. The rain slowly lessened.

Then she had the feeling that she'd been here before.

The feeling grew stronger, and she realized that yet more of her dreamphone amnesia was lifting. Yes, Lungo Muso had taken her here before.

The rain finally stopped. The clouds cleared and she saw a moon emerge, round and full, and shining like silver. And in the moonlight, she got a much better look at the land below.

Farms and pastures. And the ocean. Down by the village there was a harbor with some large sailing ships.

From behind a nearby oak tree a figure emerged. The figure wore a long black cape and had a rough animal head.

It was Lungo Muso.

He approached her through the moonlight, his eyes glowing amber, and offered her his arm. He wanted her to come with him.

They started down the hill. The house down there was made of ivory-colored stone, was three stories tall, had a west wing, east wing, a coach house, ornamental gardens, ponds, trees, two arboretums, stables, and two large conservatories. It was a huge house, a mansion. Sitting in the middle of the large front yard was an ugly square ship, like the one that brought their food-bricks every year, humming, steaming, glowing with lights.

Its ramps were swarming with New Ones.

"New Ones?" she said, turning to Lungo Muso.

Lungo Muso nodded but didn't explain what New Ones were. He was an Old One, she knew that, she remembered that from somewhere, but she still didn't know what New Ones were.

She gazed again at the square ship as they drew nearer. She saw New Ones strong-arming people out of the house, people from the old time, men in powdered wigs, women in colorful dresses. She recognized these things, understood that these people were from the old time, but wasn't exactly sure how she understood. She glanced at Lungo Muso. Had Lungo Muso taught her this? The New Ones put leashes around the necks of the old-time people and led them up the ramp into the square ship. They were being taken prisoner. She could hear their cries and screams.

"What's going on?" asked Felicitas.

Lungo Muso didn't answer. He offered her his arm again.

She took it, and they rose into the air, and she didn't know how she could fly, but she was up in the air, floating, and she could see the ground below.

They left the commotion at the big house behind them.

They floated over farms, past a mill, along a brook, and finally into the village.

The moon was bright upon the square.

A crowd had gathered by the harbor and she saw more New Ones, slick and small, and all identical, hardly at all like the savage-looking Old Ones.

Felicitas and Lungo Muso settled next to an alehouse. People stood all around, but no one seemed to see them. A few streetlamps flickered over the dirt road.

Twenty-two village infants lay in a large wagon under armed guard crying for their mothers. Shrieks of despair came from the mothers in the crowd.

The New Ones pulled the wagon to the edge of the harbor and began throwing infant after infant into the water. Several Old Ones, looking much like Lungo Muso, watched the massacre, but did nothing to interfere.

Two young men broke through the cordon and fired at the New Ones with flintlock pistols. These men were immediately killed by searing blue *uominilupi pistola* fire. She couldn't understand. Why were the New Ones killing these babies? Why were they throwing them into the harbor? She felt sick to her stomach. She looked to Lungo Muso for an explanation but he simply stared at the horrible scene.

As the baby killing continued, several explosions came from the harbor, and the sailing ships—war frigates—started to sink. She caught sight of a flag waving from a mainmast, a configuration of red, white, and blue crosses. Why did that flag look familiar? She turned just as another sailing ship was blown to bits. Why would the New Ones, who were obviously so much more powerful, feel compelled to sink these primitive wooden warships? What possible threat could they pose to the *uominilupi,* who rode out of the sky in big square ships? She could hardly think straight. The infants were crying. She looked at Lungo Muso again. Was he not going to do anything? She had to stop this. She couldn't let them kill those babies.

Lungo Muso looked down at her and his amber eyes narrowed. He shook his head. He was trying to tell her that there was nothing she could do. Yet she had to try.

She ran forward, thinking she might push the New Ones

into the harbor. But no one seemed to see her. She walked right up to the murderers. She pushed them, trying to stop them, and though she could feel the thick leather of their battle armor, she could in no way influence their movements. She pushed, shoved, and hit for nearly a minute but it was as if she weren't there.

Then she felt a hand on her shoulder. Lungo Muso had come up from behind.

He tried to talk to her but his voice came out as a series of snarls. He gave her a tug. She glanced once more at the brutal scene, then turned away, badly shaken, on the verge of tears.

Lungo Muso took her back to the alehouse. He knelt beside some barrels and scratched some glyphs into the dirt. She stared at the glyphs, and meaning rose out of them like mist from a morning field.

"We stood upon the river bank and watched our vanquishers destroy all we loved," she read. "We could move the plough, string the bow, and make everywhere the dead things of the forest obey our commands. But those with sense, will, and perception were blind to our efforts, so we could no longer steer our course in the river but had to trust to the New Ones. Our faith was as always, that we would ply the river of time and make good the wrongs of yesteryear, so that all our tomorrows would hold true to the peaceful ways of the Old Ones."

Lungo Muso stood up and stared at her, eager for her to understand. She now had memories, of Lungo Muso coming to her when she'd been a dead girl, calling her to the room under the south wall, where the hot spring water bubbled through the fissure, teaching her the language of the *uominilupi*. She nodded.

She at last understood that while she could walk upon this road and read these glyphs, she could in no way touch or influence the events and people of this place and time. She was no more than a shadow here. She had to let the New Ones kill those babies, no matter how much she hated it.

*   *   *

An hour later, still shaken, unable to find much meaning in the episode, she climbed the spiral ramp in the south tower, this time not to Piero's workshop but to Rosario's.

When she reached Rosario's workshop, she paused at the door. She peered inside. Rosario sat at his workbench watching flames dance orange and ruddy in a shallow bowl of oil. He held a small piece of plastic above the flame. The plastic fluttered in the heated updraft.

Open books lay on the table, their pages brown and crumbling, their bindings speckled with mildew.

She took a few quiet steps into the room. Rosario continued to experiment with the piece of plastic, mesmerized by the way the flame forced it upward. Felicitas wanted to touch him. With Maritano it was different; Maritano did most of the touching. But she desperately wanted to rub the back of her hand over Rosario's bearded cheek. The faint light of *Stella Grossa* filtered through a far window and a damp wind hissed around the tower, sending a chilly draft across the floor. She looked at the books. She found something reassuring about the books.

"You'll find the volume to your right particularly interesting," said Rosario, without looking up or turning around. "Go ahead, have a look."

He turned to her.

His welcoming expression immediately turned to one of concern. Was it that obvious? Did her fear expose her so mercilessly? She tried to hide it. She didn't want Rosario to think she was a coward, but she knew she couldn't hide anything from him. Still, she made an effort.

She pressed her lips together, walked boldly to the table, and looked at the book.

He reached up and stroked her hair. His touch seemed to send a wave of warmth though her body.

"Are you all right?" he asked.

She had to get her thoughts in order. She was haunted by all the baby killing.

"I'm fine," she said. But her voice sounded meek. "What are you doing?"

He took his hand away and pointed at the page. "Take a look at that picture."

An engraving of a hot-air balloon, ornately decorated with curlicues and florets, filled the page. A basket hung underneath, and in the basket stood a man in a frilly shirt and a powdered wig, with a telescope pressed to his eye. Below, she saw sheep on a hillside and a church steeple. She shuddered. The scene was so remarkably similar to the place Lungo Muso had taken her to. This was from the old time.

"Don't look so puzzled," he said.

"I'm not puzzled," she said. "It's just that—"

"You look pale." He put his hand over hers. "And your hand is cold." He rubbed her hand, trying to warm it up. "Is it Maritano? Has he—"

"No, I . . ." She shivered. "It was . . . I had another Lungo Muso episode . . . the Old One . . ."

She moved closer, tentative in her approach. He put his arm around her. Her fear didn't seem so bad now. She wanted to look at him full in the face but she felt suddenly shy. She again wondered if she were pretty. She turned back to the book and flipped through it nervously. Words. Hundreds of them. Thousands of them. She tried to read a few but they were all in Italian. She recognized only a dozen or so per page. Rosario smiled, like *Stella Grossa* coming out from behind a dark cloud. He flipped back to the page with the hot-air balloon.

"Look at this," he said.

He held the piece of plastic above the small flame. As the plastic fluttered upward, he released it. The plastic gained altitude; then, sliding out of the updraft, it fell to the table.

"You see a connection, don't you?" he said. "Between the picture and what I'm trying to do?"

She looked at the picture closely, then at Rosario's small flame, and yes, she saw a connection, but she was so preoccupied with Lungo Muso she couldn't show more than a passing interest.

"So you had another episode," he finally said. He still had his arm around her. With his other hand he brushed the hair away from her cheek. "With Lungo Muso."

She looked up at him. "He took me to . . . to the old time," she said. She briefly explained about the mansion, the harbor, the baby killing, then recited, as best she could, the script the Old One had scratched into the dirt. "What do you make of that?" she asked. "Have you ever heard anything so strange?"

He lifted his chin and gazed out the small window. His eyes narrowed. She put her arm around his waist and pulled herself near.

"You're not the only one Lungo Muso visits," he said. "He visits me too." Rosario stroked her hair.

"He does?" she said.

He nodded. "He takes me to a giant steel bubble in the sky, and through an oval window I see some land below me. I'm so high up I can see the clouds below me too. And standing at this window is a man. He's staring down at all this land. On the window ledge there's a book. Lungo Muso always tries to show me this book but he can't keep me there long enough. Before I get a chance to look at the book, the steel bubble fades around me and I find myself back in the prison."

She turned around.

"Look at this," she said, lifting her hair. "Look at this scar." She paused while he examined her scar. "I got this last week. Some men came in the middle of the night and took me to the south tower. They cut the back of my neck open."

She turned around and gazed at him. His eyes showed nothing. He lifted his own hair and turned around. He had a scar as well.

"We've all got one," he said. "I remember nothing about how I got mine. I've tried, but I've never been able to come up with an answer." He stroked her face. "So I don't worry about it. There's lots we don't know about this prison. This tower, for instance. What exactly is it, and why is it so different from the rest of the prison? Then there's the west annex. We've never been able to get in there. It's different in design from the rest of the prison, too. No one knows why it's been so thoroughly blocked off. I don't worry about it. And I wouldn't worry about that scar, either. Some things just are. You have to accept them." He reached up and stroked her cheek. "As for Lungo Muso . . . we just don't know."

The way he was looking at her, she felt that warmth again.

And she understood she was falling in love with this man.

He was tall, elegant, and rugged looking. The red light of *Stella Grossa* colored his face orange. He leaned forward and his lips brushed against her forehead. She lifted her chin. They sent silent signals to each other. He brought his lips farther down and they kissed. Their arms shifted until they were fully embraced. Their kiss was tender, full of meaning, and she felt a passion such as she had never felt for Maritano.

When they pulled away from each other, both were a little breathless. They looked at each other. She didn't care about the scar. She didn't care about the south tower or the west annex. She didn't even care about Lungo Muso. Because right now, staring into his blue eyes, she felt like the happiest woman in the world.

9

Felicitas looked up from her hammering and watched the men dig. Six men dug shallow graves by the north wall while another six dug a tunnel against the east wall: a tunnel as backup, in case the lattice didn't work. Even with the bones of a thousand *carcerieri*, they might not reach the top.

No *carcerieri*, no *sentinelle*, not even any more searchlights to stop them, but they still had to beat the wall.

She went back to hammering, shaping a chunk of metal into another chain link, her hand numb and her arm weak.

The men dug with their hands, with pieces of mortar, even with chamber pots, dug in desperation because they knew if they didn't find a way out soon, all the food would run out, rationing would no longer do any good, and even the *superstiti* would die. Gasparo dug faster than most. He was a mountain of a man and worked tirelessly. The man's strength astonished Felicitas.

Piero stood at the west wall with Rosario, inspecting the west gate.

The dead stared across the yard from the north wall, many of them too weak to get up.

"We found a skeleton!" cried Gasparo from the tunnel. "We found an old skeleton!"

All work in the yard stopped. Felicitas left her chain links and walked to the tunnel to have a look, glad for the excuse to take a rest.

Gasparo, covered in dirt, crawled out of the hole with a skull in his hand, a skull of neither human nor animal origin, twice the size of a human skull, with large eyes, a snout, and fangs. Felicitas instantly recognized the skull as a *uomolupo* skull, an Old One skull.

Piero and Rosario came over. Piero lifted the skull from Gasparo's hands.

Piero said something to Rosario but Felicitas was too far away to hear. Rosario had a close look at the skull, took it in his hands, brushed away some dirt, turned it around, and pointed to a serrated ridge of bone at the back, like vertebrae fused to the main carapace. He said a few words, as if the serrated ridge were of particular significance, then tapped the brow, making a comment on it. Felicitas climbed to the top of a dirt mound and looked into the pit. The rest of the skeleton lay jumbled in the mud.

Just as Gasparo was taking out some more bones, a stone sailed over the dirt and bounced off the east wall. She turned around.

Maritano stood halfway to the tunnel. His pockets were full of stones. He looked at her. Was that hatred she saw in his eyes? He pulled out another stone and pitched it at her. She jumped out of the way as the stone thudded into the dirt at her feet. His skill with a stone was unsurpassed. He made an unearthly whining sound, strangely similar to some of the sounds that had come from Lungo Muso the other day. At this sound, two dozen dead rose from the north wall in an uncanny synchronization of movement and walked toward the *superstiti.*

When they were halfway across, they broke rank and fanned out over the yard, men, women, and children acting in consort. Felicitas looked closely at their eyes. Had they all suddenly come alive? No. They walked—some even ran now—but their eyes were still dead.

As they reached the dirt piles they pulled together in a tight knot, swarmed Rosario, and pummeled him with their fists.

"Rosario!" she cried.

She ran down the dirt pile and joined the melee, pulling at the dead, trying to get them away from Rosario.

A riot ensued, *superstiti* fighting, pushing, shoving; the dead fighting back, flailing with weak arms, biting and scratching. A child ran forward and, with surprising strength, yanked the skull from Rosario's hands, then slunk back through the crowd to the north wall. Maritano issued another whine, and, as if on cue, the dead stopped fighting, quickly extricated themselves from the *superstiti,* and backed away. Some of the *superstiti* pursued them, intent on exacting retribution, but Piero raised his hand.

"Stop!" he cried. "Let them go."

Felicitas ran to Rosario.

"Are you all right?" she asked.

He had a few bruises and scratches but otherwise looked fine.

He brushed the dirt off his hands. "I think so," he said.

He then stared at the retreating dead in mystification.

"They wanted the skull?" he said.

Felicitas stared at the dead. Yes, they wanted the skull.

Sometimes there was no understanding the dead.

At the end of the day, as Felicitas was finishing her work on chain links for the crane, she looked at the north wall, wondering how many corpses there would be—even with *topi* meat many of the dead still starved, or fell to the manifold diseases of malnutrition.

Felicitas picked out among the detritus three corpses. One of them was a slim young woman lying near the north archway, her bony arms splayed, her face turned toward the wall. Recognition set in.

Felicitas felt a curious mixture of panic and grief, her eyes involuntarily moistening as her throat constricted.

She put her hammer down and crossed the yard to the north wall.

When she got there, she looked down at Adriana.

Adriana lay there, her ringleted blond hair tossed gently by the breeze that filtered down from the parapets. Adriana's eyes were partially open and her chest was still. Her skin was gray and her lips were stretched back, swollen, revealing teeth that now looked too big for her emaciated face. She was skeletal in her thinness. Another corpse, another job for Piero's burial crew. Moisture collected in Felicitas's eyes and her tears fell. She wondered how she could have been so neglectful, how she could have so entirely forgotten her old friend. Spying an old blanket, she quickly pulled it over Adriana, with no ceremony, no dignity, just wanting to hide her friend, wanting to hide what now seemed like a crime on the part of the *superstiti*, to selectively starve the prison population.

She hurried across the yard to the dispensary. She knew Rosario and Piero were in there investigating some old equipment. She felt outraged. Her grief was finding vent in anger. She pushed her way into the dispensary, where at one time everyone got a food-brick, but where now only the *superstiti* were fed.

At the far end of the dispensary, Piero and Rosario examined a wall-mounted surveillance camera, one of the last still working. Did they ever get tired of examining the prison's many curiosities? She marched up to them.

"Adriana's dead," she said.

Rosario's eyes softened with compassion, and in the

warmth of his compassion she began to cry, couldn't help herself, didn't want to appear weak in front of these men, but her friend was dead, and there was nothing she could do to bring Adriana back.

Piero looked perplexed, a little uncomfortable.

"The burial crew will get her in the morning," he said.

She stared at Piero. Death was death to this man. But it was different when your best friend died.

"How can you do this?" she said, her voice rising. "How can you make them all starve?"

Piero glanced at Rosario.

Rosario nodded, took out some tools, and began dismounting the surveillance camera.

Piero put his hand on Felicitas's shoulder and led her away. Piero was going to look after this.

"Felicitas," he said, "sometimes we have to make hard choices. I know she was your friend. And we all hoped Adriana would come out of it. For your sake. We fed her as long as we could." He shook his head. "But she seemed particularly susceptible to the dreamphones and sleeping pallets. She didn't have the will to resist them the way you did." He put his arm around her shoulder. "I know it's hard for you, and I wish there were some other way."

"Yes, but you let her starve," she insisted, getting control of her tears. "It could have been prevented."

"Felicitas, it wasn't a question of . . . if the supply ships hadn't stopped coming . . . but they have, and for the last three years . . . well, our food-bricks haven't come, and we've had to ration. And even with the rationing, our food-bricks are running out. That's why we have to get out of here. We have to hope we find a food source on the outside. That's the whole point of our escape. If I decided to feed everyone, we would have run out of food long before this. I've had to be careful. I've had to choose. And the people I've chosen are the ones I can trust, who've broken free of the dreamphones, people who've come out of it." He let his hand fall from her shoulder. "I'm sorry about Adriana. A lot of people are going to die. But at least with my rationing a few of us will have a chance to live."

In her dream, Felicitas was a small girl again, no more than five or six years old. The dream was vivid. The dream sprang from the depths of her own subconscious. It wasn't a Lungo Muso episode. It wasn't a dreamphone dream. It was a real dream, a sleeping dream, a normal dream. This was a dream about her mother.

Felicitas swam in the south bath. The water was warm and smelled of sulfur. She paddled toward the edge, where a young woman, naked except for a towel around her waist, waited for her with a blanket. This woman was her mother. A few *carcerieri* stood by the door at the far end of the bath, dim gray figures in the steam. Felicitas swam toward her mother. Her mother had long red hair and a pleasant freckled face.

Felicitas swam to the edge of the pool and her mother pulled her out. Her hair fell over Felicitas's face. It smelled fresh, like wind on a summer morning. She wrapped Felicitas in the blanket and carried her to the bench.

"I've got something for you," said her mother.

Her mother glanced toward the *carcerieri* at the door, then, miraculously, magically, pulled a small book from the folds of her towel and gave it to Felicitas.

"You read it while I go for another swim," said her mother.

Felicitas nodded. Her mother kissed her, took the towel from around her waist, walked to the edge of the pool, and dove in. Felicitas watched her mother swim away. Her mother was a good swimmer, her cream-colored body sleek and sure in the steamy water, her movements precise.

Felicitas opened the book. The book had pictures of ducklings, kittens, and puppies.

Felicitas, warm and safe in her blanket, looked down at the book, loving the feel of it in her hands, and the look of the little black words at the bottom of each page. Her mother swam farther away. Felicitas turned the page and found a wolf staring up at her with gleaming eyes. She looked up from the wolf, out to the bath, and she saw that her mother was gone.

"*Signora?*" she cried.

But her mother had disappeared beneath the green water. Her mother was never coming back, and Felicitas, running to the edge of the bath, couldn't understand why her mother would want to swim away from her, or why she would want to leave her standing here at the edge of the pool all by herself.

10

Felicitas stood in the middle of the yard, agitated, unable to shake last night's dream. Her mother. *Stella Grossa,* just over the wall now, looked as if it were being pestered by a small red bug—*Stella Piccola.* The dream half convinced her that her mother might still be here, somewhere in the prison.

She stared at the inmates along the north wall, looking for a woman with red hair. None of them looked like the woman in her dream.

She walked over to the north wall and had a closer look. It was a scene of devastation. Many of the dead now lay on their sides, curled in fetal positions, their eyes staring, each of them doomed, all because they slept the sleep of the dreamphones. Adriana was already buried, one of several hundred mounds out in the yard. Maritano grinned, his broken nose giving an unsavory cast to his face, lifted a dead *topo,* and gave her a nod. She couldn't look at him anymore. How long before he, too, died of starvation?

No, her mother wasn't there. She had to be realistic. Even among the *superstiti* there was no one who looked like her mother, no one with the same green eyes or freckles or cream-colored skin. Her mother was probably dead. Yet the certainty remained: Her mother had at one time seen these same four prison walls, these guard towers, this same sky with its two suns. Felicitas would better endure the future if she could learn what had happened to her mother.

She turned around and walked back to the east wall, kicking a clump of dirt out of the way, unable to focus on anything but her dream. Piero stood by the east wall with Rosario. As usual the two were deep in discussion. There had to be a record, she thought. A record of her mother somewhere. Her eyes settled on the south tower. If there were any records of her mother, they would be in the south tower.

Glancing at Piero, now glad he was occupied, she walked across the yard and went around the far side of the dispensary.

When she got to the end of the dispensary, she looked up at the sky where a dozen birds flew by and disappeared into the mist, panicked, squawking, spooked by something. She stopped, felt vibrations in her legs, sensed the footfall of something unimaginably huge walking around outside, smelled wet fur and the odor of decaying flesh, heard a huge splash, then silence.

She waited another moment, then hurried to the south tower.

She climbed the ramp, again fascinated by the glyphs on the wall, for the first time connecting the isolated glyphs together to form larger chains of meaning.

She soon came to Piero's workshop.

She looked at his workbench. He had books on his bench. Also blank paper. There was a vial of ink made from ash and *carceriere* oil, and a pen fashioned from a shiv. Copied from an open book next to the vial onto a sheet of paper were the following words:

Hickory dickory dock,
The mouse ran up the clock,
The clock struck one,
The mouse ran down,
Hickory dickory dock.

She gazed at the words. She could read them easily—they were English words—but she had only a vague idea of what they meant. She picked up the book, worn and dirty, a hundred years old, and looked at the front cover. A creature, much like a *topo*, only not as ugly or vicious, stared at her with bright blue eyes. *The clock struck one.* She opened the book to the first page, where she found a picture of a clock. The clock had only twelve hours, not the standard thirty-three of the clock tower. What a strange book. A child's book. Maybe she had seen this book before. Maybe this was one of the books her mother had given to her.

She heard someone's footstep at the door. She turned around and saw Piero standing there, a dark figure in the dim light, his eyes severe, his mouth an uncompromising line. He looked neither pleased nor displeased to find her here.

"I had a dream," she said. She looked back at the book. "About my mother."

Piero walked into the room and leaned against the table, folding his arms against his chest. Felicitas kept looking at the book, fighting the sudden tears that clouded her eyes, wondering how a dream could make her feel so sad, how it could break her up like this. She shook the hair from her face and straightened her shoulders. She had to show Piero she was strong.

"You've been writing," she said. "Your hand gets better near the end."

Piero didn't answer. He sat down beside her.

"Felicitas . . ." he began. "Felicitas, I understand how you feel. The amnesia lifts. You begin to dream again. And you see things. You recognize things in your dreams, people you knew. Your life comes back to you bit by bit. And you realize people are missing. You want those people back, but you don't know where to find them, and it breaks your heart. I know how you feel. My heart breaks every day."

He reached up and stroked her hair in a fatherly fashion.

"I want to know what happened to her," said Felicitas. "Can we find out what happened to her using this?" She pointed to the viewscreen.

"We have only a small understanding of how that works," said Piero. "And even that took months and months. If it weren't for Rosario, we wouldn't know anything. We have so little time before the food-bricks run out and we have to direct all our energy toward escape and survival."

"Yes, but can't you find some record?" asked Felicitas. "She must have had one of these codes on her arm. Everybody has one, don't they?"

He shook his head. "I'm sorry about your mother," he said. "I wish I could remember her."

"Don't you remember a red-haired woman when you first came out of the dreamphone haze?" asked Felicitas. "That was five years ago. Maybe if you think hard enough, you can—"

"Felicitas, it was difficult for us. We had so much to learn. And we had no one but ourselves to learn from. We watched ourselves and we watched the dead." He gazed at her appraisingly. "In particular, we watched you." He folded his arms across his chest. "That's why I'm glad you came up here. I've been wanting to talk to you about something. About the way we watched you."

He lifted a power disk from the junk on the table and got it spinning.

"Not only did we watch you," he said, "but we recorded what we saw."

He attached the necessary wires to the baseplate of the disk and the viewscreen lit up.

"It's already loaded and ready to go," he said. "I was planning to show you this today."

He typed some symbols into the keyboard and a ghostly image of the prison yard appeared on the viewscreen.

"That's you, over there," said Piero. "When you were still dead. Watch what you do."

"How did you get this?"

"The surveillance cameras operate on their own freestanding power. We figured out how they worked, how we could transmit pictures to this screen here. Given enough time, Rosario figures everything out. I don't know what I would have done without him."

Felicitas watched herself walk forward from the north wall. She looked younger by maybe a year or two. Her eyes were dull and unwavering. She trudged across the yard through a fresh layer of snow.

"What do I have in my hand?" she asked.

"You don't remember this at all, do you?"

"No."

"You've got a metal pipe. I don't know where you found it. Maybe from the junkyard out back. You carried it with you wherever you went. Then about three months ago you dropped it by the north latrines and forgot about it."

The Felicitas on the screen knelt on the ground and made markings in the snow with the pipe, gouging through the snow to the dirt, making *uominilupi* glyphs.

Piero pressed a few buttons on the console and the image changed.

She was up in the south tower now, out on the ramp with Rosario and Piero. She looked older here. She watched herself trace the glyphs on the wall out there, following them with her finger. She had no recollection of this either. Piero flicked a switch and sound now came from the viewscreen.

"Listen to yourself," said Piero. "You're reading that script."

Felicitas leaned forward and listened closely.

"In the before time, in the desperation time, when our vanquishers made this . . ." The Felicitas on the screen hesitated, looking for an English equivalent. ". . . this dark-ugly time, you did not turn away or grin the grin of defeat, but ran the path, and swam the river, the river that never forgets. You didn't bare your neck for the wound, even though the end time, the final time . . ." The Felicitas on the screen struggled: the glyph in question, a fire with three lines over it, each line thick with thorns, seemed incomprehensible to her. The Felicitas on the screen made a rough guess. ". . . even though the end-final time rose like the deadfall in the forest around you. You saw me with your . . . your night eyes, saw my daunted soul, and how it burned brightly like a star through the long winter, and you kissed me, touched me, and . . . and gave me back my . . . my . . ." The Felicitas on the screen shook her head and skipped a few words. "So that I could one day rise like the cliffbird, and call to my lonely brothers and sisters, and . . . and . . ." The Felicitas on the screen shook her head again, unable to decipher the next complicated series of glyphs.

The screen flickered, then went dark. The disk stopped spinning. She turned to Piero, the blood seeming to thicken in her veins as she recalled how Lungo Muso had scratched these same glyphs into the wall underneath the south bath, glyphs about the night eyes, as if he were trying to teach her myth, or reveal to her the mystery of how all the prisoners got here and why they had been incarcerated.

"That episode I had with Lungo Muso," she said. "The first one under the south bath. That part about the night eyes. Those are the exact same glyphs, scratched into the stone in that room under the south wall."

Piero gazed at her intently. He arched his back, as if his muscles were sore.

"You understand the glyphs?" he said.

She shook her head.

"That's just it," she said. "I can't read them now. At least not

many of them. Not unless I'm in this . . . this dream state with
Lungo Muso . . ."

Piero shrugged, not concerned. "It takes time," he said.
"You have to get over the dreamphone amnesia."

She gestured at the screen.

"Are you sure my translation is accurate?" she asked.

Piero didn't answer, at least not immediately. He got up,
walked to one of his many shelves, pulled a white plastic board
with red letters from the pile, and gave it to her. At first glance,
she didn't know what it was, but upon closer inspection she
saw that *uominilupi* glyphs occupied one side of the board and
Italian words the other.

"This is a rule board," said Piero. "We believe that before the
carcerieri looked after us, the *uominilupi* actually ran this prison,
and that this board helped them communicate with the original
prisoners. Those prisoners, for whatever reason, were Italian.
Rosario and I have made a study of Italian, and we've learned
enough to translate these *uominilupi* characters. This board is
our key, and we've been able to verify your reading of the script
on the wall outside. It's accurate, Felicitas. Their language is
complex. It seems impossible that any of us should ever learn
or understand it, much less translate it into Italian or English.
The small bit Rosario and I deciphered took months and
months of painstaking work. Rosario worked with this rule
board a full year before he finally started to understand it. How
can a young girl like you learn an alien tongue like this? Now
that you're alive, you forget. We suspected you would. We all
forget. But we want you to remember, Felicitas. That's why we
need you. You've got to make us understand these glyphs.
These episodes you have with Lungo Muso, we thought his
visits might stop once you came out of your dreamphone haze,
but obviously they haven't."

She felt uneasy. The Lungo Muso episodes represented a
loss of control to her. She had no choice about them. Particularly
troubling was a new sense that Lungo Muso had chosen her for

something, that there was a great deal at stake, and that some-how he wanted her to do something about it.

"But what *are* these episodes?" she said. She got up, agi-tated, unable to sit still. "I can't call them dreams. I feel dis-placed. I feel as if I've been plucked from the normal course of things and placed somewhere else."

Piero took a few steps toward the window and gazed down at the roof of the dispensary. "We're not sure," he finally said. "But we know Lungo Muso is real. He's not a ghost. He some-how superimposes . . . at least that's the way Rosario describes it. And of course you and Rosario aren't the only ones. There's another man, Silvio, an old man, in fact the oldest inmate in the prison. I don't know whether you know him. He spends most of his time in the south bath because he says the warm water helps his bones."

"I know him," said Felicitas.

"He's been alive for three years. You should speak to him. His episodes aren't as vivid as yours. In fact, he seems to be brought to the same place again and again. But I think between the three of you, you might piece together some answers."

She stood in the south tower's central chamber late at night with a lamp of *topo* grease, transcribing every single *uominilupi* glyph onto paper with Piero's ink of ash and *carceriere* oil. Soon they would be leaving. She would never get a chance to look at this wall again.

She was up here by herself, late at night, and nobody knew she was here, carefully drawing the symbols of an alien lan-guage, her hand now aching, her eyes red and sore. She wanted to take as many of these symbols with her as she could.

She heard the creaking of metal. She peered into the gloom.

A creature neither man nor beast approached. And she knew it couldn't be Lungo Muso because there was no tingling in her arms. This had to be something else. She blinked, rubbed her eyes, thought she must be seeing things . . . had been up eight hours of the long seventeen-hour night . . . was feeling light-headed . . . but what she saw, it just couldn't be, not now, not here, not when they were so close to escape, not a *uomolupo* come to spoil their plans at the last minute. The long snout and fangs glimmered pasty white in the torchlight, and the eye sockets were hollow and black. It carried a weapon in its belt, a shiv or length of pipe. The figure emerged from the shadows, and it wasn't a *uomolupo* at all. It was Maritano, with the skull dug up from the yard tied to his head with a plastic strap.

He stopped when he was a few paces away and stared at her, not exactly into her eyes, just to the left of them, not a dead man's stare, but a cagey stare.

"You can't go," he said. His words were precise. "Piero doesn't understand. None of you can go."

She didn't know what to say. He looked awful. He had a rash all over his face, and with that skull tied to his head, he was a thing from a nightmare. He had six dead *topi* tied to his belt and smelled of rotting flesh.

"You're all going to die if you leave this prison," he continued. His voice now had a whine to it, and she realized she was terrified of this man. "Winter's coming," he said. "You'll starve. And then you'll freeze."

She backed away. She feared his assessment. "We're going to freeze and starve in here anyway, Maritano," she countered. "What choice do we have?" She glanced at the skull. "Why are you wearing that thing on your head?"

He pulled something from his belt—a makeshift leash.

"Come," he said. "I'll put this around your neck. I'll lead you back to the north wall. I don't like your new friends. Your new friends are bad."

She looked at the leash. She recalled the episode at the old-time mansion, how the New Ones leashed the humans and led them up the ramp into the big square ship.

"I'm not coming with you," she said. "Go away, Maritano. I have work to do."

He pulled the pipe from his belt. "I don't want to hurt you, Felicitas, but I will if I have to. You're wrong to leave."

He took a few steps toward her and tried to put the leash around her neck.

She leapt back, easily avoiding him. He didn't give up, kept coming for her. She scooped a rusted length of chain from the floor.

"Don't make me do this, Maritano," she said.

"Why don't you like me anymore, Felicitas?"

How could she reply? Because you terrify me? Because you're not human? Because your eyes are off-kilter and you smell like the guts of a dead animal?

Another figure emerged from the gloom. Rosario. Holding a *pistola*. She had never been so glad to see anyone in her life.

"Maritano," he said, "leave her alone."

Maritano grew still and his arms sank as if through foam to his sides. He turned around, his feet moving by increments, his legs heavy and shuffling, and faced Rosario. Rosario's eyes narrowed as he gazed at the skull on Maritano's head. He kept his *pistola* trained on Maritano's chest. The two men looked at each other for nearly a minute—perhaps this was how long it took Maritano to puzzle through the implications of this new situation—then the younger man, whining unintelligibly a few times, skulked obediently away and descended the ramp.

Felicitas hurried into Rosario's arms.

"No," said Rosario, "I don't think he's changed, at least not in the fundamentals." The two of them were still up in the tower. Her work was going faster. Rosario had brought an extra lamp and she could see the glyphs more clearly. "I think he's just a little anxious because he knows things are different now."

She looked up from her work. "Yes, but he seems . . ." She frowned. "I didn't like the leash. These New Ones in my Lungo Muso episode, they all had leashes, and I don't think—"

"Sometimes the *carcerieri* led prisoners around by leashes," he said. His brows arched. "I don't know whether you remember that."

Her eyes narrowed as she turned back to the glyphs.

"Maritano's eyes," she said. "The way he looked at me, like he was looking right through me, but gazing a little to the left . . . it was . . . and he had that pipe. He was actually going to hurt me." She turned back to Rosario. "And that skull on his head. He said I had to stay in the prison."

"He doesn't want you to go," said Rosario. "He still loves you." He turned to her. "As for the skull . . . who knows?" He reached over and stroked her hair. "Obviously it means something to him."

She met Silvio, the prison's oldest inmate, in the south bath the next day. He was sitting on one of the submerged benches close to the hot spring, his few remaining strands of wispy white hair plastered to his head by the steamy heat. His back was badly hunched.

She was naked. For the first time, she felt self-conscious about her nakedness. She looked down at her breasts. This was ridiculous. She'd never been concerned about her nakedness before. She pushed her modesty aside. Silvio lifted his grizzled chin and looked at her.

"*Buon giorno*, Felicitas," he said. "Piero said you might want to speak to me."

"*Buon giorno*, Silvio," she said. "And how are your bones today?"

He nodded. "Today, they feel not so bad. Today, I feel I could walk to the north wall and back, and not be much worse for wear." He looked at her inquisitively. "You've come to talk of Lungo Muso?"

She nodded. "If you don't mind."

He shifted on the underwater bench. "Sit," he said.

She sat down.

"I've been having these episodes . . ." she began.

And she described in some detail the episodes she had had with Lungo Muso.

"Do you have any idea what they mean?" she asked.

Silvio considered. He moved his jaw from side to side, looked as if he were chewing on something.

"No," he said at last.

"What are your episodes like?" she asked.

He shifted a bit on the bench, as if his rump were sore, then settled back down.

"Well . . . Lungo Muso takes me to this room. And everywhere around me I see these big glass tanks filled with pink liquid. There's tubes and wires hooked up to these glass tanks. I see figures floating inside these tanks, New Ones, only they're half formed." He peered at her. "Do you know what I mean when I say half formed, Felicitas?" She shook her head. "Well . . . Concetta had a baby once, only she miscarried a few months before full term. The baby had arms and legs, a head and mouth and eyes, but it vaguely resembled some kind of fish, didn't really look human. That's what these New Ones looked like. Half made. And every time I ask Lungo Muso, what are these New Ones, and why do you have to make them in tanks instead of having them born natural, he just snarls and whines and I can't understand him. Then he shows me a picture. It's a picture of a big white building. I've never seen anything like it in my life. Like a big cake. And carved into this building are millions of glyphs. The building has no doors, no windows, no way in or out. It makes no sense to me. But for some reason, this big white building gives me the darnedest fright."

Three dozen dead, under the direction of Maritano, threw stones at the lattice, which rested horizontally across the yard on three dozen workbenches. Felicitas stood in the dispensary doorway watching. The *superstiti* now slept in the dispensary, having moved in mattresses, blankets, and furniture from the cellblocks. It was safer in here, especially with the dead behaving the way they were. Maritano still wore the skull tied to his head.

The stones clanked dully against the metal but otherwise did no harm. Twenty *superstiti* stood guard around the lattice, protecting themselves with the breast plates of broken *carcerieri*. Piero fired a warning blast from his *pistola* over the heads of the dead, and the dead scattered. A few of the braver ones, Maritano included, continued with the barrage. She glanced up at the twin suns; they glowed dimly through the damp atmosphere.

Why didn't the dead just leave them alone? Why did they feel they had to attack the *superstiti* like this?

11

Felicitas sat in the dispensary with her back to one of the east windows. The heat of the two suns felt good on her shoulders. She had a hot cup of food-brick soup on the bench beside her. She was looking at the glyphs she'd copied from the south tower, trying to understand them, struggling to make sense of the swirls, dots, dashes, birds, eyeballs, and arrows.

At first only single words were understandable. *Cliffbird*—rendered with an eye, a beak, and three arrows pointing upward. It took her nearly an hour to understand this. But the amnesia finally lifted and she remembered it. *Hunter* was easier, a series of half circles clustered around what looked like a button. This took fifteen minutes. Then a phrase jumped out: *You saw me with your night eyes.* She thought she was making progress. She tried to decipher a few more phrases but the symbols again seemed strange and blank to her eyes.

In fact the harder she tried, the more recalcitrant the glyphs became. Yet she knew she was getting somewhere. She knew it was just a matter of time. Piero was right. Language was important to her. She rolled up the glyphs and put them in her bag.

She knew that tomorrow she might be able to understand a complete sentence or two.

Piero led her up a stone staircase inside the south wall. The steps were rough, covered with dust.

"That downstairs door was bricked off years ago," he said. "You can see the outline, and how the stones are newer. We knew there had to be a way up to the catwalk. Of course we couldn't do anything about that downstairs door until the *sentinelle* stopped working. We couldn't take the risk."

Piero's lamp flickered on the stone walls. Felicitas stared at the back of Piero's neck, trying to find his scar, but his hair was too thick, and it was too dark to see.

"What are you going to do about the skull?" she asked.

He stopped.

"Nothing," he said.

"Don't you find it odd, though?" she asked. "What does the skull mean to them?"

Piero thought for a moment.

"The skull is like a flag or banner to the dead," he finally said, "something they can rally around. As far as I'm concerned, they can keep it. Who needs an old *uomolupo* skull?"

They continued to climb. The air smelled dank and the walls shimmered with moisture.

Piero held up his lamp. "Here we are," he said. "Look at this."

She saw a mural scratched into the wall.

It showed a group of people standing outside the prison wall wearing clothes of hand-stitched fur. They held spears, fishing nets, and crossbows. High above the mural, some of the stone had been remortared. Off to the side she saw some short stubby trees, unlike any of the trees she had ever seen illustrated in any of the books in the prison.

"We found this a week ago," said Piero, "when we broke open the downstairs door." A grin came to Piero's face. "We don't think we'll be alone once we get outside, Felicitas. We think there'll be people out there. You look at this mural, and you look at that stone up there, and you can't help thinking that at one time there may have been an escape, that they got out through where that stone is broken up there. These people, dressed in their furs, with their spears and crossbows, may have been seen by the artist from the parapets at a time when it was still possible to get up here, before all the stairwells were bricked off."

The mural had a high degree of realism, a scene observed.

"We see the primitive way they live," continued Piero, "and we think they must move about in tiny bands, that they live a life of wilderness survival." He shrugged. "One thing's for certain. If we find them, the chances for our own survival rise immeasurably."

Later that day, a hot-air balloon stitched together from old tarps stood near the east wall tethered to the ground by a few ropes. A small cylindrical torch—Rosario's ingenious design—hung by small wires under the balloon and pumped heated air into the dirigible's opening. Felicitas remembered Rosario's book up in the south tower, the one with the picture of the hot-air balloon. The surveillance camera Rosario had taken from the dispensary dangled below the torch and balloon. A viewscreen sat on a bench.

Piero spun a power disk and the screen flickered to life.

Felicitas was curious. She wanted to see what was out there. Right now, the screen showed a few rocks and pebbles, the ground directly beneath the balloon.

"Are we ready?" asked Rosario.

Piero nodded. "Cut the ropes."

Rosario cut the ropes, and the balloon drifted skyward.

A hush fell over the yard. All the hammering stopped.

She watched the balloon's slow ascent, worried that it might not make it over the wall. The balloon continued to climb, was caught in an updraft and spiraled toward the parapets, bounced against the wall, shuddered, dipped, then continued its climb, the flame fragile yet steady, well guarded from the wind by a perforated metal cupola.

The scene on the viewscreen changed. She saw the roof of the dispensary, the group of *superstiti* standing around the viewscreen, the lattice, the dead against the north wall, the roof of the south bath, then the south tower, and finally the parapets.

A stiff breeze caught the balloon and blew it eastward. It disappeared from view over the wall.

She watched the viewscreen carefully.

The balloon swept out over sparse grass, a few bushes, and finally trees. Trees, not like the trees from the books, different trees, strange trees, short, stubby, with long slender leaves. Trees not of Earth. Trees of somewhere else.

Half of them looked dead, as if the soil weren't rich enough to feed them properly. Many had fallen over.

Rosario said, "It's veering south."

How did he know that? With nothing but trees down there, all of them the same, how could he tell which direction the balloon was heading? But then, the trees ended and water began. The lake. Rosario was right. Veering south.

Nothing but water for a long time. Then trees again. The balloon rose and fell, sometimes sweeping so close to the treetops Felicitas was afraid it would hit. She looked for birds but saw none. She looked for animals but saw none, just endless trees, and the occasional outcropping of dull gray rock, such as the prison walls were made from. No birds and animals, Earth creatures she remembered from the books. And why should there be? This wasn't Earth. This was some place different. She saw patches of snow.

They all stared at the screen, waiting, hoping they would see something out there that would tell them they would survive.

The camera passed over a dark patch in the middle of a clearing, a brief impression of fur, blood, and bone.

"What was that?" asked Piero.

"It looked like a carcass," said Rosario.

A broad smile came to Piero's face. Felicitas had never seen the man so happy.

"Good," he said. "That's good."

Maybe there were animals out there after all.

They watched for the better part of the morning.

They saw no roads, habitations, or farms, no markings of civilization or primitive society of any kind. It was an empty land, a huge land, and she found its vastness, after a lifetime in prison, intimidating. Trees, rock, and snow. Could they make a life out there?

Then the balloon passed over a river. And sitting on the riverbank they saw three small boats, unmistakably man-made, each one next to the other in a neat row, slender, leaf-shaped. Felicitas couldn't help thinking of the mural up in the south wall. People in hand-stitched fur, holding spears. There were humans outside, there had to be, and Piero was right: Humans improved their chances of survival immeasurably.

The balloon hovered over the boats for a moment or two, as if there were a lull in the wind, and a murmuring broke out among the *superstiti*. Three boats, not much, but enough to tell them that they weren't entirely alone.

Rosario took her to the generating room the next day.

The generating room was below the old south tower. The weather had turned cooler, and as they entered the tower through the big gash near the back, thunder boomed to the west and rain fell in a sudden torrent.

"It's just over here," said Rosario, taking her hand.

He led her to a doorway in the far corner. The sound of rain drummed off the metal walls of the south tower and leaked through the many perforations. A *topo* scampered out of the way as they went through the door.

They descended some stairs, Rosario holding a lamp high above his head. From below, there rose the smell of machine oil and dust.

"Careful of that step there," he said. "It's broken."

She liked this about Rosario. He was considerate, sensitive to the needs of others, willing to give. With Maritano, it was different. Maritano never gave anything because there wasn't anything to give. She felt protected with Rosario.

She negotiated the broken step, putting her hand against his shoulder for support.

Soon they reached a large room at the bottom.

Rosario lit an extra lamp.

As her eyes got used to the dimness she saw a big cavern blasted out of the rock adjoining the room. Within this cavern stood three giant disks, gargantuan versions of the power disks Piero had upstairs. The disks caught the torchlight, reflected it in shades of pink, violet, and blue. The disks were as motionless as the *sentinelle.* They were broken, covered with years of dirt.

"This is where we get our power from?" she asked.

Rosario nodded. "Just for the heat and light. The *carcerieri,* the dispensing machine, and the dreamphones and sleeping pallets have their own power. At least they did. Two of these disks broke three years ago. That last one . . . well, you know when it broke. The day the searchlights and *sentinelle* stopped working."

"Where's this other mural?" she asked.

"Right there," he said, pointing.

Beyond some chairs and benches, and above a console stretching the length of the wall, she saw a large mural, one of *uominilupi* design, full of glyphs, not primitive like the scratched-in mural of the river people Piero had shown her yesterday, but modern. In the dim lamplight, the glyphs danced out at her. More of her dreamphone amnesia lifted. Dots, swirls, strokes, arrows, curves, and dashes. Eyes, fingers, birds, fish, lakes, trees, all in tight configurations. She understood it now. And more than just a sentence or two, such as she had anticipated. She felt dizzy at the sight of them.

"I understand them," she said, dazed at the discovery. "At least most of them."

She backed away, stumbling, and sat on a thinly upholstered bench in the middle of the room, overwhelmed.

"You do?" he said.

She nodded, then studied the glyphs. A series of five curves pointing to the right, that meant go forward. The same five curves angled to the left meant go backward. She saw none of the heavy ornate and formalized glyphs from upstairs. The language on this mural wasn't poetry. It was technical.

She glanced at Rosario. He watched her in anticipation.

Finally, she took a deep breath, trying to come to grips with what had just happened.

"This is a schematic," she said. "Like the one Piero showed me for the *carcerieri*."

His eyes widened. "A schematic?"

She stared at the glyphs. "For the whole prison," she said.

"Anything we can use?" he asked.

She heard dripping water from upstairs; the rain was leaking through harder now.

"It describes a series of anti-escape systems working within the prison," she said. She pointed to five pinwheels off to the left. "Those represent the *carcerieri*," she said. "That's the primary anti-escape system." She pointed to what was obviously a representation of an insect, a glyph that looked like a beetle. "That's another system, I'm not sure what. The tangle of figure eights beside it . . . I don't know . . . that means . . . intelligence . . . or maybe brain . . . something to do with the mind." She looked at Rosario. His eyes were impassive. "Does that mean anything to you?"

"No," he said. He continued to stare at the beetlelike glyph. "Not a thing."

She looked at another glyph, three hourglasses in a row, each backgrounded by a sunburst.

"These are the *sentinelle*," she said. "And these glyphs over here represent the dreamphones and the sleeping pallets." She nodded, growing more convinced of her interpretation. "They're all anti-escape systems. If one fails, another will take its place. They're all designed to keep us inside this prison. But I guess since they've all broken down . . . and since they're all . . ." She looked at Rosario. He was still staring at the beetle. "We're not going to get any more surprises, are we?"

He didn't answer. Instead, he pointed to another symbol, a series of strokes, followed by two triangles, and two *fucili*—rifles—crisscrossed. "What about this one?" he asked.

"The dashes and triangles, that's a skyboat, like our supply ship. The crossed rifles, that's a soldier. The three squiggles indicate a connection to . . . to the prison." Her brow knitted. She wasn't completely sure of the squiggles. "Actually, I'm not sure about that . . . I'm not getting all of it."

Rosario pondered this. He rubbed his bearded chin.

Finally, he sat up straight.

"Well," he said, with false cheer. "Soldiers." He tried it in Italian. "*Soldati.*" It seemed to work better in Italian. "And beetles. We'll be long gone before we ever see a *soldato* or a beetle."

He held the lamp up higher, and as the light shifted, Felicitas saw a picture of the big white building. She exhaled. Rosario sensed the change.

"Felicitas?" he said. He put his hand on her knee. "Felicitas, are you all right?"

She moved closer. He put his arm around her shoulder, and kissed her hair.

"That glyph up there," she said, pointing. "That building."

Rosario nodded.

"Silvio's told me about it," he said.

She turned away from the glyph. She didn't want to look at it. As with Silvio, that building gave her the darnedest fright.

He pulled her closer. His touch melted her fear.

He pulled something from his pocket.

"I want to give this to you," he said. "It's a finger bowl. The *uominilupi* made it. I want you to have it."

She took it. "It's beautiful," she said.

It was roughly half the size of a soup bowl, made of a translucent green gemstone.

"Whenever I look at it," said Rosario, "I think of your eyes."

A simple statement about her eye color, yes, but so much more.

She glanced up. "My eyes are that color?" she said.

She lifted her chin. They kissed. This was a different kind of kiss. This kiss had electricity. This kiss had passion.

He put his hand on her thigh, and their kiss deepened as their lips parted. They both knew what had to happen.

He was careful and confident. There was none of the licentious intent she sometimes felt with Maritano. Maritano never got far. This was different. This was adult. She felt toward Rosario what a wife feels toward a husband. The love they shared was certain.

Their uniforms came off. The initial pain quickly subsided, soothed by his careful gentleness. She clasped his shoulder, pressed her cheek against his chest, feeling safe with him, the both of them inside the dark generating room, the rain coming down outside. She thought he might speak, that he might utter some tender words, but, looking into his blue eyes, she saw a far greater eloquence than any words might express. As he rubbed his palm against her thigh, she angled herself and stretched her other leg.

Their movements dovetailed, skin meeting skin, rhythm meeting rhythm, and she knew that this wasn't a time for words, that the deep and penetrating pleasure she experienced went far beyond words. He leaned over her and kissed her ear. It wasn't only the pleasure, either. It was the feeling of . . . of rightness—yes—a sense that this was meant to be, that the fit was there, that it had been predestined. He was a good and kind man. He possessed a depth of character and sensitivity that thrilled her. And of course he was superbly intelligent. She felt fortunate. She felt as if this man were indeed her husband.

Their motions quickened, and she felt as if she were floating. Just when she thought she would die from pleasure, there came a great release, and she shuddered. Rosario shuddered as well. The joy, for both, was exquisite. There was nothing awkward about it, nothing to hide from afterward, just the sense that they were, as husband and wife, somehow bathed in a miraculous but invisible light. She knew that when they finally left the generating room they would brighten the dark prison yard with their glow.

The lattice stood against the wall, wide enough for five to climb, finished at last, hauled into position by the crane, with supports underneath to stop it from bending toward the wall when people climbed it. Once supplies were carried to the top, the crane would be taken apart and reassembled on the catwalk. The crane would then lift the lattice up and over the wall and down the other side.

Superstiti scaled up and down, bringing supplies to the parapet. Felicitas loaded a length of chain into her pack, hoisted the pack to her back, and began the climb.

Up and down three times already, 162 rungs to the top, with metal so cold she could hardly hold it. She forced herself to climb, even though her legs shook with fatigue and her stomach growled with hunger.

When she reached the top, Gasparo gave her a hand over the parapet. He had turned the endless climbing into a game.

"I thought we'd seen the last of you," he said.

"No," she said. She admired Gasparo's tireless enthusiasm. "I'll climb until sundown if I have to."

"Take a rest," he said. "There's some fresh water over there." He gestured toward a cistern. "You're not trying to race me, are you, Felicitas?"

She had grown fond of Gasparo, thought of him as her friend.

"No," she said. "I would never try to race you. You're unbeatable, Gasparo."

The giant smiled.

"At least you have the good sense to admit it," he said.

She walked over to the cistern and ladled some water into a cup. Rosario and Piero checked over supplies near the southeast guard tower. Gasparo, thirsty as well, came over and had a drink. She glanced at one of the *sentinelle*. Four times her height and three times her girth, but old, and badly weathered. She gazed at the glyphs on its metal plating. Even its *cannone* had glyphs.

"Has anyone ever figured out how to work one of those *cannoni*?" she asked Gasparo.

Gasparo arched his dark brow. "No," he said. "Rosario's been all over them." He took another drink; he could swallow it by the gallon. "There doesn't seem to be a trigger of any kind."

She stared at the *cannone* a moment more, then looked out at the land. Her eyes couldn't get used to the vast distance. Trees and a lake, such as had been relayed by the surveillance camera, but also mountains far to the east, their peaks jagged and covered with snow. To the south, a vast tree-covered promontory reached out into the lake. To the north and west, more trees. The mountains, through the mist, looked like a mirage, distant and unattainable.

"It's breathtaking," she said.

Gasparo nodded. "It's what we've worked for."

She heard shouting coming from down below. Men pulled on ropes—they were hauling up a heavy load. Gasparo walked over to have a look. Felicitas followed.

The men hoisted a tarp-covered skid; the tarp had a gold glyph stitched into the fabric. She recognized the glyph, the *uominilupi* symbol for prison.

"What's under there?" she asked Gasparo.

"Food-bricks," he said. "All we have left."

"That's it?" she said. She couldn't conceal her alarm. "That's all we have?"

"Three hundred fourteen of them," replied Gasparo. "Enough for a week. You can see why we've picked up the pace in these last few days."

II

ESCAPE

12

At dawn, having slept lightly the whole night, Felicitas got up and walked to the dispensary door where Silvio stood guard. Rosario had spent the night in the south tower devising a map from the surveillance camera footage, and was still there now. Silvio looked up at her from his wrinkled old face.

"You're up early, Felicitas," he said.

"I'm cold," she said. "I need to walk around."

She looked out at the yard. The mist was thick, rose out of the ground in ragged tendrils, slithered down the east wall like a heavy gray tapestry, making the air smell wet. She couldn't see to the north wall. Silvio glanced out at the mist.

"Have you ever seen it like this?" asked Silvio.

Felicitas peered into the yard where she saw the indistinct silhouettes of the nearest burial mounds.

"I won't go far," she said.

"If any of those dead give you trouble," said Silvio, "call

me." He patted his *pistola* with his arthritic hand. "I'll give them something to think about."

She left the dispensary, her footsteps light, her eyes wide, and advanced into the yard. She heard the noise of dripping water from the dispensary eaves and the lapping of waves coming from the lake outside. In this mist, all sounds were muffled, and even her own footsteps came to her as from a great distance.

She glanced at the east wall. The lattice rose out of the gloom, a gridwork of metal oblongs braced against thick wall supports and scaffolding, disappearing up through the mist like a ladder through the clouds.

She stopped as she came to the first of the burial mounds, saw only those mounds immediately before her, nothing beyond, the fog obscuring the rest. She listened again. And she grew perplexed. She should have heard the morning sounds of the dead along the north wall. They were always up before first light. But it was quiet, too quiet. She should at least have seen one or two heading toward the south bath for water. But she saw nothing, heard nothing.

She picked her way through the burial mounds, taking care to step around them. She strained to see through the mist. Up ahead, the north wall emerged as if shrouded in a dozen draperies of cobweb, the mortar lines blurred and indistinct, the cracks and chips in the stone barely visible.

She stopped when she was a few strides away. She looked for sleeping bodies but saw none. There weren't even any corpses. The dead had disappeared.

She looked to the left, peering through the mist, her curiosity overcoming her fear, then to the right. There was no one in sight, no movement, no indication that the dead had even spent the night here.

She walked slowly along the north wall, heading toward the east wall, surveying all the junk the dead had left behind: blankets, mattresses, chamber pots, *topo* carcasses. She turned around and walked the other way. She walked all the way to the west wall, where she discovered more blankets, chamber pots, and the remnants of a fire. Adrenaline eased into her bloodstream and she felt her shoulders rise. How could they disappear like this?

She approached the main door of the north cellblock, drawn by the mystery of their disappearance, and entered through the archway. She glanced at the long unused north bath, where she saw a layer of thick scum in the bottom, then looked down the northeast corridor. She ventured into the northeast corridor, her ears alert to the smallest sound, her eyes growing quickly accustomed to the dark, her apprehension melting away in her determination to find out what had happened. She knew she should go back, that she was taking a chance coming in here by herself, but she had a tough little kernel of courage that forced her forward.

All the cells were empty. Some of the mattresses had been taken away, and the cell doors were open. She half expected Maritano to jump out of the shadows, skull tied to his head, ready to force a leash over her head. But there was no one here. She listened, hoping she might hear the workaday mumbling of the dead coming from the cells up ahead. But all she heard was the sound of water dripping. The emptiness unnerved her.

She swung quickly around and looked at the cells across the corridor, her courage disappearing. She was now afraid that she might see gloom-shrouded figures crouched in dark corners waiting for her.

So she went back outside.

And she remembered the guards.

What about Nestore? What about Nazzareno? Both had been standing guard at the foot of the lattice. And what about Ruggiero, who had been on guard duty up on the parapet last night? Wouldn't they have seen something, or at least heard something?

She hurried across the yard to the east wall, weaving through the burial mounds with quick silent steps.

When she got to the east wall she cried, "Nestore?" She peered behind a stack of tents. "Nazzareno?"

She took a few steps closer to the pile, put her hand on top of the tents, and looked around the corner past some shovels to the fire. The fire was out, just a pile of ashes now.

Nazzareno and Nestore were nowhere to be seen.

She raised her face toward the parapet, resting her hand against the lattice. "Ruggero?" she called.

No answer.

The guards were gone too.

Piero walked fast, his *pistola* drawn, his cape billowing in the wake of his stride. Felicitas rushed to keep up with him.

"And you got no answer at all?" he asked.

"No," she said.

He shook his head. The mist was still thick. They stopped at the foot of the lattice.

When he saw that Nazzareno and Nestore were indeed gone, he said, "Let's go check the north wall."

At the north wall, it was the same: nobody there. Piero looked first one way, then the other, his brow knitting in perplexity. He turned on his heel and headed toward the west wall, kicking blankets and pots out of the way, his stride enormous, his prison boots crunching through the debris.

At the west wall he said to her, "Did you see anything? Anything at all?"

"What, down here?" she asked.

"Yes."

"No," she said. He seemed suspicious of the west wall.

He stuck his *pistola* in his belt, lifted his chin, took a deep breath, and looked up at the wall, his eyes narrowing, his head moving slowly one way then the other as he scanned the hundreds of windows that gaped like eye sockets in a skull.

"I've never liked this cellblock," he said. "The way it joins the west annex."

Felicitas remembered what Rosario had told her about the west annex, how they had never been able to get in there, how they had no idea what might be on the other side of the thick walls.

They walked back to the east wall, and in his urgency Piero showed no respect at all for the burial mounds, walked right over them, hopped from one to the next, as if they were rocks in a stream he was trying to cross.

Felicitas wove her way around them, running to keep up.

When they came to the east wall, Piero laid his hands on the lattice and shook it, checking for damage, climbed a few rungs, crawled like a spider from side to side, inspected the end supports and wall brackets, made sure none of the bolts had been loosened.

"Is it okay?" she asked.

He looked down at her. "It's fine."

He jumped to the ground. For a fifty-year-old, he was surprisingly spry. A frustrated crease came to his brow.

"How could they just disappear?" he asked. "Silvio should have heard something. Silvio's a good man. He doesn't fall asleep. If he gets too tired he walks around. He should have heard something. Last week they wanted to smash the lattice to bits. They threw stones at it. Now they leave it alone."

He shook his head, then glanced up the lattice, where mist, now congealing on the metal, beaded into moisture droplets all over the rungs.

"Come along," he said. "We better see if we can find them."

They climbed.

When they were halfway up they couldn't see the ground anymore, only an uninterrupted layer of mist.

At the top, they crawled over the parapet onto the catwalk and discovered that the crates of food-bricks had been broken open and the food-bricks scattered all over the place. More than half of them were missing, stolen by the dead.

"Ruggiero?" called Piero.

"Look at our food," cried Felicitas, dismayed to see their already small stock depleted.

She hurried over and gathered the loose pieces.

"Nazzareno?" Piero called.

He walked to the northeast guard tower. Felicitas picked up bits of food-brick. What would make the dead do this? Why would they leave half the food-bricks here if they were all starving to death? And how were the *superstiti* going to survive once they left the prison with only this small bit of food left?

"Felicitas!" called Piero. "Come here!"

She got to her feet and hurried along the parapet.

Piero stood by the cistern.

"*Dio non voglia!*" said Felicitas. The Italian words jumped reflexively to her mouth.

And no wonder.

On the lip of the cistern, with all the details of line and fingerprint clearly visible, she saw, like a ghoulish detail from a nightmare, a man's handprint perfectly formed in blood.

13

Piero formed search parties immediately.

"Gasparo, I want you to take Felicitas, Silvio, and Concetta and search the west cellblock. Arm yourself. Rosario and I and some of the others are going to check the north cellblock. You others check the east and south cellblocks. If you see the dead, fire. The rest of us will come running."

Felicitas, Gasparo, Silvio, and Concetta searched the southeast corridor of the west cellblock first.

Even before they got halfway down the corridor, Felicitas felt odd. She thought she might feel the tingling in her arms, as if she were going to have another episode with Lungo Muso, but she didn't. This felt different. She was unnaturally aware of the things around her. She tried to remember if she had ever felt this way before, but she drew a blank.

The west cellblock looked abandoned. As the four *superstiti* proceeded cautiously southward along the main floor corridor, she was glad Gasparo was with them, someone large and strong, someone who would give them a fighting chance against the dead should they happen to run into any.

Most of the cell doors were open. The shadows were thick, broken only by dim fingers of sunlight penetrating through the windows high above, illuminating a huge crack in the cellblock ceiling, reflecting off the perpetual damp that collected on the buttresses. The wood chips smelled rancid and the stone floor was littered with garbage.

"Where have they gone?" asked Gasparo irritably.

The big man was impatient, anxious to find not only the missing *superstiti* but also the dead.

As much as Felicitas tried to ignore the strange new feeling, she couldn't.

"I feel funny," she said.

Gasparo turned to her. The two oldsters stared at her with concerned eyes. Concetta put her hand on Felicitas's wrist.

"Are you unwell, dear?" she asked.

She looked at Concetta, then at Silvio. It was like a premonition, nothing like the tingling she had in her arms, more like a foreboding. She had the unspecific sense that there were people all around them.

"No, I . . ." She shook her head. She seemed to hear people whispering. "Do you hear that?" she asked.

She was still at a loss to explain it, yet now she recognized it, something she had heard from when she had been a dead girl, voices whispering, and also a ticking sound, a machinelike sound.

"Hear what, dear?" asked Concetta.

"That noise," she said. "That whispering. That ticking."

Yes, a whispering, a ticking, only she was hearing it with her mind, not with her ears.

"What noise?" asked Gasparo, casting a nervous glance up at the dark galleries.

It was like an omen, and she wanted to run.

She took a few steps away from the group, moved toward some stairs, feeling as if her mind were somehow opening up to her this whispering sound, that maybe it was a language of some kind. Was the whispering coming from up there, on the second gallery?

Then she heard the clang of a cell door high above. They all heard it. The wind? Her curiosity prodded her forward. She took a few quick steps up the stairs.

"Felicitas!" said Gasparo.

But she had to go. The whispering, she had to find out what it was.

She climbed the stairs. She stopped when she was three steps from the top, turned around, and stared at the others, pre-occupied. She tried to understand and translate the signals that were being dropped into mind as gently as snowflakes on a calm winter day.

"You hear that, don't you?" she said.

"The wind blew a cell door shut," said Gasparo.

"Not that," she said. "The murmuring . . . the whispering . . . that ticking sound, like a clock . . ."

A memory of this whispering, this ticking floated through her mind, of being sensitive to it, of responding to a stimuli only she could feel, as if there were an extra component to the way she sensed things.

Then, whining broke out all around them. The whining of the dead. Like a hundred dogs begging for food. The premonition. How could she do that? How could she sense the dead before they actually showed themselves?

"Felicitas!" cried Gasparo. "Get down from there. They're coming."

A dozen dead walked out of the darkness from the end of the cellblock, no longer shambling and listless, but forthright, their stride full of ominous purpose.

The gaunt figures passed a shaft of light and she saw that Maritano was leading them. He still wore the skull tied to his head, and he was now armed with a *pistola*. Ruggiero's *pistola*?

Nazzareno's? The strange feeling of premonition passed, wiped out by her fear.

Gasparo took a few bold steps toward the oncoming group.

Silvio and Concetta stayed where they were, drawing their weapons, nervous, but prepared to fire if they had to.

"Maritano!" called Gasparo. "We have no wish to harm you."

Maritano didn't respond, kept coming toward the *superstiti*. Felicitas climbed the remaining few steps to the second level and drew her own weapon. Was she going to have to kill someone? She had a tactical advantage from up here, but the thought of killing someone, especially someone she knew, left her cold.

"Where have you taken Nazzareno and the others?" called Gasparo. "We want them back."

By way of answer, a hail of stones arched from the dead and rained down on Gasparo and the two oldsters. Silvio and Concetta lifted their arms over their heads, trying to protect themselves. The stones clattered to the floor.

Gasparo abandoned negotiation.

He lifted his *pistola* and fired.

One of the dead slumped over in a smoking heap.

And that was all it took.

The dead charged.

"Felicitas!" cried Gasparo. "Fire!"

She moved forward, and, using the railing as support, leveled her weapon at the advancing dead. She hesitated only a moment, then fired. But she missed. She steadied her arm and took careful aim again, sighting down the barrel, maneuvering three fingers onto the big trigger, trying to let the weapon do its work, hoping she would be able to control its recoil.

But before she could fire again, someone jumped her from behind and yanked her away from the railing. She jerked her shoulders, freed herself, and whirled around, her anger flaring.

"Anteo!" she cried.

It was Anteo, the man who had come with Aldo that night

in the north cellblock to offer her a book, the man who had been so dead he hadn't even been able to speak.

"Come, Felicitas," he said. "Come with us. There's no point resisting."

Her eyes widened. "You talk now?" she said.

He had a tight hold on her shoulder. "Maritano wants you," he said.

"And your eyes, they're . . ."

She looked at his eyes. They had the same cagey off-center stare that Maritano's did, possessed a glittering and hard brightness that was unnatural.

He pulled her toward the stairway, yanking a leash from his belt with his left hand.

"Leave me alone," she said.

She hit Anteo's arm with her *pistola* grip, but he wouldn't let go.

So she bashed and bashed, but it was as if he were impervious to pain. She yanked, but no matter how hard she yanked, he wouldn't let go. How could he be this strong? Especially when he looked so starved? She glanced over the railing, was going to call for help, but saw that Gasparo was trying to keep back a whole crowd of them. Silvio and Concetta had leashes around their necks now. She was on her own.

She bashed Anteo's arm again.

"Felicitas, why do you fight us like this?" he asked.

"Let me go!" she yelled.

She had had enough.

She jabbed the barrel of her *pistola* into Anteo's stomach and, feeding off her anger, fired.

Anteo's eyes opened wide. The blast flung him into the air. A warm spray of blood flecked Felicitas's hands and face.

Anteo landed with an odd noise, halfway between a crack and a pop, against the railing, then flopped down to the second-gallery floor, where he landed on his side, his body as limp and twisted as a damp blanket, his left hand still clutching the leash.

The rest of the dead and *superstiti* were far down the corridor now. Blood gushed from Anteo's stomach, spreading in a dark pool over the stone, filling the damp air with its visceral smell, steaming in the dank cold of the cell block. Felicitas, charged on adrenaline, took a defensive stance, and aimed her *pistola* down the corridor.

Though the scene was lit up by muzzle flashes, it was too dark to make out any but the vaguest outlines of the fighting figures. She couldn't see well enough to shoot.

"Gasparo!" she called. She had tears in her eyes and she was shaking. "Silvio! Concetta!"

She stepped closer to the railing, peered down the corridor, now letting the *pistola* drift down to her side so that she felt the heat of its freshly used barrel against her leg through the fabric of her prison uniform.

"Gasparo?" she called again, afraid that she was now truly alone.

She turned around and looked at Anteo.

He stared up at her with half-closed eyes, his irises no longer off center, but even and straight, and with a strange dark ring around them. The puddle of blood spread out in an ever widening pool, finally formed a rivulet in one of the crevices between two floor tiles, ran over the edge of the gallery, and dripped to the first floor below in a small red waterfall, landing with a soft splatter. She heard one of the other search parties running down the corridor from the direction of the north cellblock. Maybe it was Piero.

Then she heard a scratching noise come from behind Anteo's head.

A sudden outflow of blood bubbled from his mouth and something crawled out from behind his neck, a large insect, a beetle, made of metal, slick with blood and brain tissue.

It scurried away on mechanical legs into the darkness.

When it disappeared, she looked down the corridor, feeling numb. She saw Gasparo. Gasparo running back all by himself.

Silvio and Concetta were gone.

She reached up and touched the back of her head.

And she thought of the glyph of the beetle on the mural in the generating room.

Felicitas sat with Piero, Rosario, and Gasparo in Piero's workshop up in the south tower.

"We tell everybody eventually," said Piero. "We wait until they gain their footing. When they first come out of the dreamphone haze, they're confused. They have this amnesia. They're afraid. We wait until they understand."

"Understand what?" said Felicitas. "That they can be taken from their beds in the middle of the night and have their heads cut open?"

"No," said Piero flatly. "That it's for their own good. It's hard to tell the difference. The dead, when they have these things in their heads, come alive in their own peculiar way. You've seen it. So we have to make sure. We have to check by incision. We've had to screen, Felicitas. Surely you can understand that. We perform our procedure, we make sure you're one of us, one of the *superstiti,* and then we give you time."

"You should have told me sooner," she said. "You should have told me right away."

"No, Felicitas," he said. "You and Maritano . . . the friendship the two of you had . . . we couldn't be sure we could trust you. You kept on seeing Maritano, even after the dreamphone haze lifted." Felicitas remembered coming down from the south tower after her most recent visit with Maritano and finding Piero looking at her suspiciously from the junk pile out back. "And even at that early juncture we knew Maritano was rallying the rest of them against us in some way. We thought you might inadvertently tell Maritano the reasons and rationale for our screening. There's been a big change in Maritano. And we've had to be careful. If we let him appreciate and understand the reason for our surgical screening, he'll sabotage it any way he can. Your friendship with Maritano . . ." Piero shrugged. "That was a special kind of risk, and we dealt with it by not telling you about these . . . these beetles."

Felicitas stared at Piero sullenly. "You can trust me," she said.

"That might be true," he said. "But when you first came out of it, you were confused. You were afraid. And you visited Maritano." Piero leaned against the table and gazed at her calmly. "Even back then, he was starting to organize. Tell him why we screen, and like I say, he'd do everything he could to stop it. All the dead have had the procedure, but none of them knows why. The incision tells us who gets to eat and who has to starve. Let Maritano know that, and our secret nighttime procedures would be a thing of the past. Can you blame us for taking precautions?"

She nodded. She could accept his reason. "Okay," she said.

"And we wanted to give you time," he said, as if he were now trying to appease her. "Time to remember. To make new associations. To make new friends." He glanced at Rosario. "We didn't want to scare you. Mechanical beetles crawling into the back of your head. Mechanical beetles controlling you. That's frightening. We wanted you to get through the transition period as smoothly as possible."

She contemplated Piero. "So this beetle," she said. "It controls?"

"All our observations suggest it," said Piero. "And your reading of the prison schematic down in the generating room confirms it. It's an anti-escape system. And it's been triggered by the demise of the *carcerieri.*"

Rosario slid off his stool and stroked her hair with the back of his hand.

"We think these beetles," he said, "these implants, as Piero and I call them, have subjugated the dead in a way the dreamphones never did. And Maritano seems to be the fulcrum. For one reason or another, the implants have chosen him as a . . . an operations center. Maybe there's a reason behind it, maybe not."

Piero walked over to a large shelf by the window, rummaged through the junk, and returned with a broken implant. She noticed Gasparo staring at the implant with quiet horror.

"I hate those cursed things," said the giant. "I sleep with a piece of tarp around my neck. They're sly, sneaking out of drains and down from window ledges in the middle of the night. I can't think of anything worse than having one of those things in my head."

Piero set the implant on the table before her. "This one's broken," he said. He pointed to glyphs on the back of the implant. "Can you read that?" he asked.

Felicitas lifted the implant and had a close look at the glyphs. They were small, simplified but technical.

"This glyph is the one that means human," she said. "And here's the one I showed Rosario in the generating room, the one that means brain. Other than that, I don't know."

She handed the implant back to Piero.

He pulled a small retractable blade from the underside of the implant.

"This is razor sharp," he said. "It uses this to cut its way through the base of the skull. The resulting wound is then sutured by these threading pods, leaving no scar. Three prongs attach to the cerebellum, two to the occipital lobe, and two to the Sylvian fissure. We learned this by looking at a victim, a man named Bettino. Rosario will tell you more about Bettino. But if you're interested, there's a book on the brain over there. It's in Italian but there're some good illustrations."

Piero let go of the blade. It sprang back into place and he put the broken implant on the table. He looked at Rosario. Rosario's features softened and he gazed at Felicitas.

"Bettino was the first," said Rosario. "At least the first one I saw. He used to be my cellmate. This was about a year ago. I was alive. Bettino was still dead. The evening lockup was still the same, but by that time there was no potency left in the dreamphone drug. One night I stayed awake. I saw one of the implants crawl out of the drain and bury itself in the back of Bettino's neck. You probably don't remember Bettino. He's dead now. We tried to help him but we ended up killing him instead. We found some old books in the infirmary on the basics of surgery. The books were in Italian. It took me a long time to learn the principles of anesthetic, incision, and suture. Our plan was to remove the implant from the back of Bettino's skull. Unfortunately, the implant wouldn't let us. It had a protective mechanism, grappling claws that latched onto his brain. When we pried the implant from Bettino's brain stem, we took a chunk of brain with it." Rosario shook his head. "It's too bad." He sighed. "But we learned a lot. Bettino didn't die in vain. We found out how these things work."

Piero held up the implant. "In fact, this is the same implant we took from Bettino's skull," he said. "We've tried to catch more, but we hardly ever see them. They move only at night and only through the drainpipes. You were lucky to see Anteo's." He turned to Gasparo and gave the big man a teasing grin. "You've probably seen Gasparo checking all the drains and downspouts in the dispensary at night." Piero chuckled. "Now you know why."

Gasparo frowned. "I'd kill them all if I could."

Felicitas lay on her mattress wide awake staring at the dispensary ceiling. The ceiling was dimly lit by firelight. Rosario slept next to her. Far off in the forest, a few *mostri* bellowed. She felt the thud of their gargantuan footsteps reverberating through the dispensary floor. This time of year, they always came to the prison. Rosario shifted, turned, opened his eyes, and finally sat up.

"Are you all right?" she asked.

He turned to her. "I thought you were asleep."

"I was for a while," she said.

He nodded. "I'm fine," he said. "I just feel . . ." But he trailed off.

He got up, walked to the fire, warmed his hands, then turned around and gazed at the sleeping *superstiti*. The stark features of his face seemed etched into place by the shadowy firelight. He walked around the fire, his eyes cast outward, looking at each and every member of the group. He nodded at Piero. Piero stood guard at the door.

Rosario looked anxious, as if something were bothering him.

"Rosario?" she said.

He turned to her.

"Are you warm enough?" he asked.

"What's wrong?" she asked.

His face was expressionless. "Do you want me to build up the fire?" he asked.

"No," she said. "I'm fine."

He nodded and turned away.

"What is it, Rosario?"

He turned back, his eyes narrowing.

"I don't know," he said. "I just feel . . ." His brow squeezed into a frown. "I somehow remember this." He gestured at the dim dispensary. "Like I've been here before. Like maybe Lungo Muso has brought me here." He took a deep breath, trying to steady his anxiety. "I'm sensing something, but I can't tell what."

She wondered if he were experiencing the same sense of premonition she herself had experienced earlier in the day.

She watched him walk back to the fire, where he sat down cross-legged. He picked up a small piece of *uominilupi* gadgetry and turned it around in his long-fingered hands. But he wasn't looking at it. He was staring, brooding.

She closed her eyes. She had to sleep. There would be another search tomorrow.

But then she opened her eyes, and every muscle in her body tensed.

What was that noise?

A low steady hum. She sat up. Rosario got to his feet, stood by the fire, and stared out the nearest window, his eyes intent. Some of the other *superstiti* stirred in their sleep. This wasn't at all like the faint thuds and bellows of the *mostri* outside the prison walls. This was machine-like, getting louder. The windows rattled. Some of the children woke up and began to moan in fright.

Then the yard was filled with white light, ten times as bright as the searchlights.

Rosario left his spot by the fire and joined Piero at the door. Felicitas pulled on her boots, and, without tying the laces, hurried over, afraid but curious, her mouth dry, her palms cold.

Up in the sky, through the rain and mist, she saw a bright light. The light grew, and the noise got louder, and she knew what this was, had seen one before, back in the days when she had been a dead girl: a scout ship. She tried to make out some detail, but all she saw was the light, like a smear of burning lime across the sky.

A few others joined them. Gasparo squeezed his huge frame through.

"Is it them?" he asked.

Piero stared at the light. And in his eyes Felicitas saw a new urgency.

"It's them," he said.

Felicitas couldn't help thinking of the other glyph she'd seen in the generating room; the *soldati*. Soldiers.

"Is it going to land?" asked Gasparo.

But the light backed away. The noise grew faint. The mist swirled around and finally swallowed the light altogether.

The ship disappeared into the night, leaving them all feeling anxious, fearful, and vulnerable.

14

The next afternoon, twelve superstiti returned to the west cellblock.

"Felicitas was up there," Gasparo told Piero, pointing to the second level, recapping his story. "Anteo attacked her from one of those cells there."

Piero contemplated Felicitas; he now knew about the strange premonition she had experienced.

"As for Silvio and Concetta," said Gasparo, "they were swarmed before they had a chance to use their weapons. They had leashes around their necks in no time. I fought like a mad dog to save them but one of the dead smashed me over the head with a big rock and I fell to the ground right over there. That's my blood on that buttress. Like I told you yesterday, I must have been unconscious for at least a minute or two."

Piero tapped his chin with his fingers a few times and stared at the blood.

"You saw them heading down that way toward the drainage pool?" he said. "Is that correct?"

"That's correct," said Gasparo. "Some went up there, too."

Piero glanced up at the galleries. "I knew they had to be in here somewhere," he said.

Francesco, the man who looked after the books up in the east cellblock, spoke up. "I think we should go back and get some more people," he said. "I don't think twelve is enough. What if we run into trouble?"

Francesco was another of Piero's *consiglieri*. Some speculated that Francesco and Gasparo were brothers. Certainly they were the same tall height, but Francesco was spidery, whereas Gasparo was bullish.

"Twelve is all I can safely spare, Francesco" said Piero. "I finally understand what the dead are trying to do," he said. His blue eyes narrowed. "They want to get us away from the lattice so they can destroy it. They think if they can get enough of us looking for Nazzareno and the others, we won't have enough to protect the lattice. And we can't let that happen. So we choose our numbers carefully." He looked at Francesco. "Twelve should be enough."

Francesco didn't look convinced.

"But there's a hundred forty-four of us," he insisted. "Surely we could spare a few more."

"No," said Piero, "we can't. You have to remember, we have twenty-five children. Then we have thirty-one old people, people who are past the age when they can . . . well, look what happened to Silvio and Concetta. That was a mistake. My mistake. And I'm not going to let it happen again. Twelve has to be enough. That way we leave plenty of people guarding the lattice."

Felicitas walked down the main-floor corridor of the west cellblock with Rosario, Gasparo, and Francesco. Piero had taken a team to the top two levels, while another man, Canziano, searched the middle two levels with a third team.

As they neared the end of the corridor, she saw the drainage pool, a wide shallow pool where the overflow of the south bath trickled down a sleek stone wall. Pond scum floated in dim green circles on the surface. The foam near the drainage wall looked curdled and the air smelled of algae.

"You see where that wall juts out?" said Rosario, pointing across the pool. "That's the west annex. See over there where we've tried to hack the stone away?" Felicitas spied a cavern-like opening in the wall. "That wall's got to be at least twenty feet thick."

The stonework rounded in a large curve above the pool. Higher up Felicitas saw a series of lights, now with no power, strung along some hooks, and above that, an oblong of what looked like glass suspended by some wires attached to the vaulted ceiling: a viewscreen, only a big one.

"Any idea what's in the west annex?" she asked.

"No," Rosario said. He sighed. "So far we've only been able to speculate. We think that the *uominilupi* prison staff might have stayed in there, back in the days before the *carcerieri* ran the prison, and that they might have used that screen up there as a way of communicating . . ." He stopped, looked closely at her. "Felicitas?" he said. "Felicitas, what is it?"

She stared at the west annex, listening, not with her ears but with her mind again. Listening, because she heard that sound again, the whispering, the ticking. She knew the dead were nearby.

"They're here," she said quietly, as if she were resigned to it. "They're hiding up in the galleries."

Rosario looked up at the galleries, his pupils wide in the darkness, his shoulders rising, his lips tightening. Felicitas took a deep breath. The feeling got stronger. She could sense their dead dull minds all around her, heard the monotonous and machinelike ticking of their implants. She was bewildered. The feeling left her exhausted. How could she do this? How could she sense them like this?

"Up there?" he said.

"Yes," she said.

And as if on cue, the dead whined from the upper galleries, like a hundred whimpering wolf pups.

Rosario turned to her.

"How do you do that?" he asked.

She shook her head. "I don't know . . . I don't . . . I just . . ."

A splash came from the drainage pool. One of the dead had thrown a rock into it from above.

The four *superstiti* drew their weapons.

Felicitas looked at the drainage pool. She was getting a strong feeling from the drainage pool now. Her brow creased. That couldn't be right. How could the dead be in the pool? Yet the sense was there. The dead were in the fetid water. Especially a sense of Maritano. Submerged beneath the green pond scum.

She moved closer to Rosario, clutched his arm.

"They're under the water, too," she said.

"They are?"

They both looked at the water.

Maritano rose like a prehistoric creature out of the drainage pool, the skull tied to his head, the pond scum clinging to his uniform, his hair hanging limply around his shoulders. He had a *pistola* in his hand. Marco and Ottavio, Maritano's own *consiglieri*, her old friends, rose out of the water behind him.

How could this be? How could they breathe underwater? How could they be waiting for them all this time under that pond scum?

The three dead in the pool moved forward, trudged up the slant of the drainage pool, waist deep, then thigh deep, then knee deep, coming toward the *superstiti* step by step, their legs lurching, the water dripping from their prison uniforms, their boots squelching on the damp stone.

High above in the upper galleries Felicitas heard some shouting, whining, and a few *pistola* reports. She looked up and saw hundreds of dead leaning over the railings.

"They're cutting us off from Piero and Canziano," she said.

Maritano stopped at the foot of the stairs, glanced at the

upper galleries where the sound of the fighting intensified, then looked at Felicitas.

"Your friends upstairs are having some fun," he said.

Felicitas spoke up, suppressing her bewilderment, her voice clear and sure.

"We've come for Silvio and the others," she said. She took aim at Maritano's head. "Where do you have them?"

"Put your weapon down, Felicitas." Felicitas stared more closely at Maritano. He was articulate, didn't mumble, spoke well, as if he too were now alive. "There's no hope for you if you try to fight us."

"Maritano, why are you doing this?" asked Rosario.

There came more *pistola* reports from the upper galleries, the sound seeming to roar as it echoed from wall to wall, the muzzle flashes looking like dim lightning on the vaulted ceiling.

Maritano climbed the stairs, a patient grin on his face, as if he were dealing with the question of a fool.

"You can't leave the prison," he said. "You're prisoners of the *uominilupi*. You've committed crimes and you've got to be punished."

He continued up the stairs with deliberate and proprietary steps, as if he owned this part of the prison.

Gasparo lifted his *pistola*.

"Maritano, one step closer," said the big man, his deep voice booming like the lowing of an ox, "and I'll blow you apart."

A grin came to Maritano's face as he looked at Gasparo.

"Gasparo, you disappoint me," he said. "Think things through." Maritano gestured at the surrounding galleries. "Look around you. You're surrounded. You're outnumbered. Your friends upstairs are learning the hard way. Do the smart thing. Put your weapon down." He glanced tenderly at Felicitas. "And that means you too, Felicitas. There's no point in fighting us. You can't fight us. We have the New Ones on our side."

Rosario and Felicitas looked at each other. The New Ones? What could Maritano possibly know about the New Ones?

Maritano continued up the stairs, unhooking a leash from his belt, gripping the railing posts to help himself up the slippery steps, water draining from the hollow eye sockets of the skull like tears.

Gasparo shook his head, exasperated—Maritano wasn't heeding his warning. He raised his weapon and, without further warning, fired.

His shot went wide, and the *pistola* charge scattered in a shower of sparks over the drainage pool. But his shot was like a trigger to the rest of the dead, a signal, the catalyst that turned this from a peaceful confrontation into a violent one.

Before Gasparo could fire again, hundreds of rocks rained down on them from the upper levels.

A rock the size of an orange bashed Felicitas in the head. She fell to her knees, stunned by the blow. Three or four walnut-sized rocks struck her in the back, and she thought the dead were going to stone them to death.

She heard the sound of *pistola* fire erupt all around her, and, glancing up, saw Rosario and Francesco blasting away at Maritano and his *consiglieri*. Maritano and his men took cover behind the drainage pool embankment.

Twenty or thirty dead came down the gallery stairs and swarmed them.

A half-dozen dead attacked Gasparo, two on each arm, one around his neck, another holding on to his legs, like bloodhounds on a grizzly bear, their eyes glittering askew with the mania of their implants.

Another stone hit Felicitas in the head. Blood trickled through her hair and fell from behind her ear in a series of quick drops to the floor.

She tried to get up, but was kicked again and again, her ribs taking the brunt of the attack, her shoulders and hips sustaining a good number of blows as well.

She finally crouched in a fetal position, wrapping her arms around her head, hoping to protect herself, hoping that Maritano would give the dead the signal to stop. But the kicking continued. She glanced to the left, saw a riot of scuffling feet, was now afraid the dead were going to kick her to death.

But then two strong hands grabbed her by the shoulders and pulled her free. Maritano's hands. He dragged her over to the railing, wrenched her arms behind her back, looped a piece of twine around her wrists, forced a leash over her head, pulled out his *pistola,* and pressed the barrel under her chin.

"Enough!" he shouted, raising his hand.

The fighting on the first floor stopped; upstairs it still raged. Piero was making a battle of it.

Rosario, Gasparo, and Francesco saw that they had no choice. If they didn't surrender, Maritano would shoot Felicitas through the head.

A woman collared Rosario with a leash and yanked on it tightly. He grudgingly accepted it. Leashes were shoved around the necks of Gasparo and Francesco. There was nothing they could do. The fighting went on unabated on the upper levels. Piero wasn't going to be able to help them. He had troubles enough of his own.

All their weapons were taken away from them: four more *pistole* for the arsenal of the dead.

Rosario looked at Felicitas. His face was a mess but his eyes burned with defiance.

"Don't worry," he said. "We'll get out of this."

The dead forced the four *superstiti* down the steps toward the drainage pool.

Felicitas tugged on the twine binding her hands, and to her surprise, she felt it loosen. Perhaps Maritano believed the leash was enough for her. She tugged again and the twine fell away. Even so, what could she do? Perhaps the leash was indeed enough. She couldn't attack, certainly couldn't get away, but there must be something . . . something she could do to help the situation.

She paused, pretended to stumble against the railing. She had just enough time to leave a clue behind.

Maritano turned around.

"Watch your step," he said, with an off-key cordiality that made her skin crawl.

She gave him a nod, angling herself so she could hide the railing behind her. He peered at her more closely. She couldn't help noticing nine little circular scar marks on his forehead. What were those marks? She glanced away, looking out at the water.

"Don't be so frightened, Felicitas," said Maritano. "You're a good swimmer. You'll have no trouble with this."

"We're going under the water?" she asked.

The *pistola* fire was dying out on the upper levels.

He didn't reply, just dragged her deeper and deeper until the water came up to her neck.

Were they going to drown them now? Rosario, Gasparo, and Francesco were dragged in behind her.

"It's under here to the left," said Maritano. "Don't mind the filth. It can't hurt you."

Into the water Felicitas went, deeper and deeper through the malodorous lumps that floated on the surface, until she was pulled beneath the surface. She held her breath, forced herself to follow Maritano. The sound of *pistola* fire disappeared as her ears finally dipped into the water. And she remembered the subsurface passageway in the south bath from her dream. Could there be one in this drainage pool as well?

Maritano finally dragged her into an underwater culvert. Yes, an underwater passageway. He seemed powered by uncanny force. He dragged her through the underwater culvert at great speed.

And when they emerged on the other side, they were in the west annex.

15

Maritano led her up the ramp of the west annex drainage pool. The ticking and whispering of her premonition became background noise as she looked up at the west annex. It was half the size of the west cellblock, with the standard five upper galleries. Dozens of dead stared down at her from several of these galleries, while others sat around in small groups on the first floor gazing at her with off-kilter eyes. She turned around. Marco and Ottavio led the others out behind her. She saw Silvio sitting in a holding pen off to the side. Most of the first floor of the west annex consisted of open-sided holding pens, like Francesco's holding pen full of books up in the east cell block. She looked for Concetta and the others in these holding pens but saw only Silvio. Silvio, sitting in a pile of wood chips, watched them, his eyes wide, as if he hadn't recovered from the shock of his capture.

"This is where we've been hiding," said Maritano, turning around, smiling at her. "This is our new home." He glanced down at her hands. "You've lost your twine," he said.

"Maritano, why don't you let us go?"

"Because you've committed serious crimes, Felicitas, and you must be punished."

She was again struck by how articulate Maritano sounded. She looked at the nine little puncture marks on his head.

"Come with me, Felicitas," he said, giving the leash a tug. "Your friends will be fine. You'll join them later, once I'm through with you. I have much to teach you."

She turned again, frightened, and looked at Rosario—she was going to be separated from the others.

Rosario strained on his leash. "Where are you taking her?" he demanded.

Marco pulled his club out and struck Rosario over the head.

Rosario sank to his knees, stunned, put his hands to his brow, steadied himself, shook his head, then struggled to his feet, a gash showing crimson on his forehead.

"Don't worry, Rosario," said Maritano. "Felicitas will be safe."

Maritano pulled her up some steps to the second level. He took her to a room—there were rooms on these upper levels, not cells, not holding pens, but actual rooms, as if the accommodation in the west annex were meant to be more comfortable.

Her fear turned to anger.

In the room, a few lamps of *topo* grease sat on a shelf burning dimly. The furniture—three chairs and a sofa—looked soft and comfortable, and was covered with a shiny but tough material. Twenty dead *topi* lay on a white table next to a bowl of blood, and boxes of junk were stacked against the back wall.

He led her to the head of the table, turned around, and put his hands on her shoulders. His hair hung in a tangled mess around his face, coming out from underneath the *uomolupo* skull in snaky strands, and his ears were bent comically at right angles by the lower edges of the carapace. He smelled. The left side of his forehead bulged. She stared at this disfigurement, wondering if it had anything to do with the nine puncture marks. He leaned forward and tried to kiss her, but she backed away. He then put his hand on her breast. She pulled away, recoiling from the unwanted intimacy.

"Don't you like me anymore?" he asked.

She frowned.

"Maritano, why are you doing this?" she asked. "Why are you kidnapping us like this?"

His lips parted, showing crooked brown teeth. He slid his arms around her and pulled her near. She tried to push away but he held her tight. She thought that if she resisted too much she might provoke him into doing something violent, so she let her body go limp, hoping that her complete lack of affectionate response would make him stop.

"Maritano, this isn't right," she said. "So much has happened. The prison has done something to you. There's a schematic down in the generating room, and it's—"

He brushed his lips against her cheek. The skull's teeth touched her head. "You smell good," he said.

"Maritano, I've changed," she said. "Everything's changed. I've been trying to tell you that." She felt exasperated. "I don't feel the same about you anymore." Her lack of response didn't matter in the least to Maritano, so she tried pushing him away again. "Do you have to hold me like this?" she asked. "And why do you wear that thing on your head?" She looked into his eyes. "And why are your eyes like that? Why do you have those nine marks on your forehead? What have they done to you?"

He let go of her and considered her words, raising his chin, his eyes continuing to stare just left of center, a faint grin lifting the corners of his thin lips as a droplet of water formed on the skull's right bicuspid and fell to the floor.

He then walked to the head of the table, dipped his finger in the bowl of blood, and drew a *uominilupi* glyph on the white surface.

"I finally know who I am, Felicitas," he said, his tone contemptuous.

She recognized the glyph. A diamond with a single stroke on the penultimate point and two dots above: father-leader, wise man, sheriff, protector, holy man, all of these things.

"These marks on my forehead," he said, "they'll go away. But right now I'm glad I have them. They tell me who I am." He tapped the glyph on the table. "That's who I am," he said. "This is what I've become. This is what I should be. I know more than Rosario will ever know. I know who put us here, what they're like, and what they've endured. You think Rosario's smart, but does he have any idea that the *soldati* are coming? Does he know the New Ones are on the way? Rosario's a fool. You should forget him. Compared to me, he's as ignorant as a child."

Her fear came back. The *soldati*? They were coming? Did the glyph of the crossed *fucili* in the generating room hold true then? And the New Ones? Coming as well?

She glanced again at the marks. Maybe he had a different kind of implant. "You've let them brainwash you, Maritano."

"I know how to survive, Felicitas. They taught me how to vanquish my vanquishers. They taught me to rise like the cliff-bird."

She stared at him, surprised by the familiar words.

"Listen to Rosario all you want," he said, "but you'll never know anything unless you let me teach you. I can tell you why the Old Ones had to make the New Ones. Can Rosario teach you that? I don't think so. You might as well ask a man with no legs to teach you to walk. I can teach you about the river of time. I can teach you about Reymont and Machiavelli."

Felicitas stared. River of time? Reymont? Machiavelli? She had no idea what he was talking about.

"Maritano, could I go back to my friends now?" she asked.

"I want you to join us, Felicitas," he said. He looked at the shelf to his right. He stepped to the shelf and pulled down an implant, different from an ordinary implant, a larger one, twice the size of the one Piero had shown her, with nine prongs, matching exactly the nine puncture marks on his head. "This will help you see the way of the New Ones. It's a counselor."

"Do you have one of those things in your head?" she asked.

He pointed to the sofa. "Lie down," he said. "It attaches to the forehead. It won't take long, only a few minutes. And then you'll know everything."

She backed away. "Maritano, I don't want that thing in my head."

"You're a prisoner of the *uominilupi*," he said. His voice was hard now. "You were convicted of murder. You will be punished, then rehabilitated. You will be taught the ways of the New Ones. There's no point in struggling. The *soldati* will be here in a few days, and they will force you to cooperate. The New Ones will be here by midwinter. There's no point in trying to resist them. If you don't do as they say, they'll execute you."

She put her hands up. "Keep that thing away from me," she said.

"Please, Felicitas," he said. "Lie down on the sofa."

He grabbed her by the shoulders and pushed her down on the sofa, the same odd grin coming to his face, his lips shrinking to a thin but intense line as he sucked them in between his crooked brown teeth.

"Maritano, don't do this to me," she cried. "I don't want that thing in my head. I'll join you. I'll do anything you want. But please, don't put that thing in my head."

"Let the counselor do its work, Felicitas," he said.

He held her down. She couldn't break free.

Maritano pressed the counselor to her forehead.

"Please, Maritano, please!"

She had tears of panic in her eyes, felt a fear that was like a thing alive, clawing to get out, understood that if she allowed Maritano to put the counselor in her head she would be as good as dead, a girl again robbed of her identity, a girl under the control once more of the *uominilupi*.

"You'll thank me for this, Felicitas," he said.

The small mind-control machine whirred, and the nine prongs began to drill into her head.

But they made only the smallest of skin punctures before something clicked inside and the drilling stopped.

The counselor shuddered and withdrew its prongs.

Like so much of the other machinery in the prison, the counselor had broken down.

Maritano shook his head. "Don't worry, Felicitas," he said. "We'll find a new one."

When she told Rosario about the counselor, and how Maritano was going to find a new one, Rosario's eyes narrowed.

"We'll be out of here long before that," he said.

Felicitas told him about the *soldati* and the New Ones, about Reymont, Machiavelli, and the river of time.

"Reymont," he said. "Machiavelli." He shrugged. "Who knows?" He peered at her anxiously. "And he really said that the New Ones will be here by midwinter?"

"Yes," she said.

"And that the *soldati* would be here in a few days?"

"That's what he said."

He shook his head. "Then we've got to get out of here," he muttered.

Felicitas glanced at Silvio, who was sleeping in a corner.

"Did Silvio say what happened to the others?" she asked.

"Yes," said Rosario. "He says they took Concetta last night. Into that room at the top of those stairs." Rosario pointed to a broad set of stairs at the end of the annex. At the top there was a door opening out onto a small mezzanine. Rosario shook his head again. "He doesn't know what they've done with her, but he hasn't seen her since." Rosario dabbed delicately at the gash on his forehead. "As for the others, he doesn't know. He hasn't seen them."

She snuggled closer to his side, thinking.

After a minute she said, "Why do you think they've come here?" she asked.

"Who?" he said.

"The dead," she said. "Why do you think they've come to the west annex?"

He nodded, thinking about the problem. He gazed out the bars of the holding pen. A few torches burned here and there. So did a couple of fires.

"You look out there," he said, "at the west annex, and you can see that it's different. They have some holding pens down here, yes, but other than that, it's rooms everywhere. I think it's like we speculated, that the *uominilupi* stayed here when they themselves ran the prison, before they automated it. We've always thought the *uominilupi* might have run the prison a long time ago. And the west annex makes a good stronghold." He brushed back some of her hair and inspected one of her cuts. "And I . . . I think it might have some symbolic significance to them." He took a deep breath and folded his hands over his right knee. "The implants make the dead associate strongly with the *uominilupi*. This west annex, it's a *uominilupi* place, and they find that appealing. Their implants force them to find it appealing. It's the same with that skull, isn't it?" He put his arm around her shoulder. "It's a symbol to them."

She gazed out at the vast cavernous structure. She was still perplexed.

"But how did they find it?" she asked. "You and Piero searched for a way in and you never—"

"Their implants," he said. He raised his eyebrows. "Their implants tell them everything, don't they?"

They sat silently for a while. Then she asked, "What about the river of time?"

Rosario shook his head. "I have no idea, Felicitas."

*   *   *

She had another dream that night. About her mother.

They were in a cell. Felicitas and her mother were sitting on the edge of the sleeping pallet. There was something different about her mother—a light in her mother's eyes that had never been there before. Her mother wrapped a bandage around her arm. Felicitas looked at her arm, thinking she must have a cut or scrape, but there was nothing wrong with her arm.

Two *carcerieri* entered the cell and grabbed her mother. The *carcerieri* dragged her mother out of the cell, and her mother didn't resist but went willingly, calmly, holding her chin high, striding next to the two automatons with her customary dignity. Felicitas slid from the sleeping pallet and followed, but the *carcerieri* closed the door before she could leave the cell. All she could do was stare at her mother through the bars, hoping to get one last look.

Her mother waved, a pale hand in the misty dimness, and finally disappeared.

Felicitas woke up.

She woke up to find Rosario sitting next to her, his eyes intent on something out in the annex behind her, his back straight, his shoulders squared, his muscles as taut as a spring-coil.

She turned around.

Marco and Ottavio entered the holding cell, their *pistole* drawn. Maritano came in behind them and looked at Felicitas. Beneath the skull, he was sneering.

"I don't like you sleeping next to Rosario," he said.

He yanked her to her feet. In an instant Rosario was up next to her trying to pull her back, but Marco and Ottavio quickly advanced on him, grabbed his arms, and pushed him against the metal slats of the holding pen.

"Where are you taking me?" she asked.

He pulled some rope from his belt and bound her hands behind her back.

"Back to my room," he said. He looked at Rosario, a quiet but seething expression on his face, as if Rosario were an object of great disgust and hatred for Maritano. "I can't have Rosario near you. Rosario's bad for you. He's filling your head with lies. You'll wait in my room until I find a counselor."

Maritano left her in the room by herself.

She heard him slide a timber brace into place under the outside latch. She stood in the middle of the room, listening, then, with quiet steps, approached the door and peered out the small window. The timber brace was thoroughly wedged under the outside latch. Not the best security, but effective. The latch had a large thumb level that when depressed lifted the door's internal bolt. By wedging the timber underneath, it couldn't be depressed, and the internal bolt couldn't be lifted. She looked at the inside latch. It was all the same piece with the outside latch. She turned around, and, with her hands still tied behind her back, jiggled the latch, testing it. The latch wouldn't budge. She shook it, yanked it, finally kicked it, but it wouldn't move.

She again looked out the small window to the second-floor gallery. She could see over the railing into the main annex. If she strained, she could see the drainage pool. Above, she saw three more levels. To her left, the gallery walkway curved to a large set of steps leading down to the first floor of the annex. At the top of these steps was a door, the same door Rosario had pointed out earlier. The door was open and she saw a number of dead sitting in there on a low wooden bench, firelight flickering on their faces, their off-kilter eyes seeming to collect the light so that their irises glowed with a deep but unnerving luminescence. They were eating. Some ate stolen food-bricks. Others ate *topi*. Some ate larger pieces of meat. Were they able to get outside and hunt? Was there an exit in the west annex? And what were they eating? She remembered the carcass from the balloon reconnaissance.

She finally left the door, realizing any attempt through the door, at least for now, was futile, that until more of the dead went to sleep, even the noise she made shaking the latch would attract attention and send them running. She walked to the middle of the room and stopped, distracted by her own thoughts.

If Maritano finally got the counselor into her head would she be able to fight the nine small implants the way she'd fought the dreamphones? She shuddered. She was afraid of the counselor. At the same time, she was curious. What would she learn from the nine implants? The English, the Italian, the New Ones, the Old Ones—would all those questions be answered? And would it tell her anything about that big white building that frightened her so much?

She continued across the room and looked out the window. No bars, no glass, just a rectangle through the stone, big enough to crawl through. But the drop was sheer, right down to the rocks and the lake, and she'd kill herself if she tried to jump.

It was raining now. It came down steadily, pushed sideways by the west wind, and in the phosphorescent light of the rain clouds she saw whitecaps out on the lake, a relentless procession of small but fierce waves crashing onto the stony beach. Lightning lit the sky . . .

In the flash of lightning she saw a lone figure standing on the shore of the lake, shadowy and indistinct . . .

Her shoulders rose in fear. One haunting glimpse, enough to make her think the river people might be out there after all. The lightning flashed again, flickering for a few seconds. No, not one of the river people. This time she made out the ears and the shaggy head. It was Lungo Muso, standing there in the rain all by himself.

Her arms began to tingle.

She backed away from the window and gripped the chair. The lamps flickered strangely, with the small flames drawn upward as if in a sudden updraft, and she grew suddenly breathless and faint. She sank to her knees. She felt as if she were becoming unstuck again. She felt her hair rising around her, as if the same updraft affecting the flames was now touching her, trying to pull her upward as well. She took a deep breath, struggling to control her fear. Here we go again, she thought.

She closed her eyes . . . and she felt herself spinning out the prison window in a gentle wind . . .

16

When she opened her eyes she was in a large room—a room not from the west annex, but a room from an earth interior. A room, once again, from the old time.

On a table sat some papers and a feather quill. Lungo Muso, now looking misty, stood next to this table. She looked down at her hands. They were no longer tied behind her back. She rubbed her wrists to get her circulation going again.

Out some double doors she saw a man in a doublet and a ruff collar, well into his sixties, leaning over a balcony railing, peering through the darkness, his shoulders tense, listening intently to the sound of approaching horses. The memory came back. That book in Francesco's library, with its picture of a horse. Lungo Muso had taken her here before.

"Felicitas," said Lungo Muso, "there's nothing you can do about this." Lungo Muso could talk now? "We are shadows here. You can touch these papers and this quill, but you can't touch that man. You can in no way change what you're going to see here."

She looked out the window.

A wagon rolled to a stop in front of the building, and New Ones and old-time soldiers in chain mail and armor jumped out. The man on the balcony retreated into the shadows. He hurried to a telescope on the balustrade, unclasped it from a tripod, then shuffled inside, his legs seeming to creak along, as if his knees were arthritic and giving him a great deal of pain.

When he reached the middle of the room, he lowered himself stiffly to one knee, pulled up a floorboard, and hid the telescope underneath.

Then someone banged on the downstairs door.

"Signor Galilei!" a voice called. "Signor Galilei, open up!"

Signor Galilei put the floorboard back in place, hiding the telescope, and hurried to the table. He stacked the sheets of paper as quickly as he could, but his fingers seemed to be as stiff as his legs, and Felicitas could see that his hands were bent and crippled, and that it was costing him a great deal of toil to get the sheets stacked.

"Signor Galileo Galilei, I order you in the name of the Church to open this door!"

A loud thud came from downstairs. The soldiers were using a battering ram to break down the door. With a dozen sheets stacked, Galileo rolled them into a long tube, tied them with a ribbon, and placed the roll on top of a rafter near the door. The thud came again. Felicitas heard the door crash open. She heard heavy boots on the stairs, the rattle of chain mail, and the muffled whining of New Ones. She heard soldiers coming down the hall and finally heard them kicking at the apartment door.

Galileo looked up in terror.

The thin wooden door exploded, broken open by a final kick of an armored boot.

Soldiers and New Ones filed into the room. An officer of the Church followed, a well-fed man in scarlet vestments, a large gold crucifix hanging around his neck, a black pointed beard on his chin.

"Father Coseni!" said Signor Galilei. Galileo bowed. He was trembling. "What a pleasure."

Father Coseni looked around the room, his eyes fierce and darting, and his gaze finally rested on the remaining papers on the table. He pointed at the papers.

"We have told you about this, Signor Galilei?" he said.

Galileo's hands went up in an involuntary gesture of prayer.

"Father Coseni," he said. "These papers . . . they are nothing . . . they're an old man's whimsy . . . a harmless pastime. This is just—"

Father Coseni signaled his troops.

The soldiers walked across the room and dragged Galileo to a spot on the floor just beneath the central rafter. Without so much as a word of warning they forced a noose over his balding head, ripped his ruff collar away, and tightened the noose around his throat.

"Father Coseni, please, I beg you, the work I do is solely intended to—"

"The pope has ordered a direct decree against these . . ." Father Coseni gestured disparagingly at the diagrams and the writing. ". . . these black arts."

"But Father Coseni, even our friends here . . ." Galileo looked fearfully at the New Ones. "Even they concede that they come from beyond the stars. Even they—"

"And so they do," said Father Coseni. "But they know their place. They understand their secondary position to Man. And we now know that they are sent here by God, such as they have explained to us, come to help us understand His word and His law better."

Father Coseni nodded at his soldiers.

"Father Coseni, I beg you—"

The priest again held up his hand. "If you must speak, Signor Galilei, perhaps it should be in the form of prayer."

A soldier brought a chair to the middle of the room. The

New Ones whined among themselves. Two of the soldiers hoisted Galileo on top of the chair. Another threw the end of the rope up over the central rafter. The lieutenant secured it to the bed.

When the rope was taut, the lieutenant walked over to the chair and, without ceremony, kicked it out from under Galileo's feet, the same way he might kick a dog in the street. Galileo's body fell with a quick jerk. A feeble grunt came from the old man's mouth as the noose tightened around his throat.

The room dissolved around Felicitas . . .

She was back in the west annex now, in the upstairs room.

She took a moment, trying to calm herself, trying to accept and understand the brutal murder of Galileo Galilei. What did it mean? She had no idea. But she was sure Lungo Muso had taken her there for a reason.

She walked to the door and peered out the window.

Except for a few torches burning here and there, the west annex was dark. She couldn't see anybody standing guard anywhere. It was late. She thought that this might be a good time to try the latch again. She looked down at her hands and saw that they were still untied.

And she knew then, beyond all doubt, that Lungo Muso was real, that he had left this . . . this small gift, free hands, a chance, an opportunity to find her way out of here and help the others escape from the holding pen downstairs.

She tried the latch but it was still stuck. She looked around the room and spied an old stone, about the size of a head, sitting in the corner. She walked to the corner, lifted the stone, carried it back to the door, and poised it above the latch. The latch, a simple curved handle, looked old, as worn and corroded as the metal of the south tower. She lifted the rock and banged the latch. It broke right off. As it was continuous with the outside latch, she heard that latch fall off as well. The timber brace tumbled away. She lifted the broken inside latch, stuck it in the hole, and jimmied the internal bolt upward. She gripped the edge of the door and pulled. The door opened easily.

She crept out into the corridor.

She pressed her back to the wall, hiding in the shadows of a buttress. The reek of wood smoke hung in the air, and down below she saw that there were still a few open fires burning. She glanced at the room where the steps curved down to the main level, where she'd seen the dead eating earlier. The door was still open but the room was now dark; she couldn't see anybody eating in there anymore. She glanced the other way, where a series of switchback stairs led to upper levels. No one. She moved cautiously to the rail and looked down into the annex. Only a few people huddled around the fires down there, while others slept in wood shavings here and there, huddled three and four in a bunch to keep warm.

She stole back across the corridor, closed the door to Maritano's room, shoved the outside latch back in and propped the brace against the jamb, making it look as if she were still inside.

Then she forced herself to take step after step away from the room, shaking the images of Galileo's brutal murder from her mind, keeping her back to the wall.

She descended the steps . . . and just as quickly stopped.

In the annex below, Maritano emerged from a room behind the drainage pool, followed by Marco and Ottavio. They marched around the drainage pool and descended some steps into the main part of the annex. She darted down the remaining few stairs and ducked into the doorway of the eating room. Except for a few glowing coals in the fire, the room was dark. She crept behind the door and pushed it halfway shut. She peered down the steps to the first floor.

Maritano held something in his hand, and his stride was purposeful, ominous; as he passed one of the fires down there she saw the distinct nine-prong configuration of another counselor. She closed her eyes and her whole body weakened with fear. Another counselor, the end of her freedom, the end of her new and hopeful future on the outside. She opened her eyes. She had to act, had to think of a plan, knew that the longer she delayed the more likely her chances of failure.

Maritano crossed the large open space on the first floor. He was coming this way, and she understood her predicament clearly. He was coming to put this new counselor into her head. When he discovered she wasn't there, he would mount a search, and she would be discovered before she had a chance to free Rosario and the others.

She backed farther into the room. A log shifted in the fire. She swung around at the sound of it. The flames flickered to life and the room brightened.

She was so terrified by what she saw she could hardly move: ten of the dead sat on a wooden bench staring at her with half-closed eyes.

She thought they would pounce on her but they just sat there, staring, their fingers and faces greasy from whatever they'd been eating. They slouched on the bench, their chins resting forward on their chests. For several seconds she couldn't move. And then she realized that they were insensible. They may have had their eyes half open but they couldn't see her at all. They were like machines that had been shut off.

Aldo was there, the man who had promised her a book. He looked well fed now. More important, he had a *pistola* stuffed into the waistband of his prison uniform. She looked more closely. He was truly insensible, neither awake nor asleep, as if he had indeed been switched off like a machine. He couldn't see her, couldn't hear her, had no idea she was in the room; he sat there on the low wood bench breathing heavily, as if trapped in this stuporous state by too much eating. She glanced at the *pistola* in his belt again, and she knew she now had a chance.

She nimbly picked her way around the fire, turning off her fear as much as she could, shutting out the visions of Galileo's murder, concentrating solely on the movements of her body. She had to get that *pistola*.

She stopped when she was halfway to Aldo. Stopped because she saw the burned remains of Concetta's prison uniform on the floor, the uniform with the embroidered bird on the front, Concetta's symbol of freedom. She felt sick. She now understood why all these dead people looked so well fed.

She scooped the remains of Concetta's uniform off the floor, stuffed it into the waistband of her uniform, then strode to Aldo and pulled the *pistola* from his belt. She tried not to think of what might have happened to Concetta, resisted being trapped by her fear, or handicapped by horrific speculation. Aldo moaned but remained insensible as the waistband of his prison uniform snapped snugly back against his abdomen. She sensed the ticking of his implant inside his mind but she shut it out and moved with stealth toward the door.

Maritano was coming up the stairs with Marco and Ottavio, his face set, holding the counselor before him with a kind of reverence, as if its value were beyond measure. The three dead men walked right in front of her, curved left up the remaining few steps to the second level, and continued toward the braced door. This was her chance. Their backs were turned.

With quick quiet steps, she darted across the small mezzanine and descended the steps two at a time, her feet as light as air, to the main level.

On the main level, she ran as fast as she could across the annex floor, the *pistola* gripped tightly in her hand, her first and middle fingers awkwardly poised above the big trigger. As she neared the holding cell, she saw a dead man standing guard at the door.

She didn't give him a chance. She aimed her *pistola* and fired.

The blast of the *pistola* boomed through the large stone edifice and lit up all the shadows in a blinding flash. The guard crumpled to the floor in a smoking heap while the groups of sleeping dead huddled in various spots around the main level lifted their heads and looked in the direction of the holding pen.

The *superstiti* inside the holding cell jumped to their feet.

Rosario ran to the bars.

"The lock!" he cried.

"Stand back!" she said.

She fired at the door. A huge chunk of metal popped out of the lock's casing and clanked to the floor, glowing red hot for a moment before it quickly dulled to gray while it hissed on the damp floor. She lifted her leg and kicked the door open.

She heard shouting from the second-floor gallery, Maritano's voice, irate, vengeful, frustrated. He had been alerted by the *pistola* fire. And he was coming after her.

"Felicitas!" he cried, stretching out each syllable.

His voice was like a howl, unearthly, as if someone had just stabbed him through the stomach with a shiv, full of violent emotion. The voice seemed to physically claw at Felicitas. She struggled to summon her wits.

"Let's get out of here," she said.

The *superstiti* filed out the holding-cell door. Rosario leaned over the dead guard and pulled the *pistola* from his belt.

Maritano whined shrilly again. "Felicitas!" Like the whine of an injured dog. "You can't leave! You don't know what you're doing!"

The *superstiti* ran for the drainage pool. She stuffed her *pistola* into her belt, dove into the water, and breast-stroked across the pool. She glanced back; her fellow *superstiti* were right behind her. Through the darkness she saw the dead running toward them down the stairs, not lurching or shambling, but running in a quick and organized column, as if the implants had given them not only a greater eloquence with their tongues but a keener agility with their bodies.

Maritano pointed. "Get them!" he shouted.

A few *pistola* shots flamed over their heads, and a *pistola* round splashed into the pool right next to her.

"They're coming!" she cried.

"Everybody under!" cried Rosario.

They all dove.

She found her way to the culvert easily. She came up for one last breath of air, was about to dive again, but then somebody jumped into the drainage pool from the small platform above and grabbed her by the collar. She was hoisted above the surface and yanked toward the edge. She whirled around and saw a man with a hook nose, a bulbous chin, and the usual off-kilter eyes looking down at her.

His arms were thick, hairy, muscular, and he had a peculiar sour smell she found terrifying. She tried to pull away. But his grip, like Anteo's grip, was unbreakable. He let go of her collar and grabbed her by the hair. She reached for her *pistola* but the man knocked it out of her hand and it sank beneath the water.

"Help!" she called.

Rosario fired at the oncoming dead with his *pistola*. Silvio and Francesco were trying to find the culvert. Gasparo came to her aid.

The giant lunged through the water toward her.

He pounded the man's arm with a sledgehammer stroke of his large fist, breaking the man's grip instantly, then lifted the man bodily out of the water, high over his head, and threw him against the stone edge of the platform. The man winced in agony and fell face down into the water, unconscious. He floated there for a few seconds, then sank.

Felicitas turned to Gasparo.

"*Grazie, signore,*" she said. "You're a true friend."

"Let's dive, *bella,*" said the big man. "They're coming." The big man waved to Silvio and Francesco. "Come on, you two!" he called. "The culvert's over here.

Francesco and Silvio waded over. Felicitas and Gasparo dove.

She kicked and stroked with all her strength, feeling her way through the culvert. The water was cold, filled with unseen clumps of pond scum, and the sides of the culvert were thick with slime. She tasted algae in her mouth. She kicked and stroked, hoping everybody else was right behind her, that they would all make it, and that Rosario in particular would have the good sense to stop fighting and make his escape.

A minute later she emerged into the west cell block's drainage pool.

She broke the surface, saw lamps all around. Piero stood at the railing looking down at her. She felt weak with joy to see that he was still alive after the horrendous battle of yesterday.

She called up to Piero. "They're coming!" Gasparo and Francesco broke the surface. "The dead are coming!"

Silvio broke the surface behind her, then Francesco, then Rosario.

Piero swung round to his band of *superstiti*.

"Draw your weapons!" he cried.

The *superstiti* drew their weapons and took up positions.

Felicitas helped Silvio up the steps. The old man, out of breath from the swim, seemed oblivious to what was going on. Gasparo clutched the railing, pulled himself up and over, grabbed an extra *pistola*, and took up his own position. Rosario and Francesco did the same.

Moments later the first dead appeared.

The *superstiti* fired at will.

Every time the dead surfaced, they were gunned down.

Felicitas hated it. But she also understood the need for it. There could be no more delays. They had to get out of the prison. Their food was nearly gone. The *soldati* would be here in a few days. They couldn't have the dead standing in their way any longer.

The dead toppled into the water, pitched and tossed by the *pistola* fire as if they weighed next to nothing, their wet uniforms sizzling with each strike, the smell of burning flesh filling the air.

And when it was over, their corpses crowded the drainage pool, and the water was red with their blood. Felicitas tried to pick out Maritano's body but she couldn't see it anywhere.

Rosario turned to Piero.

"How did you know?" asked Rosario. "How did you know to wait for us here?"

Piero contemplated Rosario. "Your wife has more ingenuity than we give her credit for." She knew he used the word *wife* loosely, as a term of affection, not as one of consecration. In the prison, there were no consecrations. Piero grinned at Felicitas, reached in his pocket, and pulled out the *uominilupi* finger bowl. "She left this on that ledge over there. We knew you had to be around here somewhere. So we just waited."

17

Felicitas, Rosario, and Piero sat
around a small fire when they got back to the dispensary. Gasparo and Francesco were comforting Silvio. Everyone understood what the half-burned uniform meant; and because Silvio and Concetta had been together for nearly thirty years, the old man needed a great deal of comforting.

"I think we have to assume that Nazzareno and the others are dead," said Piero.

Felicitas recapped for Piero her conversation with Maritano and told him about her new encounter with Lungo Muso: Galileo's hanging.

"He could talk this time," she said. "I could understand him."

"That's just your dreamphone amnesia lifting," said Piero. "I'm sure you could always understand him. You're just remembering how, that's all." He rubbed his hands together, holding them close to the fire; the nights had become cold. "I think Lungo Muso's trying to tell you something."

"Yes, but he's showing me in bits and pieces, and none of it makes any sense. I wish he'd explain about the big white building."

"Maybe bits and pieces is the only way he *can* show you," suggested Rosario.

"This Galileo," said Piero. He looked at Rosario. "Why's that name familiar to me?"

"He wrote a book," said Rosario. "On astronomy. I have it in my workshop."

"And what about Machiavelli?"

"He was a diplomat from a long time ago on Earth," said Rosario.

"And who's this Reymont?"

Rosario shook his head. "I have no idea."

"And the river of time?"

"I have no idea about that either," said Rosario. His eyes narrowed. "Though there's that line in the *uominilupi* script in the south tower, the part about the river that never forgets. Maybe that has something to do with it."

Piero brooded as he gazed into the fire. "I guess it really doesn't matter," he finally said. "I'm more concerned about the *soldati*." He looked at Felicitas. "Maritano said they were really going to be here in a few days?"

"Yes," she said.

"Then we're going to have to make our escape as quickly as possible," he said. "I want to be long gone by the time they get here."

After the cold night, Felicitas was glad to get moving again. The rain had cleared and *Stella Grossa* and *Stella Piccola* shone weakly over the south parapet. She had a bite of one of the remaining food-bricks, washed it down with a cup of water, and climbed the lattice.

She tried to forget Concetta and the others—there was nothing she could do about them now. She glanced at Silvio. The old man had been up all night staring into the fire. Gasparo still sat beside him, handed him a bit of food-brick, but he refused.

Gasparo glanced her way, his eyes concerned, then came over.

"He's got to eat," said the big man. "He's going to need his strength."

Felicitas stared at Silvio. She took the remainder of the food-brick from Gasparo. "I'll make him some soup with this later," she said. "Right now, I think we better leave him be."

Gasparo nodded. "I'll keep an eye on him," he said.

"So will I," she said.

She left the barricade and climbed the lattice.

At the top, she approached Piero and Rosario, who were helping reconstruct the crane.

"What do you want me to do?" she asked.

Piero stood up, arched his back, and looked around. Finally he pointed.

"You can sort those scraps of cloth and tie them into bundles," he said.

She did as he asked, though much of this work had already been done by Concetta.

After sorting a while, she stood up, rubbed her hands together to keep them warm, and stared out at the land. She heard the lapping of water from behind the south wall.

She glanced at the nearest *sentinella.* It stood next to the southeast guard tower, ten feet tall, with one big eye on a ball-like head, and a complicated series of crud-coated sprockets meshed into the chain-drive below. She looked particularly at its *cannone.* As always, she was drawn to the glyphs.

She walked over and had a closer look. Gasparo was right: There was no obvious trigger mechanism.

She looked at the glyphs on the weapon's casing, saw faces, figures, trees, birds, stars, moons, lines, strokes, curves, gashes, and dots. She read. This was a certain weapon serving a certain purpose with a certain power and range, had been installed under the patronage of a certain father-leader belonging to a certain pack, and had been blessed by a certain priest.

Then a particular glyph caught her eye, three curves followed by an arrow: an action glyph. She ran her finger over the glyph and a small compartment opened, revealing switches underneath.

Her eyes narrowed, and she turned around and glanced at the other *superstiti*. Why had this never been discovered before? She turned back and flipped a few of the switches.

The weapon whirred, operating on a surge of unexpected power, swung around, and aimed midway up the west wall. Felicitas jumped back.

A thunderous blast came from the *cannone* and a huge fireball flew over the parapet and slammed into the west wall. Stone exploded into the air and rained down on the dispensary like hail. Smoke rose from the west wall, propelled upward by the concussion of the blast.

When the smoke cleared, she saw a big hole in the west wall three times the size of any of the windows, yet not all the way through, as if the *cannone*, though powerful, wasn't yet strong enough to blast through the thick stone wall.

Piero and Rosario hurried over from the half-built crane.

Piero looked at her, his eyes bright with excitement, then studied the west wall. Dust from the blast settled over the yard, the heavy particulate sinking fast while the smaller and finer powder hung like a gray pall in the prison yard. Other *superstiti* gathered at the parapet to look. Piero examined the *cannone*, more particularly the panel of switches, touching them experimentally with his fingers, his eyes narrowing in concentration.

"What did you do?" he asked. "How did you find this?"

"I just touched these glyphs," she said.

Rosario said, "I've gone over every single *cannone*. I've never found anything like this."

"How did you get it to fire?" asked Piero.

"I flipped these two switches," she said.

Piero inspected the switches again, then tried them himself. Nothing happened. The *cannone* remained dead to his touch.

"You try it," he said to Rosario.

Rosario tried. Nothing.

"Was there a special way you did it?" asked Rosario.

"No," she said.

The two men looked at each other. Then Piero turned to her.

"Why don't you try it again for us?" he said.

She shrugged. She flipped the switches. The *cannone* whirred, just as it had before, swung marginally to the right, and fired.

A huge ball of flame roared across the yard and exploded above the west gate.

The two men stared at her.

"Why does it work for you and nobody else?" mused Piero.

Felicitas and Francesco, the man who guarded the books in the east cellblock, went down to the generating room a little while later.

Everyone was taking a last look around. Rosario and a team of six *superstiti* checked the east cellblock while Gasparo had a team in the north block. Piero continued to supervise on the east catwalk.

As Felicitas and Francesco descended the stairs to the generating room she again got a faint whiff of machine oil.

"I've only been down here twice," said Francesco.

"Are you really Gasparo's brother?" asked Felicitas.

"I don't like it down here," said Francesco. "It's so damp. I'm a bit like Adriana that way. I hate the damp. I'm sorry about Adriana, Felicitas."

He put his hand on her shoulder. Not that his sympathy was unwelcome, she just felt uncomfortable with his hand there. She got the sense he was trying to make it mean more than it really should.

"You and Gasparo are so tall," she said, moving quickly ahead into the generating room.

He let his hand drop away.

"Well . . . I suppose . . ." he said. "But I'm more like a stick. Do you like tall men, Felicitas?"

She wasn't sure how to answer. Finally she just said, "Height isn't a factor."

"No," he said, as if he were happy about this. "And it shouldn't be. There's a book up in the library." He called the holding pen full of books up in the east cellblock the library. "It's about earth insects. Do you know what insects are?"

"Yes."

"There's a picture of a long thin insect," he said. "A praying mantis, they call it. I often think of myself as looking like a praying mantis. I even like the name."

Was it particularly flattering to compare oneself to an insect? Felicitas thought it might be a good idea to change the subject.

"Would you mind standing guard over here?" she said, pointing to the foot of the stairs. "And give me your lamp. I'm going to need two."

"You want me to stand in the dark over there by myself?"

"In case the dead come."

"Of course, Felicitas," he said. "I'll do whatever you say."

She stared at him as he strode away and finally shrugged.

She went to investigate the generating room mural one last time.

She looked at the pinwheels—the glyph representing the *carcerieri*—and now saw that a series of linking cuneiforms connected the *carcerieri* directly to the glyph of the beetle and the figure eights: the implants. Were there enough implants for every single prisoner? That's one of the things she wanted to find out. She looked more closely. There didn't seem to be any indication of number. So she followed the series of linking cuneiforms to the next glyph: the dashes, triangles, and crossed *fucili* of the *soldati*. This glyph was double-linked: to the *carcerieri* on one side, and to the hourglass and sunburst glyph of the *sentinelle* on the other. She now noticed something new about the *soldati* glyph: a series of keylike markings connected it to what was obviously a representation of *Stella Piccola* and *Stella Grossa*. The *soldati* were close to the twin suns? In orbit? She wasn't sure what the word meant, but she knew she had seen it somewhere before, in one of the English books, and that Lungo Muso had once explained it to her.

"You and Rosario," said Francesco. His voice drifted out of the darkness like a small weak bird. "You're rather fond of him, aren't you?"

She glanced toward Francesco, annoyed that her concentration had been broken.

"We're husband and wife," she said.

"Oh," he said. "Oh . . . well . . ." He sounded thoroughly dejected. "I didn't know," he said. "I had no idea."

"There's nothing here that says when the *soldati* will arrive," she said. "But they're not that far away."

Francesco didn't respond.

Felicitas looked at the glyph of the big white building. Despite the damp coolness in the generating room she felt suddenly warm. The white building stood alone, with no key-forms or cuneiforms connecting it to any of the other systems. It dominated.

"Congratulations," said Francesco.

Felicitas turned to him. "What?"

"Congratulations," he repeated.

"For what?"

"You and Rosario," he said. "I didn't know you were husband and wife."

She got up. She wasn't going to learn anything else from the mural.

"I won't keep you down here in the damp any longer, Francesco," she said. "Let's go back upstairs."

*   *   *

Up on the parapet she found Rosario giving books to the children. She watched him from beside the water cistern.

He knelt beside each child, a gentle smile on his face. He said a few words about each book. A book was something light and easy for a child to carry.

Once he had given the book to the child, the child would run off, face grave but joyous, and stow the book into his or her bag.

When Rosario was done distributing the books, he walked to the inside parapet and gazed down at the yard. He was good with children. He was still smiling. He enjoyed children. Yet now his smile faded. He grew pensive, melancholy. She couldn't stand to see him this way.

She walked over. He glanced at her, gave her a nod, tried to smile again, but his smile wouldn't stay.

She slid her arm around his back.

"Are you sad about something?" she asked.

He looked beyond the south parapet to the lake. A steady wind blew from the west, churning the water into small gray waves. The sky was patchy with thick clouds, but here and there the light of the twin suns shot through, etching beams through the air, glittering on scraps of lake.

"I'm not sad," he said, with some resignation. He put his arm around her shoulder and kissed her forehead. "I have no reason to be sad." He looked into the yard. "But this prison, it was . . . this was our home, wasn't it? And as hard as things were . . . well, everything hasn't been entirely bad. I fell in love with you here. I came to understand a great deal about myself here. My parents died here. There's a lot that happened to all of us here, and it's worth thinking about."

Felicitas stared at the yard: the familiar drab walls with the vacant dark windows; the archways leading to the cell blocks; the *sentinelle* with their big spherical heads and massive *cannoni*. These were the things she had seen every day of her life. She knew Rosario was right. This was home. She felt some of his melancholy. She pulled him nearer.

"We'll find a better home, Rosario," she said. "This place . . . it isn't safe anymore. We'll find a much brighter home . . . out there." She gestured toward the distant chain of mountains in the east. "Now that we have each other, things will just keep getting better, no matter where we are."

Even at high noon, when the suns were at their strongest, it was still cool on the catwalks, and there was really no place to escape the wind.

Gasparo and Francesco worked the crane, hauling up a bundle of tents, while Felicitas leaned over the parapet and watched. She was cold, didn't know when she would ever be warm again, but that didn't matter, not when freedom was just hours away. A group of children played tag among the stacks of extra clothing. Clouds moved in, obscuring the feeble light of the twin suns. The mountains far to the east were shrouded in mist and it looked as if a snowstorm whirled around the top of the tallest one, circling it with a flossy halo of ice.

The chain creaked as the tents spun upward. Two young women steadied the tents as they came up over the wall, guided them to a spot next to the cistern, then untied them and carried them to the outside parapet. Gasparo and Francesco moved the crane into position over the lattice. They were ready to haul the last load—the lattice itself.

Piero climbed on top of a crate. He raised his hands to get everyone's attention, his face windburnt and rosy, his eyes glittering with excitement, his chin held high as he composed his lips into a benevolent and optimistic smile.

"My brothers and sisters," he called.

Superstiti gathered around. Rosario looked up at Piero, a grin on his face. Felicitas left the parapet and stood beside Rosario, slipping her arm around his waist, pulling herself close. He kissed her on the cheek.

"I guess this is it," he said to her.

She glanced up at Rosario. Her husband's previous sense of

melancholy was now gone. She pressed her cheek against his shoulder.

Piero began.

"Today we venture into this new world," he said, pointing to the woods beyond the prison, "a world we know little about. The balloon reconnaissance showed trees, snow, rock, and a carcass. We also saw three boats on the bank of a river. We know there are people out there. You've all seen the mural up in the south wall. We think these people are hunters. We think they fish. Who knows if we can find them? We can only try." He lifted his arms, as if he were trying to convey to everybody just how big and unknown the outside really was. "Farther along, we may find towns or cities. Then again, we may find nothing at all. What's important is that we have this chance."

Gasparo and Francesco cinched the top rung of the lattice in several different spots, using sturdy ropes, and walked back to the crank handles.

"What's important," continued Piero, "is that we have an opportunity to survive, not as dreamphoned prisoners of the *uominilupi* but as a free people." He lifted his hands. "But being free doesn't mean we get to do whatever we want. Don't think only of yourselves. Think of everybody else. Never forget the importance of the group, how each and every one of us must work for the group as a whole." He looked across the yard to the west wall. "And let's not forget those who have already lost their lives for the sake of the group. Keep them in your memory always."

But even as he spoke, the whining of the dead erupted out in the yard.

Rosario lifted his chin and peered over the parapet.

"It's them," he said. "I knew they would try something."

The dead hurried across the snow-covered dirt, an unruly mob of two hundred or more, their whining echoing from wall to wall, most of them thin, so undernourished they looked too frail to run. When they were halfway across, Felicitas again sensed the whispering and ticking of their implants.

Rosario took her by the hand and led her to a rack of *pistole.* "Take one," he said.

She nodded. "I hate this."

"We all do," he said. "But it's necessary."

They hurried to the inside parapet.

The dead passed the clock tower, then the dispensary, their uniforms hanging in great loose folds around their bony frames, their faces pale. Felicitas saw Maritano near the back, the skull still tied to his head. She aimed, automatically spurred by her loathing, and fired.

The weapon was unwieldy in her hand, the trigger so big she could hardly manage it, a trigger designed for *carceriere* hands, and the *pistola* jerked each time she fired. She kept missing Maritano.

The dead swarmed over the barricade and charged the lattice.

"Are they going to climb it?" asked Rosario over the din.

She saw no point in wasting fire on Maritano. He was too far away.

"I don't know," she said.

So she fired on those directly below her. She had to close her eyes. She didn't want to see who she was killing. After a few seconds she forced her eyes open.

"They used to be my friends," she said to Rosario.

"They have those things in their heads now," said Rosario. "Killing them is a kindness.

Piero ran to the parapet, armed with two *pistole,* and blasted away, his eyes frantic, his shoulders rising up and down like pistons with each recoil.

"Secure the ropes!" he cried. "They're going to pull it down!"

The dead had no intention of climbing the lattice. They just wanted to destroy it.

"We're going to be stuck up here?" said Felicitas.

Dozens of dead crowded the lattice, compelled to this work by their implants, their movements unnatural, as if their limbs were being moved by puppet strings. They moved not so much as human beings but as corpses brought to life. The lattice shook, making it difficult for Gasparo and Francesco to secure the ropes. Felicitas fired again, but she fired without any expertise or intent, simply fired because she knew she had to. She didn't like killing people. Each time she fired, she felt horrible. Yet she continued—she knew the alternative was to end up like Concetta.

As quickly as the dead were killed by *pistola* fire, others came to replace them.

"There's too many!" cried Piero.

The lattice lurched away but didn't have enough momentum, and banged back into the wall. Felicitas was sure the lattice would break, especially because it had been ripped free from its underlying support and scaffolding. But it stayed in one piece.

Below, the dead looped ropes around the lattice. Several *superstiti* grabbed its top in an effort to keep it tight to the wall, but it lurched away again, breaking free of their grasp. The strain made the metal creak.

"It's going to go!" cried Rosario.

The lattice swung upward, away from the wall, bending this way and that, as if it were made of rubber, not steel, slowed as it reached the vertical, looked as if it might come crashing back to the wall, but then . . .

Then the lattice fell the other way into the yard, two tons of metal, like a giant tree made of *carcerieri* bones.

"Nooooo . . ." cried Piero.

The dead fled from its path. The *superstiti* watched in horror.

The lattice, stretching nearly to the west wall, hit the ground with a resounding clang.

And broke into hundreds of pieces.

18

The yard below was quiet.

All the dead had returned to the west wall. The *superstiti* had lit a number of fires up on the catwalk and had erected a few tents. A light rain polished the stonework. Night was nearly here, and it promised to be a cold one.

"We have one chance," said Piero. Felicitas sat next to Silvio as they listened to Piero, had her arm around the old man, was trying to soothe Silvio. "We'll lower everything by crane."

Rosario raised his eyebrows. "People included?"

"People included."

"But that could take days," said Gasparo.

"If we start now, it won't take more than two."

"But the *soldati* could be here in two days," said Felicitas.

Piero turned to Felicitas. "We'll just have to hope they aren't." He turned back to Rosario. "We'll go in shifts, four to a team."

"There's still one difficulty," said Rosario. "How's the last man going to get down? Who's going to lower *him*?"

"I'll be the last man," said Piero. "I'll put the chain against the wall and climb down."

"No," said Rosario. "You should be one of the first to go. Everything's new out there. People are going to be nervous. They're going to think of the *mostri*. You should be down there with them, just to give them confidence. I'll be the last man down." He put his hand on Piero's shoulder. "You're not getting any younger, Piero." His grin broadened as he gently teased Piero. "I'll go. I'll be less likely to hurt myself."

Felicitas woke up early. She looked out the tent flap, saw the rain clouds moving west, leaving the diaphanous light of *Stella Grossa* and *Stella Piccola* glowing in the clear morning sky. Piero sat by the fire. After a night of rain and thunder, the quiet unsettled her. Rosario lay asleep beside her. Only the sound of the crane broke the stillness, the crane going constantly all night, lowering supplies and people, the crank handles creaking and creaking in a low dirge of desperation. She pulled on her uniform and went outside.

Now, over the creaking of the crane, she heard another sound, not unlike thunder, echoing through the red mist from a great distance.

Piero lifted his head, his eyes intent as he stared toward the source of the sound, and the workers stopped turning the crank handles on the crane.

The rumble rolled over the hills across the lake, where the last shreds of night clung to the sky, a hiss with the deeper tones of a growl, a sound she remembered from her childhood. Piero got up and walked to the inside parapet. Far in the distance, Felicitas saw a teardrop of white light flickering like a candle; she couldn't understand why the *soldati* had landed all the way over there, behind some hills on the horizon. They should have descended into the landing pit outside the prison.

She walked to the inside parapet and joined Piero.

"The *soldati*?" she asked.

"They must be," said Piero, stroking his beard.

They stared toward the southwest, watching the afterglow shrink behind the hills.

"Why would they land all the way over there?" asked Felicitas.

Piero shook his head vaguely. "A miscalculation?" he suggested.

"How long will it take them to get here?" asked Felicitas.

"A day," said Piero. "Maybe less."

"Can we finish everything?" asked Felicitas.

Piero turned around and stared at the pile of supplies, then faced southwest again, where the last of the ship's afterglow faded from the sky.

"We'll have to," he said.

By late afternoon, with the shadows thick in the trees, Felicitas sat in the harness, ready to be lowered. She gave Rosario a kiss, then nodded at the two men operating the crane.

The men turned the crank handles, lifted her into the air, then swung her over the parapet.

Piero would be next; he had guards posted on the roofs of the southeast and southwest guard towers, watching for the *soldati*, ready to bang chamber pots should they see anything. The west wall was silent. No sign of the dead.

With a creak, she descended the wall.

The outside wall, badly weathered, more so than the inside stone, had been cracked and broken, the edges of various fractures polished smooth by the wind. A few saplings clung to larger dirt-filled crevices, their leaves now gone, the first victims of winter. As the chain spun gently away from the wall, she saw two dozen *superstiti* staring up at her. Others sorted supplies into six different piles at the edge of the wood. A group of children played hide-and-seek among the trees, exuberant in their new freedom.

They were half finished. They might make it after all.

As she reached the ground, Gasparo came forward and steadied the harness, halting its spin.

"That wasn't so bad, was it?" he said.

"No," she said. She looked around the woods, feeling as if she had stepped into a dream. "It's so big out here."

Gasparo smiled. "A lot of room," he agreed.

"And smell the air," she said. "Have you ever smelled air so fresh?"

He helped her out of the harness. "Who's coming next?" he asked.

"Piero."

"So he's finally leaving the old brick pile, is he?" said the big man. "I think he's going to miss it."

Gasparo let the harness go and it made a quick ascent.

Felicitas looked around, trying to get used to the actuality of her freedom, reached down, picked up a few brown shoots of grass, and nibbled experimentally. They tasted bland and she spit them out. She peered into the trees, then out to the lake, then finally to the hills beyond. A barren and bereft land. Would they find any food before the cruelest of the winter months struck? And where were the river people in all this bush and rock?

Up above, she heard the crane creaking. Rosario helped Piero into the harness. The two men working the crane lifted Piero and swung him out over the wall. A great smile came to his face, as if he were enjoying the ride. He dangled in the harness, came down slowly, and as he got closer she felt that everything would be all right, that with a man as resourceful as Piero, whose confidence never faltered and who always knew what to do, they would survive.

He was halfway down when up on the guard towers the alarms sounded. The *soldati* had been spotted, and were approaching through the forest toward the prison.

"Run!" cried Rosario from the top of the wall. "Hide! They're coming!"

The crane rattled, and Piero all but plummeted to the ground, slowing just as he reached bottom, his eyes wide with sudden fear.

Felicitas stared up at Rosario, feeling as if she had suddenly become detached from everything. A great panic that was both a desolation and a fear rose in her chest. Rosario was still up there. Piero tumbled into the grass, the harness still attached. She stared at Rosario with a kind of dumb wonder as she listened to the lookouts striking their chamber pots, half believing that there had to be a mistake, that what the guards actually saw was perhaps a beast or a large species of bird. Yet the tinny rhythm was insistent, a dire tattoo of danger and alarm. How could this happen, just when salvation had been within their grasp?

Piero ran to her and gave her a good shake, trying to rouse her.

"We have to hurry," he said.

"But Rosario's still up there," she said.

"We're going to get caught if we don't hurry," he insisted.

Rosario shouted down the wall as the guards continued to bang their pots. "Go with him, Felicitas!" he called. "Don't wait for me. Go on, get out of here!"

She continued to stare at Rosario, her eyes filling with tears, then took a confused look around. Women hurried with children into the woods, and the men, as prearranged, made off with the supplies, heading east toward a distant hill on the other side of a small valley. Piero pulled her by the arm and she stumbled over the grass away from the prison.

"Easy, Felicitas," he said. "One foot after the other. You're free now."

"Yes, but Rosario's still up there. I can't leave him."

"There's nothing you can do for him now."

An explosion came from the other side of the prison. And

she knew it couldn't be a beast or bird. She knew it had to be the
soldati.

She allowed Piero to lead her away.

"Run!" cried Rosario. "They've blown open the west gate.
Get away while you still have a chance!"

Piero yanked her, and they ran into the woods.

A *soldato* came around the corner of the prison, gray and
well armored, a machine twice the size of a *carceriere,* armed
with a *fucile,* bounding with thick, triple-jointed legs over the
grass, its rectangular feet throwing up chunks of half-frozen
mud. Broad-shouldered and broad-chested, the *soldato* thun-
dered to a stop at the top of the hill, scanned the retreating *superstiti* with glowing white eyes, took aim, and fired. The
charge, a small blue fireball, flew over their heads and burst
among the trees, setting several alight. Felicitas and Piero rolled
to the ground and took cover behind a small hummock. The
soldato was old, just like the *carcerieri,* covered with grease and
dust, and looked as if it had been sitting in the deployment bay
of an assault craft for a hundred years. The *soldato* took aim
again, but something went wrong and it brought its *fucile*
straight up, turned around three times in a lumbering pirouette,
swung its weapon all the way down, and fired into the ground
at its feet, blasting a sizable hole into the mud. But then it
swung its weapon up in the proper direction and fired again.
And just as the huge blue ball of flame blasted away a tree, five
more *soldati* appeared around the north wall, and together, all
six pursued the *superstiti,* shooting at will, more intent on
killing the escapees than recapturing them.

19

Felicitas woke early the next morning in the branch of a tree, feeling sore, as if she'd slept with her limbs bent out of shape. Even before she opened her eyes, worry and sorrow took their place beside her fear, and she knew she had lost Rosario. Yet at the same time she couldn't admit to the hopelessness of the situation. She didn't want to open her eyes. Images of last night's rout flashed through her mind, of men, women, and children running blindly through the dark forest pursued by the colossal *soldati;* the constant flash of *fucile* fire; the smoke, noise and confusion. She couldn't understand it. The *soldati* behaved erratically. Some prisoners they killed, others they captured, and still others they let go completely.

She opened her eyes and saw the devastation.

Where were they? Somewhere far east of the prison, on the slope of a lightly treed hill. Twenty-five dead and wounded lay on the ground. Her eyes clouded with tears. Who gave the *sol-*

dati the order to kill? Was death their intent, or like so many of the *uominilupi*'s other machines, had the *soldati* become dangerously inconsistent because of their decrepitude?

Piero knelt over one of the *soldati,* the only one destroyed last night, trying to pry the chest plate from its console. Felicitas sat up and shivered in the cold wind. She sat there for several minutes, working through her fear, resolving that sometime, somehow, she would go back to the prison; she and Rosario would be together again.

She picked her way along the branch to the trunk. A woman crouched nearby, weeping over a dead child. Everywhere, there came the sound of moaning. She climbed halfway down the trunk, then jumped the rest of the way. She still didn't understand it. Why the wild pursuit, why all the killing, and why the sudden retreat, especially when the *soldati* were impervious to *pistola* fire? The only one disabled had been tripped in a large snare, and battered with rocks. Was their programming really so unpredictable, or was it just badly deteriorated? Maybe the electrostatic charge of the *pistola* barrage had in some way altered or damaged their programming.

She walked to Piero and put her hand on his shoulder. He hardly noticed, continued to pry at the chest plate. What did he expect to find in there? Certainly nothing that could bring all these dead back to life. In a sudden fit of anger he pounded the chest plate with his fist.

"It won't budge," he said. "Help me up. My legs are sore and this cold has made them stiff."

Felicitas helped Piero to his feet. He looked around at the killing ground with bleary eyes, like a man who has lost his confidence, his shoulders stooped, his hair disheveled, and the bones showing through on his face.

"What are we going to do?" she asked.

His eyes settled on the woman weeping over her dead child. Then he looked up at the sky. It was clouding over and it looked as if it might snow.

"I wish this weather would clear," he said.

Now wasn't the time to ask about Rosario, or whether they might go back to the prison to get him.

"Are you all right?" she asked. The rims of his eyes looked red. "You look a little . . ."

He turned to her. She saw that he was exhausted, that he was suffering from battle fatigue.

"You don't know how hard I've fought for this," he said. "I was convinced, absolutely convinced, that I could beat the *uominilupi*. You can't imagine what great joy I took in watching their machines fall apart one by one. I believed if I could only last long enough, the prison would crumble around me, and I would be free."

He picked up a rock and banged the chest plate of the dead *soldato*.

"We'll have to find shelter," said Felicitas. He stopped pounding and stared at her. "Those clouds look threatening." That was better. One step at a time, never more than a single step. "Everybody's cold." With each step, she would defeat the doom she felt. "And the supplies have been scattered. Everybody's waiting for you to say something. You should get up and say something."

He looked away, disheartened, and struggled to his feet.

"I'm sorry about Rosario," he said. "I know how you must feel."

He walked away, climbed a nearby boulder, and raised his hands to get the people's attention.

Felicitas turned and stared into the misty trees while the *superstiti* gathered around Piero. He was sorry about Rosario? What did he mean by that? In deciding life and death, Piero might have had the ultimate say on the food-bricks. But he wouldn't have the ultimate say on Rosario. She turned around and gazed at Piero. The wind tossed his hair.

She was free, but without Rosario, she was miserable in her freedom.

*   *   *

They moved east, away from the prison over the next three days.

The sky remained overcast. The land grew hilly. At times, the soil was thin, rocky, could support no more than a few stunted trees. They crossed several brooks, so were never without water. Food was another problem. The forests and dales seemed so silent that at times Felicitas thought they must be devoid of wildlife. Then they would see something lumber through the bushes, and they would chase after it, but none of them were expert hunters and the beast would inevitably get away. Or a flock of strange birds would fly overhead and they would shoot at them. But the birds were often too far away, and even if they managed to kill one they could never find it in the bush afterward.

They tested all sorts of plants, roots, and tubers but all of them turned out be inedible. So they had to rely solely on foodbricks, and these were running out fast. They weren't going to last more than another few days.

Sometimes Felicitas helped the children along. The youngest, a girl of five, Giovanna, was a small child with a pale complexion, dark serious eyes, and an unruly head of curly black hair. Not that Giovanna needed help—she was an energetic little girl—but because she had no mother Felicitas often carried her for a hundred yards at time, about as far as anyone could carry a five-year-old, simply because the child needed comfort, and was afraid of this big open world.

More often than not, Felicitas helped Silvio. The old man found the uneven ground hard on his ankles and knees, and he often took Felicitas's arm for support.

"I miss the south bath," he said. "You don't know how good that water sometimes felt, Felicitas. But this . . ." He looked around at the sparsely treed hilltop. ". . . this is different. It's hard on my legs, but I find it interesting. I forget about my legs.

Look at those hills over there. That outcropping of rock. It looks like a face."

Felicitas gazed at the rock in question. Slabs of gray rock—the same rock that the prison was made from—formed themselves into a heavy brow, a square nose, and a blocklike chin. Some trees grew on top. The trees looked like hair.

"You seem . . . better," said Felicitas.

She was thinking about Concetta.

The old man's lip drooped a bit, but then he looked up at Felicitas, and his eyes were no longer so preoccupied, as they'd been for the last few days.

"I miss Concetta," he said. "I'm still going to cry for her. But she was a sensible woman, Felicitas. She never let me mope. I broke my arm a few years ago, and the *carcerieri* fixed it, but it hurt a lot while it was healing. After a while, it didn't hurt so much. But I still complained about it. I'd grown into a habit of complaining. Even when it was completely healed, I complained about it. Concetta broke me of that habit." He glanced far ahead, to where Piero was walking with Francesco. "Complaining's no good for you. Neither's self-pity. No, I won't pity myself. Concetta wouldn't want me to. I won't say that I haven't been mourning her for the last couple of days. I wouldn't be human if I didn't. I've been mourning her all the time. I still am. But I know she'd want me to take an interest in all this." He looked around at the land. "So that's what I'm doing." He looked up at Felicitas and smiled. "She didn't teach just you young ones, you know," he said. "She taught a lot of us older ones as well."

Felicitas's hunger gnawed at her constantly. By the third day she felt so weak she wondered if she would be able to find the strength to search for food. She was beginning to think Maritano was right, that they were all going to starve to death out here. She thought of the prison and wondered if the *soldati* had brought more food-bricks.

She paired herself with Gasparo. As they foraged away from

the main group toward a series of low-lying hills in the distance, she glanced up at the big man. She wanted him to reassure her somehow. He carried his pack on his back, in case they should find anything they might be able to eat. He looked down at her, tried to smile, managed to lift the corners of his lips for a moment or two, but the smile crumbled, and she saw the dull glitter of desperation in his eyes.

"Are you all right?" she asked.

He took a deep breath, sighing. "All these brooks we keep crossing," he said. "They must empty somewhere. Piero thinks they empty into the river. He thinks the river is that way." Gasparo pointed to the northeast. "We're slowly heading in that direction. Maybe we'll find the river people."

"I'm hungry," she said. "I feel dizzy."

"I remember reading a book," said Gasparo. "It must have been a couple hundred years old, all yellow and falling to pieces. It was called *The Gentleman Angler.* It was about fishing. You get a pole with a line on it. On the end of the line there's a barbed hook, and you put some bait on this hook and cast the line into the river. You catch fish that way." She nodded. She seemed to remember this technique from somewhere. "I must have read that book fifteen or twenty years ago, when I was still dead, but I've never forgotten it. Then you see the picture up in the south wall, of the river people using nets to catch fish. That's all I want to do, Felicitas. Catch fish. I picture myself on the banks of this river with a fishing pole. Once we get there we'll be fine. I'll catch all the fish we need. These brooks are getting wider. I think we're going to be there soon."

But she could tell he was forcing himself to be optimistic.

"Why don't you check this pond?" he said. "Who knows, you might find some fish. I'll go around this hill and see what I can find over there."

They separated.

She walked to the edge of the pond. The water was dark, like tea, and covered with a film of ice. Gasparo was right; the river people, they had to find them. But would that be possible in this vast land? She peered across the pond. What was that sticking up out of the bank on the far side? The first step would be to find the river, then the river people. She walked around the edge of the pond.

A bone, six times the size of a man, with patches of moss, protruded from the reeds. A *mostro* bone. She looked into the dark water, hoping she might see fish, but she saw nothing but the mulchy bottom and a few underwater plants. She reached into the pond, pulled the plants out, and tasted them. Bland, but at least not bitter. She put them into her bag. She would let Piero decide.

Then she heard Gasparo crying for help from the other side of the woods, his voice pitched higher than she had ever heard it, filled with a bone-chilling timbre that penetrated deep to the pit of her stomach.

She turned from the pond and hurried up the hill.

At the top of the hill she saw Gasparo among some trees clutching the back of his neck, twisting and turning wildly, as if something were attacking him. She ran down the hill and into the trees. She forced her way through the tall grass and thick undergrowth until she stood next to him.

An implant was on the back of his neck.

"Get it off!" he cried.

Gasparo tried to pull it off, but the barbs on its feet latched onto his skin, and the retractable blade had already made an incision.

"Gasparo . . ." She felt helpless. She remembered Bettino. If she tried to pull it off, she might take half Gasparo's brain with it.

Automated forceps pried the flaps of skin away, a screwlike mechanism penetrated the base of his skull, and turning counterclockwise, the mechanism drew the implant in until it was flush.

"Please, Felicitas, you have to . . ."

Gasparo was so breathless he could hardly speak.

He knelt, clutching madly at the thing, but with all the

blood, he wasn't able to get a good grip. He caught his breath and looked up at her with pleading eyes.

"Get it off me!" he cried. "Use your shiv!"

"Gasparo, I don't know if I can."

"It crawled out of my bag!"

Even as she spoke the threading pods went into action, pulling the flaps of skin over the entire mechanism, working quickly with articulated joints, suturing the wound shut, spitting out thread from an unseen cavity.

Gasparo sat on a boulder, scared but otherwise fine, his hair matted with blood, a bulge on the back of his neck. Piero stood over the large man inspecting the incision, lost in thought. Francesco stood nearby, his spidery hands on his hips, his thin brown hair hanging in limp strands around his long narrow face. Brothers or not, Francesco and Gasparo had become good friends over the last few days, and Francesco's eyes were grave with concern. Felicitas stood next to Silvio; she and the old man had something in common now. As Silvio had lost Concetta, so Felicitas had lost Rosario. Felicitas pulled her blanket around her shoulders. Many of the forty other *superstiti* were now wearing their blankets. The wind was strengthening, turning yet colder. To be hungry all the time made the cold seem worse.

Piero finally stood up.

"And you don't feel any different?" asked Piero. "You haven't had any strange thoughts or ideas? You haven't heard any of the other dead talking to you? Because I sometimes think they must talk to each other using these implants."

Now that the implant was activated, Felicitas could hear its dull ticking in her mind. She still didn't understand this ability she had.

"No," said Gasparo. "I feel a little groggy, that's all. Other than that, I'm fine." He shrugged, his brawny shoulders bulking under his prison uniform. "Maybe it hasn't started working yet. Maybe it takes a while. I'll rip it out with my own hand the minute it does."

Piero sighed. "It's not as easy as that, Gasparo. Remember what happened to Bettino? Let me see your eyes. Lift your head."

Gasparo did as he was asked, as submissive as a lamb. Piero looked first in one eye, then the other, and shook his head.

"I don't see anything," he finally admitted. "Your eyes look normal. But that doesn't mean . . ." He glanced away, searching for words. "How are we going to know, Gasparo? You see my dilemma, don't you? I don't want to kill you. You've shouldered more than your fair share of the burden, and you've been an invaluable help to the whole enterprise. But if you start working against us . . ."

"Piero, I swear to you, I'll take my own life if I should turn against you. I hate them as much as you do. I would never let you down."

A fragile smile came to Piero's face. "I know you wouldn't, Gasparo," he said softly. "You've been with me right from the start. It's just that . . . once it starts working—if it starts working—you might feel differently. Maritano might be able to talk to you directly, through your mind. I'm nearly convinced that's the way the implants work. You might be sly. And how will we know? I'm going to have to take your weapon."

Gasparo immediately handed over his weapon. "You'll be able to tell by my eyes. They'll be off-kilter. If you see that, kill me outright. Or better yet, tie me down and see if you can get any useful information out of me. Maybe I'll be able to shed some light on this white building Felicitas keeps telling us about. I might even understand the murder of Galileo and why the New Ones threw all those babies into the harbor."

"You're a big man, Gasparo," said Piero. "You wouldn't be easily subdued. I should bind your hands now, only I need every one of us looking for food. No, I think the best thing is for someone to watch you. Someone who's had a lot of firsthand

experience." He turned to Felicitas. "That would be you, Felicitas. Because of your encounters with Maritano, you perhaps
have a better understanding—"

She nodded. "I'll watch him."

"Good." Piero turned back to Gasparo and put his hand on
the big man's shoulder. "Maybe it's a broken one," he said.
"Maybe it won't work." He let his hand fall. "We'll just have to
hope for that."

They traveled northeast, following the natural drainage patterns of the land toward what they hoped would be the river. At
the top of every hill they were sure they would see it, but all
they found were more trees. At one point, it snowed, not much,
but enough to make them realize that winter was nearly here.

They found shelter for the night in a thick cluster of trees
near a brook. No sign of pursuit, and now that they were far
from the prison, Piero believed no one would find them. Gasparo behaved normally, though Felicitas still kept watch on
him. The *superstiti* pitched tents, lit fires, and tried to forget
about all the loved ones they had lost. Some of the older women
got the children settled for the night. Several children were crying because they were so hungry. Felicitas's mood darkened.
She felt a great emptiness at the prospect of having to spend another night without Rosario. And she was apprehensive about
the *soldati*. She thought the *soldati* might get the prison running
again, that they would restore the dreamphones and sleeping
pallets. And where would that leave Rosario?

When she raised this possibility with Piero, he continued to
stare into the fire for a while, then finally lifted his eyes.

"Felicitas," he said. "I've thought about Rosario constantly.
I keep asking myself, how can we get Rosario out of that place,
and I haven't come up with an answer yet."

"But what if they dreamphone him again?"

"We'll just have to hope they don't," he said. "And besides,
what can we really do? We're a small band now. There's only

forty-four of us. And only a handful would be any use against the *soldati*. Consider the odds. Twenty-five killed last night, six of them children. It doesn't make sense. We're forty-four. We're free. We've escaped. We have a definite gain. Do we risk it all on a suicidal attempt to save the others?" He shook his head. "No," he said. "I don't think we do."

20

That same evening, Gasparo wanted to wash the matted blood from his hair. Under Piero's orders, Felicitas accompanied him to the brook.

While he knelt on the stony bank lapping water onto his hair, Felicitas was again overcome by a sense of premonition. She sensed Gasparo's implant, yes, but this was different, this had that same plurality of sound that her previous encounters had had. A fleeting sensation, to be sure, one that passed quickly, but which left her staring uneasily into the bushes across the brook. She took a deep breath. Was there someone out there?

She knelt beside Gasparo, cupped water in her hands, and drank. The feeling was gone. The water from this brook tasted far sweeter than the water they got from the south bath.

"How do you feel?" she asked Gasparo.

"Tired," he said. "And dirty. If the water weren't so cold, I'd give my whole body a scrub."

She stood up. She was relieved. He still seemed normal.

She looked back at the camp. Six fires blazed in the growing darkness, orange pools of light sending embers into the air, reassuring in this wilderness night.

And once again she got that feeling.

She turned around and peered into the bushes across the brook, and in the dusky light she saw a face, pale and indistinct among the leaves.

"Gasparo," she whispered.

She felt her neck muscles tensing.

He looked up at her from his washing. "What?" he asked.

"There's somebody over there."

She took a few steps into the brook, heedless of the cold water. She recognized the face. Marco's face.

"It's Marco," she said.

Gasparo stood up. "Where?"

But he was gone, a sapling springing forward to hide his face.

"How could the dead have found us all this way?" she asked.

"And you're absolutely sure it was Marco?" said Piero.

She nodded. "I got a good look at him as I was crossing the brook."

Francesco spoke up. The thin wiry man had now become Piero's chief *consigliere* in light of Gasparo's compromised condition.

"And did you see any others?" asked Francesco. "Did you see Maritano?"

"No," she said. "Marco was the only one."

Piero nodded.

"Francesco, take a party across the brook and see if you can find footprints."

Francesco quickly organized a group of five men and they hurried in the direction of the brook, torches high above their heads.

"Maybe I should go with them," suggested Gasparo.

"No," said Piero. He approached Gasparo and, with un-friendly eyes, stared at the big man. "What's going on, Gas-paro? Are you communicating with them?"

Gasparo's eyes widened in distress. "Piero, I swear to you . . . I have no idea . . . I would never . . . the dead have some-how been able to follow . . . but I swear to you, I haven't be-trayed you." He pounded the back of his neck angrily. "This thing, it's not working. I'll be okay." He lifted his chin. "Look at my eyes. My eyes are normal. I've seen their reflection in the brook." He nodded. "I'm okay. It's not going to work. It's bro-ken, I'm sure it is."

"Then how did the dead find us?" asked Piero. "You're communicating with them somehow. That snow covered all our tracks. You've been communicating with them. Through your implant."

"Piero, that's not true, I'm just the way I was. Nothing's happened to me. I'm just good old Gasparo, the man who can lift anything."

Piero put his fists on his hips.

"Don't you understand, Gasparo?" he said. "You're a risk."

"Then kill me!" said Gasparo. "Kill me right now. If that's what it takes to prove my loyalty. Draw your *pistola* and kill me this instant. I would willingly lay down my life for you and the others," said Gasparo. "You know that."

Piero stared at the big man.

With startling quickness, Piero pulled out his *pistola* and jammed it against Gasparo's temple. Gasparo's eyes squinted shut and he clenched his jaw in a sudden spasm—but he didn't pull away. He stayed there, preparing himself for death. He shook for a moment but then grew still. All the *superstiti* stared, horror-struck.

"Go ahead," said Gasparo. His voice was despondent but calm. "Get it over with."

Piero slowly lowered the weapon. He stared at Gasparo, considering the big man's reaction.

"It hasn't started working yet," he at last concluded.

There came a rustling through the trees.

Francesco and his party returned. The men were grim-faced. Francesco carried something in his hand. As he entered the glow of the firelight, Felicitas saw that it was a *topo* carcass.

"We found this," said Francesco, showing it to Piero. "There's got to be a dozen over there. Plus a small campfire. And we found footprints as well."

"How many?" asked Piero.

Francesco shrugged. "Hard to tell," he said. He looked apprehensively at the surrounding bush. "I don't know how they can be so quiet. It's like they're not even there."

Lungo Muso took her on a small journey that night.

This time he didn't go to Earth, he stayed on the prison world. She knew this because there were two red suns in the sky.

They stood on a vast snowy plain. And before them rose the big white building. She felt cold with fear as she looked at the building.

"Behold the river of time," said Lungo Muso.

The white building was the river of time?

The Old One stooped and drew a glyph in the snow: three thorny lines above a fire. She recognized the glyph. It came from the script up in the south tower. It was the glyph she had such trouble with. End time. Final time. End-final time.

Lungo Muso looked at her. He pointed at the glyph.

"You must understand this glyph above all others, Felicitas," he said. "It is this glyph that tells the tale of your doom. It's this glyph that you must overcome. It is this glyph that you must finally defeat."

Lungo Muso dissolved in a thousand crystals of snow.

And Felicitas was left standing there on the cold plain.

Staring at the big white building. Wondering what it all meant.

* * *

She slept uneasily after that, and woke early.

Five *superstiti* stood guard at the edge of the camp, watching for the dead.

She got up and told Piero about the episode.

"What do you think it means?" she asked.

Piero blew gently on the embers of the fire, then sat up.

"Lungo Muso's definitely trying to tell you something," he finally said. "There's something going on, and you seem to be the key. That glyph, that end-final time, it bothers me."

"What should I do?" she asked.

He stirred the embers in the fire with a stick. "There's not much you *can* do," he said, "at least not right now. We'll wait until Lungo Muso makes himself clearer. In the meantime you better go down to the brook. I see Gasparo heading that way."

At the brook, Gasparo knelt on the stony bank a short distance downstream, splashing his face with water. A few others did the same upstream, while others dipped pails into the brook to bring water back to camp. Some of the children threw stones into the water. She got on one knee and looked into the water. She saw three brown fish dart by and disappear into the rapids on the other side.

She stood up, electrified by the sight of them, her mouth suddenly watering, her stomach lurching in anticipation. She was so hungry he could have eaten them raw.

"I saw fish!" she called to Gasparo.

She thought Gasparo would jump up and run to her side, thought he would be excited, especially after reading *The Gentleman Angler,* but he just turned his head, remaining on one knee, and looked at her, his face curiously slack, his eyes off-kilter. Some of the children stopped throwing stones and stared at the giant.

And she knew it had happened. Gasparo stood up and looked at her.

"Fish?" he said, as if he hadn't understood.

He took a few steps toward her. She backed away, reached for her *pistola,* and aimed it at his chest.

He stopped. The other *superstiti* at the riverbank began murmuring among themselves, nervous to see the big man's eyes looking so strange.

"Felicitas?" he said.

"Gasparo . . ." He seemed to have no idea what had happened to him. She wasn't afraid. She felt sorry for him. "Gasparo, can you not feel what's happened to you?"

He looked at the brook, but there was something forlorn about his eyes. "I want to fish," he said.

His simple manner unnerved her. She knew he was a threat, and she steadied the gun as best she could. She tried to pull the trigger but her hand simply wouldn't close around the bulky firing mechanism. This was Gasparo. This was the big man with the booming voice whose superhuman strength had proven invaluable in all their endeavors. This man was her friend. She tried to look beyond her own feelings. But she hesitated.

"Felicitas, I don't know what's happened," said Gasparo. He rubbed the back of his neck. "I don't feel the cold. And I don't feel hungry." He looked across the brook into the woods. "Is someone calling me? Do you hear that voice?"

She looked into the woods, tensing, searching for faces among the leaves, swung her *pistola* in that direction, then back at Gasparo.

And in that instant, he bolted. In getting her to look across the brook, he had purposely distracted her. She fired, but her hesitation had cost her. She missed. She fired again but she was so upset, and so caught off guard that she missed again.

Those along the bank scrambled for cover. She heard others come running from the encampment. Some of the children started to cry. She fired again but he was already into the trees and she couldn't see him anymore.

She knew she had blundered badly.

*   *   *

Piero's face reddened, his jaw stiffened, but the expected out-
burst didn't come. "You hesitated," he said, his voice flat, without inflection. "You knew the implant had started working and
that he might possibly pose a threat, but you hesitated. You
knew the dead were in the vicinity, and you . . ."

He shook his head and rubbed his brow with his thumb
and forefinger.

He rose from his stone and walked to a nearby tree, where
he rested his hand on the trunk.

Francesco spoke up. "What if it stops working?" he said.
"What if in a day or two we find him and he's perfectly
normal?"

Felicitas was beginning to understand; everyone was thinking of themselves. Piero was thinking of everybody else. He ignored Francesco's remark. Francesco's words were the biased
words of a brother.

She stood there with her head bowed. A small mistake. Was
it fair that she should be singled out like this when anybody
could have made the same mistake? She looked at Piero, mus-
tering as much nerve as she could.

"He tricked me," she said. "He made me think there were
people across the river. I swung my *pistola*—"

"You should have killed him outright," said Piero, "without
hesitation, like I said to." He sighed and shook his head. "I'm
sorry, Felicitas, I shouldn't be so . . . but was I wrong to trust
you? After how well you did in the west annex?"

"I'm sorry, Piero," she said. "He was my friend and I . . . the
second he ran, I fired. I fired three times, but he got away."

"You let him get away," said Piero.

"No," she said, "I didn't." She bowed her head. "He just
managed to . . ." She looked up at him. "Maybe he'll get lost in
the woods. Maybe he'll—"

"I don't think so," said Piero. Exasperation crept into his
voice. "He's going to find those other dead and lead them back

to us. Thanks to you, our survival is now a minute-by-minute proposition." Piero waved his hand at the woods across the brook. "Gasparo's out there now, and he's one of them. He knows we're heading for the river. He knows that finding the river people is our only chance. And he'll tell Maritano. On the way to the river we'll be ambushed. The dead will be waiting for us somewhere."

A small mistake. But a deadly one. She saw that clearly now.

Piero looked at her forlornly. She could tell he was trying to be as fair as he could with her, but he was having a difficult time.

"What am I supposed to do?" he asked. "Can we safely go to the river now?" He shook his head. "I don't think we can. How can we go to the river if they're going to be waiting for us? About the only possible thing we can do is track east and hope we reach the river farther downstream, away from them. Because if we don't reach that river, we're dead."

21

It snowed a few hours later. The land rose, the trees thinned, and the clouds came down low and thick, touching the tops of the surrounding hills. She caught up with Piero. They were in a shallow valley. Piero wouldn't look at her, kept his eyes forward. But at last he glanced at her.

"Are you tired?" he asked.

"No," she said. "But Silvio is. And some of the children have to be carried."

The snow gathered in small drifts on the ground.

"We go until dark," said Piero.

"Piero, I'm sorry," she said. "I'm sorry about Gasparo. But he got me looking across the river and I—"

"It's all right, Felicitas," he said. But she could tell he was still unhappy with her.

"What's done is done," he said, his tone softer. "I sometimes think everybody has to act as coldly and ruthlessly as me. But I know they can't. I can't help thinking . . ." He stopped, turned, and stared at her. "Those who are close to me . . . you, Rosario, Silvio . . . I think of you as . . ." He looked away. "I don't know . . . as a kind of family." His eyes seemed to burn with a strange light. "And you get certain expectations of the people who are close to you, who you think of as your family. I've watched you grow, Felicitas. I've tried to give you that . . . that sense of belonging to something, because I knew it would be good for you." He shrugged listlessly. "Unfortunately, I'm not well suited . . . I'm not sure if I know how to be a . . . a father, or a guide, or even a good teacher . . . I was just trying to do what was right. I don't know why I should expect any more from you than I should from anybody else."

She put his hand on his arm. "I have memories now," she said. "I remember the time you've spent with me . . . how you've tried to be . . . you know . . ." She looked away. "And I appreciate it. I know you've taken special care with me. When you found out I read the glyphs—"

"It's more than just the glyphs, Felicitas." He was silent for a moment. "It's been . . . that is, I feel . . ." He shook his head. "It's more than just the glyphs with you, Felicitas. I was so happy when you came out of the dreamphone haze. It meant I didn't have to make you starve. It meant I didn't have to watch you die."

She nodded, understanding. "You care about me," she said. She knew he would never say it himself.

"I care about everybody," he replied.

But she knew what he meant.

Someone called out. "Piero!" It was Francesco.

Piero stopped and turned around. Francesco pointed toward the low hills to the north. Felicitas looked in that direction.

She saw thirty or forty dead standing a mile off on top of a hill looking down at them, barely discernible through the snow, an unsettling long-distance encounter in this near empty land. Tendrils of gray stretched downward from the low clouds, hiding the dead. A minute later, the tendrils passed on, and the dead were gone.

Felicitas felt worse than ever about hesitating with Gasparo. The consequences were now tangible. They were being followed.

"They're waiting," said Piero. "When we're weak, when we're nearly starving, when we're so cold we'll do anything to keep warm, that's when they'll strike."

They moved east for the rest of the afternoon, trying to keep hidden behind a series of hills. Piero kept them strung out in a fairly loose column, with the strongest fighters at the front and back. The large gradual hills gave way to a series of smaller, steeper ones, and the trees began to grow more thickly.

Felicitas ranged ahead, acting as an advance scout, believing that with her sense of premonition she was better equipped to give the group warning. She was desperately trying to make up for her mistake. She climbed one of the small steep hills and glanced back as the bulk of the group reached the top of hill behind her. From this perspective, the group looked small, specks on a rolling sea of hills that stretched on and on, people adrift in a vast wilderness with the river their only lifeline. If they didn't find the river soon, they would be lost.

She continued on.

At the bottom of the hill she found a brook. The brook was frozen over. She tried to sense the dead, tried to hear the mind-control machines ticking away in their heads, but all she heard was the wind moaning through the trees and rustling through the dead brown grass that poked up through the patches of snow.

She veered north, ran beside the frozen brook—ran, even though she was weak with hunger—because she wanted to make sure their northern flank was safe. Then she backtracked, scurried south along the brook. She sensed nothing. The dead were keeping away for now.

Francesco emerged from behind a stand of trees to her right.

"I thought I might catch up with you," he said.

"I'm trying to sense them," she said.

He joined her at the brook. "Any luck?"

"No," she said. "I think they must be too far away."

At the top of the previous hill, the first of the group appeared.

"Do you mind if I walk with you for a while?" he asked.

Her eyes narrowed. She tried to divine Francesco's purpose.

"No," she said. "I don't mind."

The two walked up the next hill, ahead of the group, finding their way through the trees.

"I'm sorry about Rosario," said Francesco.

She took a deep breath, her jaw stiffening. Francesco was waiting for her to say something, but she found she couldn't.

"He was always watching out for you when you were a dead girl," said Francesco.

She glanced at him. "Was he?"

"You couldn't have chosen a better man for a husband," he said. "I'm sorry he got left behind."

Her eyes momentarily clouded with tears. "I am, too," she said.

He sighed, an uncomfortable sound, and rubbed his hands together, as if they were cold.

"Did you know that I developed a fondness for you as well?" he finally asked.

She felt her lips squeezing together as her shoulders rose. She glanced at him. Tall. Spidery. Thin. A praying mantis. Amiable, well-meaning, but . . .

"That's flattering, Francesco," she said.

"You were always coming to read the books," he said. "And I grew quite fond of you . . . I just wanted to let you know that . . . I know it's too soon after Rosario . . . he and I were always best friends . . . but I just want you to know, that is, I thought it might be good if I . . . ." He squared his shoulders and gathered his wits. "I just want you to know that you still have someone watching out for you, Felicitas."

She took a deep breath. "That's kind, Francesco," she said. "But I'm sure I'll be able to watch out for myself."

They camped next to a stand of trees. It was a miserable night, cold and damp, and the children whimpered in their sleep.

Francesco tried to sleep next to Felicitas, even tried to touch her, but she didn't feel that way about Francesco. He was a sensitive man; he understood and accepted her feelings.

"I'll wait," he said. "I know I can't compete with Rosario, but I'm a decent man, Felicitas, and there's not many men to choose from. I think you would make a good wife. I think you have qualities that make you—"

"I appreciate the compliment, Francesco," she said. "But have you not seen the way Innocenza watches you? I think maybe you should try to sleep next to Innocenza."

Francesco cast a dubious glance at Innocenza. She had to be near forty, a kind woman, but with an unfortunate abundance of facial hair. Francesco squinted at the suggestion.

"I don't think so," he said. "You're far prettier. And you have something about your eyes . . . I've never seen such eyes as yours." He shrugged. "If you get cold in the night, let me know. Two under a blanket is warmer than one. I won't try anything, I promise. I just want to make you feel better. You look so sad."

They continued east the next morning, sticking to the trees, hoping the trees would hide them, their food-bricks now nearly gone. Many of the children were so tired they again had to be carried.

They discovered huge *mostro* tracks frozen in the mud.

Felicitas walked around the first track, wide-eyed with wonder. Most of the others were just plain scared—the tracks were twelve paces long and four paces wide, and a meandering rut between the tracks couldn't be anything else but the mark left by a long thick tail. She looked at Piero, remembering all those distant cries heard from inside the prison. She recalled the outside bars of the west gate, finally understood what the outside bars were for—to stop the *mostri* from getting into the prison. And she remembered the thudding vibration in the ground of *mostro* footsteps.

Piero glanced around the group, sensing their anxiety. Not only did they face starvation, death by exposure, recapture, and possible execution, they now had a *mostro* wandering about whose single footstep was enough to crush any of them.

Piero stepped into the first of the large prints and spread his arms.

"You don't have to be afraid of this," he said, smiling. "You should be happy about this. This animal has to eat. And if we follow its tracks, we might find its food. And maybe its food might be something we can eat. Such an animal is bound to be cumbersome and slow. Why should we be afraid of this beast? Think of the meat a beast like this could provide if we can kill it. Why should you be frightened? There will come a day when we hunt such beasts, and live off their meat and flesh, and make houses from their bones."

As Piero spoke, Felicitas moved to the edge of the group and peered into the forest.

What was it? She had that feeling again. Of premonition.

She sniffed. What was that smell? A familiar smell. A smell from the prison. The smell of jail rot.

Then she saw a figure emerge from the mist in the forest. His face was pasty white, and his eye sockets were empty. Maritano. With the skull still tied to his head.

Twigs snapped, some bushes rustled. The dead had at last caught up with them. The dead had finally chosen their moment.

She swung round to Piero.

"They're here," she said.

Piero stopped talking and looked into the forest.

Maritano strode from the trees, followed by Marco and Ottavio. Thirty others stepped out from behind bushes. They all looked well nourished, as if the *soldati* had taken good care of them. They wore new brown uniforms, had their heads shaved, and were armed with new *pistole*.

Maritano stopped at the edge of the wood.

"Put your weapons down," he said. "There's no point fighting us. You're marked. You can't hide."

Felicitas peered at Maritano. What did he mean by that? In what way were they marked?

The *superstiti* turned to Piero. Nearly at the end of his patience, Piero leapt out of the *mostro* footprint, his face turning red, his brow knitting, yanked his *pistola* from his belt and, as if he meant to fight the dead single-handedly, fired at the nearest, blasting a sizable hole in his chest. The man slumped down dead.

All the dead drew their weapons and took aim, as if they'd been expecting this.

Felicitas stared at Piero in disbelief.

Was he mad? She scrambled to the other side of the track as other *superstiti* drew their *pistole* and dove for cover. Did Piero want to get them all killed? Silvio and Francesco jumped to the ground and crawled beside her.

"What's he doing?" she asked.

Francesco said, "He's fighting. What else can he do?"

"But there are children."

The dead opened fire. Yet they didn't shoot to kill. They fired expertly over the heads of the *superstiti,* creating panic, instilling fear. Children, terror-crazed, broke free and ran in all directions, some of them stumbling in the snow, others tripping over roots.

The dead captured the weakest and smallest children first, looping leashes around their necks. The *superstiti*'s own *pistola* fire, sporadic to begin with, petered out. Some of the women tried to rescue the children, but they, too, were captured.

"Run!" Piero called.

He sped off into the forest.

The *superstiti* bolted in all directions.

"Are we just going to leave them?" asked Felicitas.

"What choice do we have?" asked Silvio.

Felicitas reluctantly joined Silvio and Francesco and ran off into the forest. Piero was far ahead of them. The man was doing anything he could to elude capture.

She crashed through the saplings and bush, her heart pounding, even as the ramifications of this ambush took hold. She was guilty. Gasparo knew they would try for the river. And the dead had indeed found them. She was guilty, and she could barely stand it. Silvio and Francesco followed closely behind her. Would they ever get to the river now? What were they going to do? How could they expect to survive? So far, they'd seen no sign of the river. They were nearly out of food. She glanced over her shoulder.

The dead captured yet more *superstiti*. Felicitas stopped. She had to go back and try to rescue some of them.

"Felicitas, no!" cried Piero.

She stared at the melee.

The dead looped a leash around Innocenza's neck, and much to Felicitas's shock, threw the rope over the lower branch of a tree, hoisted it, and peremptorily hanged her. Felicitas drew her *pistola* and fired. Instead of hitting one of the dead, she nearly hit one of the *superstiti.* So she stopped. And she stared, wondering what she could do.

Some they captured, some they killed. It made no sense. They were as erratic as the *soldati.* The things in their heads must be malfunctioning.

With so many now captured she saw that there was no helping them. There was nothing else she could do but run.

She caught up with Piero and the others.

"Are we just going to leave them?" she said.

"There's a gully into those hills ahead," said Piero. "We might be able to lose them in there."

"But what about the others?"

"Never mind the others," he shouted. "Just run!"

So she ran like she had never run before.

Ran because she now saw that Maritano had left the rest of the group and was coming after her, targeting her. Did he have a counselor in his bag? Was he going to try and put one of those things in her head again?

"You go ahead," called Francesco, seeing that Maritano had singled her out. "I'm going to try and stop him. I'm not going to let him get you, Felicitas."

"Francesco, don't!"

But Francesco turned around and fired at Maritano. The ground was slippery, he couldn't get his footing, the angle wasn't the best, and he missed.

Maritano returned fire. He fired his weapon with the same expertise and skill with which he threw stones. A blue ball of flame leapt from his *pistola* and sliced Francesco in half. At the sound of the blast, Felicitas glanced back. Her throat buckled at the carnage, but she kept running, up through the gully, higher and higher, knowing that if she could only reach level ground she might outrun Maritano.

"We have to keep you safe, Felicitas!" shouted Piero. "Run!"

Why was he so concerned about her safety in particular? She ran past Piero up the hill, glancing back every now and again, hoping that at least some of them could escape.

Silvio was losing ground. Maritano caught up to the old man but instead of putting a leash around his neck he simply pushed him out of the way. Silvio fell to his knees and crawled quickly away into the underbrush.

Felicitas and Piero scrambled through a treacherous gauntlet of boulders up the hill. Maritano caught up to them, was right behind them, gained on them, and was able to close the distance easily, even on this steep incline, as if his counselor were giving him extra strength.

At last they reached the top. They found a break in the trees, open ground, good for running, with more trees a hundred yards away. Felicitas bolted. She was fast, agile, bounded like a gazelle. The fifty-year-old Piero kept right behind her.

"You run to the left!" he called. "He can chase only one of us."

She ran to the left. She thought Piero would run to the right, but glancing back, she saw him turn and face Maritano. Maritano stopped, confused by the tactic.

"Felicitas!" called Maritano. "I want you!"

Maritano ignored Piero, tried to dart around him. But Piero wasn't going to let him by.

Piero tackled Maritano, sacrificing himself so Felicitas could get away. *We have to keep you safe, Felicitas.* He was thinking about Lungo Muso. He was thinking about the New Ones. He was thinking about the big white building.

She didn't want to disappoint Piero again, so she ran and ran, stopping only when she had reached the cover of the trees on the far side of the break.

She hid behind a bush and watched.

The two men tumbled in the snow, pummeled each other, struggled to disarm each other. Maritano was younger, better fed, better rested. Piero fought valiantly for nearly five minutes, but finally gave in.

Maritano overpowered Piero, pushed him to the ground, and forced a leash over his head. There was nothing he could do.

Piero, the architect of their freedom, was once again a prisoner.

Felicitas hurried off into the forest to hide.

22

She hid for most of the after-noon, and when she was sure it was safe to come out, she walked farther into the forest. She was alone and it was getting colder. Her hands and feet were numb, and she couldn't feel her nose or cheeks.

The light faded.

She shivered. She found a spot in the leeward side of a tree and pulled her blanket around her shoulders. The material was so thin it did little to stop the cold wind from getting through. Besides her blanket, all she had was her bag, her glyphs, the finger bowl, a bit of food-brick, and her *pistola*. Should she go back to the *mostro* track to see if she could find any extra equipment? No. They would be waiting for her.

She had to do something to stop this cold or she was going to freeze to death, but if she lit a fire the smoke would bring them running.

But finally she got so cold she had to light a fire.

She got to her feet and walked east, away from the *mostro* track, hoping she might find the river. That felt better. The walking warmed her, made her feel as if she might survive on her own, at least for a little while. As she walked, she picked up pieces of kindling.

Just before nightfall she came to a gorge. She followed a ledge down into the gorge until she found a recess protected from the wind by stone slabs. She stacked her kindling near the rock face, gathered some small logs that lay about, and lit them with her *pistola.*

The flames danced up, hissing in the damp. She stuck her hands close to the fire. A painful yet pleasurable warmth emanated through her fingers. Heat radiated to her frozen cheeks and nose. She would sleep here for the night. By her small fire. She would force her fear away. And tomorrow, she would find the river.

Her sleep was unsettled, and the cold woke her often.

Somewhere deep in the night, it started to snow again, and, waking up, she replenished her fire. She moved into the rocky recess as far as she could, tried to get comfortable, and drifted back into fitful sleep.

She dreamed. And again she dreamed of her mother.

She was in the south bath. She couldn't have been more than nine. They were out on the central island and her mother was peering at her, the same way Piero peered at her that day so long ago when she first came out of the dreamphone haze. Her mother was asking her if she were alive. She tried to answer, because, yes, she felt alive, especially whenever her mother was near, but the dreamphones had turned her tongue to lead, and she couldn't articulate her feelings, couldn't tell her mother just how much she loved her. She saw her mother's clear green eyes. Her mother stroked Felicitas's hair. Marietta. Her mother's name. It came to her now, as she shivered in her sleep, another bit of dreamphone amnesia lifting. Marietta was trying to tell her something. They were going on a journey. The journey would be long and there would be much hardship.

Marietta looked down at Felicitas's arm; the bandage was still there. Why did she have a bandage? Then she felt vibrations through the water. *Soldati* appeared on the tiled deck. They lifted their *fucili* and fired indiscriminately into the crowd of swimmers. She saw Francesco torn in half. She saw her mother torn in half . . .

And she opened her eyes . . . only to discover snow falling on her face. Only to understand how much she missed her mother. Only to realize that she was a seventeen-year-old girl out here all alone in the middle of the forest in the freezing cold with no one to help her.

She got up, put more wood on the fire, took out her glyphs, and read them out loud. She could read the words but she still wasn't sure what they meant.

"In the before-time," she read, *"in the desperate time, when our vanquishers made this dark-ugly time, you did not turn away, but ran the path, and swam the river, the deep fast river that never forgets."*

She smiled. You did not turn away but ran the path, swam the river. There was courage and hope in such words. But was that river really the river of time, such as Rosario had suggested?

"You saw me with your night eyes, saw my daunted soul, and how it burned brightly like a star through the long night, and you kissed me, touched me, and . . . and . . ."

She broke off, overcome by sadness. Rosario. You kissed me. Touched me. She turned away from the glyphs. And she saw Rosario standing there in the gloom. A fragment of a dream? Not the Rosario she remembered but a Rosario with the life gone out of his eyes, the sleeping pallet pallor returned to his cheeks, a dead Rosario, an unthinking Rosario.

The dream fragment disappeared.

She continued on: the cliffbird, the lonely brothers and sisters, the sky, earth, and water, trying to understand just what

Lungo Muso had in mind for her, now clutching at the hope that if she could run the path and swim the river she could somehow find a way back to Rosario.

"*But in vanquishing our vanquishers,*" she read, "*we ourselves became vanquished, and never again found the way of peace, but had to stand guard against our foes, so that our hearts changed, our blood changed, our sinews changed, and we lost the way, lost the silent current, where our ancestors still burn in the everlasting night.*"

She rolled up the glyphs, put them back in her bag, and pulled out the finger bowl. Did she really have eyes the color of this green gemstone? She held the bowl up to the firelight and looked at the glyphs carved on the side. For the first time she understood the ornamental and formal symbols.

She sounded out the words.

"*I called to you in the light of the moon, and through the darkness you came to me.*"

As usual, a metaphor. For love, for devotion, for commitment.

Lungo Muso will show me the way, she thought. I will run the path and swim the river.

And I will at last rise like the cliffbird.

23

In the morning, she climbed out of the gorge into the surrounding forest. She had to go back to the *mostro* track to see if she could find any supplies. Though it had stopped snowing halfway through the night, she now saw, through the short stubby trees, thick dark clouds moving in from the northwest, not just more snow but a real winter storm. She would need shelter. She could only hope that she might find a tent back at the site of the ambush.

Innocenza, murdered for no apparent reason, still hung in a nearby tree. A few other corpses lay scattered among the trees, each now covered with a light dusting of snow. Two of them were children.

Felicitas gathered what supplies she could—some food-bricks, two blankets, and fortunately a tent. She put them in her bag, hoisted her bag to her back, and left quickly, spooked by the silent tableau of death, afraid that the dead might still be somewhere nearby, even if she couldn't readily sense them.

She continued east for a while, then headed straight north. She had to get to the river. She had to find the river people.

The storm hit not long after. She kept going, holding in her mind like a bright flame her newfound freedom. Yet against the blizzard her resolution faltered and the true nature of her predicament settled around her with the desolation of a lost hope. Freedom. The freedom to starve. The freedom to freeze. The freedom to die all alone.

Freedom, she thought, was an ambiguous proposition at best.

By nightfall she had lost her sense of direction. The sky had been overcast all day and the suns hadn't been there to guide her. The river was nowhere in sight.

She found shelter in the leeward side of a tree-covered hill, erected her tent low to the ground so it wouldn't blow away, then searched for firewood. The blizzard, if anything, worsened.

She stacked some wood and lit it with her *pistola*. In seconds she had a bonfire, a big one that sent huge clouds of smoke into the air as it battled the dampness of the snowflakes. She needed a big one if she was going to keep it going in this blizzard. She set up her tent close to the fire. What warmth! Far warmer than her small fire last night.

She crawled into the tent and pulled her blankets over her shoulders. The blankets steamed in the heat. Was there any point in leaving this tent ever again? Why not just stay here until she died? Her food was running out, and she was all alone. What good were the glyphs now? What good was Lungo Muso's plan, if, indeed, he had a plan? What did she have to do with Galileo's murder? What did she have to do with Reymont and Machiavelli, whoever they were? She cried. She would never see Rosario again. She would never see Piero again. The great doom of the white building would descend upon her and she would be swallowed. The end-final time would finally sweep her away.

If nothing else, she would simply freeze to death.

*   *   *

She fell asleep.

And she dreamed again. Her old dreamphone dream.

She ran after the young woman through the rain, the scarred hands floating in front of her. The woman's auburn hair flew in the wind. She chased the woman up a hill into the moss-hung trees.

She was just about to kill the woman again when the woman turned around. And it wasn't the woman from her dreamphone dream . . . no, not at all . . . it was her mother, as if her mother understood just how desperate she was, how much she needed help . . .

Marietta raised her arms, beckoned to Felicitas, and a reassuring smile came to Marietta's face. Felicitas went to her mother, and her mother folded her in her arms, and all her guilt over that young murdered woman disappeared.

For the first time in her life, Felicitas was free from that haunting face in the rain, from that woman with the *uominilupi* identification tag stapled through her ear.

The cold woke her several hours later. Not only the cold but also the noise of the wind howling, of her tent flapping, and of the rattling of ice crystals against the tent fabric.

She sat up, and, peering through the flap, looked at her fire, now burned right down, a feeble flicker glowing at the heart of a charred snow-covered mass of logs. She shivered in the cold and blew against her hands. She looked up at the dark sky.

Then, over the wind, she heard something, a distant boom, and felt a faint tremor in the ground. The footfall of something unimaginably huge.

Her back stiffened. She heard another boom, this time closer, like the beat of a large drum, then heard the cracking of a tree. She got to her knees and crawled to the tent flap. She heard

three more booms in quick succession, then a lugubrious bel-
lowing cry, deep and resonant, blending with the wind.

Felicitas scrambled out of her tent, was about to douse her
fire, when she heard another tree crack not twenty yards off.
She forgot the fire. She ran. *Mostro.* All her childhood terror of
them came back. She didn't feel safe near the fire. Some said the
reason the *mostri* came to the prison was because of the light.
She thought of the *mostro* footprint back at the ambush. Maybe
this was the same *mostro.*

She ran up the hill, stumbling through the snow, leaving
everything behind her at the campsite. Another two booms reverberated through the ground, the branches of the tree above
her shook, and snow came tumbling down on her head. She ran
to the top of the hill, no longer feeling cold, simply wanting to
survive for the next minute, the next second, forgetting the
helplessness of her situation in her overpowering need to live.
She smelled the *mostro,* like old wool left out in the rain.

At the top of the hill she stopped beside a thick tree and
looked back at her camp.

How pitiful her camp looked, that small scrap of tent, a
flicker of fire, meager protection against this immense storm,
such insignificant and ultimately futile shelter in this wilderness. She heard another boom. Then for a long time she heard
nothing.

She dug a burrow in the snow and crouched next to the tree.
As seconds lengthened into minutes, the adrenaline eased from
her bloodstream and she felt the cold again. She looked up at
the sky, hoping she might see some sign of morning, but all
was dark, and she knew dawn was still hours away. She peered
into the forest, searching for the *mostro.*

In the faint light coming from her fire she saw hundreds of
tree trunks, any of which could have been the leg or tail of a
mostro. After careful scrutiny, she convinced herself that they
were just trees, that her imagination was making her see things.

She stayed in her burrow. She hadn't heard any retreating

booms, nor felt the thud of footsteps, so she knew that the
mostro still lurked nearby. She dozed, slipped back into her
dream again, basked in her new feeling of relief, in the certainty
that she hadn't killed that young woman after all.

She opened her eyes and saw that her fire had burned even
smaller. How long had she dozed? She wasn't sure. The wind
had shifted and the stench of wet wool had disappeared. She
stood up and took a few steps forward. She gazed into the darkness. Was it still here? Or had she missed its departure?

No, she hadn't missed its departure.

Its tail swung out of the darkness to the left, so quickly, so
unexpectedly, she hardly saw it coming. The tail was covered
with long ropy strands of fur. It hit her with numbing force and
she fell face forward into the fur, stunned and winded. Before
she could come to her senses, she discovered her wrist had become tangled in the fur. She was trapped in the tail.

The tail went swishing away and Felicitas was dragged
through the snow. Then it reversed direction and she grabbed
on to the fur because she was heading right for a boulder. Before the tail reached the boulder, it rose high into the air, well
above the treetops, hoisting Felicitas along with it.

She clung with arms and legs now, her jaw clenched, her
eyes wide as the tail swung back and forth above the trees,
knowing if she fell from this height she would die.

She heard the boom of the creature's footsteps as it moved
quickly away from the campsite. Despite her fatigue and nearly
uncontrolled fear, she knew if she left her campsite—particularly if she lost her *pistola*—she would have no hope of surviv-
ing. So she struggled to get her hand loose from the thick
ice-coated fur.

The tail came down as the *mostro* gained speed, finally
dragged along the ground again. Felicitas wrenched her hand
free and rolled into the snow. The creature continued on. Felicitas looked up, her heart beating so fast she was beyond fear.
She tried to get a good look at the creature, but all she saw was

the tail, thick and gargantuan, disappearing through the squalling snow.

She got up and returned to her camp, her legs shaky, taking deep breaths to calm herself. How was she going to survive out here if something like that could happen?

Back at camp, she built her fire and crawled into the tent.

For a long time she couldn't get to sleep. She was afraid the *mostro* might come back.

But slowly her eyes closed, even as the wind outside lessened, and she once again slipped into her dream of beautiful, sweet, and peaceful absolution.

She slept right through after that, and when she woke, the wind had stopped and the snow had ended.

She crawled outside and stood up. Though the flames had all but disappeared, smoke billowed in copious amounts from her fire, unfurling straight up through the trees. She saw the *mostro*'s tracks, twelve paces long. She saw all the broken trees and the burrow she had dug on top of the hill. In the sky, *Stella Grossa* and *Stella Piccola* fought to get out from behind clouds.

She walked over to her fire and threw handfuls of snow on the remaining embers—she didn't want the dead to see the smoke. She finished her last piece of food-brick. She rolled her tent and blanket up and slung them onto her back. Then she sat down on a fallen tree and wondered if she should go back to the prison. The escape had failed. She was the only one left out here. True, Silvio had managed to crawl away, but he was most probably dead by now. What was the point of staying out here when she was going to die? Better go back to the prison, if she could find it. She would submit to the dreamphones, if the *soldati* had restored them, resume her old life as a dead girl, and hope that some day they might get another chance.

But then she heard the sound of water. And not just a brook or a stream. Real water. Big water. She peered through the trees.

She couldn't see anything. But the sound was unmistakable. Not a brook. Not a stream. This was no inconsequential trickle, not with such a breadth of sound. It had to be a river.

It had to be *the* river.

24

She packed her gear and walked toward the sound of the river. Despite her exhaustion, her steps were light, and she felt excited by the prospect of finding the river.

She descended a ridge into a small gorge, then climbed a hill.

When she reached the top of the hill, she saw it. The river.

It was wide and fast-flowing, sparkling in the intermittent sunshine, and fringed with snow. She gazed up and down its length, hoping to find some sign of the river people.

But the river was empty.

She walked downstream a good part of the morning, hoping she could find them.

Near noon, she discovered a large stone marker on top of a high bluff next to the river, each stone meticulously stacked to form a pyramid. A few Italian words had been scratched onto one of the larger stones, words she didn't understand. She crouched, brushed some snow from the pyramid, seeking further clues, but found only an engraving of a large misshapen beast crawling out of the river.

She stood up and looked downstream. From up here on the bluff she had a good view. And what she saw made her heart jump.

To the southeast, several columns of smoke rose into the air. She shook with sudden, uncontrollable joy. But just as quickly, her joy disappeared, and she realized how far that smoke was. It would take her two days to get to those fires, and she didn't have two days. She had no food. She was already weak. She was already starving. The terrain was so difficult and the cold so intense she would tire and die before she reached those fires.

But she had to try. She had found the river people. She had to go to them. She couldn't let her dream—Piero's dream—die.

Before she took another step, she heard a noise in the bushes behind her.

She swung around.

She took a sharp breath, startled by what she saw.

Three men stood on the higher edge of the bluff above her, watching her, men she had never seen before, not dead, not *superstiti*, different men, dressed in garments of fur, armed with bows and arrows.

The youngest stepped forward and said, *"Non aver paura. Noi conosciamo la divisa. Voi siete dalla prigione. Vieni con noi. Abbiamo trovato degli amici vostri."*

She couldn't understand him, but she recognized the language as Italian.

"I'm sorry," she said. "I don't understand you."

Could it be she was finally going to get an answer to why there had been so many Italians in the prison? The river people. Did these three men represent a part of her history?

The youngest spoke again. *"Abbiamo visto il fumo,"* he said. *"Non aver paura."* He smiled, took a few more steps toward her, and offered his hand. *"Abbiamo trovato degli amici vostri. Essi ci hanno parlato di voi."* His smile broadened further. *"Felicitas,"* he said. *"Felicitas. Che bel nome. Vieni con noi."*

If she recognized nothing else, she at least recognized her name.

And she concluded that the only way they could know her name was because they had found some of the other *superstiti.*

Felicitas and the three men walked through the snow down a steep path toward the river's edge.

The three men made further attempts to communicate with her, but she couldn't understand more than a few words.

At the bottom of the steep path, they walked along the river-bank, and the youngest offered her meat, only this meat didn't have the gamy taste of *topo.* This meat was orange, sweet, and succulent, unlike anything she had ever tasted.

Soon they came to a shallow backwater.

A slender, leaf-shaped boat, much like the ones she had seen from the balloon reconnaissance, bobbed in the water, tethered to a tree. With the help of the young man, she climbed into the boat and sat down. One of the older men wrapped an animal fur around her.

Once she was settled, the rest of them got in and the young one pushed off, digging to the bottom of the shallows with his oar, sinking it into the mud to gain purchase, then paddling on alternating sides till they reached the river.

The current took them downstream at great speed. Under the big fur she soon stopped shivering.

As they came to some rough rapids, and the boat lurched up and down, the young man turned to her, smiled, and said a few words. If she didn't understand their actual meaning, she at least recognized the tone of reassurance in his voice, knew that they were words of comfort. She smiled back to let him know she was all right.

They traveled downstream, following the river as it curved

southeast, then due south, then southwest, describing a large arc through the land. The clouds cleared and she saw the mountains to the east. Other than that, she saw nothing but bush and forest from horizon to horizon.

Early in the afternoon they reached a fork in the river, and after negotiating some brisk rapids, the three men steered the boat to the right, taking the smaller of the two rivers westward, back toward the prison.

After another hour she saw a giant fur-covered carcass several stories tall lying on the riverbank, and a collection of hide-covered huts beyond. Sixty men and women crawled over the beast, butchered it with various knives and saws, carted away hundred-pound chunks of meat on crude sleds, lowered bales of fur by rope. Dozens of big brown birds spun and dove over the carcass, thieving scraps, squawking rudely over the susurrating whisper of the river. She couldn't help wondering as she looked at the huge carcass: Was this the *mostro* from last night?

Smoke drifted into the sky from sundry cooking fires, and looking closer, Felicitas saw a whole village of men, women, and children dressed in fur and dried animal skins, clothing such as the mural in the south wall had depicted. She looked at the smoke. This was the smoke she had seen earlier that day. She had at last found the river people.

They drew up to the shore and the young man helped her out of the boat. Then the three men lifted the boat onto the bank and turned it over.

They led her along a well-worn path past the carcass into the village, where children played in the snow, women stretched hides, and several men constructed a curing shed out of poles and twine. She followed them along a brook to the largest of the huts, a dwelling place big enough for twenty people or more.

The young man pulled aside the flap and they went inside.

Her eyes got used to the dark. A small fire burned in the center, and standing by the fire, with ten other men, was Piero.

Her eyes narrowed and she took a closer look because at first she thought she must be mistaken, that she *had* to be mistaken, because wasn't Piero a prisoner of the *uominilupi* again? Hadn't Maritano forced a leash around his neck? But then Piero turned to her, and she knew that it was true, that those bright blue eyes could belong to no one else, that this had to be Piero, brought to her by some miracle she didn't as yet understand. And she saw Silvio as well, sitting on a bench drinking from a cup. Escaped. Both of them. Her friends. Alive.

Piero said, "Felicitas?"

Piero left the fire and hurried to her.

"It's me," she said, feeling tears come to her eyes.

Silvio got up from the bench and hobbled over. Her chest swelled with relief, not because she was at last safe but because Piero was safe, because the man who most deserved freedom was at last free.

She ran to both of them and embraced them.

"You're alive," said Felicitas, still bewildered. "You're free."

"And so are you," said Piero.

"We knew you would make it," said Silvio. "Piero told them you were out there. He told them to look for you."

She stroked the old man's wrinkled face. "You're here," she said. Then she looked up at Piero. "How did you ever—"

"You must be cold," said Piero. "And hungry." He stroked her hair. "They found me late last night . . . they were out on the river and they . . . they had lights on the river and I called to them. And they found Silvio a day ago. He was sheltering under a big tree by the river. I guess we all had the same idea. Get to the river."

"Yes, but how did you . . . the dead were armed. They had you on a leash. You were outnumbered forty to one."

"I . . . I just couldn't let them take me . . . I couldn't let them . . ." He stopped. He seemed puzzled by her question, as if he wasn't sure of the answer. But then his eyes brightened. "I escaped," he said, as if that would explain everything. He shook his head, amazed by the simplicity of his answer. "I escaped."

* * *

After a long rest, some food, and more expressions of joy and amazement about being together again; after Felicitas had told her story, Piero his, and Silvio his; and, finally, after Silvio had settled himself down for a nap (the old man was exhausted from his ordeal) Piero and Felicitas went for a walk along the river down to the carcass.

"That man over there is Urbano," said Piero. "My Italian isn't good, but from what I understand, Urbano is their leader, at least for this particular hunting expedition. His people respect him. He's been good to me so far. He's a good leader."

Felicitas stared at Urbano. He was an older man, at least as old as Piero, and wore a suit of white fur.

Piero nodded a greeting to Urbano.

"Come on," he said. "I'll introduce you."

They walked over, and in broken Italian Piero introduced Felicitas to Urbano. Urbano took her hand and kissed it, and said something in Italian to her. She turned to Piero, hoping for a translation.

"I'm not sure," said Piero. "Something about your eyes. He says he'll talk to us later. Right now he has to supervise this butchering."

Felicitas nodded at Urbano. *"Grazie, signore,"* she said. *"Grazie."*

Piero and Felicitas walked on.

"He knows about the prison," said Piero. "And he knows of the *uominilupi* too but only as legend. He says they haven't been seen here for generations and generations. He doesn't concern himself with what happened hundreds of years ago. His great joy is hunting the *mostri*. He's the best hunter they have. He's told me some of his hunting stories. He says they come to this place every year to hunt the *mostri*, and that the *mostri* migrate in this season along the river to feeding grounds farther south, where the weather is warm. The weather here is cold enough to keep the meat frozen. They smoke some of it.

They salt some. All they have to do is kill one of these beasts and they have enough to feed them all winter."

"Has he given you any idea about who they are?" she asked. "And where they came from, and what connection they might have to us? They all speak Italian."

Piero stared at the birds flying above the carcass.

"There are some old stories about the prison," he said, "but it's been so long since Urbano's heard them he isn't sure what they are anymore. He knows his ancestors originally came from the prison, that there was an escape hundreds of years ago. But no one bothered to record anything. They were too busy trying to stay alive. They've come a long way since that original escape. Urbano doesn't concern himself too much with the history of it. His father was a hunter. So was his grandfather. That's his true love. I know they call themselves the *popolo,* the people. He says there was an escape eight or nine years ago too. The escapees are now living in their town." Piero peered at her. "Do you remember that, Felicitas? An escape eight or nine years ago? I don't. I don't see how it's possible. We were all still dead then. But Urbano's sure of it. He knows some of the escapees personally. He says they speak English."

"No," she said. "I have no recollection." She looked at Piero curiously. "The *popolo* have a town?" she said.

He nodded. "Yes," he said. "They call it New Florence."

"New Florence," she said, trying the name.

Piero stared at her for a few seconds. Then they walked a little way. Felicitas watched the activity in and around the *mostro* carcass. The *popolo* had erected a crude climbing lattice, much like their own prison lattice, against the side of the *mostro.* The smell was horrendous.

"How do they manage to kill the *mostri?*" she asked.

"They chase them into the river," said Piero. "The *mostri* are cowardly and run from anything. Once the hunters bully one into the river, it gets mired in the muck on the bottom. When it's good and stuck, five or six hunters crawl into its ear and build a fire near its brain. They secure the firewood in place with grappling nets so the beast can't shake it loose. Sticks and stones, and a little bit of fire, Felicitas. That's how they do it. They've been using the same method for hundreds of years."

"They've been here that long?"

"That's what Urbano says."

"So they really don't know much about the *uominilupi*?"

"Again, there are old stories. Urbano says there've been some skeletons discovered, just like the one we found in the prison. And they have some old artifacts in their town hall."

"Have they told you about this town?" she asked. "New Florence. Where exactly is it?"

"It's near the mountains."

"And do all the *popolo* live there? Are there any other towns?"

Piero gazed up at the sky. In this valley they were well protected from the wind, and the sunshine was nearly warm.

"The *popolo* think there might be one far to the south across the badlands. There are old stories. But no one's traveled across the badlands for the last hundred years, so no one knows for sure." He shrugged again. "These are simple people, Felicitas. They farm, they hunt, they gather. They've domesticated some of the birds, and a beast of burden they call the *speranza-bestia*, the hopebeast. None of them are really interested in where they came from, not when they have to work so hard to live. Urbano says there are a few *insegnanti* in the city, teachers and academics who study such things, but what happened hundreds of years ago doesn't mean much to most of these people. They live their lives. Generations come and go, and there's not much change from one to the next."

"You just won't let it go, will you," said Piero.

Felicitas, Piero, Silvio, and Urbano sat in one of the huts with twenty other *popolo*, huddled around their own small fire, wrapped in fur, eating chunks of *antilope* meat—this was what the *popolo* called the giant beast outside, as good a name as any on this world without names.

"Why should I?" said Felicitas. "I love him. If that's selfish, then that's selfish. He's my . . . my husband. I can't leave him. And now that we have an opportunity, a real opportunity to set him and the others free, we've got to make the most of it." She looked at Urbano, conscious of the fact that he couldn't understand a single word of English. "We have to make Urbano understand."

"Felicitas, you haven't thought it through," said Piero. "Yes, we have numbers now, but let's not forget what we're up against. The *soldati* have secured the prison. They have *fucili*. And they're programmed to kill. Look how many they've killed so far. The *soldati* are a formidable mechanized army. Now look at the *popolo*. They have bows and arrows. If you think they're any match for the *soldati* . . . well, they're not. And the prison itself is impregnable."

Felicitas stared at Piero, fighting back her frustration.

"Yes, but the mortar's crumbling everywhere," she said. "I'm sure we could find a way in."

"Even if we did, we can't be sure that Rosario's alive," said Piero. He put his *antilope* meat aside. "And if he's still alive, he's most probably dreamphoned."

"What does it matter if he's dreamphoned?" she asked. "All of us were dreamphoned. Get him out and I'm sure he'll recover."

"Felicitas, think. The *superstiti* were only a fraction of the entire prison population. Even when the machines stopped working, three-quarters stayed dead. Not many of us came out of the dreamphone haze. The same thing's going to happen this time. Three-quarters are going to stay dead."

"But he's valuable, Piero," she said. "He's brilliant. Think of the contributions he can make. Look at the way he understands everything. Talk to Urbano. Tell him about Rosario. You know enough Italian to get through to him. Please." She couldn't stop the tremor in her voice. "I don't want to lose him."

Piero's face reddened. "Why do you think I have any influence over Urbano?" He glanced at the leader, who smiled amiably. "Urbano does what he wants. He's the leader here, not me. He's not going to expose his people to danger if he doesn't have to. And the prison scares him. It's more than just a pile of stone to him, Felicitas. The *popolo* are superstitious about the prison. Not only that, winter's coming and the weather's going to get worse."

"Then I'll have to go myself," she said. "I'm not going to leave Rosario there. He doesn't deserve to rot in that place. None of them do."

Her voice was strained. Piero stared into the fire.

"I can't let you do that, Felicitas," he said. "You're needed here. You can read the glyphs now. And let's not forget Lungo Muso. He's trying to tell you something. He's got plans for you. He needs you. He's shown you the glyph, the end-final time. Something's got to be done. Something bad's going to happen otherwise."

"I'm free now," she said stubbornly. "I've asked for your help. You're not going to give it to me. What choice do I have? I'm going back to the prison. Lungo Muso will just have to wait."

"All right, all right," he said. "But how do you expect me to convince Urbano?"

"Tell him how useful Rosario will be. Tell him Rosario's a *genio.*"

Piero picked up his stick of *antilope* meat and warmed it over the fire. "And if he refuses?" he asked.

"Then I go myself," she said. "It's as simple as that."

25

Felicitas stood outside Urbano's hut, waiting.

The river swept by beside her, its bank now glazed with ice. In two weeks the river would freeze completely. The *popolo* would have to be out of here before then. She wasn't sure if two weeks would be enough to get Rosario out of the prison, or to even find a way into the prison.

She turned from Urbano's hut and walked to the outdoor fire. She was now dressed in fur, but she still had to stand by the fire to keep warm.

Two women roasted one of the big brown birds over the fire, turning it slowly on an iron spit. She nodded, smiled, and held her hands out to the flames. The women didn't attempt to speak. There was no point. They spoke Italian and she spoke English.

She gazed westward past the trees to the opposite bank, knowing that somewhere far beyond those hills on top of a small barren summit overlooking the lake stood the prison.

Was it really so hopeless? She heard people emerge from Urbano's hut. She turned around.

Piero walked across the snow toward her, his steps measured, his face set, his hands deep in the pockets of his new fur
coat. Urbano stood at the entrance, his face expressing a mixture of concern, pity, and apprehension. As Piero reached her,
he put his hand on her shoulder.

"We're going to the prison," he said.

She felt exhilarated. "I knew you could convince him," she
said.

A crease came to Piero's brow, and he raised his hand, cau-
tioning her.

"Felicitas, I wish I could believe in this . . . this adventure the
same way you can."

"We're going to get him out of there, Piero," she said. "I
know we are. And he's going to be all right."

He let his hand fall, and as he looked at the women roasting
the bird, his eyes grew solemn.

"Urbano says we leave tomorrow," he said. "We're taking
five of his best hunters. He says this fork of the river empties
into the lake a few miles south of the prison. I wish we'd known
that earlier. We would have found the river a lot sooner. We
travel by boat. We should get there in two days."

Felicitas looked at Urbano. "He doesn't look pleased."

Piero turned to the hunter. "He's worried about the weather.
If the weather turns colder . . . well, then freeze-up starts. At
that point, I don't want any arguments, Felicitas. We leave. We
go to New Florence with the *popolo.*"

Silvio was too old and too exhausted for a return journey to
the prison, so he was going to stay in the village.

Felicitas saw the old man standing on the riverbank as she
practiced paddling in a boat with a young hunter. She turned to
the young hunter and pointed to Silvio. The young man nodded. He brought the boat to shore.

Felicitas stepped out and joined Silvio on the riverbank. He was dressed from head to foot in fur, and now used a sturdy stick as a cane. The long trek from the prison had exacerbated his sore knees and ankles.

"Has Piero told you?" she said. She was still breathless with enthusiasm. "We're going back to the prison. To free Rosario."

Silvio at first didn't reply. He watched the young hunter steer his narrow craft out into the rapids with the deft use of his paddle.

"That boy has skill," he said. He looked up at her. "Will he be going to the prison with you?"

"Yes," she said.

Silvio nodded. "Piero's told me all about it," he said.

"Rosario and I are going to be together again," she said.

Then she thought: Silvio and Concetta will never be together again. Maybe her enthusiasm, this chance she had, was a source of pain to Silvio.

"I'm sorry," she said. "I didn't mean to . . . I know you must miss Concetta."

"I do and I don't," he said. "Now that I've finally had a chance to sit down and rest, I'm remembering all sorts of things about her. I don't think I'll ever get over all of this amnesia, but I . . . I had such a sweet memory of her just now, as I was standing here on the riverbank. A memory from many, many years ago." A melancholy grin came to the old man's face. "It was summer. I think we had the bi-solar eclipse that year, so it was warm. Concetta and I climbed to the roof of the dispensary . . . oh, now let me see, yes, it has to be at least thirty years ago . . . and only *Grossa* was up in the sky, and we lay there together all afternoon basking in the sunshine. Then a *carceriere* came and beeped at us. As we climbed down I found a small blue flower growing out of a dirt-filled crevice between the tiles up there. Who knows how it got there? Maybe a seed blew in over the wall. I gave it to Concetta. That's when we started thinking of each other as husband and wife. When I remember that flower . . . such an odd shade of blue . . . I nearly feel that Concetta's right here next to me," he said. He looked up at her from his humped shoulders. "So you see, Felicitas, I'm not so badly off. I had a good long life with Concetta." He patted her hand. "And I can only wish the same for you and Rosario."

"I know we're going to get him out," she said.

He neither affirmed nor denied her conviction. They strolled along the river for a while in silence. Some children were having a snowball fight in a nearby thicket of trees.

Silvio began to work his jaw back and forth. She knew he had something on his mind.

"Don't worry," she said, second-guessing him, "I'll be careful."

"I'm sure you will, my dear. You're as capable a girl as I've ever met."

"Silvio, if there's something you want to say, why don't you—"

"I just hope you've been properly grateful to Piero," said Silvio. To her surprise, the old man sounded annoyed. "It wasn't easy for him, begging Urbano like that. He begged Urbano for nearly two hours, and he did it for your sake. I hope you know that. And I hope you realize just how much Piero cares about you. He might not show it, he has a hard time showing things like that, but he sacrificed a great deal of his dignity and his own better judgment for you, and I hope you thanked him for it." The old man stopped, looked up at her. "He cares about you, Felicitas. More than you could ever guess. And I hope you don't disappoint him."

Light snow came down from the sky when they left the next morning.

They traveled in three boats, moving swiftly downstream with the current. The land was wooded and hilly, with the stubby trees close together, and every so often she saw an outcropping of gray rock, jagged and imposing against the predominant greens and browns of the forest. The river bubbled and rippled, a deep and nearly metallic blue, and was so clear she could see the bottom.

They surprised a strange ground bird, really just a feathery ball with long legs and a beak. After squawking a few times, the bird darted into the woods with its wings folded on its back, and, dodging the close-packed trees, disappeared over a hill.

After lunch, Felicitas was given a chance to paddle. At first she found it hard, but as her muscles limbered up she soon found the dip and pull hypnotizing. She paddled until her arms were sore and her hands were blistered.

As the light faded from the sky Urbano directed the group toward shore, and they soon set up camp. The men cut some branches and constructed a large lean-to, big enough for all of them to sleep under.

When most of the others had gone to sleep, Piero and Felicitas sat up by the light of a small fire talking. The snow had stopped and the wind had died, and it promised to be a calm and noiseless night under the lean-to, a good night for sleeping.

"What do you think this New Florence will be like?" asked Felicitas.

Piero drew his left leg up and folded his hands over his knee. "Urbano tells me they have a few thousand permanent inhabitants," he said, "and that it's mainly a market town. He says it grows a bit each year. There's a school there now. And a temple. And the town hall I was telling you about, where they keep the *uominilupi* artifacts. I'm glad you're curious about it, Felicitas. New Florence is your future. The prison is your past. You should leave the prison behind you."

She looked away. He always came back to this.

"You know I have to go," she said.

"Felicitas, let me tell you a story. Four years ago, when you were still a dead girl, and when Rosario and I and the others first began to understand what had happened to us, I knew a woman, her name was Angela, and I called her my wife. I called her my wife for the same reasons you call Rosario your husband." Piero's lower lip stiffened as he stared into the fire. "Together we had a child. We named her Isabella, and she was a beautiful child, with yellow curls and the happiest blue eyes. She was the first child born to those of us who were alive. We protected her from the *carcerieri*. She was a child who was never dreamphoned, or put in the sleeping pallets, a perfect child, a pure child, the first of a free generation." The rims of Piero's eyes reddened. "But the prison's never been a healthy place. Isabella got sick and died. So did Angela. I kept blaming myself, thought that if there were only something I could have done I might have saved them. But then I realized that it wasn't my fault, that death was death and loss was loss, and that there was nothing I could do about either of them."

"I'm sorry," said Felicitas. "I had no idea."

"Don't be sorry. I've learned to accept it. And I've tried to gain something from it." The fire settled in on itself, sending up a swarm of sparks into the night sky. "Isabella still represents to me everything I find most important in life. So does Angela. And so I haven't really lost them. Nor have you lost Rosario. If we can't get Rosario back, maybe this is the way you should think about him. Ask yourself what he represents to you. How did he change you? What did he teach you? Take these things from him and he will live forever."

At sunset the next day, the river, now carrying with it a milky residue of silt, emptied into the lake.

The prison loomed before them, two miles beyond the promontory, forbidding, a massive oblong of crumbling gray stone. Urbano and the rest of the *popolo* gazed upon the prison with apprehension. Felicitas felt no fear. Staring up at the ugly edifice, she felt only small, helpless, and disheartened. How could she defeat such an daunting structure?

They crossed the lake in the last two hours of daylight.

They camped by a marsh, just southeast of the prison. The hunters found a rich supply of antennaed shellfish to eat in the half-frozen mud of the marsh.

Felicitas spent long hours searching the walls of the prison for a way in. On the second day, it started to snow, a wet sticky snow that frosted the wall, making detection of any likely way in difficult. She took a spear and scraped the snow and ice away from the stonework, hoping to find crumbled mortar or a major crack, something that might help them make a good start in penetrating the wall. She urged the others to do the same.

In the first couple of days, they heartily cooperated, especially when it became apparent that the *soldati* weren't going to come out and blow them to pieces. The prison appeared deserted, and except for the occasional brown bird that perched on the parapets, showed no signs of life, mechanical or otherwise.

"The *sentinelle* aren't working," said Felicitas to Piero. "We would have been able to hear them moving along their chaindrives. So that probably means the dreamphones aren't working either." Her enthusiasm was desperate. "In fact, I'm certain the dreamphones aren't working."

On the night of the third day, Felicitas asked, "Why do you suppose the dead don't come out and capture us?" She nibbled at her shellfish. "You'd think Maritano would be out here with his leash."

Piero stared into the fire. "There's no consistency to the way they act," he said. "Those things in their heads are faulty. And maybe the *soldati* are using the dead for something else right now."

The suns came out on the fifth day, the air warmed, and the ice fell away from the prison walls in great chunks. This made their search easier. They found a few spots where the mortar looked so badly crumbled they thought they might get in. A spot up on the south wall looked especially promising, where a single large stone had been replaced by many smaller stones.

"That's got to be level with that wall mural," said Piero. "I wonder if that's where those other prisoners got out eight or nine years ago."

Unfortunately, this spot was too high for them to reach.

In other spots, despite crumbling mortar, the stones were so large that not even everyone's strength combined could budge them.

On the sixth day she inspected the west gate. The gate was now repaired. Even the scorch marks from the explosion were gone. She spent all day looking for a switch or panel for the west gate, even searched with a torch once it got dark, but found nothing. With desultory steps she made her way back to the camp.

That night Piero said, "The weather's turning colder. Urbano says freeze-up's going to start in a few days. He says we can't stay much longer. You see that, don't you, Felicitas?"

"I want to see if we can get up to those windows in the west annex," she said. "That room where I found Concetta's uniform. If we could reach that window we would be able to get in."

"Felicitas, how are you going to do that?" he asked. "It's straight up."

She looked at him defiantly. "I'm going to climb," she said.

The next day she attempted to climb the wall of the west annex.

The wall was so scarred by wind and rain, so chipped, gouged, and cracked that she found many good toeholds, enough to give her hope. Piero and the others waited below. The rocks were coated with frost, and as the suns came up, the prison glistened, casting eerie reflections of broken light onto the lake.

Her hope faltered at the top of the buttress. There weren't as many cracks and crevices up here. But she didn't give up. Straining every muscle, she crawled up the wall of the west annex, ignoring the cold, thinking only of Rosario, moving carefully until she was several yards above the buttress. The wind kept sweeping her hair into her face. She pulled herself up, gripping the stump of a dead sapling, angling her feet to fit the grooves of the mortar, never looking down. Far above, she saw the window of the room where Concetta had lost her life. She gripped a jagged edge of stone and pulled.

"Felicitas!" called Piero. "Come down. It's too steep. You're going to fall."

"No, I . . . I think I can . . ."

She placed her foot against the broken sapling and pushed, hoping it would hold. And she suddenly remembered that day long ago when the searchlights went out and the *sentinelle* stopped working, and Piero had placed the uncompleted lattice against the wall and climbed—climbed even though there was no way to reach the top, climbed out of principle. Her eyes clouded with tears. She knew she couldn't go on. Piero was right. It was too steep.

"Stay there," called Piero. "I'm coming to get you."

"No!" said Felicitas. "You'll never make it." She'd already lost Rosario. She didn't want to lose Piero as well. "I'm coming down."

Coming down because she finally understood Rosario was gone and there was nothing she could do to get him back. Stone by stone, crevice by crevice, she descended the wall, her fingers stinging in the cold, her body taut, her muscles strained to the limit. Coming down because she finally had to accept the impossibility of her plan.

The irony was cruel.

After struggling so hard to get out of the prison, she now couldn't find a way back in.

When she woke up the next morning, she felt numb. Wrapped in fur, she was the only one left under the lean-to, and she could hear the men moving around outside, packing supplies and loading the boats for the long journey back to the hunting village. She threw the furs off, sat up, and ran her fingers through her hair. Her muscles ached from her climb and her hands and fingers were blistered from gripping the rough stone surface.

She crawled to the fire where she found a lukewarm cup of

tea waiting for her. She drank a few sips mechanically, hardly tasting it; then, with sluggish, automatic movements, much like the movements of a dead girl, she left the lean-to.

Down at the marsh, Urbano offered a few scraps of shellfish to her, but she didn't feel like eating, and shook her head. The marsh was slick with a thin coating of ice. Urbano shrugged and went to help the others. She looked around for Piero and saw him standing at the edge of the lake shaking out one of the furs. Snow tumbled from the sky, obscuring the edges of the prison across the marsh, and the trees creaked and moaned as they wavered in a strengthening wind.

She picked up a bundle, walked down to the shore, and stowed it in one of the boats. She looked at no one, spoke to no one, tried to carry her failure and her heartbreak with as much dignity as she could.

Soon they were ready to go. Piero came up to her.

"I'm sorry, Felicitas," he said.

She couldn't say anything. She felt tears coming to her eyes. She turned away, not wanting him to see her tears, knowing that her tears would cause him distress. He put his hand on her shoulder. She stared at the lake, now churning with small gray whitecaps.

"I'm all right," she said, without turning.

"Let me help you into the boat," he said. "You're unsteady."

He helped her into the boat and they pushed off.

When they were no farther than a dozen paddle strokes from shore, she heard a sudden whispering up on the catwalks—the *sentinelle* once again rattling along their chain-drives. She glanced back at Piero.

"They've got them working again," she said. "I guess that means they have the dreamphones working as well."

He shook his head sadly. "I'm sorry, Felicitas," he said. "I'm truly sorry."

III

FREEDOM

26

The *popolo* dismantled their temporary hunting village and left for New Florence. They loaded hundred-pound chunks of meat into boats, disassembled the huts and stacked them in a cave halfway up the hill for next year's hunt, and bundled the children in fur for the long ride home. The mood was festive. The hunt had been a great success and everyone would have enough to eat this winter.

But Felicitas felt anything but festive as they finally pushed off into the river. The sunny sky, the glistening snow, and the frolicking current of the river as it tumbled over rapids or dodged around boulders did nothing to dispel her bleak sense of defeat.

They traveled upstream until they came to the fork in the river. Here they took the east tributary for several days. The weather turned colder and colder. As the mountains drew closer, Felicitas showed little interest in any of the people or the things around her. Her grief took hold like a disease. She didn't think about the future, tried to get through each day, each hour, each minute any way she could.

New Florence came into view on the morning of the sixth day. A large earthen wall four times the height of a man stood around the town, and an impressive assortment of stone and wood buildings rose from within, some nearly as tall as the prison guard towers, others squat and low. The trees had been cleared outside this wall and the land fenced and squared into fields and pastures, now fallow under the snow.

The flotilla of boats drifted up to a dock at the foot of the town, where the river widened into a calm pool. To the left beyond the dock she saw a broad busy street. She got her first glimpse of the hopebeast, a hoofed creature that reminded her of the horses of earth, such as the books in the prison had described and illustrated, but with shaggy gray fur, and a small hump on its back. To her right, on the other side of the pool, she saw seventeen stone slabs on a hill erected in two concentric semicircles. In the east she saw the mountains, closer now, jagged, covered with trees. Despite the majestic vista of this impressive range, she looked at the mountains with dull uninterested eyes. She felt numb.

She was free.

But she didn't care anymore.

Felicitas, Piero, and Silvio were billeted in the west wing of the town hall, a warm and airless place smelling of grease and smoke.

A parade of different officials came to meet them, most notably a man named Fortunato, the *sindaco*, or mayor. Urbano the hunter accompanied these officials on their visits. Felicitas hardly paid any attention, stayed to herself much of the time, and spent most of the first two days sleeping, discovering that sleep was the best way to combat, and, at least to a small extent, dispel her sorry lack of spirits.

Bread, meat, and drink were supplied. Silvio developed a

hacking cough he couldn't seem to shake. The old man tried to cajole Felicitas, but there wasn't anything he could do.

"Maybe you should try some exercise," said the old man. "I find a walk will make a person's mood brighter. Certainly all that walking Piero made us do helped me with the loss of poor Concetta. Why don't you come out with Piero and me? We're going to explore the town."

"No," she said. "I think I'll just stay here. If I can only rest . . . I'm so tired, Silvio. If I can rest I think I'll feel better."

Felicitas didn't eat breakfast and brooded for most of the morning. She sat by the great stone hearth while Piero and Silvio explored the town. She sat still. She found that when she sat perfectly still, with her eyes closed, her mind would empty, and she would make herself, in a sense, a dead girl again. It was one of the few ways she could deal with her pain.

On their fourth day, Silvio took a turn for the worse. Though Piero proposed another walk in town, Silvio was too ill to go.

"I think I'll stay with Felicitas," he said. "You go ahead, Piero."

Silvio stayed with Felicitas in the town hall, kept to his bed, got up only to eat and bathe. His cough grew more persistent, and through the course of the afternoon he developed a high fever. During this fever, he slipped into a fitful and delirious sleep, and Felicitas grew so worried she had one of the town hall runners fetch the doctor.

While she waited for the doctor to arrive she watched Silvio. At the height of his fever he seemed to have a profoundly disturbing dream.

He lay there twitching, muttering a few words every now and then, sitting up occasionally, showing every appearance of being awake, but really still asleep.

"Yes, I see now," he mumbled.

He muttered these same words several times, as if to someone in his dream. She wondered if she should wake him up.

He was still dreaming when the doctor got there. Piero had returned to translate for the doctor.

"No," said the doctor, through Piero "Don't wake him. Sleep's the best medicine. And dreams are often cathartic. He'll probably feel better when he wakes up."

Silvio woke at sunset. Piero had again gone out into the town. A brittle red light shone through the windows of the town hall and fire flickered feebly in the hearth. Silvio stared at her with wide astonished eyes.

"He came to me again," he said.

Her eyes narrowed. "Who?"

"Lungo Muso. And I understood him this time."

She leaned closer, her eyes widening.

"Did he take you to that place again?" she asked. "Where they have all those glass tanks full of half-formed New Ones?"

Silvio nodded. "Yes, he did. And he was able to speak to me. He finally told me why they make New Ones. He finally told me what their purpose was." The old man raised his fingertips to his lips and pondered. "The New Ones can work the river of time. Yes, that's what he said." He looked at her. His eyes were keener than they'd been all day. "Remember how you told me about the English infants in the harbor, how you tried to stop that . . . that infanticide? But you had no effect? And then you told us about Galileo, and how Lungo Muso said you could do nothing to stop his hanging? That you were just a shadow in the old time?"

"Yes."

"You couldn't change or influence anything in the old time." Silvio nodded, more to himself than to Felicitas. "But the New Ones can. You were at temporal odds with your surroundings, a person not of that time, and so unable to alter the events of that time. Not so with the New Ones. Lungo Muso told me the New Ones can change anything they like, that they can touch the old time just as easy as they can touch anything in the here and now. That's what they were built for. To cheat the temporal odds. That's what they use them for. To make changes to the past. He kept telling me they were the true journeymen of the river. And he told me the river of time was one and the same with the big white building. They use the big white building to travel up and down time." He looked startled. "That's how he was able to take you into the past, Felicitas. That's how he was able to show you all those crazy things."

Officials took the *superstiti* to the town square, St. Mark's Square, just behind the town hall, where a large crowd of *popolo* had gathered. Silvio had rallied, though he still had his cough. It continued cold outside, and the crowd had to stamp their feet to keep warm. The sky was clear and the twin suns shone with muted pinkness.

"What's going on?" asked Felicitas.

"I don't know," said Piero. "Urbano hasn't told me anything. Neither has Fortunato."

After another ten minutes, a group of eighteen townspeople emerged from a stone building on the south side of the square. The crowd broke into spontaneous applause. Silvio looked up at Felicitas, bewildered.

"Who are these people?" he asked.

"I don't know," she said.

She stared at the people. What had they done to deserve such applause?

Piero's eyes widened. "I recognize the man with the gray beard," he said. "His name's Vittorio." An astonished smile came to Piero's face. "These are the prisoners Urbano told us about."

A woman stepped forward from the group. Felicitas peered at the woman. There was something familiar about this woman . . . long red hair, with threads of silver, a pale oval face, startling green eyes, the gemstone green of the finger bowl . . . Felicitas took a few apprehensive steps toward the woman. The woman looked at her. Then they just stared at each other, groping toward recognition.

Felicitas felt a quavering in her body. The woman approached her tentatively.

When they were no more than a few paces apart, they scrutinized each other. Piero approached, curious about the encounter, and appraised the woman.

In his usual bold manner, he said to her, "This is Felicitas."

The woman's eyes widened and a shudder of surprise passed through her body.

"I'm Marietta," said the woman.

Something expanded inside Felicitas, an emotion so large that she felt she wasn't big enough to contain it. The dreams came flooding back: her mother in the south bath with the book about small animals, her mother taken away by the *carcerieri,* her mother finally telling her that the journey would be long and that there would be many hardships. Marietta looked eight or nine years older. Recognition came, and Felicitas superimposed the older face she saw onto the younger one she remembered.

"Signora?" said Felicitas. The term of affection came unbidden to her lips.

"Figlia?" said Marietta, responding in kind.

"Is it really you?" said Felicitas. "After all these years?"

Tears came to Felicitas's eyes. She stepped forward and rested her hands on her mother's arms. She felt as if she had been holding up a great burden, and was now finally able to put it down.

"Felicitas," said her mother. "I never thought I'd see you again."

Felicitas was so overwhelmed, she could hardly speak.

"I . . . woke up," she stammered. "I came to . . . and the dreamphones had stopped working . . . and I could hardly remember . . ."

Marietta embraced her daughter.

"Felicitas, we tried . . . we really tried . . . but we . . . your father and I, we . . ."

Emotion made clear expression difficult for both of them. How could either of them explain all the gaps, sketch in the history of nine years at this sublime moment?

"Is my father not here?" asked Felicitas. "I haven't had any dreams about him. I haven't . . ."

Marietta cast a despondent glance at the crowd.

"I thought he might be with you," she said. "But I can see he's not."

Marietta then noticed all the *popolo* looking at them, and she stood up straight.

Switching to Italian, she said to the crowd, *"Questa e mia figlia, Felicitas."* She turned to Urbano. *"Signore, vorrei ringraziarla per tutto ciò che ha fatto. Le ne saro per sempre grata e Le manterrò la mia massima stima."*

Urbano raised his hands, modestly denying the importance of his role in saving the three *superstiti. "Signora, Io ho fatto ciò che qualsiasi altro avrebbe fatto al posto mio."*

The crowd began to applaud again. Not only for Urbano but for Felicitas, Piero, and Silvio. Felicitas gave them an unsure smile and waved. She turned to her mother.

"What did you say to them?" she asked.

"I just thanked Urbano," she said. She stroked Felicitas's hair, her eyes now glistening. "And I told them you were my daughter."

A few days later, Felicitas moved into her mother's small house at the edge of town, a two-room dwelling with a stone floor, a loft for sleeping, and a fireplace. A steaming kettle hung on a tripod in the fireplace. Felicitas saw her future glimmer weakly through her shroud of heartache. She was glad to be with her mother but she still missed Rosario.

"You peel the bark like this," said her mother. Felicitas's mother peeled a chunk of bark away with a sawing motion of the knife—the stubby trees had their uses after all.

"You see this white layer of flesh between the bark and the pith? You cut it away in chunks. It cuts like cheese. You see how easy it is?"

Felicitas took her own knife and helped her mother cut away the white flesh in chunks.

"So what happened after my father injured his arm?" asked Felicitas.

"He took the skin right off," said her mother, "arm code and all. The *carcerieri* couldn't identify him anymore. So they just left him alone. And slowly he came out of it. He began to understand how the prison worked."

"But how did you get out? When Urbano told us there'd been an escape eight or nine years ago . . . we couldn't remember anything, not with the dreamphone amnesia. How could you get past the *carcerieri*? How could you get past the *sentinelle*?"

Her mother nodded, gathering her thoughts as she prepared to recount the story.

"High in the south wall there's a passageway," she said. "You have to climb a broad set of steps to get to it. At one time the *uominilupi* used it to climb to the catwalks, but the stairs are bricked off near the top." She chopped another piece of white flesh out. "Nine years ago, a large stone fell out up there."

Felicitas remembered the spot up in the south wall where one large stone had been replaced with several smaller ones, the spot near the mural.

"Your father discovered this," said Marietta. "He chose fifty of the dead and wrapped their arms in strong cloth so that the *carcerieri* wouldn't be able to identify them. He tied my arm up. I came out of it. So did the eighteen others you saw in the square. Your arm was wrapped but you remained dreamphoned. Even so, we had to take you. You were our daughter. We couldn't leave you. We made a rope. Most of us got down. Your father was last. He was going to carry you on his back. I went down next to last. At the final moment, the *carcerieri* discovered us. I got down but you and your father were caught."

Marietta glanced at Felicitas's work.

"You have to cut deeper, *figlia*," she said, "right through the green membrane to the pith. You'll see why in a minute."

"So what did you do?" asked Felicitas.

A wistful expression came to her mother's face.

"We waited," she said. "Ten days we waited. We watched the hole up in the south wall, hoping the two of you would come down. But then the *carcerieri* repaired the hole, and we knew there was no hope. The *popolo* found us two weeks later and brought us here."

Felicitas thought about this as she worked on the bark of the tree.

"So you have no idea what happened to my father?" she said.

The middle-aged woman looked at Felicitas. "No," she said. "When I heard about you and the other *superstiti*, I hoped he might be with you."

"I can't remember a man with an injured arm in the prison," said Felicitas.

"I'm surprised you remember anything at all," said Marietta. "The dreamphone amnesia . . . it's so overwhelming." She put her knife down and moved the bulk of the trunk away. "That about does it," she said. She broke a bit of white off. "Taste that."

Felicitas tasted the white. She made a face. "I've never tasted anything so bitter in my life," she said.

"And if you eat enough," said Marietta, "you die. Now taste some of the green."

Felicitas tasted some of the green. "That's even worse."

Her mother smiled. "Isn't it awful? But at least you don't die from it. You just get sick." She turned a piece of bark over, green side up, and lifted a small wooden mallet. "Here's the trick."

She bashed the bark with the mallet, pounding the green into the white. To Felicitas's surprise, the bark turned orange.

"I don't know who discovered this," said her mother, "but the *popolo* wouldn't have survived without it. You have to bash it well. You have to make sure all the toxins are fully neutralized. There, you see? It turns pink. Taste that bit there."

Felicitas tasted the pink: a rich nutty taste, wholly satisfying.

"That's good," she said. "And you won't get sick?"

"No. You can eat as much as you like. It's a staple. The *popolo* call it *pane,* bread. Here's another mallet. You can help me. Then we'll drop it in the pot and make soup with it."

For the next while the women hammered away. When they were half done, Felicitas put her mallet down.

"What about the *popolo*?" she asked. "How did they get here? Piero says they originally came from the prison like us. At least that's what Urbano told him."

Her mother put her mallet on the sideboard and smiled at Felicitas.

"You were always curious," she said. Marietta picked up a rag and wiped her hands. "There are stories, Felicitas. And who knows if they're true? Time has a way of changing stories. Most of us in town believe the *popolo* came from the prison, yes, though there's no written record of any escape. We have artifacts from the prison. You can see them on the second floor of the town hall."

"Urbano told us about them."

"Books, mostly," said Marietta, "all crumbling to dust, all of them in Italian. There's a few old uniforms, and several pieces of glyph-covered machinery nobody's figured out. I think Fortunato will want you to look at them. As for this escape a long time ago, I don't know. The *insegnanti* say it happened five hundred years ago."

"And do you think the *popolo* originally came from Earth?" She was thinking of all the books she had seen up in the room guarded by Francesco in the east cellblock. "Before their incarceration?"

"The books in the town hall certainly come from Earth. So most of the *popolo* think they come from Earth, too. Your episodes with Lungo Muso would seem to support that. You ask any of the *insegnanti* and they'll tell you that's where we're from. But a lot of people are mixed up about Earth. They've never read anything about it so they make up their own notions. Some say if you follow the river out to the sea you'll find it on the other side of the ocean. Others say you have to travel across the badlands. Our priests say the only way to get to Earth is if you die, and your soul will be transported there. And then there's Raffaele. Has anybody told you about Raffaele yet?"

"No," said Felicitas.

Her mother seemed suddenly reluctant. "Maybe we should just continue making our *pane,*" she said.

"*Signora,* tell me about Raffaele."

Her mother looked down at the *pane.*

"Well, he . . . he lives up in the mountains, and he watches the stars and the suns . . . and he's got some books on astronomy. No one knows where he got them from." She lifted her dishcloth, stared at it, but then did nothing with it. "He . . . he believes you can get to Earth using one of the *uominilupi* skyboats." Marietta's eyes narrowed and in a hesitant quiet voice she said, "He also knows about this . . . this Lungo Muso you tell me about."

"He does?"

Marietta looked at her daughter. "I really didn't want to tell you, the doctor says you shouldn't get excited, but I—"

Felicitas felt her blood quicken. "He knows about Lungo Muso?" she said.

Marietta nodded solemnly. "He says Lungo Muso has visited him often," she said. "I was a little surprised when you told me about Lungo Muso."

"He exists, *signora,*" said Felicitas, emphasizing her words.

"I know he does," she said, quick to placate her daughter. "But he's not the best thing for you right now."

"What does Raffaele say about Lungo Muso?" she asked.

Marietta hesitated. "Well . . ." She inclined her head, and looked doubtfully at her daughter. "I'm not really sure, but . . . Raffaele lives in a cave up in the mountains . . . and in this cave, there's a pool . . . not an ordinary pool, a special pool . . . and the water glows in this pool. Raffaele says he can see Lungo Muso in this pool, that Lungo Muso talks to him through this pool. Except for a few of the more eccentric *insegnanti,* most people call Raffaele a heretic and a fool. The priests certainly don't like him. He claims that this pool is a device of the *uominilupi,* that he found it by accident deep in a cavern when he was mining there one day."

"I'm going to have to visit him," said Felicitas.

Lines of worry appeared on her mother's brow. "He's visiting relatives down on the coast right now," she said. "Maybe you should forget about Lungo Muso for a while. Until you get your strength back."

But Felicitas was relentless.

"Did Raffaele ever say anything about the white building?" she asked. "The one I was telling you about?"

Marietta pursed her lips. "He knows of it," she said. "And the *pastori* say they've seen it . . . but I really don't think—"

"The *pastori?*" said Felicitas.

"Our herdsmen," explained Marietta. "They roam the plains north of the badlands. *Figlia,* why don't we talk about something else? The white building's not good for you right now. You get this strange look in your eyes when we talk about the white building." Her mother gave her a worried look, stroked her cheek. "Maybe you should forget about the white building. You should think of happy things. You're young. And you're free now. You should let your freedom pull you along." She took a deep breath and looked at her daughter with concerned eyes. "You should put Lungo Muso and the white building behind you, *figlia.*"

Felicitas shook her head and stared at her mother. "I wish I could, *signora,*" she said. "I wish I could."

27

Felicitas sat by the kitchen win-dow in her mother's house watching her mother's hopebeast nose its way through the snow searching for grass. Finding nothing, it shuffled toward the back fence, stopped, turned, looked toward the house, walked a few paces to the right, then peered out to the street, its ears turning forward.

A few moments later, Piero, mounted on his own hopebeast, appeared from around the side of the house. Her mother's hopebeast bleated, stomped a few times, shook the snow from its humped back, and cantered to the stable.

She watched Piero get off his hopebeast and lead it to the stable. He had spent the last week in the south, with the plains people, the *pastori*. Confined to the prison his whole life, he now seemed intent on wandering as far as he could.

Felicitas got up, hung the kettle on the tripod above the fire, opened the door, and stepped out to the stoop.

Piero emerged from the stable.

"Buon giorno, Piero," she called. She forced herself to speak

Italian. She needed the practice. "You've finally returned from the plains."

He walked across the yard, dressed in thick *mostro* fur, his feet crunching through the snow, his breath frosting over in the crisp air.

"I have, indeed," he said, replying in Italian. "And I've brought some . . . some perplexing news." He looked at her appraisingly. "Your Italian has improved."

"I've been working hard," she said.

Working hard, she thought, as a way to forget Rosario.

"Has your mother been helping you?" asked Piero.

He approached the stoop and knocked the snow off his boots.

Felicitas nodded. "She must have been one of our teachers in the prison," she said. "She makes it easy."

Piero gave her a hug and a kiss.

"You see where you get your talent for languages from," he said. They went inside. "Your Italian sounds better than mine. In a week or two I'll be taking lessons from you."

She smiled, but as with everything, could feel no real pleasure in Piero's compliment.

She glanced at Piero. His initial jocularity had disappeared and his eyes grew serious. She surmised the nature of his thoughts.

"This isn't a friendly visit, is it?" she said. "This perplexing news you have . . ." She trailed off.

He didn't answer immediately. He took off his cape, his scarf, and his gloves, and held his hands to the fire.

She didn't press him. She spooned some tea into the kettle, placed a plate of *pane* on the rough wood table, then sat in the chair across from him. A smile came to Piero's face, but it was an ambiguous smile, and it quickly dropped away.

At last he said, "The *pastori* know of this white building."

She took a deep breath.

"Yes, my mother told me," she said.

He leaned forward, put his hands on his knees. "Renzo was there just last month," he said.

"Renzo?" she said.

"One of the *pastori*. A herdsmen, a breeder of hopebeasts, one of their chiefs. He was there last month and he saw . . . there have been . . ." He looked at her, trying to find the right word. "There have been disturbances," he said. "Disturbances in the sky. He's seen things."

Apprehension congealed like a ball of ice in her chest. The white building. Coming back to haunt her. She remembered the picture Lungo Muso had drawn, successive slabs of white piled on top of each other in a diminishing sequence of size, no windows, no doors.

"Disturbances?" she said.

Piero turned his attention to the fire, stirred it with the poker, and added a few thin logs. Fire sprang from the logs and steam unfurled from the kettle spout.

"They call this white building the outpost," he said. "I don't know why they call it that. Maybe because it's so far north. Maybe because it's the last recognizable landmark before they turn their herds back. But they say the outpost is ten times the size of the prison, shaped just like you say it is." He put the poker back and stretched his legs. "Covered with glyphs. No windows, no doors, no way in or out. Renzo says many *pastori* have tried, but no one has ever succeeded. He was there with his herd at least six times last summer, and each time these . . . these disturbances became greater."

Felicitas was now curious. "Did he describe them?" she asked.

Piero shrugged. "He called them . . . ghosts, phantoms. Whole cities of phantoms. They appear on the tundra for an instant, then disappear. The sky warps and bends above this outpost, skyboats flicker for a second or two, then disappear. He sees people. He tries to touch them but he can't. They're shadows. He shouts at them but they don't hear. They can't see him. They don't know he's there."

Felicitas was silent. She took the water from the tripod and poured it into the teapot.

"They're coming," she said quietly. "Just like Maritano said they would."

"Who?"

She looked up at him, stopped pouring the water. "The New Ones," she said.

For a long time neither of them spoke. While they waited for the tea to steep they stared into the hearth, where the logs, glowing red, collapsed by increments, sending embers up the flue. Piero picked a chunk of ice out of his fur pants and tossed it into the hearth. It sizzled in a wisp of smoke.

"Renzo also said he saw fire," murmured Piero. "At least a mirage of fire."

Her arms tingled, as if Lungo Muso were somewhere nearby. "Fire?" she said. She felt suddenly taut.

"A vision of fire," said Piero. "Everywhere. Stretching for miles and miles over the tundra, reaching all the way to the prison, engulfing New Florence, spreading to the badlands, leaping across the sea, rolling through space to Earth. He sees men, women, and children running through this fire. They flame up like torches, become nothing more than fuel for it. He sees blackened skeletons and charred corpses. He sees death." Piero caught her gaze and held it. "He sees the end-final time, Felicitas."

She looked out the window. New Ones, not born like humans or Old Ones, but grown in giant glass tanks, coming to destroy them. The message settled in her mind. Looking out the window, she saw, for the first time in weeks, lurking among the trees at the end of the yard, Lungo Muso, in battle dress, the silhouette of his ears discernible against the dying red light of day.

"Felicitas?" said Piero.

She pointed. "He's here," she said.

Piero looked out the window, then turned to her, puzzled.

"Who?" he said.

"Lungo Muso," she said.

He looked again, but finally shook his head.

"I've never seen him," he admitted. "But I believe you." He sighed, as if he were casting about for the right words to explain things. "Felicitas, all my life . . . at least since I've been . . . ever since the dreamphone haze lifted, I've been fighting. It's all true, everything Lungo Muso has told you. And I see that I'm going to have to fight again. So be it. Why did he choose you, a seventeen-year-old girl? It's hard to tell. But I think you have the . . . the night eyes. Like it says in the script. I think you can see things, especially anything and everything to do with the *uominilupi*. I think that's what they mean by night eyes. I've always believed this about the *uominilupi*, that there's a component to their minds that can somehow reach out and touch things. It's the same with their machinery. Their machinery, in a sense, is alive. Remember how you were the only one who could work the *cannone*? There's a mind-machine connection to the way the *uominilupi* build things. True, I can work the *pistole,* and I can work the viewscreen, and Rosario and I even figured out how to work the viewscreen and the surveillance camera as part of the same system. But neither of us can operate the more potent machines. We haven't made that connection. You have. That's why you could work the *cannone*. And you were able to anticipate the dead in the west cellblock when we searched for Silvio and the others because of this connection. You were sensitive to their implants, to those little mind-control machines we hate so much." Piero's eyes narrowed. "I bet you can guess what I'm getting at. Renzo sees fire. Lungo Muso draws the glyph of death. The New Ones are coming, they could be—"

She cut him off. "You're going to this . . . this outpost, aren't you?" she said. "The white building. And you want me to come."

His eyes grew pensive as he stared at the fire. Then he looked up, an apologetic grin on his face, and poured tea.

"All I want to do is live," he said. "I don't want to be faced with threats anymore. I've had enough threats to last a lifetime.

Here's this end-final time we learned about in the *uominilupi* script. I've listened to everything you've told me about Lungo Muso. I've written it all down. I've listened to Rosario and Silvio, and though I'm not exactly sure of the details, I'm convinced the New Ones are on their way to kill us, that they're going to use the outpost in some way to bring about this end-final time. The script in the old south tower speaks of vanquishers. I believe the New Ones are our vanquishers. I believe Lungo Muso is trying to stop them."

Her eyes narrowed as she recalled everything Lungo Muso had ever shown and told her.

"Felicitas . . ." said Piero. "Felicitas, you must. Think of the children you see playing in St. Mark's Square." He gestured toward the hearth. "Now look at that fire. Look at the way the logs blacken and glow. Think of children burning in that fire. Think of women burning in that fire. We know you hold the key. We know you can stop it. You have to come with me. You must. You have to stop it because you're the only who can."

Silvio came to visit the next day.

"Have you heard?" he asked. And then immediately started coughing.

"Your cold is worse again," said Marietta. "Come sit by the fire."

Felicitas's mother helped Silvio into a rocking chair, fussing over the old man as if he were her personal property, quickly draping a shawl around his shoulders, even smoothing out his windblown hair.

"You're kindness itself," he said, fumbling over the Italian.

"We should call the doctor," said Marietta.

"I'm fine," insisted Silvio.

"Heard what?" asked Felicitas.

The old man's eyes narrowed.

"A few soldiers from the St. Mark's garrison spotted a half-dozen dead two miles upriver yesterday."

* * *

Felicitas and Piero studied the artifacts on the second floor of the town hall.

"This is all old weaponry," said Felicitas, reading the glyphs at a glance. "All of it's broken except for this," she said, pointing at a short lancelike weapon.

Fortunato, *sindaco* of New Florence, an old man who had a full head of red hair, looked at her in astonishment, then stared at the weapons, his face filling with apprehension, as if he couldn't believe they had unwittingly housed such dangerous relics all these years.

"Weaponry?" he said.

She lifted the lancelike weapon. It had an arm brace on the end of it. The mayor took a few steps back.

"This brace closes around your forearm here," said Felicitas. "You grip this lever. It's all in these glyphs here."

She lifted the weapon and the brace automatically closed around her forearm.

"Do we need a demonstration?" asked Fortunato, trying to remain as calm as possible.

Felicitas's curiosity overrode her prudence. She gripped the lever. And in a flash of insight, she understood what Piero meant by the *uominilupi*'s mind-science, the mind-machine connection. She aimed the weapon at the hearth, she thought the thought, and a fireball boomed from the end of the ancient piece into the hearth. Fortunato jumped back. Logs scattered and the custodian scrambled to gather them before the thick tapestries on the walls caught fire.

"*Dio non voglia!*" said Fortunato. "How did you do that, *bella*?"

"I . . . I'm not sure . . ." She looked at Piero. "I think what you said . . . I just had to think the thought and—"

Piero came over.

"Let me try it," he said.

Felicitas gave him the weapon.

The mayor stepped forward. "Is it really necessary?" he pleaded.

Though the brace closed around his forearm, Piero couldn't get the weapon to fire. So he gave the lance back to Felicitas.

"Here," he said. "Try again. You have the night eyes."

She aimed the weapon. She thought the thought. And . . . *boom!* The weapon fired. The custodian, now disgruntled, ran to gather the logs again.

There were books to be studied—Earth books from the old time—books about agriculture, carpentry, masonry, and metal working.

"Some of these came when our ancestors escaped so many centuries ago," said Fortunato. "Others just appeared one day. You see how old they are. We've taken steps to copy them out fresh." He puffed up, proud of his foresight. "We have at least two copies of each book now."

They studied these books. The suns shone through the windows. The windows were made of beveled glass, which broke the light into the colors of the spectrum. Felicitas noticed something odd about her skin. In this broken light, it sparkled.

"Piero," she said, "look at this."

He came over.

"My skin sparkles in this light," she said.

He looked at her skin curiously. "Were you in the glassworks recently?" he asked. "There's a lot of glass dust in there."

"I was there our third day here, when we got that tour. But I've had several baths since then."

Piero held his own arm up into the prismatic light. His skin sparkled as well.

"Look at that," he said, amazed. He turned around. "Fortunato, Renzo, Urbano, come over here."

The three men came over.

"Look at this," said Piero.

Felicitas and Piero held their arms in the broken light. Their arms sparkled. The two New Florentines and the *pastori* chief did likewise, but their skin stayed the same.

"Try washing in this basin over here," suggested Fortunato.

Felicitas and Piero washed in the basin, scrubbed and scrubbed until their hands and arms were pink.

But when they came back to the prismatic bands of light, the result was the same: Their skin still sparkled.

28

Raffaele returned from the coast the next day.

Felicitas rode her mother's hopebeast east through the town. She was bundled in a fur coat and leggings to protect against the cold. She gave the east gatekeeper a nod, then ventured beyond the protective earthworks until she came to the river.

Here, the river wound north. She crossed the bridge. The planks, slick with hoarfrost, reverberated to the sound of the hopebeast's hoofs. As the hopebeast snorted, its breath steamed in the cold morning air. She left the bridge and followed the road.

After a few miles, the road turned into a track and, twisting this way and that, climbed the mountain. This was White Mountain, so named because there was always snow on its peak, winter or summer. Trees pressed in close from either side of the track, great outcroppings of granite protruded here and there, and several fast brooks ran right through the track.

At last she came to a clearing, and within the clearing against the gray rock-face she saw a cave where a small fire flickered just to the left of the entrance. A dozen fish hung on a rack smoking over this fire.

She turned her hopebeast toward the cave.

When she got a little closer, she called, "Raffaele?" She waited for a reply. "Raffaele, are you here?"

She got off her hopebeast and tied it to a tree.

A moment later a man appeared. He was dressed in a rough wool tunic spun from *mostro* fur—standard apparel in New Florence—and thick leather boots to his knees. He was in his forties, and didn't look at all like a heretic or a fool, such as he had been characterized in town. On the contrary, he looked intelligent, with a lean quick face, a strong brow, and a thin but wiry build. He wasn't wearing a coat, and his arms were bare. He had pale arms, with coarse black hair all over them. What marked him as different was his left eye—it was coated with a thin gray membrane.

When Raffaele saw her, a fatalistic grin came to his face.

He gave her a wave, as if he had known her all his life. Felicitas couldn't understand this. She'd never met the man before.

"So you've come at last," he said. "The girl has arrived."

As they entered the cave, Raffaele told her that he had seen her a hundred times, that Lungo Muso had shown her to him again and again.

"You are the one," he said. "The girl who can see with the night eyes. I knew you were coming. Lungo Muso shows me a girl, she's in a prison yard, she's insensible, her eyes are dull, yet she etches the most exquisite glyphs into the ground with a pipe. Lungo Muso shows me a girl holding a green finger bowl, a girl all alone in the forest, a girl riding on the tail of a *mostro*. The girl is you."

The entrance of the cave widened into a main chamber.

Rough wood furniture stood around an open fire. A hole had been chiseled through the roof for smoke to escape. Paintings of hopebeasts and *mostri* decorated the walls, and hundreds of books stood on shelves.

"I'm interested in the pool," she said.

But he seemed not to hear. "Sit over there," he said.

She sat down. He glanced around the room as if he were looking for something, but, giving up, turned to her.

"I used to be a miner," he said.

"Yes," she said, "my mother told me."

"I had a wife and a family, but they all died in a rock slide," he said. "We were in here mining. For copper. There was nothing I could do. That's how I got this eye. A rock sliver." His face grew slack, his good eye pensive, as if he were overcome with sadness. "After they died," he said, "I started seeing Lungo Muso. I tried to get a new wife but none of the women in town trusted my talk of Lungo Muso. That's why I live up here by myself. I haven't the patience for people in town anymore." Raffaele shrugged. "I try to make them understand, about the outpost and all, but they don't believe me. I guess some of them might change their minds, now that you're here."

Felicitas shifted on the uncomfortable wooden chair.

"And when was the last time Lungo Muso came to you?" she asked.

Raffaele took a few steps forward and slumped down on a bench.

"A week or two before I left for the coast. He takes me places." He peered at her cautiously. "Has he ever done that to you?"

She nodded. "He's taken me to Earth," she said.

Raffaele leaned forward, put his elbows on his knees. The man seemed weary, as if he'd lived too long with his burden.

"He's taken me to Florence, the old Florence on Earth, in the old time, to a big house, and there's a man in armor sitting at a table and he's surrounded by New Ones and Old Ones. The New Ones are forcing this man to sign something. I have no idea what it is. Then Lungo Muso takes me to the workshop of a *genio* named Leonardo, and I see this *genio* blown to bits by *fucile* fire. Then I'm out over the ocean and I see some ships scuttled by the New Ones. I ask Lungo Muso what it means but he's never been able to talk to me. All does is snarl."

It was as if Raffaele couldn't stop talking. Now that he'd started, the pressure of keeping it to himself all these years was too much. He was going to talk, had to talk, and Felicitas simply tried to understand, as best as she could, everything he said.

"He takes me to a small English village where a boy experiments with a tea kettle. Who knows what it means?" Raffaele seemed downright frustrated now. "And then he takes me to Germany where a young man experiments with small rockets. I don't understand. He takes me to a sandy strip of land near a beach where two men are trying to fly a box with wings. Why? I don't know. I've tried to find the answers in these books," he said, waving his hand toward the books, "but I haven't found them yet. He finally takes me to a small room somewhere in Italy, and there's a man sitting at a table, and he's writing with a quill, and I'm able to glance over his shoulder, and I see that he's scribbled his name." Felicitas thought of Galileo; but it wasn't Galileo Raffaele was talking about. "His name is Niccolò Machiavelli," said the New Florentine. "Who is Niccolò Machiavelli?" asked Raffaele. "How should I know? I ask Lungo Muso, but of course he just barks or grunts. How am I supposed to understand barks and grunts?" Raffaele shook his head. "I think he must mistake me for a cur." He gestured toward the books. "I look for Machiavelli in these books, but I can't find him. Lungo Muso shows me this man again and again, as if this man is the key to the whole thing, but I don't get it. I haven't been able to put it together."

And Felicitas thought, Machiavelli. Just like Maritano said. The name somehow unnerved her.

Raffaele got up and scratched his back, looking more perplexed that ever.

"Where's the pool?" asked Felicitas.

Raffaele stared at her, as if he weren't sure he could trust her. He pointed to a great crack in the wall at the back.

"That way," he said. He was suddenly circumspect, suspicious.

"Can I see it?"

Again, he debated with himself. Finally, he said, "I've endured a decade of ridicule."

"I won't ridicule you, Raffaele," she said. "I believe you."

He considered this, then finally shrugged. "Come this way," he said, his weariness bringing a great sag to his shoulders.

He led her around the fire past some earthenware jars, pushed several bunches of herbs out of the way, and, taking a lantern from a hook on the wall, entered the opening at the back, holding the lantern high above his head.

The cave narrowed considerably, became no more than a dank passageway. Felicitas felt cool wind on her face and heard the sound of flowing water below. Raffaele turned to her.

"There's a river at the bottom," he said. "We won't be going that far. The pool's just up here. Watch your step. This ledge is narrow. I've always meant to rope it off. I never have."

The passageway widened. The rock face, rich in copper, had turned green with oxidation. Up ahead she saw some light . . . the glow . . . the luminescence of the pool . . .

Faint at first, but growing brighter with each step, violet, blue, and pink, shimmering in a dim rainbow upon the rock face.

The floor of the passageway rose and the walls and ceiling closed in, narrowing to a bottleneck. They both had to crouch through.

Once through, the cave again widened.

And there it was. The pool.

Perfectly round, too regular, too even, the work of intelligence, not geology, small, no more than five or six paces across, with an upraised lip of stone around it. She was mesmerized. She walked to the edge and got down on her knees.

"I wouldn't touch it if I were you," warned Raffaele. "That's not really water. It's plasma or something. I made the mistake of touching it once and it nearly killed me. Knocked me right out." Raffaele approached cautiously and peered into the pool. "Every so often I see Lungo Muso down there staring up at me. Sometimes he climbs out and shakes the plasma off his fur like a dog shaking off water."

She looked at Raffaele. "You just found it here one day?"

He pointed to the bottleneck opening. "I was in here with my pickax pounding away. My pickax went right through where that opening is and I found this cavern back here. The pool was just as you see it. A few days later, I saw Lungo Muso standing next to it. That's how it all started . . . the trips . . . the excursions—whatever you want to call them."

She turned back to the pool. The plasma glowed, swirled, pulsated. She looked at the upraised lip of rock surrounding the pool, brushed away some of the dust, and found some glyphs, badly worn but still discernible.

"Have you ever seen these before?" she asked.

He nodded. "The dust keeps falling from up there," he said indicating the ceiling. "I've got things living up there, I don't know what they are, things with wings, not bats, I know what bats are. I used to clean the glyphs but I can't read them anyway so I decided there was no point. I haven't cleaned them in a long time."

She read the glyphs: *"We step around and behind, but never across. We run the circle but never the line. We start where we finish, and finish where we start."*

Yes, she could translate, but she couldn't interpret. She looked at the plasma. The pool was a beginning; the pool was an ending. As she stared into the pool, the colors shifted and changed, and the tingling came to her arms. In the plasma she saw clouds, then stars, and finally fire, the vast inextinguishable fire Renzo, the *pastori* chief, had spoken of, reaching across the space, consuming everything, the instrument of the end-final time.

"Felicitas?" said Raffaele.

She hardly heard him. The fire faded, leaving behind a diaphanous mist, and through this mist there emerged a figure. She recognized the figure—the shaggy head, the ears, the indomitable amber eyes. It was Lungo Muso. The mist cleared, and she saw Lungo Muso staring up at her through the plasma. He raised his hand, reached to her, beckoned her. He was pleading, and she knew she had to go to him. She had to help him, wanted to help him. So she reached out, heedless of Raffaele's warning, and dipped her hand into the plasma, knowing there was still much to learn.

As her fingertips touched Lungo Muso's, the cavern disappeared around her and she found herself floating next to the Old One.

She was stepping around and behind, bending the line so she could start at the finish and finish at the start, twisting time, guided by Lungo Muso's able hand. The pool. A way in, a way out, connected to the river. The river of time. The Old One, using his night eyes, dropped these thoughts into her mind, and she absorbed them the way a plant absorbs sunlight. Here she was, traveling with Lungo Muso again, but this time it felt different. This time he conveyed to her his great sense of urgency.

They traveled through the stars, through time, using the pool as a transfer point. He explained this to her as they floated next to each other. The pool was yet another part of their mindscience. She shouldn't be startled by how fast they traveled or how bizarre everything looked, he told her. If she wasn't exactly unsettled, she at least felt disoriented, and found herself clasping Lungo Muso's hand tightly.

They landed on a barren and hostile world where a desert of broken rock and sand stretched to a distant horizon. She saw soldiers, human ones. They surrounded a pool just like the one in Raffaele's cave. She looked up at Lungo Muso, hoping for an explanation, but he simply gestured toward the soldiers around the pool. She watched, trying to make sense of it, absorbing without trying to analyze. The soldiers erected several posts around the pool. Flashing lights blinked on the top of each post.

One of the soldiers twisted a handle on a control box, then took cover with the others in a ditch. The lights glowed, formed a nebulous mass between the posts, and the plasma in the pool was drawn upward into this light. The plasma then sizzled, bubbled, and finally disappeared.

She tried to puzzle it out. Why would these human soldiers want to destroy one of Lungo Muso's pools? Did they view the pool as a weapon? And did that mean there was a larger conflict between the humans and the *uominilupi?*

Before she could think of any answers, Lungo Muso whisked her away to a jungle world. Human soldiers performed the same task, vaporizing a *uominilupi* pool, as if these pools were particularly dangerous and needed to be destroyed wherever they were found. The pools were transfer points. The humans were trying to stop the *uominilupi* from moving around.

With breathless rapidity, Lungo Muso took her to a snow-bound world. The same operation was taking place. By sheer repetition, he was expressing the importance of these pools. But she still wasn't sure why.

To an airless cratered moon; the pool again vaporized by human soldiers.

Again and again, to world after world; human soldiers were seeking out these pools and destroying them.

Lungo Muso turned to her. "The New Ones are coming," he said with his night eyes. "They have to use the old ways. They have to hop from stone to stone. They will reach the river of time, out where the worlds are few, and the stars are distant. And they will annihilate. They will destroy. They know not the ways of the Old Ones. They cannot reconcile. They will kill any and all who are different."

The pools, a way to get around quickly, through time and

space. But now destroyed by human soldiers. The New Ones using the old ways.

She stared at Lungo Muso, and speaking with her own night eyes, said, "Do you mean they come in skyboats?"

He nodded.

And now that she had at least an idea of their mechanical means of arrival, she pondered their reason for coming. To annihilate. So it was true. She felt suddenly weak with fear. The end-final time was upon them. And it was going to be brought about by the river of time, the big white building, the outpost.

"We must hurry," said Lungo Muso.

Space curved above them, the stars stretched into thin white lines, and she again went behind and around.

She found herself standing in a giant steel bubble in front of an oval of glass. She understood she was in a skyboat, a human skyboat. She looked through the oval of glass, and knew that this was Rosario's episode, the one he had told her about the day they first kissed. She looked out the oval where she saw a black sky and endless stars, and a planet below, not Earth—she knew the land masses of Earth from the old globe in Francesco's library—but another planet. This indeed was Rosario's episode.

She looked around for the book Rosario always said Lungo Muso tried to show him, and saw it lying on a bedside table.

She saw a man sleeping in the bed. A small man with a pointed beard, his forehead furrowed in a frown, as if he were having a bad dream.

"This is James Kenneth Reymont," said Lungo Muso.

Reymont. Just like Maritano said. The name now seemed to have a palpable weight in Felicitas's subconscious. And she was more afraid of it than ever.

"He is the one," continued Lungo Muso. "He's the terminus of the thread, the final strand. There he sleeps," said Lungo Muso. "The colonel. The conqueror. The renegade. And there lies that book." He pointed at the book. "How can a slender volume like this have such a profound effect on our lives? We thought that with massive temporal surgery we might solve the problem, but we now see it all comes down to this book." He looked at her. "Go ahead," he said. "Have a look."

Felicitas walked to Reymont's bedside table and lifted the book. The author, a name she immediately recognized, was Niccolò Machiavelli. This was it. The book. The one Lungo Muso had so desperately tried to show Rosario again and again. And here was the connection between Reymont and Machiavelli. She looked at the title. *The Prince.* Then she looked at Lungo Muso. He nodded, an odd movement, neither assent nor affirmation.

"You've seen it before," he said. "When you were a dead girl. You've read it. All the books . . . I brought them to the prison through the . . . the pool?" He named it as she named it, as Raffaele named it, so they could understand each other. "That's how all the books got into the prison," he said. "That's how they all got to New Florence. As a way to help you." He nodded at the book. "Open it," he said. "Reymont's underscored several passages."

She turned first to the table of contents. She read over some of the chapter headings. This particular edition was in English. *On New Principalities Acquired by One's Own Arms and Skill. On Cruelty and Mercy. On Whether Fortresses are Useful.* The book was badly dog-eared, looked as if it had been read a hundred times. She flipped through the yellowed pages till she came to some underlined quotes. *A prince must concentrate solely on the profession of war. He mustn't let any other object distract him.* She flipped again. *A prince with a moral conscience will come to ruin in a world full of so many wicked men. A prince must discard his moral conscience if he wishes to stay in power.* She flipped a third time. *Men are thankless, unfaithful, and greedy. Most of all, they are liars.* And she flipped a last time, to a sentence that was underscored so heavily and with such passion that the pen had actually gone through the page. *A prince always has a ready reason for breaking his promise.*

Now she looked at Colonel James Kenneth Reymont. About

sixty, short, bald, no more than a hundred pounds. Was he the reason she was in prison? Was he the man who could tell her why there were just Italians and English in the prison? This man who had been so influenced by Machiavelli's slim volume? She now remembered the book, from when she'd read it as a dead girl. But she still didn't understand, at least not completely. Pieces were still missing.

She turned to Lungo Muso.

Lungo Muso nodded. "Yes, Felicitas," he said. "It is he." He gestured toward James Kenneth Reymont. "Meet the vanquisher."

Lungo Muso took her to the snowy plain again.

Far in the distance she saw the white building—the outpost—rising out of the tundra into the dusky winter sky. The wind was high, and the snow on the ground drifted, but she hardly felt the cold. She thought of Reymont. What did that small and decidedly weak-looking man do? What chain of events had he initiated? They stood on this bleak and treeless slope, gazing upon the outpost—the river of time—and she at last understood that James Kenneth Reymont was in some way responsible for everything that had ever happened to her.

She glanced at Lungo Muso, hoping he would explain. But he looked tired, weak, as if he couldn't maintain this excursion through Raffaele's pool much longer. With some effort, he raised his hand and pointed to the white building: a series of oblongs stacked one on top of the other in diminishing sequence of size, such as she'd seen again and again. As he pointed, flame issued from the top. The sky swirled, and a dozen violet funnel clouds appeared.

"This is where you start," said the Old One, "and this is where you end." He let his arm drop. "This is where you must go," he said.

The flame expanded into an all-encompassing wave. The

wave rolled toward them. She wanted to run away, but Lungo Muso put his hand on her shoulder.

"You are the journeyman," he said. "Only you can stop the fire."

She stared at the oncoming wall of flame.

"But *how* can I stop it?" she said.

The Old One knelt. He drew the glyph in the snow again. Three thorny lines with a fire underneath. The end-final time. But now she saw it with a new understanding.

All she had to do was shift the emphasis. *Time.* That was the important part. Time reaching backward, time reaching forward, a death so wide, so broad, it leapt into the past to preempt existence, sprang into the future to strangle potentiality.

Lungo Muso nodded. He seemed relieved.

"You at last see with your night eyes, Felicitas," he said.

On her way down White Mountain, Felicitas met Piero riding toward her across the east bridge.

"Your mother said I would find you here," he said.

The suns were higher now, and the hoarfrost had melted from the bridge planks.

"I was with Raffaele," she said.

She told Piero about her episode with Lungo Muso.

"Then it's much as we suspected," he said. "The New Ones are on their way and they mean to destroy us. But that's not our only problem." They rode in silence for a moment. "I was north on the river with the St. Mark's garrison this morning," he said. They left the bridge. The sound of the hopebeast hoofs grew instantly muffled on the soft dirt road. "We found a camp," he said.

She felt her shoulders sinking.

"The dead?" she said.

"I wish I could tell you otherwise," he said. "We had a little bit of snow up that way. They left fresh tracks. We chased after them. We actually saw them on a hill, but we couldn't catch up to them."

Piero reined in his hopebeast, bringing it to a halt.

Felicitas did the same.

"How many were there?" she asked.

"I saw three, but I think there were more. The prints they left . . . I don't know, about six." He turned to her, hesitating. "Felicitas, I saw . . ." He shook his head. "I saw Maritano. There was no mistaking that skull. Even from that distance. He's still wearing the cursed thing." Piero spurred his hopebeast, and they continued slowly along the road. "I can't imagine how they tracked us all this way."

29

Silvio's cough got so bad again that Felicitas and Marietta had to move him into the town infirmary.

"I'll be able to administer my embrocations more effectively at the infirmary," said the doctor. "And he'll have round-the-clock care."

The town infirmary, a commodious log structure with a peaked roof and an indoor water well, sat at the end of a cul-de-sac just off St. Mark's Square.

Even in the first day the old man's cough improved. If he was still occasionally racked by violent spasms, the spells were less frequent, and he could sleep for longer periods. Rest, the doctor insisted again, was the best curative.

As mother and daughter sat beside the sleeping convalescent, Marietta said, "You've been quiet, *figlia.*" Marietta gazed at her daughter with melancholy indulgence. "You've rarely spoken since you visited the mountain."

Felicitas watched a nurse walk by with a tray of *pane* soup.

"*Signora* . . ." She didn't want to upset her mother. "*Signora,*
I was with Lungo Muso again. When I was up on White Mountain with Raffaele. What Raffaele says about the pool is true. It's
a device. Of the *uominilupi.*"

Her mother nodded. "And what did Lungo Muso say this
time?" she inquired.

Felicitas fiddled with the sleeve of her tunic.

"He showed me things," she said. "I know what's going to
happen. He told me the New Ones would arrive in skyboats."
She pointed out the tall narrow windows where pink sunshine
lit the cul-de-sac. "All this . . . New Florence, the prison . . . the
reason we're here . . . this is all the end result of forces far
greater than any of us can . . ."

She stopped. She saw her mother's eyes glistening.

"Don't go," said Marietta.

"*Signora,* I have to." She again looked out the window. "If I
don't go, we'll lose all this."

Her mother nodded. "I understand, Felicitas."

Felicitas wasn't sure she did.

"Lungo Muso says I'm the one," she said. But she realized
that no matter what she said, her mother wouldn't want her to
go. "I don't understand half of what he tells me, but I trust him.
He's weak. He tells me what he can. I have no idea what I'm
going to do once I get to the outpost. But I have to go." She
leaned forward and put her hand on her mother's arm. "Please,
signora, you have to understand. Time is running out."

Her mother smiled and brushed away her tears.

"And you go with Piero?" she asked.

Felicitas nodded.

"Then I know you'll be safe," said Marietta.

She presented Raffaele to Mayor Fortunato and his town councilors the following day.

Raffaele was fidgety as they sat in the town hall watching
the leaders gather.

"I haven't been inside the town hall for years," said Raffaele.

She patted his hand. "They should have believed you long before this," she said.

A few more councilors filed into the chamber.

"You don't know how good it feels to be around people again," he said. "I might tell you I like my life up in the cave, but ever since my family died . . ." He rubbed his opaque eye. "I'm glad you came here today with me, Felicitas. I'm glad you're going to speak for me."

"You're a decent man, Raffaele," she said. "You're the only man who"—she gestured at the artifacts on the special display table—"who cares about all this, who knows what it means. Someone else might have bowed to the pressure. You might have denied Lungo Muso. But you kept insisting. Maybe that's why Lungo Muso's chosen you. He knows he can count on you."

Raffaele lifted his chin, pleased with this praise.

"No one's going to tell me to disbelieve what my own eyes have seen," he said.

"Which is why I think you should come on this expedition," said Felicitas. "They've chosen Urbano. And he's just a hunter. Why shouldn't they choose you? You've had direct contact with the Old One." A grin came to her face. "Not only that, I like you."

"You just feel sorry for me."

"You've been unfairly treated," she said. "Why shouldn't I feel sorry for you? People are going to take you seriously now." Her grin broadened to a comradely smile. "I'm going to make sure of that. We who have gone on excursions with Lungo Muso must look after each other."

He nodded fondly. "We must indeed," he said. "You look after me, Felicitas, and I'll look after you. That's how it should be. That's how it *will* be. We're honorary Old Ones."

"Of course we are," she said.

Fortunato brought the meeting to order and Felicitas got up to speak.

Though her Italian still wasn't perfect, she could speak it well enough to make herself understood in front of the assembly.

She nodded graciously toward the officials.

"Mayor and councilmen," she began, "you see before you a man who has been vilified by your community. You see a man who has been ridiculed so often that he must live in a cave on White Mountain all by himself. He is a man who has been called heretic and fool." She swept her arm toward Raffaele. "But this man is no heretic," she said. "And he's no fool either." She took a few steps toward the assembled councilmen. "I've had the privilege of speaking with Raffaele about his time on White Mountain. For ten years Raffaele has been telling you about the Lungo Muso. For ten years he has been telling you about the outpost. He has warned you about the end-final time. But you all laughed at him."

She stared at the council, letting the point hit home.

"Then a young woman came to New Florence," she said. "That young woman was from the prison. And this young woman knew about Lungo Muso, too. She knew about the outpost. She knew about the everlasting flames that are coming to destroy us. And you must have asked yourselves, how can Raffaele and this girl tell the same story when they've never met each other before?"

She stopped and looked at each and every councilman.

"Councilmen, we tell the same story because the story is true. And because the story is true we have asked you to support this expedition to the outpost. You have so far chosen the members of the expedition wisely. Your inclusion of several *pastori* is particularly prudent. But I now ask you to include Raffaele. His intelligence, his knowledge, his warmth and kindness make him an excellent choice. He has been touched by Lungo Muso. He understands. He knows how dangerous the outpost is. He knows what's at stake."

The mayor and councilmen stared at her. They then conferred for several minutes.

She went back to Raffaele and sat down.

"You speak so eloquently," said Raffaele. "It's true what Piero told me. You have a way with words."

"I speak only as I feel," she replied.

"Then you must feel strongly," he said.

She turned to him. "You know what I like most about you?"

"I'm surprised to be liked at all, after ten years as a hermit."

"I like your lack of conceit. You're an example to me, Raffaele. You've made me understand the truth, and just how important it is."

At the front, the mayor and his councilmen took their chairs. Felicitas got up and approached them.

"Well?" she said.

The *sindaco* cleared his throat.

"This council offers our sincerest apology to Raffaele," said Fortunato. "A public apology will be posted in the square, in all the guild halls, and at all the gates." He leaned forward, folding his hands. "And we agree to your request, Felicitas." He turned to Raffaele. "As he is privy to the teachings of Lungo Muso, and knows about the outpost, he would make an excellent addition to your party. We therefore approve your recommendation and will make the extra equipage available."

They used the parade ground adjacent to the St. Mark's barracks as a staging area for the expedition.

Felicitas and Piero stood at the far end of the target range. Renzo and the other *pastori* were practicing with bows and arrows, sharpening their hunting skills under the direction of Urbano—they would supplement their diet on the way to the outpost with wild game.

Piero held Felicitas's *pistola* in his hand, the only *pistola* to make it all the way from the prison to New Florence without getting lost or confiscated by the dead. It wasn't working anymore.

"I don't know what's wrong with it," said Piero. "I was

practicing with it just this morning. The last time I fired, it made a strange hiss. Then it wouldn't work."

He lifted the weapon, aimed at one of the targets at the far end of the range, and pulled the unwieldy trigger. Nothing happened. He gave the *pistola* to Felicitas.

"You try," he said. "Maybe with your night eyes . . . it might respond the same way the *cannone* in the prison responded."

She took the weapon, aimed, and pulled the trigger. Nothing happened.

"It's gone," she said. "I guess all we have is the lance now."

The expedition party consisted of Felicitas, Piero, Urbano, Raffaele, Renzo, and five of Renzo's ablest riders. Ten people altogether, each riding a hopebeast, with five extra hopebeasts to carry supplies and equipment.

They set off at dawn the next day, exited the town through the north gate, and followed the North Road through rich bottom land, past farms and pastures. Everything lay under a thin layer of snow. The air smelled crisp, and on this cloudless day Felicitas could see right to the top of the mountain peaks to the east.

Piero rode beside her. He adjusted the pack on his saddle and turned to her.

"I'm sorry Marietta couldn't come," he said.

"I'm just as glad she's staying with Silvio," she said. She looked at him with concern. "Do you think he'll be all right?"

"With Marietta looking after him, he'll have no choice," he said. He glanced toward a stand of trees at the back of a field. "I'm a little worried about Maritano, though," he said. "We found another campfire yesterday. After I left you at the range. This one was three miles downstream. It was they." He reached across and tapped the antique *uominilupi* weapon she had in her saddle scabbard. "I'm glad this lance still works."

Soon they came to the last farm.

The trees closed in.

They followed the river valley as it curved northwest. The terrain was hilly, cut with gorges, and several times they had to dismount and lead their hopebeasts. At one point, Renzo got off his hopebeast, pulled an arrow from his quill, and felled a large brown bird. Two of his men cleaned it and soon had it roasting on an open fire.

After eating the bird they set off again.

They traveled no more than an hour when Renzo led them sharply to the left. This brought them to a mountain pass. Only a small amount of snow had accumulated here, and they were able to spur their hopebeasts to a trot.

They finally arrived at a small lake. This lake marked the end of the mountain pass.

"We'll camp here for the night," said Renzo.

"A good enough spot," agreed Urbano.

"I'll post guards," said the *pastore.* "I caught a glimpse of the brown ones an hour ago." Renzo called the dead the brown ones because of the brown uniforms they wore. "We should be safe here."

Piero spoke up. "You saw them?" he said.

"They were on that ridge several miles back. They think they know how to hide. They think they walk silently. But they don't know my eyes. They don't know my ears."

"Why didn't you tell us?" asked Piero.

Renzo shrugged, as if it were a matter of small concern.

"I counted six in all," he said, "including the one who wears the skull." He patted his dagger. "They're no match for my riders."

"Renzo, they're armed with *uominilupi* weaponry," said Piero.

"Piero, it's not the kind of weapon," said Renzo. "It's the skill with which it's used."

Later that night, with the campfire burning and the stars thick in the sky, Felicitas said to Piero, "Maritano knows we're traveling to the outpost." Piero glanced up from his *pane*. "He's going to try to stop us," she said. "The New Ones are using the dead as puppets." She glanced around at the *pastori*. "Do you think Renzo will be able to protect us?"

Piero contemplated the stern-looking leader. Renzo sat on his hopebeast at the edge of the encampment staring into the forest.

"I hope so," he said. "But if he can't, we'll just have to protect ourselves."

They ate their *pane* in silence for a minute. This was a kind of hard-biscuit *pane,* not particularly palatable, but it traveled well.

Piero said, "How do you know the New Ones are using the dead as puppets?"

"Because Lungo Muso has been talking to me all afternoon," she said. "While we were in the pass."

They set off before first light the next day.

A trail terraced the mountainside on the opposite side of the lake. They reached a smooth stretch of saddle terrain near the top by noon. They traversed this saddle terrain until they got to the other side. The wind howled, stinging Felicitas's cheeks, turning her fingers numb.

It took them the rest of the day to get down the other side of the mountain. She was so tired by the time they reached the bottom that she had to coax herself to stay awake long enough to help unload supplies.

They made camp in the middle of a small pasture.

"Why don't we camp in those trees?" asked Felicitas. "We'll be out of the wind."

Renzo glanced nonchalantly toward the saddle terrain.

"Because they're up there," he said. "The brown ones. They followed us. I'd sooner stay out here in the open, where we can see them coming."

* * *

The dead made no attempt to show themselves that night.

"You see?" said Renzo. "They're cowards. They won't attack us."

"Renzo," said Piero, "they've already killed. Back at the prison. And Felicitas thinks they mean to stop us. She thinks they're controlled by the New Ones."

"They're just men," said Renzo. "They can be killed, just as easily as you or I."

In the morning they traveled through another pass. It snowed steadily all day.

A little after lunch, Raffaele reined his hopebeast next to Felicitas's. His film-covered eye seemed to be bothering him in this cold.

"I don't feel him, Felicitas," he said. "What good am I to this expedition if I can't feel Lungo Muso? I've never been this far away from the pool before. I can't feel him at all."

She looked up at the sky. "He's waiting," she said. "Look at those clouds, those dark ones over there. Do they look strange to you?"

Raffaele looked. "Not particularly," he said.

She stared. "I don't know," she said. "They were . . . shifting. They were bending out of shape."

As they continued through the mountain pass, Sabino, a tall lithe youth, a little older than Felicitas—Renzo's younger brother—kept looking at her. Though he was handsome, she wasn't particularly flattered, and did nothing to encourage him. He was dark, with shoulder-length hair and exotic eyes, yet compared to Rosario he was unformed, had no depth of character. She felt nothing but a fond sisterly regard for Sabino.

The pass narrowed.

Renzo became ever more watchful through the course of the day.

The pass deepened, turned into a gorge. Through this gorge ran a fast shallow brook, not yet frozen over.

"We ride in the brook," said Renzo. "We'll lose the brown ones in the brook. Sabino, you take that trail over there." Sabino's face reddened—Felicitas could see that he didn't want to be separated from her. "Try to decoy them. Antonio, I want you to double back and head into the mountains. Meet us at Flat Rock." Renzo glanced up at the slope behind him, his eyes like slits. "I thought we'd lost them, but I guess we haven't."

The main party rode for the next two hours in the brook; this way they didn't leave any tracks behind them. The snow came down harder, and Felicitas could hardly see the mountains around them. The temperature got colder and colder and she often held her gloved hand in front of her face to keep her cheeks from freezing.

Renzo led them upstream until they arrived at a pool.

"Bring your hopebeasts out here," he said.

They walked their mounts onto a shoal of rocks extending outward from the bank into the pool. Renzo then had them get back into the water and led them once again through the brook. They made many such detours over the next few hours.

They finally turned around and backtracked a good distance.

Then they left the brook entirely. The snow fell heavily now.

"They'll never find our trail in all this snow," said Renzo.

After leading them into another gorge, Renzo had his riders sweep over their tracks with branches. Renzo then led them farther into the gorge.

The gorge ran west for miles, then curved to the north, and in this circuitous way, they finally veered back in the direction of the outpost.

The snow stopped late in the afternoon and the clouds cleared. Felicitas glanced at the sky every now and again, thinking it might bend or warp, or show another aberration. But all she saw were some high thin clouds, some birds, and the pinkish glow of *Grossa* and *Piccola.*

The trees this far north were different from the ones around the prison, taller, with fewer branches, and the branches were covered with thick green scales. Eventually these trees thinned out, and by the time the expedition came to Flat Rock, they grew in widely spaced clusters of two or three—dashes of green in the surrounding white.

Flat Rock, a smooth sheet of black granite sheared from the adjacent mountain by a rock slide, tilted south, got the full rays of the two suns, and acted as a heat conductor. Any accumulation of snow quickly melted from its surface. It was as big as the prison but not so tall, just twice the height of a man, and worn to a tabletop smoothness by wind and rain.

They made their camp next to Flat Rock, sheltered from the north wind on its leeward side. Renzo posted a guard on top of Flat Rock, and another in the valley.

As the suns set, Felicitas saw Sabino appear on a ridge to the west, a lone mounted figure, black against the red sky.

A short while later Antonio appeared from the east.

Both were tired and cold. Most of all, both were famished, and sat down to eat right away.

Renzo looked up at the mountains.

"If they find us now," he said, "they're magicians."

30

After supper, Sabino came up to her, his face set, his dark eyes defensive.

"Your weapon," he said. He pointed at her antique firearm. "How does it work?"

Felicitas lifted the weapon and got up. "Come," she said. "I'll show you."

Renzo watched them. Sabino wasn't fooling anyone. Everyone knew what was going on. Felicitas wasn't going to be unkind. She knew the boy liked her.

"What do you call it?" asked Sabino, his tone sullen.

"We call it a lance," she said.

"Lance," said Sabino, testing the unfamiliar English word in his mouth. "An ugly name," he concluded.

"This brace goes here," she said, "near your elbow. It closes by itself." The lance hummed as the brace closed around her arm. "You grip this lever like so." She gripped the lever. "Then you take aim." She lifted the barrel, a batonlike tube tapering to a rounded point, and aimed at a boulder halfway down the slope. "And when you're ready to fire, you just . . ." How could she put this to Sabino? "You just think the thought, and the weapon should . . ."

She visualized the discharge.

A moment later, a fireball rocketed from the end of the lance and blew the boulder to bits.

Sabino jumped. Then he looked at the weapon doubtfully, as if he weren't convinced of the sense behind the weapon's method of operation.

"You just think it?" he asked.

Renzo interrupted. "Sabino, the girl is special. She can think the way the *uominilupi* can. She has the night eyes, such as Piero's described to us."

"I know she's special," said Sabino. "I know she has the night eyes."

"Then why do you think you can learn?" asked Renzo.

But Sabino ignored his brother.

"Teach me," he said to Felicitas. "How do I think this . . . this thought. Tell me how I should—"

"Here," she said, giving him the lance.

Sabino took the lance, held it at arm's length, examined it, then gripped the lever, angling the brace so it was near his forearm. His face now hardened. He wanted to show her he was used to handling weapons. The brace hummed and closed around his forearm.

He turned to his brother, his face brightening with vindication.

"You see?" he said. "It's not so hard."

His brother simply watched.

"The brace works for everybody," explained Felicitas.

Sabino's shoulders sank. "Oh," he said, his pride deflating. "Well, I'm sure I can make the lance work," he said. He lifted the weapon and aimed. "Is there a certain way I have to grip this lever?" he asked.

"No," said Felicitas. "Just hold it the same way you might hold a hammer."

He checked his grip, then nodded to himself, certain he was holding it the right way.

"Now what do I do?" he asked.

She smiled nervously. "Don't point it at me," she said.

He swung it quickly away. "Sorry!" he said. "I didn't mean to . . . I'm sorry."

"It's all right," she said. "Aim it at that rock."

He aimed the lance at the rock.

"Now," she said, "when you're ready to fire, you just . . . this is hard to explain, but you just think the thought . . . maybe think of shooting an arrow from your bow."

He paused, thinking about it. "An arrow from my bow," he said. "That's good. I'll try that."

His face settled and he looked so grim she nearly laughed. He blinked a few times, in anticipation of the weapon firing, but the lance refused to work. Finally, he lifted his chin and stared at the batonlike barrel in consternation.

"It's not doing anything," he said.

"Try again," she said.

So he tried again. He composed his face into such a warriorlike expression that his brother Renzo finally *did* laugh.

Sabino glowered at Renzo. "If you think it's so easy," he said, "you try it."

"I don't think it's easy, Sabino," said Renzo. "I think it's impossible."

Sabino spit on the ground in disgust, then sighted the lance directly at the rock. He jerked his arm a few times, as if he thought that would get the lance to work. Nothing happened.

"Sabino," said Renzo, "I told you. The girl is special. She has a connection to their machinery. She visits the past with Lungo Muso. She goes to different worlds. Piero has tried to work the lance. So has Urbano. So have I. None of us have succeeded. Why do you think you should be any different?"

"Because the three of you are old and simple men," said Sabino, "and I'm young and smart, like Felicitas."

Felicitas tried to defuse things.

"It's all right, Sabino," she said. "If you can't work it, it doesn't mean—"

"I feel it coming," he insisted. "It's almost there. I sense the thing's power in my arm."

Sabino lifted the weapon, more determined than ever. He tried to fire the lance, but again the lance wouldn't work.

He turned to her in frustration.

"What am I doing wrong?"

"You're not doing anything wrong," she said. "It's just not responding. I don't know . . . I guess you have to be . . . I've known Lungo Muso a long time and I—"

"Let me try again," he said.

He closed his eyes, clenched his jaw, and held his breath. His body shook, as if he were trying to lift a thousand-pound weight . . . and, to her astonishment, the sky lit up, and she thought Sabino had finally made the lance fire. But then the old feeling of premonition overwhelmed her, she heard the ticking and the whispering, and she knew he hadn't made the lance fire, that in fact he had been fired upon by the dead, and that the sky lighting up had been the flash of *pistola* fire.

Sabino's arm disappeared in a splash of blood and the lance fell to the ground. The boy's face turned white, his eyes opened wide, and he staggered backward.

"What?" he said, looking at his arm.

"Sabino!" Felicitas cried.

His arm wasn't there anymore. All she saw was a blackened stump below the elbow.

Sabino's heel caught on the edge of a rock and he fell to the seat of his pants. Blood dripped from the stump.

"My arm," he groaned.

The boy sat there, his legs akimbo, and looked at what was left of his arm, his eyes glazed, as if he wasn't sure what had happened.

"Sabino!" she said again.

Renzo jumped from the top of Flat Rock and landed next to Sabino. He quickly tied a leather lace around his brother's severed arm, making a tourniquet. He then dragged Sabino into a small ditch.

From behind the nearest trees, six dead appeared: Maritano, still with the skull tied to his head, Marco, Ottavio, two others she didn't recognize—and Gasparo. Gasparo, now wearing a brown uniform, his head shaved, a *pistola* in his hand. Gasparo, standing next to Maritano, as if Maritano had chosen him, out of spite, because of her mistake, because of her hesitation, for his new number-one *consigliere*. The dead fanned out around the edge of the campsite. Gasparo remained by Maritano's side, as loyal to Maritano as he'd been to Piero.

"Felicitas!" called Piero. "Get down."

She ran to the ditch beside Renzo and Sabino, still unnerved by the sight of Gasparo. She shook her head, struggled to regain her wits.

"Get your weapon," hissed Renzo.

Yes, her weapon. She had to think clearly. She couldn't let an attack like this confuse her.

Pistola fire erupted all around them.

She inched out of the shallow ditch on her stomach toward her lance.

Two *pastori* emerged from the tent while two others leapt from their guard positions on top of Flat Rock. All four launched a volley of arrows at the dead, giving her cover. The dead scattered. The arrows sang through the air. An arrow hit Ottavio in the shoulder, skewering him—the barbed point went right through, came out his back.

Felicitas, now some distance from Renzo and Sabino, grabbed her lance, and, keeping as low as she could, mounted it on her arm. Piero, Urbano, and Raffaele took up positions with their own bows and arrows. The hopebeasts tugged at their reins, skittish, ready to bolt, bleating mournfully. She glanced toward the edge of the encampment to see if the dead were advancing, but they kept their distance, held back by the swarm of arrows.

"Felicitas," called Maritano. "Tell them to stop! There's nothing you can do to beat us."

From her prone position on the snow and rock, she looked at Maritano. He and Gasparo had moved to the right, now knelt behind one of the few trees in the area. Maritano stared at her through the dusky light of the dying day, the skull glowing with its own preternatural light on top of his head. He singled her out, as always, for special attention.

"Give yourself up, Felicitas," he called again.

She ignored him. She looked at the brace. Blackened and half melted. She wasn't sure she was going to get it to work.

Maritano tried again. "You can't stop the New Ones," he called.

"Yes we can," she called back, still fiddling with the brace.

"They're coming whether you like it or not."

"Let them come," she called. "We'll be ready for them."

As she tried to secure the brace around her forearm, she caught movement out of the corner of her eye.

Gasparo was loping toward her from behind the tree, obeying Maritano's order. She struggled frantically with the brace, but the weapon had been so badly damaged, the brace wouldn't close. Some of the *pastori* shot arrows at Gasparo, trying to keep him away from her. One of the arrows got him in the leg, but he hardly noticed. She finally gave up with the brace. She clutched the lever, hoping the lance would work without the brace, and aimed at Gasparo.

But before she could shoot, the ground exploded directly in front of her.

Maritano was firing. Not trying to hit her, just trying to keep her in one place. Dirt and rock leapt into her eyes. A diversionary tactic. She lifted her hand to her eyes, tried to wipe the dirt out. She couldn't see. She aimed the lance blindly, thought the thought, heard the weapon fire, felt it jerk, but with her eyes closed, her shot went wide.

She forced her eyes open, hoping to get off another shot.

But she was too late. Gasparo was already there.

He ripped the lance out of her hand, tossed it to the ground, scooped her up, and slung her over his shoulder, jackknifing her at the waist. He carried her over the rough ground toward Maritano.

"It's time to come home, Felicitas," said the big man.

She pounded at Gasparo. "Put me down!" she cried.

She saw Urbano and Piero running after her. Piero raised his weapon . . . but hesitated.

"Felicitas, I can't . . . I might hit you!" he called.

"Just shoot!" she called.

She'd sooner take her chances than be Maritano's special prisoner again.

Piero raised his weapon, but again he hesitated.

"I can't," he said. "The outpost."

She understood. They couldn't risk losing her under any circumstances. She was the only who could beat the outpost. It was up to her. She had to somehow fight this giant of a dead man by herself. But how?

She saw the arrow sticking out of his leg, the shaft protruding from his muscular thigh like a quill, blood soaking through his brown pants. She reached down and, gripping it with all her strength, yanked it out. He seemed not to notice. It was as if he were numb to pain. She stuck the arrow between her teeth, clutched the back of his shirt, and pushed herself up. Pivoting her abdomen on his broad shoulder, and using the arrow like a knife, she stabbed him in the left eye, hooking her arm around to the front of his face in an awkward but effective lunge. He grunted in pain and surprise. He reached up, stunned by the suddenness of the attack.

He lost his grip.

Felicitas wiggled free.

She fell to the ground, and, juiced on adrenaline, jumped to her feet and ran away.

She bolted toward the *pastori*.

She got no farther than a few yards before Maritano tackled her from behind.

She fell to her stomach. He fell on top of her, his arms around her hips. She clawed at the ground ahead of her, trying to pull herself away, but he clutched her fur tunic and pulled her back. Piero and Urbano were now running toward her. Surely they would save her.

But then, as if receiving a silent command from Maritano, Marco opened up with a withering hail of *pistola* fire, and both Piero and Urbano were forced to take cover behind a boulder.

"Felicitas, please," said Maritano. "Please listen to me."

"Let go of me!" she screamed.

He got up, sat on her legs, and pressed his hands against the small of her back, keeping her pinned.

"They've fixed the prison," he said. "You'll like it a lot more now." He was pleading. "It's working much better now. Everybody has food. It's warm. The lights are back on. Why don't you come home, Felicitas?" he said, the whine creeping into his voice. "Why don't you please come home?"

"Get off me, Maritano!" she said.

"I've brought a counselor with me," he said. "We'll let it do its work. And then you'll finally understand. You'll be happy. We'll both be happy."

She knew there was no reasoning with him.

She found a fist-sized rock and, wrenching herself around, whacked him on the side of the head.

His head jerked to one side, and a bright red gash appeared on his temple, but other than that, he didn't seem to feel it. With the skull still tied to his head, he was a vision from a nightmare.

"You can't get away from us, Felicitas," he said. "No matter how hard you try. Your skin, it sparkles. You're marked. The scout ship marked you. We'll always be able to find you."

She understood. The scout ship. Coming in the night so long ago above the prison yard. Out of the clouds, a bright light, a loud hum, the dispensary shaking, not really a scout ship, but a probe of some kind, marking them with this sparkle, something that allowed the dead to track them, another anti-escape system.

"Maritano, you don't understand," she said. "The New Ones . . . they've turned you into . . . and the outpost, they're going to change the outpost. They're going to use it to spread the fire . . . and I don't care what the counselor tells you, the New Ones aren't going to spare anyone. Not even you. They're going to—"

"I've brought a counselor with me," he repeated, cutting her off.

"I want you to listen to me, Maritano," she said. "I want you to—"

"I'm taking you home, Felicitas," he said, his voice hardening. He looked at Piero and Urbano, who still crouched behind the boulder, then at the *pastori*, who continued their barrage of arrows. "I'm taking you home and no one's going to stop me. I'm going to make love to you. I finally understand about love, Felicitas. The New Ones have taught me about love. I can make you happy."

"That's what you think," she said.

She smashed him again with the rock. *Pistola* fire hissed everywhere, arrows flew through the air, *pastori* shouted war cries, smoke filled the air, and Gasparo groaned in agony over by the tree. She swung again, hitting Maritano in the ear.

He tried to grab her arm but she jerked it away and swung yet again. She knew it wasn't Maritano's fault, but she was so angry, she couldn't stop herself. She reached up, even as he again tried to grab her arm and pulled the snout of the skull over his face, blinding him then, using all her strength, swung yet once more.

He was stunned by the blow. She raised both arms and pushed. He lost his balance and fell over.

"That's what I think of your counselor," she said.

The skull tumbled from his head. She slid out from between

his legs. Maritano struggled to get to his knees again. She sprang to her feet and ran away. Maritano just knelt there. He could have killed her. He could have drawn his *pistola* and shot her in the back. But he didn't. He hesitated, just as she had hesitated with Gasparo. Some of the old Maritano was still inside. Some of the old Maritano still loved her.

She ran for cover and crouched behind the boulder with Piero and Urbano.

She looked around, saw a corpse lying by the tent.

"Antonio's dead?" she said.

Piero nodded. "Marco got him."

She glanced toward Sabino. Renzo was still by the young man's side. Both of them were lying on their stomachs in the small ditch.

"And Sabino is still alive?" she said.

"Yes."

One of the *pastori* ran from the tent and crouched behind the boulder with them.

"I brought you a bow and arrow," he said, handing the weapon to Felicitas.

She nodded gratefully. She looked at her lance, which was at the edge of the campsite. She couldn't risk getting it now. She would get it later.

She gripped the bow and threaded an arrow onto the string. She pulled back and let the arrow fly, aiming for Maritano. Despite the way he might have spared her, her anger wouldn't let her alone. The arrow went wide. He watched it go by. Then he turned to her.

He looked at her with off-kilter eyes, a pitiful sight. She found it difficult to steady the next arrow. He looked so . . . so betrayed. What was he thinking? What were they making him think?

Finally, he got up and retreated.

He made some whining sounds. Gasparo got up, holding his eye, and lurched after him. The others followed. Some of the *pastori* came out of their hiding spots and launched some arrows after them, but it was getting dark, and there was no way to see if any of the arrows hit anybody.

She stood up and stared after the dead. They retreated up the mountain into the deepening gloom. Who could say whether they would attack again?

Renzo called out, "Save your arrows." His men turned to him, reluctant to stop their attack, but obeyed his command. "You're just going to lose them in this darkness."

She was out of breath.

Piero stood up next to her and put his hand on her shoulder.

"He still loves you," he said.

She stared up at the mountains, where the dead trudged single file along a narrow pass.

"They know how to find us," she said. "He told me how they do it."

He looked at her. "How?" he asked.

She explained to Piero about the sparkle dust, how the scout ship had marked them.

"I knew there had to be something special about that ship," he said.

31

Piero and Raffaele carried Sabino into the tent. The young man's eyes were half closed, his coppery skin had turned the color of a fresh mushroom, and he moaned continually. Felicitas crawled into the tent after them.

They put him on a fur. She peered past Raffaele's shoulder, trying to get a better look.

Renzo came into the tent carrying a burning stick, the end glowing red hot, and held it out to Felicitas.

"Hold this," he said. "Keep blowing on it. Keep it hot."

Felicitas took the stick and blew on it.

"I'm going to cauterize," said Renzo.

Renzo extracted some oval-shaped leaves from a pouch and stuffed them into Sabino's mouth. Sabino opened his eyes and looked up at his brother, still dazed.

"Chew, Sabino," said Renzo. "Chew!"

The young man chewed, but with no energy, his head lolling to one side as his good hand spasmodically gripped the fur blanket he was lying on, his tongue and lips smacking as he tried to moisten the wad of dry leaves. His eyes started to close. Renzo gave him a small slap.

"Stay awake, Sabino," he said. "You've got to chew these. These leaves will help with the pain."

So Sabino chewed again.

And as he chewed, Piero explained to Renzo about the sparkle on their skin.

"That's how the dead were able to track us so far," said Piero.

Renzo nodded. "The ways of the brown ones are indeed devious," he said.

After Sabino had chewed the leaves for five minutes, Renzo took a deep breath and prepared himself.

He took the burning stick from Felicitas. The tip was now white hot, about two inches across, narrowed to a fine point, the perfect instrument for sealing Sabino's wound.

"Piero, Raffaele," he said, "hold him down."

The two men held the young *pastore* down. Renzo pressed the glowing tip to the stump of Sabino's arm, and immediately Sabino arched his back in agony, roused from semiconsciousness by the searing pain. The tent filled with the scent of burning flesh. Sabino groaned.

"It would have been a lot worse without the leaves," said Renzo.

Sabino's chest heaved. The young man bit down hard on the wad of leaves. His eyes opened wide.

Renzo finished cauterizing the stump, then poured cold water over it.

Sabino's breathing grew easier and the young man finally passed out, overcome by the ordeal.

Renzo, relieved it was over, straightened his back, wiped the sweat from his brow with the back of his hand, then looked out the tent flap, his eyes misting over with a far-off but predatory look.

"Tomorrow I find the brown ones," he said, his eyes now like stones. "Tomorrow I make them pay."

Felicitas and Piero looked at each other. Piero spoke up.

"Won't that take time?" he said.

"They will pay," insisted Renzo. "I'll take my riders and I'll hunt these killers down. You and the town dwellers head straight north while we're gone. We'll find these killers, we'll do our work, and then we'll catch up with you."

They spent an uneasy night.

Felicitas and Piero sat around the small campfire just outside the tent.

Though she felt drowsy, Felicitas didn't sleep. She was sure the dead would return. She forced herself to stay awake so that her night eyes would feel them coming through the darkness down the mountains. The sky flashed bizarrely to the north, puckered into several small funnel clouds, then returned to normal.

"Look at that," she said to Piero.

Piero looked up at the sky. "We must be getting close," he said.

Felicitas stared at the mountains, dark hulking shapes blotting out the starlight, wondering where Maritano might be. She drew her fur wrap more closely around her shoulders and shivered.

"Maybe we should go inside," suggested Piero. "You're cold. You can't be expected to sit out here all night just because you have the night eyes." He gestured at the guards. "These men will spot the dead if they come."

"They might spot them," said Felicitas, "but I can feel them."

"You should try to sleep," he said.

She looked at Piero. She reached over and put her hand on his arm.

"Don't worry," she said.

He tried smiling but he couldn't manage it.

"I wish I could help you in some way," he said. He stared at the fire. "This outpost . . . it seems unfair that you should have to do it all alone."

She knew he wanted to protect her. Yet he was right, there was nothing he could do for her once they got to the outpost. She would have to do it all herself.

"I'll be fine," she said.

"I wish you would sleep," he said. "If you sleep now, you'll be alert tomorrow."

She nodded. "I'll sleep," she said. "If it makes you feel better, I'll sleep."

But she slept for only three hours.

When she woke up, the wind was blowing harder outside, making the tent snap like a flag. Renzo was still sitting next to Sabino. Piero lay asleep beside her. She sat up and looked at Sabino.

The young man breathed shallowly, quickly, and his eyelids kept flickering. She looked at Renzo.

"Let me stay up with him for a while," she said. "I'll watch. You rest. The night is long and you haven't put your head down once. You rest and I'll look after him till morning."

Renzo hesitated, but finally nodded.

"You don't mind?" he said.

"I can't sleep anyway," she said. She looked apprehensively at the roof of the tent. "This wind bothers me."

Renzo took a deep breath. "Can you sense the brown ones at all?" he asked. "With your night eyes?"

She sat still for a moment. "No," she said. "They're nowhere near."

"I've been a fool," said Renzo. "I should have taken the brown ones more seriously. I was sure we could lose them."

"The sparkle on our skin," she said. "You couldn't have known."

"I should have taken more care."

"You took a lot of care. You did everything you could. But

Piero and I are marked. No matter what you do, nothing's going to stop them from finding us."

Renzo looked at his brother. "He's so young," he said. "I should have made him stay home. But I thought this would be good for him. Now he's lost his arm."

She sat vigil for the next several hours. The wind shrieked and made the tent snap fiercely. At one point she thought she heard the dead whining, but as she could feel no premonition, no sense of their implants working inside their heads, she concluded it must be the wind. Over the wind she sometimes heard the hopebeasts bleating in the dark.

The men changed guard every two hours. She watched them come and go, wondering how they could sleep when the tent flapped so loudly. She was afraid the tent might blow away, but the *pastori* shored the guy ropes and the poles with extra rocks, and it stayed in place.

Just before dawn, Sabino stirred. He looked up at her with feverish eyes. She glanced at this stump. It was now red, puffy, and a thick discharge oozed from the end.

"Felicitas?" he said.

She filled a cup of water. "Here," she said.

She held it to his lips. He took a few small sips.

"Is this a dream?" he asked.

"No," she said.

"Then why do you glow?" he asked. "Why do you sparkle?"

She looked at her hand. Lamplight, reflecting through the water bottle, had brought the strange sparkle to her hand.

"I was marked," she said.

He nodded, accepting it, even if he didn't understand it. He drank again, some water spilling around his chin.

When he was done, his head flopped back. Even this small effort had exhausted him.

"I've never seen a girl with green eyes before," he said. "Where I come from, all the girls have brown eyes."

"I get my eyes from my mother," she said.

"And your hair. It's so long. In the south, the girls cut their hair. The hopebeasts eat it if they don't. I like the way you've tied yours back. It makes you look . . ."

He winced, overcome by pain. Beads of perspiration formed on his brow. Felicitas hated to see Sabino so badly injured. A violent chill shook him and he coughed a few times.

She said, "Is there a girl back home that you . . ." She shrugged. "You know, someone who's special?"

He shook his head. "No," he said. "I have too much work to do. With the herd. My brother keeps me busy. But he says that the elders . . . they're arranging something for me." He smiled, a weak self-deprecating smile. "I've never kissed anyone before," he said. "Can you imagine? I'm nineteen years old and I've never kissed anyone. That's how busy Renzo keeps me."

She leaned forward. She put her hand on his dark hair. His eyes widened . . . and she pressed her lips to his. She kissed him tenderly.

"There," she said, pulling away. "Now you have."

His eyes were wide, serious.

"Thank you," he said.

She ran her hand over his forehead.

"Go to sleep," she said. "Sleep, and you'll feel better in the morning."

An hour later she felt the tingling in her arms.

She knew she was going to have another Lungo Muso episode.

She left her spot next to Sabino and crawled out the tent flap.

Lungo Muso stood by the campfire wrapped in a cape, the light of the flames dancing over his brutish face. Two *pastori* sat on either side of the fire, guarding the campsite, but they didn't see Lungo Muso, even though he stood right in front of them.

She realized that she had become unstuck again. The guards couldn't see her. Lungo Muso approached her. The sky swirled with a dozen violet funnel clouds.

"Come," he said, extending his hand.

She took Lungo Muso's hand, and together they floated upward.

Flat Rock, the mountains, and the forest receded below them. They entered one of the violet funnel clouds.

The funnel cloud twisted and curved, spiraled and coiled, and the walls shimmered with mother-of-pearl light. She was carried by an unseen current, and after a few minutes she felt herself descend. The mother-of-pearl light dimmed and the funnel cloud snaked all the way to the ground, carrying Felicitas and Lungo Muso with it. It left them there, in a new locale, the way an ocean wave might leave a piece of driftwood on a beach.

She looked around.

She was in the prison . . .

Her legs felt suddenly weak. She looked up at Lungo Muso, wondering if she could trust him after all. Why would he bring her back here? Was he going to imprison her again?

He put his hand on her shoulder and looked down at her with calm eyes.

"Have no fear, Felicitas," he said. He gestured at the prison's four bleak walls. "These walls can't hurt you. These walls can't trap you. This is not the place of your captivity. This is the prison as it existed two hundred years ago. I bring you back not to imprison you."

He pointed at the west gate.

"Behold the west gate," he said.

A dozen New Ones escorted seven Old Ones through the gate. The Old Ones were shackled and chained. She recognized the middle one, Lungo Muso, a much younger Lungo Muso, his teeth bared, his eyes glaring. The Lungo Muso beside her pointed to the north wall.

"Now behold the human prisoners huddled against the north wall," he said, "fearful of this procession. They haven't seen Old Ones in a long time. The New Ones have taken over. And they don't know why the Old Ones are being brought here."

He nodded toward the Old Ones.

"That is my younger self," he said. "Taken prisoner by my own sons and daughters, by the New Ones. And this you must understand: The New Ones are the true journeymen of the river of time, such as Silvio has told you. They overcome the swell of the current, ride the rapids, and tame the unruly compass of time. But they have betrayed us. They have turned against us."

Felicitas watched the New Ones march the Old Ones to the south cellblock.

"Why are the New Ones putting you in prison?" she asked.

Lungo Muso's shoulders sagged.

"Because they're afraid of us," he said. He watched the procession. "We never wanted to hurt anyone," he said. "All the murder and genocide, that came from the New Ones, after they grew up, after they overmastered us. From the outset, we wanted to negotiate with Reymont, to demonstrate to him that we had the river of time, that if need be, we could go back into his own planet's past and arrange events in such a way as to pre-empt his journey to our five home worlds. We wanted to let him know we could stop the eventual human migration into space as a way of protecting ourselves from his belligerent rule. We never wanted murder. He had to know that we could use the river of time as a weapon. But the New Ones had other plans. We wished to use the river as a weapon of peace, not as one of war."

She looked up at him with wide eyes. "You used it as a weapon?" she said.

He nodded sadly. "We had no choice," he said. "When we went back, it was a blunt surgery at first. We searched for any scientific flowering, anything that might directly lead to the development of human space travel and, consequently, Reymont's arrival at our five home worlds. We wished to stop our vanquisher. You know your history. I made you read the books when you were a dead girl. We went first to your Italian Renaissance, a remarkable scientific flowering, and imprisoned those individuals who might plant the seeds of such a space migration. The impulse to colonize goes hand in hand with the impulse toward space migration, and nowhere was that impulse stronger than on the island nation of Great Britain. We then sank the British fleet. We took many Britishers prisoner. We curbed that nation's expansionist tendencies. I've been trying to show you these things, but your amnesia's made it difficult. This is why there are so many Italians in the prison. This is why there are so many English."

She watched the New Ones and Old Ones disappear behind the south tower.

"And did you stop Reymont from coming to your . . . your home worlds?" she asked, feeling her way through this new information.

He shook his head. "No," he said. "Our initial surgery was too crude. Your Italian Renaissance, the British fleet . . . well . . . it didn't work. We had to find a more exact thread, something that was particular to Reymont. And that exact thread, of course, turned out to be Niccolò Machiavelli. *The Prince.* A book that influenced Reymont's every course of action while at the Five Worlds."

She stared at the Old One. "But you . . . you couldn't have succeeded . . . even if you did find that thread. Even if you knew about Machiavelli, you couldn't have . . . or else we wouldn't be here right now, would we?"

"Correct."

"But if you knew what to do . . . if you knew the connection between Reymont and Machiavelli was the one you were looking for, why didn't you—"

"Because the New Ones stopped us before we got the chance," said Lungo Muso. "The New Ones were afraid. The

New Ones realized we were going to let them die out once they had stopped the human migration into space for us. Our own sons and daughters turned against us, before we had a chance to negotiate with them. They were creatures cloned from our own cells, designed to circumvent the temporal imbalances that keep you and me from affecting and influencing the past. We weren't going to make any more of them. And they couldn't submit to that. They wanted continuance. So they made their own birthing tanks. They cloned themselves. And they plotted against us." He shrugged. "They rebelled."

He lifted his cape in front of her face.

When he lowered it, she saw a different scene. The prison, another day, another month, another year.

Old Ones were shooting at New Ones. Humans were running everywhere, trying to keep out of the way. The *carcerieri* had been disabled, stood like statues around the yard.

"What's going on?" she asked.

"This is where I escape," he said. "This world," he said. "You can't imagine how distant it is. We had to hide the river of time here, hide it from Reymont, where he would never think to look. But in bringing it here, the New Ones defeated us. The New Ones overwhelmed us with their numbers. We couldn't send garrisons out here fast enough to protect the river." He gestured at the younger Lungo Muso, who crouched behind the clock tower with a *pistola*. "My younger self has come to this prison world to regain control of the river. Before the New Ones can use it to kill everyone. Their fear is so great, they see genocide as their only solution. And genocide not only for the Old Ones. Genocide for everyone. For all intelligent life."

He lifted his cape again. A small jump through the river of time.

She arrived at the next bend.

The prison again. Now silent. All the New Ones were dead. Lungo Muso was still alive. So were three of the other Old Ones who had come with Lungo Muso.

"We used Raffaele's pool," he said. "The pool was like our

private boat. We traveled along the river of time, evading the New Ones with it, using the river with impunity, tapping into its power, yet always remaining beyond the grasp of the New Ones. With the pool, we can stabilize time locally, and thereby evade not only the New Ones, but also combat any unruly temporal paradox. Time is so full of paradoxes. And the pool protects us. Should the New Ones, with the river, try to preempt my existence by killing my parents, I can stabilize time locally and continue to live. We've made many such pools, hoping to fight the New Ones. But just as fast as we made them, James Kenneth Reymont destroyed them."

Lungo Muso lifted his cape again.

When he let it down, she saw a different scene.

With the battle over, the Old Ones now repaired the prison. All the machinery damaged in the battle was put to rights.

"We couldn't leave you with no one to look after you," said Lungo Muso. "Before we escaped, we repaired the prison and made it work by itself again."

He lifted his cape one more time.

When he let it down, he said, "Behold. You stand in the outpost, as it existed two centuries ago."

The river of time flowed before them. Galleries overlooked the river.

She looked over the gallery railing to the river below.

Violet plasma filled the river, the exact same plasma that filled Raffaele's pool. The river flowed away from them, bubbled up like a natural spring from an unknown source behind them.

"You know my story," said Lungo Muso. "I came to this prison world to regain control of the river. I was captured and imprisoned. I escaped. And now I finally come here to the river to make one last desperate attempt. Look at all the New Ones I've killed," he said, gesturing. "Here you see my final battle."

A hundred New Ones bled into the river. The blood of the New Ones was one and the same with the plasma of the river. Everywhere she saw signs of battle. Smoke hung in the air and corpses lay scattered everywhere.

The young Lungo Muso was wounded, bleeding badly. The young Lungo Muso's blood was red blood, real blood, the blood of a visceral creature. He lay on his side, propped on his elbow, slumped over the raised edge of the river. The raised edge around the river looked much like the raised edge around Raffaele's pool, with glyphs all over it.

"This is where I die," said Lungo Muso.

She looked up at him in sudden surprise. "You die?" she said.

He nodded.

They walked up to the dying Lungo Muso. A hole had been blasted through his battle armor.

"I know I'm dying," said Lungo Muso. "The funnel clouds in the sky close off one by one as the New Ones try to block my exits. They think they finally have me. I see visions of the end-final time before me. If I don't regain control of the river, the New Ones will send the end-final time to destroy us. It's not their fault. They wish to be safe. And the only way they think they can be safe is to destroy everybody else. They are really children and they don't understand. You see me there. I've come all this way and I've failed. What can I do now? Is there some way I can go back in time and make it work? I'm mortally wounded, I'm dying, and the New Ones are going to turn the outpost into their weapon of eternal flame. How can I get the river back? Who can help me?" He put his hand on her shoulder. "Is it possible that one of our human prisoners might help me, a human who can somehow cross the bridge?" He nodded. "This must be my course. You see me there with barely a dozen breaths left. I'm about to die. I have to do something and I have to do it fast."

The wounded Lungo Muso rubbed a few glyphs on the raised edge of the river, the glyphs seeming to act as controls. A series of concentric rings emanated through the river. The wounded Lungo Muso climbed over the raised edge of the river and toppled into the plasma.

"Come," said Lungo Muso. "We go back to the prison."

He lifted his cape and they traveled back to the prison.

They stood in the prison, in the chamber under the south wall, the same chamber where Lungo Muso had taught her to read the glyphs. A younger Lungo Muso, still imprisoned, not yet escaped, contemplated the corpse of the older Lungo Muso, the one she'd just seen killed at the outpost.

"I presented my corpse to my younger self," explained Lungo Muso. "This was my final desperate plan. You see how my younger self ponders. I knew I wasn't going to make it. I knew that in finally reaching the outpost I would meet my death. So the next time I escaped I had to find another way." He put his hand on her shoulder. "And I found you, Felicitas. I searched two hundred years into the future and I finally found you. And not a moment too soon. I knew it would take the New Ones at least two hundred years traveling the old ways to send a new garrison. You were a dead girl, yes, barely sensible of your existence, but after watching you for a while, I saw how all the machinery in the prison responded so easily to your touch. I understood. I took you to my chamber and began your education."

"But why me?" she asked. "I'm only a girl of seventeen. You should have picked someone like Piero or Rosario."

"I picked you because you have the night eyes," he said. "I picked you because you belong to a particular segment of the prison population, because your brain is different. You have been modified, Felicitas. Your kith and kin have changed you. You have the night eyes. Some of the others do, too. Silvio. Rosario. Even Raffaele, to a small extent. You are modified. They've changed you. They made you so that you can talk to me."

Before she could ask any further questions, Lungo Muso's strength seemed to fail. Whatever tenuous thread of plasma kept them here shredded.

"What about Reymont?" she asked. "Why did he come to your home worlds in the first place?"

But he couldn't answer. He was too weak.

He finally disappeared.

And Felicitas flew through a violet funnel cloud back to her own time and place.

She found herself sitting in the *pastori* tent again. Next to Sabino. And Sabino wasn't breathing.

Sabino had died during the night.

Renzo and Urbano hacked their way through the frozen ground and made two shallow graves. Renzo uttered a few words in Latin and the other riders filled the grave with rocks, dirt, and snow. Felicitas stared at the two mounds—Sabino and Antonio—and remembered all the burial mounds in the prison yard.

Renzo, a hard man, wouldn't speak to anyone.

Only when all the supplies were gathered, and the tent taken down, and all traces of the camp obliterated did he convey his plans.

"We'll go as far as the tundra with you," he said. "From there, you ride due north until you come to a shallow valley. There are no trees. Wait for us there. Camp there. If you go any farther, you're sure to get lost. My riders and I will return once we find Sabino's killers. We'll come for you and take you the rest of the way to the outpost."

32

There were only four in the party now: Felicitas, Piero, Raffaele, and Urbano.

Felicitas saw a snow-covered treeless plain rimmed by bare mountains stretching from horizon to horizon before them. This was the tundra. The wind blew fiercely. It got so cold they had to stop and take out extra furs. Felicitas wrapped her face in a thick fur scarf.

As they traveled north over the tundra, the sky shimmered with bands of violet light, seemed to bend and stretch, as if it were being refracted through a large concave lens. Small funnel clouds appeared.

Felicitas told Piero about the funnel clouds in her episode with Lungo Muso last night. She told him how the Old Ones, using the New Ones to manipulate history, had tried to stop Reymont's arrival at the five home worlds of the *uominilupi* by stunting the development of human space travel.

Piero pondered this for a while. "So they got into our past

and tried to clip our wings," he said. He pointed to the funnel clouds. "I suppose the outpost must make those."

"I don't like them," said Urbano. "They remind me of the flying *mostri*, the way they dip. I keep thinking they're going to come and pick me up."

"Urbano," said Raffaele, "they're not alive. They're part of the outpost. You should be in awe. Think what a grand design this outpost must be if it can make the sky dance like this."

"It's nothing but a black art," said Urbano. "This sky, it's an omen."

"No," said Felicitas, "it's not. It's just a kind of . . . a kind of weather. It's just time and space, trying to sort themselves out." She felt these thoughts slip into her mind, knew that Lungo Muso was somewhere nearby, speaking to her with his night eyes. "It's just a . . ." She decided she liked Renzo's word the best. "A disturbance."

"Anything I can't skewer with my spear I don't trust," said Urbano.

"You have nothing to fear, Urbano," said Piero. "These funnel clouds won't touch you. You haven't got the night eyes. If they're going to touch anybody, they'll touch Felicitas."

They continued northward.

Through the morning, the sky grew more unruly. It twisted into swirls, ridged into waves, changed color, flashed. It rumbled, howled, and wheezed.

Funnel clouds finally touched down a short while later, leaving bizarre apparitions behind. The group reined their hopebeasts in and watched.

They saw a city with no roads, just canals. People floated in gondolas. Several *uominilupi* skyboats hovered above.

"Lungo Muso's brought me here," said Raffaele. "I've seen this place before. You see those New Ones over there? They're taking prisoners."

New Ones herded humans up ramps into skyboats.

"I hate this," said Piero. "I hate to see prisoners of any kind. I hate those leashes."

Urbano pulled out his bow and arrow. "Are you sure they can't touch us?" he asked.

"Urbano, these are just . . . just time storms," said Felicitas. Her brow furrowed. "At least that's what Lungo Muso . . ." The Old One was again slipping thoughts into her mind. "They can't hurt you."

"Those little brown whelps . . . the New Ones, as you call them," said the hunter, pointing, "let them come. I'll teach them a thing or two."

He strung an arrow onto his bow.

"It's a strange sight, to be sure," said Raffaele. "I feel I could take a few steps and be wet up to my neck in that canal."

"It's not real," said Piero, getting off his horse. "And I'll prove it."

Piero strode toward the disturbance, walked right through it, disappeared for a few seconds, and came out the other side.

"You see?" he called. "It's nothing but light. It's all pink inside. It's just another *uominilupi* contraption. We have nothing to fear."

He got back on his hopebeast and they moved on.

They continued to see mirages through the rest of the morning—time storms, as Felicitas insisted on calling them.

They saw deep space, endless stars, and their own twin suns, looking like little red pellets, as if seen from a great distance.

They saw what they finally concluded had to be a more modern-day Earth, an Earth at war with itself, with tanks, planes, and artillery.

"We had a book in the prison that described these things," said Piero. "I read it a long time ago, when I was a boy, but now it comes back to me."

"I'd like to get my hands on one of those weapons," said Urbano. "Think how easy it would be to kill the *mostro*." He pointed at one of the tanks. "I wonder how you aim that. I wonder if it works like a catapult."

They finally saw a tsunami-size wave of fire roll toward them.

Felicitas eyes filled with terror. Flames. Everywhere. Destroying everything. The end-final time. Even the hopebeasts grew skittish, and for a moment she thought the flames must be real.

But then the fire rolled over them harmlessly, and she knew it was just another mirage, another time storm.

By the time they made camp, the time storms had ended, and the coming of the night brought calmer skies.

"I wonder if the outpost feeds off the energy of *Piccola* and *Grossa*," said Piero. "I wonder if that's why the time storms have stopped for the evening."

Later, when they sat around a campfire, Urbano said, "What if these disturbances get stronger tomorrow?" He nibbled irritably on a piece of hard-biscuit *pane*. "What if by the time we get to the outpost the things we see in these mirages actually come out and hurt us?"

Raffaele stared at the hunter patiently. "You worry too much, my friend," he said. "Why in the name of the seventeen stones would they get any stronger?"

"Because we'll be close to the outpost. We'll be nearer to the source."

"The source of a rainstorm is a little white cloud," said Raffaele. "Why should a time storm be any different? I'm sure the closer we get, the milder these . . . these mirages will become."

Piero shook his head, amused by the argument. "You can speculate all you want, *amici*, but until we get there—"

"The mirages *are* going to get stronger," said Felicitas, her voice flat, so certain that all the men turned to her.

"What do you mean?" asked Urbano.

"They're charging it up . . . the New Ones, they're making it ready for the big change . . . they're sending it signals from their skyboats, even before they arrive."

"But, *bella*," said Raffaele, "how do you know this?"

"Because Lungo Muso has been speaking to me all afternoon," she said. She gazed beyond the fire into the dark tundra. "I don't know if we can wait for the *pastori*. We may have to find the outpost by ourselves."

"Does Lungo Muso say these New Ones will attack us?" asked Urbano.

"No."

Urbano drew his knife. "Because if they do," he said, "I have room on my trophy wall for at least a dozen of them."

"I wish Lungo Muso would tell me more about Reymont," said Felicitas. "I wish I knew how and why my brain acts differently than everybody else's."

Piero leaned forward and put his hand on her wrist. "I'm sure he'll tell you everything," he said.

Urbano threw his piece of hard biscuit into the fire.

"I hate these wretched hard biscuits," he growled. "I need meat." He got up and checked his quiver of arrows. "I'm going hunting," he said. "There must be something to hunt out there," he said. "I saw tracks earlier. I'm going to get us a proper dinner."

He marched from the campfire, mounted his hopebeast, and spurred the animal into the icy wasteland.

"I certainly admire that man," said Raffaele, staring after the hunter. "He's a tough one. But he's a good man to have along on a trip like this. I was getting sick of the hard biscuit myself. I hope he finds a bird of some kind. There's nothing I like better than a good piece of pan-fried bird."

"Maybe you should get some sleep, Raffaele," suggested Piero. "You're on late watch tonight."

Raffaele stared at Piero, not without some suspicion.

"Okay," he finally said. "But you'll wake me up if he comes back with something good to eat. Don't eat it all yourself. I'd hate to miss out on a piece of pan-fried bird."

Piero nodded. "We'll wake you," he said.

After Raffaele had settled himself in the tent, Felicitas saw that Piero was thinking about something.

"What is it?" she asked. "What are you thinking about?"

A crease came to Piero's brow and he tossed a stick from their small supply of firewood into the fire.

"I can't help thinking about Maritano," he said.

She cocked her head.

"What about him?" she asked.

"You were always with him as a child," he said. "And when the two of you grew up, you were always together then, too. That's one of the reasons I stalled so long before telling you about the implants." He stirred the fire. "It's strange, though," he said. "I can't help thinking that the New Ones have connected to Maritano the same way the Old Ones have connected to you. You were so close as children, but now you seem exactly the opposite, and dead set against each other."

She frowned. "He still thinks we're close."

Piero shook his head. "I know he does," he said. "I wish there was something we could do for him. I feel sorry for him. He was always so contrary. He was always fighting with the other children. And his stone throwing, the way he practiced and practiced. And the way he was continually hunting for *topi*. He was good at hunting." He waved his palm at the tundra. "We could have used someone like him. But they've ruined him."

Wind gusted over the tundra, blowing crystals of ice through the campsite, making the hopebeasts bleat.

"Do you think Renzo will kill Maritano?" she asked.

He looked up. "Yes." He exhaled, looked into the fire again, his eyes growing pensive. "You sound concerned." He shrugged. "But it's in your character. That's where I'm lacking. I can't see Maritano as a fellow prisoner anymore. I can't see him as the lonely sad boy with the bad teeth and the crooked nose." He tossed another stick into the fire. "All I see is a skilled hunter who wants to kill me. All I see is another threat."

* * *

An hour later, when the sky was nearly dark, Urbano rode back into the camp.

He rode at a walk on his hopebeast. He sat upright in his saddle, his face expressionless, a dead white bird hanging from his saddle horn. The hopebeast walked right to the edge of the camp, dragging its feet through the snow, its eyes blinking dumbly, its breath coming and going in exhausted gasps, as if it had been ridden out. Urbano stared down at them. His eyes looked dull, his lids were half closed, and ice covered his beard. His mouth hung open.

Felicitas got up from the campfire and approached him.

"Urbano?" she said. "Urbano, are you all right?"

He fell forward in his saddle, toppled over the saddle horn, and tumbled to the ground. His back smoked.

Piero jumped to his feet and ran past Felicitas to the stricken man.

"Urbano!" he cried, kneeling next to the injured hunter.

Felicitas followed cautiously.

Then she stopped and stared into the darkness, where the snow-covered moguls and dunes, barely visible in the starlight, rolled away into the distance.

"They're out there," she said. "I can feel them."

"He's been shot by a *pistola*," said Piero. "He's gone."

She continued to stare into the darkness. The dead, out there, only five of them now . . . she couldn't pick up Ottavio anymore, knew Ottavio must have finally succumbed. She saw dark shapes running crouched from snowdrift to snowdrift, advancing in a zigzag fashion toward the campsite.

"Piero," she whispered.

She pointed.

He looked, then nodded.

They hurried back to the campsite and doused the fire.

Felicitas got her lance ready while Piero woke up Raffaele.

Raffaele came out of the tent looking bleary-eyed. He armed himself with a bow and arrow.

In the darkness, Felicitas saw the dead coming, dim shadows against the snow.

The large man to the left had to be Gasparo. She could see the dead with her night eyes, heard their implants industriously giving them commands, sensed the counselor whispering into Maritano's ear. The dead had no idea she and the others were ready for them. They held, at least for the moment, the advantage.

"Let's get it over with," she said to Piero.

There was no more hesitation. She'd learned her lesson from Gasparo.

She lifted her lance and fired, killing outright one of the dead. Piero and Raffaele let fly with arrows.

Beyond the edge of the encampment, she saw Maritano and his *consiglieri* scramble for cover. They took up positions and returned fire. Under a massive barrage of *pistola* fire, Raffaele crawled next to her.

"We're outgunned!" he shouted over the din. "I'm going to see if I can get that dead man's *pistola.*"

"Raffaele, no!" she cried.

But before she could say anything else, he was gone, crawling on his stomach into the darkness toward the downed man.

Felicitas and Piero gave him as much cover fire as they could. She took careful aim, thought the thought, and a small fireball jetted from the end of her weapon. The fireball nicked the head of one of the dead just as he was taking up another position. The heavy charge was enough to blow his brains out, and he fell down dead.

Piero pointed. "Raffaele's got a good idea," he said. "I'm going to try and get that other man's weapon. We'll stand a better chance if I do."

Though fearful of his plan, she nodded. "I'll try to keep them pinned," she said.

Piero crawled away. He maneuvered around and behind the hopebeasts. The hopebeasts tugged at their reins, jumped and bucked, but couldn't get free from their heavy ground pegs.

When Piero was safely behind the hopebeasts, he got to his feet and ran up a small slope.

But as he reached the top, someone jumped out from behind the other side.

"Piero!" she cried.

It was Gasparo.

The big man jumped on Piero and together they tumbled down the slope in a cloud of churned-up snow. Gasparo, her mistake coming to haunt her again. They rolled right into the middle of the hopebeasts. The animals nickered and pranced about, trying to avoid them.

She got to her feet, knew she had to do something to help Piero, but ran no more than a couple of paces toward him when a volley of *pistola* fire exploded all around her. She fell to the ground.

Maritano was forcing her to take cover, keeping her away from Gasparo and Piero.

She tried to see through the panicked hopebeasts. She inched forward, dragging herself on her elbows. She gazed out at the surrounding snowdrifts, looking for Raffaele, hoping the New Florentine had at last recovered a *pistola,* but she couldn't see him, and was afraid that he might have been killed.

"Raffaele!" she called. "Help us! We need—"

"Felicitas, why do you fight us this way?" called Maritano. "You know you can't fight us. We've got you outnumbered."

She ignored Maritano. Maybe she could fire over the heads of the hopebeasts. If she could create enough panic . . .

She steadied her lance and fired above the nervous animals. They pulled madly at their reins and several broke free. This produced the diversion she hoped for.

The loose animals stampeded.

She got to her feet and ran.

But she got no farther than a few steps when Maritano lunged out of the darkness and once again tackled her from behind.

He yanked the lance out of her hands and threw it into the snow.

"Felicitas, are you going to make us follow you forever?" he asked.

"Maritano, please."

She turned around and struggled to push him away.

"The great day is nearly here," he said. "Why do you want to stop it?"

She heard a *pistola* report. And she stiffened. A single report, not followed by any others, coming from over there, behind the remaining hopebeasts.

"Piero?" she called.

"Felicitas, forget about Piero. Piero has the starving deaths of hundreds on his hands."

She propped herself up on her elbows. "Piero, can you hear me?"

She received no reply.

"We'll help you gather your hopebeasts, Felicitas," said Maritano. "Then we'll go home."

"Piero!" she cried again. "Piero, answer me, please!"

But the only answer she got was Gasparo, a hulking lone figure, walking out of the remaining hopebeasts, a *pistola* hanging from his hand.

"Piero, please!" screamed Felicitas, tears coming to her eyes.

"He's dead," Gasparo reported.

"And the other one?" inquired Maritano.

Gasparo turned and stared dumbly out into the tundra. "Out there somewhere."

"Find him," said Maritano.

"Piero . . . please," said Felicitas, now sobbing.

Gasparo trudged off into the snow to find Raffaele.

Maritano looked at Felicitas with compassion. "Felicitas, Piero's committed unspeakable crimes," he said. "He's a mass murderer. Look at all the people he let starve to death. Look at poor Adriana. He should have been put to death long before this."

No point in explaining to Maritano that Piero didn't have a choice, that they all would have starved had he not rationed the food-bricks. Her hands tingled. They had the telltale feeling of a Lungo Muso episode. Yet no episode came. Instead, she felt the Old One's presence all around her, giving her strength, supplying her with the fortitude she needed to get through this.

Her body tensed, and she felt suddenly charged, as if every muscle buzzed with electricity. Her hands darted upward and locked around Maritano's throat. As Maritano so often singled her out, so she now singled out him. She saw only her hands clutching Maritano's throat. Everything else faded into the background. She watched her hands. She had slender womanly hands, not scarred ugly hands—yet hands that, after all, could strangle the life out of somebody.

A gagging sound came from Maritano's throat. She grew dimly aware of the sound of renewed *pistola* fire out in the tundra, but she shut it out and squeezed even harder. Maritano's milky gray eyes began to bulge. He pulled out his *pistola*, was going to shoot her, but she knocked it out of his hand with a quick chop and it tumbled into the snow. Maritano then clawed at her hands, tried to break her grip, but she was hooked into Lungo Muso, could feel him all around her, was now discovering another facet of the night eyes, something strong, something poignant, something that made her become one and the same with the Old One.

She dug her thumbs into Maritano's Adam's apple and squeezed with all her might. She heard yet more *pistola* fire coming from out in the snow. And she knew that Raffaele must be fighting the others. Maritano punched at her arms but her grip remained firm. Seventeen years old, didn't remember a murder, a sentencing, or a trial, but she now knew she could be a killer if she had to be. His face turned blue as more gurgling sounds came from his throat. His eyes began to run with tears. She had all the strength of an Old One. She swung him to the ground, keeping him at arm's length, her hands continuing to tighten like a vise around his throat. A new facet of the night eyes, one that gave her this new physical strength. He clawed and shook but there was nothing he could do. She climbed on top of him and placed her knees firmly astride his hips.

She gave Maritano's throat one last vicious squeeze.

And heard something snap inside.

Then she lifted her hands. And looked down at him.

He was dead.

She looked at her hands. They were covered with fur. Each had six clawlike fingers.

The vision passed, and she saw only her own hands now.

She looked up and discovered Raffaele standing next to her, a *pistola* in each hand.

"I killed them all," he said, amazed.

She looked down at Maritano, as if she were waking from a dream.

"And I killed Maritano," she said.

As *Piccola* and *Grossa* rose over the southern mountain peaks the next morning, Felicitas knelt beside Piero's corpse.

Piero's face was now white, making his beard and hair look as black as jet, and his eyes were partially open, his pupils wide and fixed. Her grief made her numb. First Adriana, then Rosario, and now Piero. The wind moaned persistently from the northwest, kicking up ice crystals from the surrounding moguls and drifts, spinning up snow ghosts that whirled across the tundra like small tornadoes.

Raffaele knelt at the top of a drift just to the south of the camp, hand to his brow, looking toward the mountains, keeping an eye out for Renzo and his riders. He turned, glanced at her. The area was strewn with corpses. Only three hopebeasts remained.

Raffaele got up and walked down the side of the drift, his feet sinking up to his ankles in the fresh powder snow that had fallen just before dawn. He knelt beside her.

"I think we should go," he said.

She nodded.

The sky funneled, a large one, one that stretched from horizon to horizon. They both stared at it. Raffaele was nervous about it. The sky had been doing this all morning, that one big funnel, like an eye in the sky. That was a distinct change. Felicitas felt nothing. Raffaele put his hand on her shoulder. Felicitas looked up at him. His opaque eye was tearing badly in the wind.

"I don't think the *pastori* are going to come," he said. "I think they must have been killed. It's up to us now, Felicitas. Let's head north. It's our only chance."

The sky now made a strange noise, like the sound of a stone thrown across ice, a high-pitched twist of a sound, squeaking and echoing from horizon to horizon. The suns turned green for an instant then went back to their normal red.

"I'd like to bury Piero first," she said. "And I'd like to bury Gasparo too." Her eyes momentarily clouded with tears. "He was my friend."

Raffaele stared at her, then nodded.

"Of course, *bella*," he said.

They hacked out two graves, hard work in the frozen ground. And as they dug the graves, Felicitas began thinking about the outpost. And the more she thought about it, the more she realized that even Lungo Muso had missed something.

Once they finished burying Piero and Gasparo, they gathered up supplies, weapons, food, what was left of their firewood, and packed everything on the remaining hopebeasts.

Then Felicitas walked over to Maritano.

"What are you doing?" asked Raffaele.

She didn't reply.

She wrenched the bag from Maritano's back. She undid the snaps on Maritano's bag, her hands so cold she could hardly move her fingers, and pulled out the counselor.

She held the mind-control machine up for Raffaele.

"I think I'm going to need this," she said.

33

The outpost came into view just as the red suns sank behind the horizon later that day. They found it by themselves. They didn't need Renzo's help after all. Felicitas could hear it whispering to her, calling to her.

It rose out of the snow-covered tundra in a diminishing sequence of white oblongs, just as Lungo Muso had always shown her, the largest on the bottom, the smallest at the top. Felicitas and Raffaele approached in silence. She had never seen a building so massive. It sat on arched pilings above the ground in the center of a shallow valley, and was surrounded by several factorylike installations and outbuildings, all of which now looked abandoned and derelict.

As she rode her hopebeast at a walk into the valley, she saw a landing pit, like the one outside the prison. This one had a square ship in it, much like a supply ship, but as with everything else, it was old, a wreck in this place of wrecks.

The sky puckered and a violet funnel cloud appeared. Then that sound again, high, like a stone across ice; it panned from one horizon to the other, starting in the east, arching over them, and finally fading in the west.

They stopped and gazed at the intimidating structure.

"No doors, no windows," said Raffaele. "Just like Renzo said." He shook his head. "How do we get in?"

She turned to Raffaele, her eyes narrowing as she thought about the mind-machine connection. "I don't think *you* get in, Raffaele," she said. She gazed at the outpost. "I think only I get in. Can you feel it?"

His brow arched in puzzlement. "Feel what?"

"Its pull," she said. "The tingle in your arms?"

He shook his head. "No," he said, as if he mildly resented her sensitivity to the outpost. "I don't feel a thing."

She pointed. "We'll go along there," she said. "Where the wind has blown the snow clear."

"That looks sheer," he said. "The hopebeasts might have trouble."

"We'll dismount. We'll lead them down."

They rode their hopebeasts a little farther along, then dismounted. Taking hold of the reins, they led the animals around a large drift and down the snow-cleared section of the slope. The sound of the wind, constantly moaning, was abrasive and fluctuated in intensity, sometimes louder, sometimes softer, whistling over hundreds of drifts and ridges, changing pitch in an eerie melody as they descended the icy incline toward the first of the factorylike installations.

They stopped at this installation. It was made of metal and was corroded in places. It showed many of the same pinhole deteriorations as the prison's south tower. Structurally and architecturally it had many of the same features.

Old machinery lay abandoned inside. And was that a *carceriere*? They went inside and had a closer look. No, not a *carceriere*, but definitely a cousin, a little bigger, manlike, but instead of digitized hands, it had paddles. Large paddles on the ends of its arms instead of hands. The paddles were covered with a frozen compound of some kind, spattered in a drip pattern. Felicitas broke some of the frozen compound off and sniffed it. Then she tasted it.

She looked at Raffaele in surprise. "Food-brick," she said. "I can't believe it. They make food-brick here."

He cocked his head to one side. "Food-brick?" he said. "What's food-brick?"

"They used to feed us this in prison." She looked around the broken-down factory. "I thought they made it somewhere else. I thought they made it . . ." She waved at the sky. "Somewhere up there, in the sky."

Before they investigated further, the loud high-pitched sound came from the sky again, and everything turned violet.

They hurried outside just in time to see an oblong skyboat descend from the sky, a ship unlike any she had ever seen, sleek, with rounded edges, looking new. It descended smoothly, directly above the outpost, its underside all aflame and billowing smoke. It sank to the top of the outpost, the last and smallest oblong in the precise geometrical progression. Unlike the other skyboats, which were either black or gray, this one was white, and matched exactly the white of the outpost.

A strong northwesterly wind ripped the copious amounts of smoke to tatters. The fire disappeared, the roar of the engine ceased, and the oblong ship came to rest on top of the outpost.

Felicitas and Raffaele looked at each other, and they didn't have to say anything, because they both knew what this was.

The New Ones had arrived.

She watched the oblong ship while Raffaele made a fire, expecting at any moment to see the New Ones emerge. But like the rest of the outpost, the skyboat had no windows or doors, at least none that she could see from where they were. She suspected that the New Ones were entering the outpost through the top, from a hatch in the bottom of their ship.

She got up and examined the arched pilings. They were about waist high, made of a corrosion-proof alloy that allowed the frigid air to circulate beneath the outpost so the outpost wouldn't melt the muskeg and sink. She put her hand against the biggest and lowest oblong. In area, this oblong had to be ten times the size of the prison. The white material shimmered under her touch, and a pattern of concentric ripples spread from her palm. She pulled her hand away, startled by the effect.

"Raffaele!" she called. "Come here."

The New Florentine stopped his fire-building and walked over.

"Put your hand against this wall."

He shrugged, and put his hand against the smooth white material. Nothing happened.

"It's cold," said Raffaele, taking his hand away.

Felicitas put her hand against the structure again. It shimmered. It sensed her. Her hand sent out concentric rings. And the longer she left it there the bigger and more pronounced the rings became. All at once the wall gave way, and she fell forward, caught off balance. Her arm disappeared up to her shoulder. Raffaele grabbed her and pulled her back. She withdrew her arm quickly, as if she had put it in an open flame, her heart pounding, her blood racing, and looked at the wall.

Then she looked at Raffaele with wide eyes. "You try," she said.

"Oh no," he said. "You're not going to get me to put my hand against that wall again."

"You have to," she said. "We have to be sure."

"Sure of what?"

"Sure that I can . . . that it's only me . . . that my night eyes aren't just a . . ."

He looked at the wall suspiciously. "That wall just tried to get you," he said.

"Don't worry," she said. "I'll pull you out." She pointed to the wall. "Go ahead," she said.

Raffaele tried again. The wall remained hard and unresponsive to his touch.

"Nothing's happening," he said, sounding relieved.

Felicitas nodded.

"Good," she said. "Then you stay here."

"Where are you going?" he asked.

"I'm going in."

"How are you going to do that?" he asked.

"Watch," she said.

She put her hand against the outpost wall.

The concentric rings appeared, the wall gave way, and she walked forward into the outpost.

Inside, the walls were made of a dark shiny material, like zinc. She was in a corridor. The corridor was empty. Illumination came from the ceiling—amorphous pods of light that followed her wherever she went. Stairways at either end of the corridor led to an upper gallery. She heard footsteps echoing everywhere but she couldn't see anybody.

Her arms tingled.

She walked toward the far stairway. A pod of light on the ceiling followed her, lighting just her immediate vicinity. She climbed the stairs.

As she neared the top, she saw, over a barrier made of the same zinclike material, a river; not just any river, but the river of time.

It flowed with violet, blue, and pink plasma. Suspended immediately above this river, something she hadn't seen in her last episode with Lungo Muso, was an equally radiant river flowing across the ceiling. Rivers top and bottom, like twin mirrors, each reflecting the other, the reflections reflecting the reflections, over and over again, so that, looking closely, she now saw a never-ending series of rivers, extending upward and downward to infinity.

She stared for a long time, awed by its beauty. And as her

eyes grew used to its spellbinding luminosity, she saw a thousand New Ones, silhouettes, all identical, crouched in exactly
the same pose of supplication on the upraised edge around the
river, all stroking glyphs in perfect unison, all, in effect, pulling
the trigger of the end-final time.

She felt the river reaching for her. With her night eyes, she
felt the New Ones, felt their fear, felt their sense of impending
triumph. They were the true journeymen. And she needed
them. They made a difference on the river of time; she was just
a shadow. Only the New Ones could change things and touch
things; their veins ran with the plasma of the river; they were,
in fact, the corporeal embodiment of the river, the tools by
which the Old Ones could change the wrongs of yesteryear.
And she had to control them. She would control them the same
way Maritano had controled the dead. With the counselor.

She gazed around the second level. Several small catwalks
led out over the river. She hurried to the nearest, keeping
crouched behind the barrier. The tingling wouldn't leave her
arms. She sensed Lungo Muso somewhere nearby but he
wasn't showing himself. She took one last look at the rivers, top
and bottom, then boldly mounted the catwalk and strode to
the end.

"*Salve!*" she cried. "*Pronto!*" she cried. "I'm up here! Look,
I'm up here!" She waved her hands. "Hey, come and get me!
I'm up here!"

Hundreds of expressionless faces looked up at her. Childlike
eyes. Identical little snouts. Tiny ears, all exactly the same. All
of them turning in unison. All of them wearing the same brown
uniforms of the dead.

She set her bag down, got on one knee, and lifted out the
counselor. She couldn't right all the wrongs of yesteryear by
herself, not when she was a shadow. It was a question of control. Everywhere below her New Ones rose from the edge of the
river and ran to the stairways. She got to her feet and pressed
the counselor to her forehead. It didn't matter if she came out
of this alive, she just had to make sure everybody else did.

The mind-control machine whirred and she felt nine tiny pinpricks on her skin. Her forehead went numb and the nine macroscopic implants drilled into her skull.

The New Ones were up on the second level now, running for her, trying to stop her. She sensed *pistola* fire whizzing past, but it was as if she were in a protective cloud. As she teetered on the edge of the catwalk, her old dreamphone dream came back, brought to her by the counselor, as a way to defeat her, and she saw the scarred ugly hands floating before her, the woman running through the rain, the hands locking around the woman's throat. She was overcome by a nearly overpowering sense of guilt, by a need to surrender and go back to the prison. But she fought it. Fought it with her night eyes. She had a way with the machines of the *uominilupi*, a way of control. Her brain was different. She fought against the counselor, with its confabulations of guilt and shame, with its caricature of a murderer meant to turn her own mind against her, she battled hard. The New Ones stepped onto the catwalk and ran for her. At the last second, she felt the balance tipping in her favor. She had control of the counselor now, and she was using it to command the New Ones.

She jumped.

She thought she would fall into the river. But she rose, rose like the cliffbird, to the river on the ceiling. Rose and fell at the same time, embracing the essential paradox, fell into the past but sprang into the future, into the endless reflections. She commanded the New Ones to obey. They jumped in after her.

And at last the counselor informed.

34

Lungo Muso had prepared the river for her coming. All of human history was illuminated. She knew of the English, the Italian, knew of the Renaissance, of the British fleet, of Galileo, and of Machiavelli. She knew of Reymont. She recognized the crudeness of the surgery the Old Ones had tried to perform, rushing in with their scalpel before they had diagnosed the problem, stopping human space travel any way they could.

Out of the violet, a world emerged.

A room paneled in dark mahogany coalesced around her. Not Galileo's room, a different room, some crossbeams overhead, a writing table in the corner, a chest of drawers against the wall, a folding screen with a painting of the Virgin Mary in front of the bed.

Standing at the arched window was a man, not Galileo, a different man, younger, in silk hose and buckled slippers, wearing a black hat that looked like a rum pudding, a ruff collar, fenestrated sleeves, silk hose, and a large black cape. Her arms tingled and she knew Lungo Muso was nearby, getting closer. She stared at the man. And she understood, as if Lungo Muso had dropped the thought into her mind, that this man was Niccolò Machiavelli, the same Machiavelli who had so profoundly influenced James Kenneth Reymont.

Machiavelli stared out the window, through which a hot summer sun was pouring in. The smell of street sewage and horse manure wafted on a breeze into the chamber. She took a few steps toward the table. She saw the book. *The* book. Manuscript pages. Written with a quill, the Italian words flowing across the pages like an army of black ants. She felt a thousand minds hovering around her, the New Ones, waiting for her, but she wasn't sure what to do. So she concentrated on this man, this Niccolò Machiavelli. She walked to the window and got a better look at him.

He was in his midforties. And he looked angry.

She glanced down at the street where she saw a market. A group of soldiers in chain mail and helmets walked from stall to stall disrupting the wares, stealing whatever they wanted and wrecking the rest. She heard them laugh, jesting with each other. They were speaking French. She again looked at Machiavelli. She saw bitterness in his brown eyes. She again felt the tingling in her arms. She knew Lungo Muso was helping her make a more exact evaluation of how the wrongs of yesteryear could be corrected.

She turned from the window. She saw Lungo Muso standing by the armoire.

"Don't be surprised," he said. "I knew we would at last meet in this . . . this studio." Lungo Muso pointed at the Italian man standing at the window. "You see him there," he said. "And you understand him, know who he is, what he's done and what he's become. Of course you do. You travel the river of time. You've lived his life, seen his life, tasted his life. And he hates those soldiers in the square. He hates the French because he sees in the French his vanquishers. Just as we see Reymont as ours. Just as the New Ones are yours. Why this small moment of time? Why did it make such a difference?" Lungo Muso shrugged. "Who can say? And why Machiavelli?" He shrugged again. "The loom of time spins in unpredictable patterns. Gaze upon him. You see that he hates those French soldiers. You see that he feels the need to do something about them. These French soldiers haunt his dreams. He despises these French soldiers for turning Italy into a battleground. All the Italian defeats have made him bitter. This was the exact thread we were looking for."

He nodded toward Machiavelli.

"This man is presently engaged upon a literary work of minor significance," said the Old One, "a commentary on Republican Rome. This work is his true love, but he now feels he must interrupt it, that he must write something that will in some way help defeat those French soldiers down in the piazza. He can't stand the endless defeats. First Fornovo, then Capua, then Valià, then Bologna, then Vicenza. He can hardly live with himself. He has to do something. He's angry. He's not a bad man, not an evil one, but he wants the French to stop raping, pillaging, and plundering. He thinks of the Medicis, the strongest house in Italy, and he concludes that if anybody can do it, they can. But he must give them a blueprint. So he abandons his work on Republican Rome, and he writes his small treatise on princely rule, little realizing that fifteen centuries later another equally bitter man would read his treatise and take its every word to heart. A small thread reaching back fifteen centuries, and this is the thread you must remove."

"You speak of James Kenneth Reymont," she said.

Lungo Muso nodded. "Niccolò Machiavelli can't possibly realize the effect his treatise will have on the young cadet. To Reymont, *The Prince* becomes gospel. The end justifies the means."

She looked up. "But why did Reymont ever come to your five home worlds in the first place?" she asked.

Lungo Muso's shoulders sagged, and he looked spent.

"The humans sent a receptor, a probe, forward into time," he explained. "And it came back with a dire warning: A catastrophic threat, of a military nature, was going to threaten not only the Five Worlds of the *uominilupi* but also Earth. Reymont was sent to organize us into an army, no easy thing, considering we're as politically fractured as Machiavelli's Italy. There already existed some trade agreements between the *uominilupi* and Terra, so we at last agreed to talk to him."

This was new terrain for Felicitas, but she assimilated it quickly.

"He tried to make an army out of the Old Ones," continued Lungo Muso, "to face this catastrophe, this military threat, whatever it was." Lungo Muso shook his head. "From the outset, he encountered obstacles. Of course he did. The Old Ones like to argue, Felicitas, it's in their nature, they can't help it. Making an army out of us, getting us to cooperate with each other, that was going to take doing. We were over five thousand packs, and every pack had their own way of doing things. Reymont first tried to negotiate with us, but he discovered we could negotiate forever. Then he was authorized to buy our support. You'd think it would be an easy thing. You'd think we would want to mobilize against whatever this threat was. But we saw no threat in the river of time, and believed the river far more sophisticated than any human time probe. So Reymont had to use force. He had to conscript us. He'd suffered enough setbacks in his military career, and he wasn't going to suffer any longer. By that point in his career, he was already a bitter man. He'd been passed over again and again for the more glamorous commands. He saw the Five Worlds as a last chance for glory. We've used our night eyes to understand him thoroughly. His job was to unite the *uominilupi,* and, no matter what it took, he was going to do it. He used *The Prince* as his blueprint. He used it to bolster his own justifications, to bludgeon the Five Worlds into unification. His offensive weaponry was far superior to anything we *uominilupi* possessed. And because his mind seethed with the double-dealing rhetoric of *The Prince,* he killed all who stood in his way, and killed them with a clean conscience. As far as he was concerned, the threat was on its way, and he was going to make the *uominilupi* into a cohesive fighting force whether we liked it or not. He fashioned himself into a ruthless colonial governor. This was his triumph. This was his greatest success. It made up for all his previous failures."

Lungo Muso held up his index finger.

"But then . . ." he said, gazing at her with his forthright amber eyes. "Then his commanders took it all away from him. The Terrans ordered him to return. No explanation was given. Maybe they sent a different probe and got a different reading. Reymont was outraged. No one was going to take his prize away. He unilaterally declared himself ruler of the Five Worlds. He cut ties with Terra and established his own sovereignty. He killed millions of us. And that's when we decided we had to fight back. With the river of time."

She stared out at the street, where a man led three donkeys with large earthenware jars of olive oil strapped to their backs away from the fracas the French soldiers were causing, thinking of everything the Old One had told her. Machiavelli continued to gaze upon the French soldiers with pure hatred.

"So I just get rid of the book?" she said.

"Our models tell us so, and our models are as sophisticated as the river of time," said Lungo Muso. "To get rid of the book, you must get rid of the cause behind the book. You must get rid of those French hooligans in the market square." He turned his head to one side, puzzled. He sniffed the air. "Do I sense New Ones nearby?"

Felicitas eyes narrowed. He sensed things just the same way she did. He knew all, saw all.

"Yes," she said. "I've brought them with me."

Felicitas told her about Maritano's counselor and how she thought she would need it to control the New Ones.

"You're a remarkable young woman," he said. He pulled an identical counselor from the folds of his cape. "You know my plans even before I tell you about them." He put his hand on her shoulder, and she knew, with the omnipotent knowing of the river, that this was their farewell, that she would never see Lungo Muso again. "I am weak now," he said. "I am from another time and place, and am fading. Even with this counselor in my own head I would never be able to control the New Ones. They've redesigned themselves so that Old Ones can never control them again, not even with a counselor. But a human can control them easily. You can control them, Felicitas. You are the rudder upon the river now. Only you can save us from the end-final time." He let his hand fall from her shoulder. "So farewell, Felicitas. Swim the river, run the path, and at last rise like the cliffbird."

What volition she suddenly had! What precision of time and knowledge. She knew everything, saw everything, felt everything.

She was in the air above a river, and the year was 1495, and to the north she saw the town of Fornovo, and on the flood plain she saw the troops, archers, and horsemen of Charles VIII of France preparing for battle against a disorganized rabble of Italian soldiers. The Italian soldiers looked doomed to defeat. But now she gave them help. Arrayed in the surrounding hills, among the farms and olive groves, were a thousand New Ones, in brown uniforms, well hidden, blending with the sun-baked grass of summer, controlled by her counselor the way Maritano controled the dead.

Charles VIII's archers sent a barrage of arrows into the air against the Italian troops. Some of the Italian troops turned and ran for the River Taro, thinking they might find safety in the water. Felicitas launched her own attack. *Pistola* fire sprang up like a thousand lightning bolts from the surrounding hills, cutting the arrows in midflight from the sky, instantly turning them to ash.

The French troops were so startled by the display they broke rank. Their horses grew skittish, and some of the animals bolted. As with the lance, she thought the thought, and another volley of *pistola* fire erupted from the surrounding hills, killing, in an instant, more than a hundred heavily armored cavalry. She sensed the thoughts of the French, and, using the newly discovered facet of her night eyes, *became* those French soldiers.

In this time of deep religious belief, such a display of force could only be construed as coming from God. French troops got on their knees and began to pray for their lives. But Charles VIII, himself in charge of the battle, exhorted his troops to fight. Yet even as the king of France, growing ever angrier, charged about on his royal mount beheading his disobedient soldiers, Felicitas let go with another volley of *pistola* fire and half the French troops turned and fled, many getting trampled to death in the flight.

The Italian troops, now believing that God Almighty was on their side, gave chase with their inferior weaponry and loose discipline, and were able to kill and maim at least another two hundred.

She slid forward in the river of time, and the years were like days, then like hours, and she sensed that all over Italy, in the disparate republics, duchies, and principalities of that politically fractured peninsula, the word was spreading that God had intervened for the Italians at the battle of Fornovo and had driven the French out.

Yet now there was another king in France, Louis XII, and he bitterly resented the defeat at Fornovo, and was determined to show Europe that when it came to God, France was His favorite. The river of time gave her this power, this knowledge, this omnipotence, to know all and see all. So Louis XII raised an army, and the French marched on Italy again. And again, Felicitas was determined to thwart the attackers.

She paddled in the river of time until she came to the year 1501. The French were gathered outside Capua on a field surrounded by thick forest, at a time when elk, bear, and wolf were still hunted in that part of Italy. There was a pause before the battle. And in that pause Felicitas came to a startling realization. If the end result of all this manipulation was to stop Reymont from coming to the Five Worlds, then she would take away the reason for the *uominilupi* fighting back. And if she took that away, why would the *uominilupi* ever build their prison? And if they didn't build the prison, then there would be no prisoners. And if there were no prisoners, there could be no Felicitas. In making this small temporal resection she would most likely blot herself out of existence. There would be no Piero. No Rosario. No New Florentines. No *pastori*. In saving them from one end-final time she might inadvertantly create another.

So it came down to sacrifice. And she knew what she had to do. It wasn't just the New Florentines she had to think about, nor the *pastori*, nor the *superstiti*. All intelligent life, wherever it might be found, would be destroyed by the New Ones, if the New Ones were given the chance. So yes, she had to take away the reason for building the prison. And that reason was *The Prince*. The way to stop *The Prince* was to stop these French invaders, even if at the end of it all, in the grandest of *uominilupi* paradoxes, she herself ceased to exist.

So she thought the thought, and the New Ones took up positions in the surrounding trees. She watched from above, an incorporeal presence in the river of time. She watched the horses, the armor, the wagons, the banners, the flags, all the pomp and majesty of a pitched sixteenth-century battle. Only this time the Italians were more confident. They'd won at Fornovo and this made a big difference to their morale.

Still, Louis XII's army was large, battle hardened, and on this sunny day, looked more determined than ever.

This time the French didn't start with their archers. This time, Louis sent his heavily armored cavalry charging across the field. Even from where she floated, Felicitas could hear the thunder of their hoofs. The Italians, under the command of Lorenzo de' Medici, charged with their own small cavalry. And that's when Felicitas thought another thought. Even though the New Ones, this time, were out of range, and their *pistola* fire scattered in a shower of sparks well before it reached the charging French cavalry, the demonstration was enough to instill in the French horsemen great confusion and fear.

Their horses reared up.

The New Ones advanced out of the trees, none of them taller than four feet, all the same, all in brown uniforms. And yes, they looked somewhat wolflike from a distance, and, sensing the thoughts of the French troops with her night eyes, Felicitas knew that they believed God had turned the wolves of the forest into these manlike apparitions. Her night eyes took an extrapolative tour up the river of time, and she understood that forever after the legend of the werewolf, the man-wolf, the *uomolupo* would take deep hold in that part of Italy, quickly spread through the Ottoman Empire, the Balkans, and then to the rest of Europe.

She thought the thought, and the New Ones fired again. If she had learned anything, it was that men didn't understand battle unless it was underlined with death. The *pistola* fire was so strong that it burned right through armor, and all but a few of Louis's cavalry were killed.

This allowed the Italian cavalry to charge into the massed French infantry well before the French archers had time to get themselves organized.

The ground ran with blood and the air was filled with the clang of metal as swordsmen battled swordsmen. The New Ones pulled back into the trees, circled around, and attacked the French flank. Volley after volley of *pistola* fire jetted from the thick foliage—lightning bolts from God—and Felicitas showed no mercy. She had to teach the French a lesson. She had to make sure they didn't come back. She had to make them understand that they themselves would be destroyed if they attempted to destroy the Italians.

Mass confusion ensued. Panic set in. Horses, infantry, archers clamored to get away from the relentless *pistola* attack. She watched the French stream away as she floated high above them, individual by individual, up the hill into the woods, par-

ticles becoming detached from the main mass of clashing, fighting bodies, running as fast as they could, trying to get away
from the manlike wolf creatures that now attacked them . . .

And after an hour, it was over . . .

All she could see down there were victorious Italian troops
picking over the corpses, taking the best swords and battle-
axes, salvaging the undamaged armor, gathering up the stray
French horses, taking what they could of the spoils of war.

Now she floated ahead in time, allowing the current to pull
her slowly through the years. Valià, 1507, historically the scene
of another French attack. But Louis XII had been cowed by the
strength and wrath of God. Forward again, to Bologna, 1511.
The town was peaceful, and there was no gathering of French
troops beyond its fortified walls. And finally Vicenza, spring,
1513. The Vicenzians went about their peaceful business. No
siege was imminent.

And now to summer, 1513, in the upstairs studio of Niccolò
Machiavelli, with the heavy mahogany paneling, the writing
table, the open window, and the sound of the market below. No
sign of Lungo Muso. But Machiavelli was there. He stood by
the window. And July sunshine streamed in like gold.

She moved around and got a better look at Machiavelli. She
sensed none of the previous bitterness. In fact, he was smiling.
She looked out the window to see what he was smiling at.

A fourteen-year-old girl, a beautiful creature, looking much
like Adriana, fed bits of cheese to a monkey in a wicker cage.
Up the street, a harlequin entertained a crowd by juggling red
boccia balls. And across the street two wool merchants in black
hose and ruff collars haggled over the price per bale, each fin-
gering the raw wool as if they wanted to hurt it. No sign of
French troops. Machiavelli was happy. A typical Renaissance
street scene. The disparate republics and principalities of his
beloved Italy, in the wake of their victories against the French,
were to a certain extent cooperating with each other.

The middle-aged man left the window and returned to his

writing table. Felicitas followed. She looked over his shoulder as he wrote.

There was nothing in his writing about how a prince should concern himself only with war; nothing there about how a prince shouldn't hesitate to lie; nothing there about how ungrateful, fickle, and greedy men were. This wasn't *The Prince,* that legendary handbook of evil. This was a commentary; a commentary on Republican Rome.

Machiavelli's lengthy analysis of republican forms of government.

A book Colonel James Kenneth Reymont would never hear of, one he would never see, and one he most definitely would never read.

35

She now slid through the years at a tremendous rate. Within the mother-of-pearl walls, time and space became close cousins. She was flung across the stars, through the hot white center of the galaxy, and out the other side.

She finally came to the outpost planet, the prison world.

The violet stream of the river dimmed, tightened into a funnel cloud. Her sense of omniscience evaporated. She was leaving the river of time. Below, she saw tundra. She saw mountains far to the south. She saw two pink suns above her. She wondered if these would be the last things she would ever see. She had now preempted the existence of *The Prince*. And didn't that mean she herself would now cease to exist?

Down she went. The snow had disappeared and everywhere the tundra was in flower. She looked for the outpost but couldn't see it anywhere. All she saw were the dilapidated installations and the old square supply ship.

As she got closer, she saw a dozen hopebeasts grazing

among the wild flowers. She saw some men come out of the food-brick factory.

Her feet touched the ground.

And she realized she was still alive, that she hadn't ceased to exist.

She looked down at her feet. Nine small implants, like bugs, lay in the moss. She touched her forehead. She felt no incisions, no scars. She couldn't understand why she was here, why she was still alive, when she should have disappeared with the New Ones, swallowed by the implacable paradoxes of time.

She saw Raffaele walk down the valley toward her. She saw Renzo and a dozen other *pastori*. She looked behind her. There was nothing but a vague depression in the tundra where the outpost had once stood. She felt a final tingling in her arms. Lungo Muso was slipping thoughts into her mind one last time. *You won't need the counselor anymore,* he said. She understood. *And I've used the pool in Raffaele's cave to stabilize time locally, to guard against the paradoxes, to secure your time-line so you can continue to live.*

The pool in Raffaele's cave. A window, a portal, a river of time in miniature. She was here, on this world, and she was going to stay. They were all going to stay. Lungo Muso had made certain of it.

Raffaele came up to her. "You're back," he said.

She looked around at the wildflowers growing up through the moss. She felt disoriented. "What's this?" she asked, pointing at the flowers.

Raffaele looked puzzled. "It's spring."

"Spring?" she said, surprised. "But I was in there only a few hours."

His eyes showed concern. "I guess when you're inside the river, time is measured differently."

She put her hand on his arm. "You waited for me all this time?"

He nodded. "I found a supply of food-bricks down there," he said, pointing to the square ship in the landing pit. "And there was some old furniture I was able to burn. You have no idea how bitter the winters are this far north. The suns disappear. It's dark all day. But I waited. I waited because Lungo Muso came to me and told me you were on the river." A grin came to his face. "He didn't bark and grunt this time. He said that because I was so close to the river I had greater powers of understanding. And then the *pastori* came. I wasn't going to leave you, Felicitas. I was going to wait for you. I was going to see it through to the end."

"And Lungo Muso came to you?" she said.

"Yes."

"And what did he say?"

"He told me *The Prince* was gone," he said. "And that Reymont was a different man."

"How so?"

"He no longer cared about glory," said Raffaele. "He only cared about orders. When his commanders ordered him home, he went home, and that was the end of it."

When she got back to New Florence, Felicitas found she had become a hero.

Her mother was relieved beyond words to see her safe home again. Silvio was back in good health, and just as overjoyed as Marietta.

On the other hand, everyone was greatly saddened by the deaths of Piero and Urbano, and a memorial service was held in St. Mark's Square, with over a thousand in attendance.

Eventually all the excitement and commotion over her return died down.

At the end of it all, Felicitas was left with what had become, to her, the central question: How and why was her brain different? Why did she have night eyes?

She spent much of her time in the town hall going over the *uominilupi* artifacts trying to find an answer. Strangely, the artifacts began to loose their physical integrity. The leather on the book bindings cracked and peeled, and the pages turned to dust. All the metal gadgets rusted right through. It was as if what had happened in the prison—the machinery breaking down, the *carcerieri* dying, the *sentinelle* and searchlights stopping—the same process was happening all over again, to every piece of *uominilupi* gadgetry the *popolo* had ever scavenged, only happening at an accelerated rate.

She climbed White Mountain to Raffaele's cave.

Together they went to see the pool.

"It doesn't glow as much," said Raffaele. "And look at these glyphs. You can hardly see them now."

"It looks smaller," said Felicitas. "It looks like it's closing up."

Within a week the pool was gone.

That's when she began making sense of things. As summer came, she was filled with a new hope. If all the *uominilupi* machinery was breaking down in New Florence, then mustn't all the refurbished equipment in the prison be breaking down as well? With the disappearance of the outpost, the *uominilupi* presence on the prison world was fading away. The *soldati* must have stopped working by now. The dreamphones and sleeping pallets would again be derelict. And the whir of the *sentinelle* up on the parapets would cease.

The time was ripe for another escape.

Mostri were sighted going north the next week, making their return migration. In New Florence the return migration meant another hunt to the western reaches of the river. Felicitas decided this would be the best time to go to the prison.

Felicitas took her request to Fortunato, the *sindaco*.

"I know it's usually a smaller hunt," she said, as they sat in the south chamber of the town hall with the light streaming through the beveled glass windows. "I know you don't take as many boats. But I propose the same number of boats. We've got to make a try. There could be survivors in the prison. And if there are, we're going to need every boat we have."

"But how can we get into the prison?" asked the leader of the *popolo.*

Felicitas leaned forward, putting her hands on the table.

"If all the *uominilupi* machinery in New Florence is breaking down," she said, "chances are the same thing is happening in the prison. Don't you see? With the changes I made, it's as if the *uominilupi* never came to this world. Everything they left here is slowly disappearing. Yet we remain because of Raffaele's pool. Lungo Muso has made it so. If all the machinery in the prison is breaking down again, it means we can get the prisoners out of there. It's our duty to rescue as many survivors as we can."

Fortunato ran his hand through his red hair, glancing out the window where a few puffy clouds hovered above the mountains.

"Their machinery might be breaking down," he conceded. "But what of the prison itself? It's made of stone. The stone is that same gray stone so common along that part of the river. It has nothing to do with the *uominilupi.* It's part of this world." His eyes narrowed. "How do we get through this stone?"

She had anticipated this objection. "There are windows in the west annex," she said. "There are no bars or glass in these windows. If we construct a climbing lattice we can reach them easily."

He raised his eyebrows. "I'm sure our carpenters might construct whatever climbing lattice you might desire," he said. "But how would we convey this lattice upstream?"

"They make the lattice piece by piece," she said. Outside, a few brown birds flew by the tall spires of the temple across the square. "It could be taken upstream section by section in several different boats. When we get to the prison we could put it together there."

Fortunato hesitated. He got up, put his hands behind his back, and walked to the window, where he looked out at the street. He turned around.

"I guess we can't let them rot in there, can we?" he said.

*   *   *

The *popolo* in the advance party reached the prison ten days later.

Even in the strong sunshine of early summer, *Stella Piccola* and *Stella Grossa* couldn't seem to brighten the dour edifice. It was like an indelible shadow in the surrounding green.

Felicitas was in the lead boat with Ignazio. Ignazio was the new hunt leader, now that Urbano was dead.

"The west annex is over there," she said, as the paddlers stroked evenly across the lake.

She took a closer look at the prison. She listened. From up on the catwalks, silence. The *sentinelle* had died a second time.

After paddling for another five minutes, they landed on the shore and approached the west annex.

The carpenters went to work putting together the lattice.

When it was done, it took every man and woman to push it up against the side of the prison.

Ignazio turned to Felicitas.

"Who goes first?" he asked.

Her lips settled. "I do," she said.

She gripped the lattice and climbed.

Here was the old stone, worn and scratched by the wind, the same dull gray that had been the predominant color of her childhood. She glanced down. Ignazio and some of the others were right behind her. The sanded wood of the lattice was smooth under her palms.

She finally reached the window. That same window of the same room where Concetta had lost her life. She crawled through the window. Once in the room, she listened. Silence.

Ignazio and the others climbed in after her. They looked around the room with wide eyes. She walked through the ash of the old fire, pulled the door open, and strode out to the main gallery. The *popolo* followed her out of the room onto the mezzanine.

A *soldato* lay crumpled on the steps, corroded badly, crawling with *topi*. A few corpses, skeletons in tattered prison uniforms, lay on the stone floor of the second gallery. Sunlight penetrated through the upper windows but did little to dispel the musty darkness. The place smelled of rot.

They descended the stairs and crossed the annex floor until they came to the drainage pool.

"Are you good swimmers?" she asked.

Ignazio stared at the pool.

"We're fair," he said. "We swim a lot in the river."

She pointed. "There's an underwater culvert," she said. "We swim through that, and we get to the other side."

Ignazio nodded. "We can manage," he said.

She stepped into the pool. The hunters followed. She feared the worst, but hoped for the best. The whole rapturous weight of her love for Rosario made her feel weak. Just the same, she dove under the water and swam with all her strength.

When she emerged on the other side, she stood up in the opposite drainage pool and looked around the west cellblock. The trickle from the south bath's drainage wall had stopped and the water in the pool had turned stagnant. She looked up at the cells. All silent, all empty. Ignazio and the others splashed up through the water behind her. Ignazio waded through the pool, walked up to her, and wiped the water from his eyes.

"A sad place to spend your childhood, Felicitas," he said.

How true, she thought.

This was the dark place of her childhood. She felt like she was walking into a world of ghosts. Here was a place full of melancholy, a place where the prisoners had been forgotten and abandoned by their jailers. Yet it remained a part of her life, and, as such, her feelings were mixed. Did she not enjoy at least some happiness in this dark place?

She climbed up the steps out of the drainage pool and into the southwest corridor. She looked around. She felt like crying.

Ignazio put his hand on her shoulder. *"Bella?"* he said.

She glanced back at the hunter.

"I'll be all right," she said. She pointed up the corridor. "We can get into the yard through that door."

They walked along the corridor, their footsteps echoing through the empty space. They passed a few more corpses. They kicked a couple of derelict implants out of the way—even the implants had stopped working. Light filtered in through the arched doorway of the west cellblock. They turned right and went out into the yard.

Seventy or eighty prisoners sat in small groups. Near the north wall she saw the remnants of a large bonfire, and in the ashes, hundreds of human skulls. All the graves had been dug up and the corpses burned. Thirty *soldati* lay broken or destroyed around the yard. The *sentinelle* stared down at the prisoners, mute and silent, their *cannoni* shouldered. Piles of refuse littered the yard. Near the dispensary a large skid of food-bricks had been broken open and scattered all over the place. The food-bricks had mold growing on them. Five corpses lay unburied near the clock tower. An attempt had been made to rebuild the lattice, but all the metal *carceriere* arm and leg supports were now thick with corrosion, and were about as strong as cardboard. The only noise in all the yard was the sound of a single person hammering.

Felicitas, Ignazio, and the others advanced into the yard. They followed the sound of the hammering. It came from behind what was left of the old barricade, the one the *superstiti* had built after the dead had made their first attack. Prisoners stared up at them from crouched positions on the ground, their uniforms now no more than rags, their eyes dull, their faces skull-like. They were starving to death. It was as if they couldn't believe what they were seeing, as if they, too, had been plagued by mirages from the outpost, and could no longer distinguish between what was real and what was illusion. As Felicitas passed the dispensary, she saw three *topi* dart by, one carrying a decayed human hand in its teeth.

She rounded the barricade and saw a solitary man hammering, trying to rebuild the lattice.

All she could see was the man's back. His hair was disheveled, matted with dirt, and he was so skinny his ribs were visible through the tears in his shirt. She felt a sudden spark of hope. Something familiar about the way his arms worked, the way he looked so sure and proficient, something competent and unflinching; something she remembered from the day she had first heard the magical sound of his laughter. Here he was, the only man left hammering, trying to escape, never letting the dream die, never giving up.

"Rosario?" she said.

The man turned around . . .

His face was gaunt and his hair hung limply over his forehead.

Rosario.

At last.

He rose from his work, his eyes showing none of the dreamphone haze, his face expressionless. She didn't want to scare him, or in any way unbalance him, because she could see that he had gone through a lot. She just stayed where she was, letting him get used to her. A huge scar showed up white on the underside of his left arm, where his arm code had been. No wonder he hadn't been dreamphoned. He looked weak. His legs shook. He stared at her.

Then he looked at Ignazio and the other *popolo,* looked at them in his old inquisitive way; and he saw that they were wearing clothes stitched out of tanned *mostro* hide, that they carried bows and arrows, that they in every way matched the mural drawing of the river people up in the south wall.

He looked at Felicitas again.

"Felicitas?" he said.

She nodded.

He lifted both arms. He took a shaky step toward her. He was dirty, but that didn't matter. She lifted her own arms. He took another shaky step. Then another. Other prisoners stirred, came to watch.

"Felicitas?" he said again. His voice was like a tonic to her. "You're here at last?"

She reached out, touched him.

"Yes," she said.

She put her arms around him, held him up on his unsteady legs.

And supporting him like this, in the shadow of the south tower, amid the fallen *soldati* and the silent *sentinelle*, surrounded once again by the four dark walls of her childhood, she knew that the *uominilupi* were gone for good, that the *superstiti* were at last free, and that this world, as open and empty as a blank canvas, was, and always would be, their home.

36

Summer had come early to New Florence.

The pasture behind Marietta's house was thick with wild-flowers, the snows on the mountains had receded to the peaks, and fish schooled massively in the river. *Pastori* rode in and out of St. Mark's Square, bartering their herds for supplies. The fields around New Florence were green with fresh shoots of cereal grass. Most special of all, *Stella Piccola* kissed the side of *Stella Grossa*. The bi-solar eclipse, something that happened every five years, was underway, and would mean an extra long growing season.

Rosario sat in a reclining chair covered in blankets just outside Marietta's back door. Felicitas sat next to him, feeding him small spoonfuls of *pane* soup. For the first time since coming home to New Florence two weeks ago, he felt like talking, had the strength to talk. He reached up and stroked her hair.

"We couldn't understand it at first," he said. "*Soldati* would suddenly stop working and fall over in the yard. The *sentinelle* halted up on the parapets. All the lights went out. Worst of all, the new food-bricks started to rot. Food-bricks don't rot. And then the heat gave out. We were so cold, Felicitas. We burned anything and everything. People started getting sick so I ordered the corpses burned."

"Rest, Rosario," she said.

He let his hand drop from her hair.

"You're more beautiful than ever," he said. "You've become a woman."

She lifted his hand and kissed it.

He didn't want to stop talking. He had kept everything in so long that he had to get it out.

"They dreamphoned us again," he said. "I cut my arm code off. I hid in the north bath. I got a bad infection. I was delirious for about a week. When I finally came out of it someone told me Maritano and his *consiglieri* had gone to look for you. With Maritano gone, we could get away with small things. We gathered up the broken lattice and tried to rebuild it. But the metal was weak. I don't know how the metal corroded so quickly." He gazed up at her. "I was desperate for answers. And that's when Lungo Muso came to me. That's when he explained everything to me. By that time, you were already in the river. He told me the changes you were making on the river would make things break down again. Temporal instability, he called it."

"He spoke to Raffaele," she said. "And he came to see Silvio again, too."

He nodded. "He told me he was pushing himself because he knew things were coming to an end." Rosario took a deep breath and scratched his blond beard. "He came to me often," he said. "And not just his regular visit, where he takes me to look at Reymont in the skyboat. These were real visits." He took a mouthful of soup, seemed to have some trouble swallowing it, but finally got it down. "This was about four months after you left, near the end of winter."

At the back of the garden, Marietta's hopebeast bleated, lifting its head as one of the ball-like flightless birds darted
through the tall grass and disappeared into some reeds near
the back.

"And he told you everything?" she asked.

Rosario nodded. "Everything," he said. "Reymont, Machiavelli, the river of time, everything. He came often. Even when
the machinery in the prison broke down, and we all started to
starve to death, he came to me."

"Did he tell you how my brain worked differently?" she
asked. "He never told me that. Did he explain why I have the
night eyes?"

Rosario leaned back in his chair. He looked stronger. The
color was returning to his face. He took Felicitas's hand.

"Your ancestors, Felicitas. That's why you have your night
eyes."

"My ancestors?"

"You, me, and Silvio aren't descended from the original
group of English prisoners, the ones from the old time. We're
descended from a much later group." Rosario stopped for a little soup, then continued. "One of the first things humans found
out about the *uominilupi* was the mind-machine connection of
uomolupo science." Rosario took another deep breath, inhaling
the fragrance of the wildflowers in the meadow beyond. "They
discovered the night eyes, Felicitas." He nodded. "It was the
British who began to genetically develop humans with night
eyes. They enhanced certain parts of the human brain, mainly
the Sylvian fissure . . . I'll draw you a picture of that later on.
This was after centuries of war with the New Ones, war stretching back to the Renaissance. They thought this might be the
only way to negotiate with the New Ones, by speaking to them
with the night eyes. But by this time the New Ones were far
more interested in annihilating us."

High in the mountains, one of the flying *mostri* soared over
a snow-capped peak, on its way to its aerie. The hopebeast at

the back of the yard glanced at the distant creature, bleated a few times, then cantered nervously toward the stable.

"The New Ones destroyed the night-eyes project and took some of the enhanced human prisoners for study," said Rosario. He patted her arm. "They all wound up in our prison. Your ancestors come from this group of prisoners, Felicitas. I must have some of their blood. So must Silvio. But you've got it the strongest."

Felicitas had to think about this. Her control of the *cannone,* her clairvoyant sensitivity to the implants of the dead, her mastery of the counselor, her use of the lance, her omniscience while on the river, maybe even her understanding of the glyphs all had to do with this enhanced Sylvian fissure, these human night eyes that had been bred into her over the centuries.

Rosario looked down the pasture, where the hopebeast, no longer nervous about the flying *mostri,* was now drinking from the rain barrel.

"And you know what the ironic thing is?" he said.

Felicitas stroked her lover's hair.

"What?" she asked.

"This original time probe sent by the humans? The one that Lungo Muso told you about?"

"Yes?"

"The one that sensed the threat against the Five Worlds from the future?"

"Yes?"

He shook his head and a wry smile came to face. "The threat was in fact the New Ones themselves," he said. "The time probe itself set into motion the sequence of events that led directly to the creation of the New Ones. A reflection of a reflection. A chance selection made by the humans' primitive time probe from among a thousand possible futures. If the humans hadn't sent the time probe in the first place, the *uominilupi* never would have made their New Ones, and none of this would have happened."

*   *   *

Midsummer.

Felicitas and Rosario stood on the hill on the other side of the river, amid the seventeen stones. Felicitas had flowers in her hair and Rosario wore his best linen tunic. The high priest stood before them in his white gown. Seventy or eighty *popolo* gathered round. *Stella Piccola* had disappeared behind *Stella Grossa*. There now appeared to be only one sun in the sky, just like on Earth. They had congregated in this holy place on this holiest of days—the day of the complete bi-solar eclipse.

The high priest raised his hands and gestured at *Stella Grossa*.

"You see now a special time in our calendar," he said. "The suns have joined and shine as one. The heat of this midsummer bodes well for a bountiful harvest. The flowers in the meadow dazzle our eyes and the fish in the pool play. The *antilope* have gone to their northern breeding grounds and the flocks in their aeries tend to their young. What better time in our year for the joining of a man and a woman? You see around you the stones that our forefathers laid," he said, gesturing at the carefully placed boulders. "Seventeen stones to represent the seventeen months, but also to intimate the seasons of life and the inevitability of change. The walls are not complete and there are spaces in between. There is no roof overhead. And for a foundation we have nothing but the grass below our feet." He brought his hands together. "It's up to you, Felicitas and Rosario, to build the rest. You have before you the tradition of our two suns to help you. You have to your left and right Marietta and Silvio, family who will support and assist you. You have above you the spirits of Piero and Lungo Muso, who will guide you. And you have behind you your community, who know of your resourcefulness and courage, and who now know of your love for each other. These are your walls, these are your roof, these are your foundation. May your marriage be the strongest of buildings, and may nothing ever cause it to break or fall, or come to ruin." A benign grin came to the high priest's face. "And now it is my duty and honor to ask you to seal and consecrate this marriage with a kiss."

They turned to each other.

Their lips came together gently.

And together they rose like the cliffbird.